THE
CANTERBURY
PAPERS

A NOVEL

JUDITH KOLL HEALEY

"Brims with authentic historical detail . . . suspenseful."

—Minneapolis Star Tribune

"Debut novelist Healey brings medieval history to life in magnificent fashion as she adds a new twist to an old legend. . . . Electrifying journey into the past." —Booklist

"The past comes alive in this stunning debut. . . . Mysteries unfold within mysteries in this skillfully layered story, which will keep readers guessing until the final engaging pages. . . . A delicious debut." —Romantic Times

"Engaging medieval suspense debut . . . most pleasurable."

—Once upon a Crime

"Be sure to get this one. It's one of the best I've read in a long time, combining an intriguing period of history, smooth writing, excellent characterization of real historic figures, and a fine plot with plenty of twists." —The Facts

About the Author

JUDITH HEALEY, whose hobby is medieval history, manages two family foundations. She lives in Minneapolis, Minnesota, where she is at work on another novel featuring the extraordinary Alais of France.

JUDITH KOLL HEALEY

The Canterbury Papers

WM

WILLIAM MORROW

An Imprint of HarperCollins*Publishers*

Grateful acknowledgment is made to reprint the poem by Omar Ibn al-Faridh from Love in the Western World *by Denis de Rougement. Copyright © 1983 by Princeton University Press. Reprinted by permission of Princeton University Press.*

A hardcover edition of this book was published in 2004 by William Morrow, an imprint of HarperCollins Publishers.

First Perennial edition published 2005.

DESIGNED BY JENNIFER ANN DADDIO
MAP BY JANE S. KIM

The Library of Congress has catalogued the hardcover edition as follows:

Healey, Judith Koll.
The Canterbury papers / Judith Koll Healey.—1st ed.
p. cm.
ISBN 0-06-052535-5
1. Eleanor, of Aquitaine, Queen, consort of Henry II, King of England, 1122?–1204—Fiction. 2. Great Britain—History—Richard I, 1189–1199—Fiction. I. Title.

PS3608.E236L67 2004
813'.6—dc21   2003053987

ISBN 0-06-077332-4 (pbk.)

12 ❖/RRD 11

To my husband,
MICHAEL

On the imagination:

The truth of the imagination leads us to compassion. These two, imagination and compassion, are the only possibility of salvation.

—W. S. Merwin
Joseph Warren Beach lecture
University of Minnesota
March 26, 2001

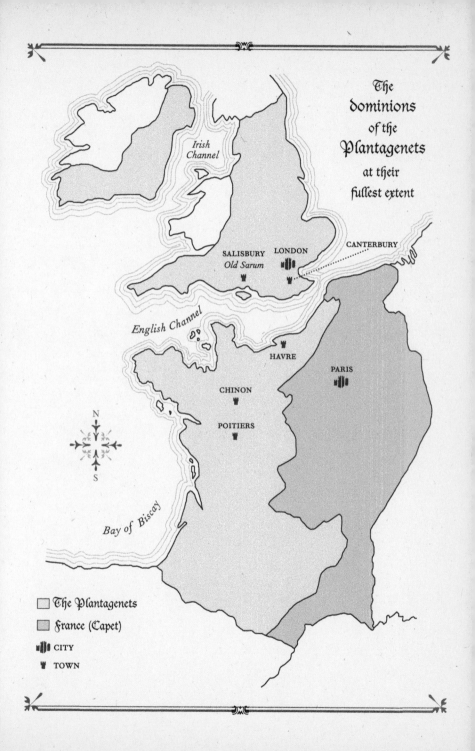

The
dominions
of the
Plantagenets
at their
fullest extent

Irish Channel

CANTERBURY

SALISBURY
Old Sarum

LONDON

English Channel

HAVRE

PARIS

CHINON

POITIERS

N

S

Bay of Biscay

☐ The Plantagenets
☐ France (Capet)
CITY
TOWN

Note on the Twelfth Century

France was still a small kingdom, even at the end of the twelfth century when this story opens. The French kings controlled the Île de France and some surrounding areas. Powerful Burgundy lay to the east, the broad lands of Aquitaine to the southwest, and Brittany and Normandy to the north and northwest, independent dukedoms or counties all.

An attempt had been made in 1137 to broaden the French kingdom when the French king, Louis VI (le Gros), and William, the ninth Duke of Aquitaine, agreed to the marriage of their children—just before each of the rulers conveniently died. Louis VII, called le Jeune, was seventeen at the time, and Eleanor, Duchess of Aquitaine, was only fifteen years old. The royal couple eventually had two daughters, but no sons. This remained a sore point with Louis's advisers and counselors, who feared for the succession.

The other power on the continent at that time was Normandy. It was from Normandy two generations earlier that Duke William (later called the Conqueror) had sailed to defeat King Harold at Hastings and to assume lordship of England. William I's granddaughter, Mathilda, vied with her cousin Stephen for the crown of England following the death of William's son, Henry I. Stephen was the victor. After a stormy civil war, and the death of Stephen's only son, Eustace, Stephen agreed to accept Mathilda's son, young Henry of Anjou, as heir to the English throne.

Meanwhile, the marriage of Eleanor and the pious Louis fared badly. In 1152 Eleanor and Louis divorced and she immediately married Henry of Anjou, who was about to become king of England.

Eleanor brought with her to her new marriage a dowry of the broad and fertile lands of Aquitaine. Henry and Eleanor thus formed a formidable alliance against Louis. This caused years of intermittent wars, notably over land in Normandy and the Vexin, although periodic attempts were also made on both sides to reach some kind of peace.

Louis married again, and again, until he had the son he so desired. From his second marriage to Constance of Spain, Louis produced two more daughters, Marguerite and Alaïs. In one of the rare moments of détente, Thomas à Becket arranged for the marriage of these two daughters to Eleanor and Henry's eldest sons. Marguerite married young Henry, called "the Young King" to distinguish him from his father, and Alaïs was betrothed to Richard, who came to be known as "the Lion Heart."

The marriage of Alaïs and Richard never took place. Eventually, much of the land of the northern continent and all of Aquitaine, Normandy, and Brittany became part of France. England went its own way, ruled for several centuries by descendants of the Plantagenet family of Anjou.

But for one century politics and power were dominated by a score of interesting, determined, and dramatic people, whose destinies seemed interwoven as if by divine design. Eleanor of Aquitaine, Henry of England, Louis of France, Richard the Lion Heart, John of England, Philippe of France, and Thomas à Becket were unforgettable characters. And so, if you believe this story, was Alaïs, forgotten princess of France.

Prologue

My last feelings, just before the hands seized me, were of my cold limbs. My last memory before darkness was of a trivial nature. I recall noticing the torches lining the cathedral walls and the leaping shadows that sprang from their fire to perform a macabre dance as if for my entertainment. They reminded me of a traveling dance troupe from Venice I once saw, tall, thin figures garbed in black cloaks and doublets, rising and falling like shafts of dark water in rhythm. The cold gusts of air feeding the torches seemed to increase as I watched, as if doors had opened somewhere. I should have been warned, but instead I paid no attention.

I was kneeling on the steps of the side altar, the very altar where Thomas à Becket had fallen under the swords of Henry's knights nearly thirty years earlier. I was not lost in prayer, as it might have appeared to an onlooker, should any such be passing through the church at this late hour. Rather I was focused on how to make my knees obey my mind and rise, so that I could carry out the purpose for which I had come, the task that forced me to spend a lonely hour on this dark, drafty April night in Canterbury Cathedral.

For although I was ostensibly on a pilgrimage to the tomb of the martyr to pray for my sins (and God knows there were plenty of those strung out like dark pearls in the years behind me), I had another reason altogether for keeping a vigil this night: I had been sent to recover Eleanor's letters.

The map stuffed into my pocket was no longer necessary. I had committed its contents to memory. All I had to do was persuade my stiff knees to disengage from the hard marble and straighten, so I could move around the altar to the masonry in back. Then it would be a simple matter to find the rosy-colored stone in the third row from the bottom and retrieve the packet of letters stored behind it. I could return to my warm guesthouse here at the abbey, and tomorrow I would be on my way back to France. Within the fortnight the letters would be delivered to Fontrevault Abbey. Then Eleanor would be happy, and I would finally get the information she had promised.

So engaged was I in that arduous task of rising that I failed to hear the slight sound behind me that would have signaled my fate. Instead I was taken completely by surprise. The only thing I felt was a strong hand around my neck, another around my waist, and—before I could cry out—I smelled the thick, sweet scent of a mandrake-soaked cloth. Unforgiving hands clapped it against my face, and all went dark.

When next I was aware, I was lying on my side in a litter of some kind, jolting along in a rough carriage enclosed by heavy velvet curtains. They smelled of mildew, and I was reminded of a damp stone tunnel under the castle at Chinon we royal children used for our play. I was covered with a rough wool blanket that scratched when I twisted. It stank distinctly of pigs.

I raised my head as far as I was able and saw that I was alone. My head felt weighty as a miller's sack of flour, and my tongue was covered in the same velvet that surrounded me. My hands were bound, but it was no matter: I couldn't have stirred a limb at that moment if they had been free. The very effort to hold my head up became too much, and I fell back on the makeshift pillow of cloaks someone had placed under me.

For a long period I could not move at all. My head felt alternately light and then leaden, and dreams wafted in and out like wisps of smoke. The shapes were familiar, but I couldn't catch hold of anything. The shoulder under me ached, probably from being tossed into this cart, but I was unable to relieve my position since my hands were pinned behind my back. I kept hearing the music of a lute, probably Marcel's lute, playing a familiar madrigal, but I could capture no more than a few notes at a time before it faded. And anyway, if it was Marcel, why didn't he stop playing and come to my aid?

An odd thought intervened: Minuit, my small black cat. I should have brought her with me on this journey. They would never remember to bring her indoors when it rained in Paris. Unbidden, tears began to spring up behind my eyes, and, like a rusty fountain finally producing, I allowed them to spill out. I had not cried in years. I was surprised I had not lost the knack.

To get better control, I tried to put my mind on some other topic. As was my practice when distressed, I set myself a problem to solve. The choice was obvious: my own situation. How was it that a princess of the royal house of France, at one time betrothed to the king of England himself, should come to find herself dragged through a cold Kent night by unknown ruffians, bound and stuffed like a wild boar in a lout's carriage? But even in my befuddled state, I knew the answer. It was the very same cause of all the difficulties that had plagued me through my entire life: It was all Eleanor's doing.

BOOK I

The Journey Out

1

The Courier

ady Eleanor was my stepmother, and the dearest friend of my childhood. To everyone else she was Queen Eleanor of England, or the Duchess of Aquitaine, or "Your Highness." To me she was simply the Lady Eleanor.

Our long and complicated history had many bends in the road, and our early intimacy had long since disappeared from view. Even so, it was hard to imagine that she meant me bodily harm. But there was no doubt in my mind that my current situation could be traced directly to the letter Queen Eleanor had sent to my brother's Paris court not a fortnight earlier.

Philippe and I were closeted together when her letter arrived. We were in his private chambers in our drafty palace on the Île de la Cité, perched on the edge of the wind-whipped Seine, when the courier found us. We were alone, without guards or servants, as was usual when he wished to badger me about some inadequacy of my performance as princess royal.

"Alaïs," I recall him saying, "I have hesitated to speak to you about this, but your behavior is becoming more and more a daily topic of discussion for the court."

With hands clasped behind his back, he paced away from me as he talked, so that his words at the end became muffled as if flung against the wind. I sighed.

The chamber suited Philippe. His passion was war, always had been. The tapestries that lined the high stone walls and provided some measure of warmth were laced with hunting scenes—men with spears, boars in flight, hounds leaping. Hunting is, after all, a form of war; at least I would think so if I were an animal. The doors that guarded the privacy of the chamber were of oak and carved with scenes from the ancient battle of Troy. Encircling the hearth was another remarkable piece of oak carved by highly skilled artisans. They had used their art to design miniature weapons—bows, arrows, knives, swords—all intertwined like a chain of malicious grapes winding around the gentle hearth fire.

"Well, what do you have to say, sister?" He turned unexpectedly and headed back in my direction. I forced my attention to the issue.

"I cannot understand, brother, why the court should gossip about me in this way. Unless it is that your courtiers are envious of my serenity in the midst of the tremendous chaos that reigns over this impending wedding."

"They say not that you are serene." Philippe's toe stubbed on a corner of one of the Smyrna carpets of which he was so proud. He cursed softly as he caught himself. At such vulnerable moments, he was not the king of France to me. I saw him only as my younger brother.

"The reports are the reverse, that your feeling about this wedding runs high. The charge is that you refuse to take part in the preparations, or even give advice when it is sought, but instead become angry when Agnès or her ladies try to involve you in their plans." He began to rub his brow, always a sign that his headaches were returning, then covered the gesture by running his fingers through his dark, cropped hair. "Alaïs, this is becoming an issue between Agnès and my royal self. She feels you are not supportive of this coming wedding between our son and the house of the Plantagenet."

I held back yet another sigh. Philippe felt caught; I could see it in his face. I knew he did not want to have this conversation with me, that Agnès had forced it on him. We cared for each other, and he mostly left me alone to brood in my own way or withdraw if it suited me. For all his faults, he was my brother. I sometimes saw in his face the broader outlines of my own as it played back to me from the metal mirror he himself had brought me from the south. We had different mothers, but the lines and shapes of our faces, long and thin, were of the father we shared, and we had the same slightly almond-shaped eyes, those eyes of the Capet house of France. His were dark, while I had been told mine were as green as the eyes of my black cat.

"Philippe, try to understand my position." I shifted on the cushions to lean forward and made a gesture of appeal with my good hand. "I don't like weddings. I don't want any part of them. I am delighted that you have arranged this marriage between little Louis and Eleanor's granddaughter." I smiled but then spoiled it by muttering, "Although why Eleanor of Castile would want to send the child Blanche from sunny Spain north to the damp fog of Paris is beyond me."

Philippe stopped in front of the small couch on which I had draped myself. "That is exactly the kind of comment that—"

"—that gets me in trouble in this court of yours," I finished for him. It was so easy to finish his remarks, because, on some subjects, they were so predictable.

"It's your court as well, Alaïs," he said, sounding wounded.

"No, it's not, Philippe. Let's not—at least between us when we are alone—keep up that fiction. I am here at your sufferance. I was sent back here like an unwanted package when my betrothal to Richard ended and Queen Eleanor found me an embarrassment. You are kind, but I am of an age where I should have my own home and county, and a husband of my own. I don't, and so I find myself your guest." I tried to speak in a matter-of-fact manner but found my voice oddly giving way to some kind of shakiness as I finished. So I stopped talking until I had more possession of myself.

"And so," I continued, speaking slowly, as if these thoughts were occurring to me for the first time, "perhaps because I never had my own wedding, it is difficult for me to enter with joy into planning this one. As I said at dinner this eve, it has occurred to me that I would be better in these days away from court. I would like your permission to withdraw for some time. Perhaps to stay with our sister Marie in Troyes until summer. She has always been willing to welcome me." I paused. "If I am away, out of sight of those who criticize me, it would not be necessary then for you to have to defend me, as you do now."

"Alaïs. . . ," he began. I was horrified to hear sympathy creeping into his voice. Who knows what emotional nonsense he would have uttered had we not—fortunately—been interrupted by the messenger, preceded by one of Philippe's marginally competent personal guards.

"Your Majesty." The short, burly figure of Philippe's head guard flung open the heavy oak door as the hinges protested. "This man insists . . . presenting . . ."

And before he could complete the announcement, the guard was gently edged aside by a remarkable-looking stranger who towered above him. The newcomer was no longer young, but he appeared still vigorous. He was dressed in traveler's garb, an ordinary tunic with no mail overshirt, leggings, a wet Lincoln green cloak, and boots spattered with mud. One keen eye sparkled with intelligence, while the other was sewn entirely shut, giving his craggy face a kind of unintended rakishness. But he held himself regally, and I saw the scarlet and white emblem of Eleanor of Aquitaine interwoven with the lions of England dressing his breast. My heart mounted into my throat, and I suddenly sat straight upright. It was Sir Owain of Caedwyd, King Harry's lieutenant and trusted knight, whom we had always called by the affectionate English name Tom.

"Sir Owain of Caedwyd with urgent messages for the king"— the guard raced through to the finish—"and the Lady Alaïs."

"Courier?" Philippe had turned at the interruption, and his voice was sharp. "What is your business with the king?" My brother disliked interruptions in the extreme, especially if he was experiencing some emotional state. Something to do with manhood, I believe.

"As your own man stated," Tom said, with the barest hint of irony, "I have letters for Your Majesty and Your Grace." He bowed low to each of us. "They are to be delivered personally and in confidence."

Tom's rumpled dress, which marked him as a servant-courier, deceived Philippe. He did not know—as I did—that Tom was an experienced courtier. Tom had been like a brother to King Henry in his younger years. Henry had even knighted him for his service. He went everywhere with us as a family, and I always felt he observed us carefully. His own manners were impeccable. Philippe was in for a surprise. I did not have to feign delight at the familiar face.

"Sir Owain," I said, extending my right hand. "Welcome to the court of Paris, dear Tom."

Tom smiled, as canny a smile as I had ever seen, and came toward me.

"You know this man?" Philippe swung his head between us with his nearsighted blink.

11

"Brother, permit me to present properly Sir Owain of Caedwyd, former lifelong friend and knight of King Harry of England himself"—I nodded to Tom—"and once a lieutenant in the king's own army. He is also a friend to France. His name is Owain, but the king always called him Tom, swearing to make an Englishman of him someday. Tom, may I present to you my brother Philippe, King of France."

I had known Tom well when I was a child at the English court. I should have recognized the thick Celtic inflection behind his labored Norman French,, even if I had not seen his beaked nose mapped with veins, the broad cheekbones, the wild thatch of red hair graying now. He had grown a red-gray beard in the fifteen years since I had last seen him, and it covered his square Welsh jaw.

But it was the sight of his hooded left eye that made me certain of his identity. I myself had seen the accident that caused his blindness when I was still a child and Tom was so young a man he hardly had a beard growing. King Harry's newest falcon had gone wild as they tried to sew its eyes shut for training, and the great bird had clawed Tom's own eye in its rage. Then both man and bird had had their eyes sewn shut. I never forgot the man's screams of pain mounting over the cawing of the great wounded bird as the barber-surgeon labored on Tom right there in the open field. I was on my own palfrey, which was pawing the ground impatiently as the shouts rent the air. The other children watched intently, the boys' faces betraying nothing. But I couldn't look. I closed my eyes and smelled the sweet field heather, wishing the echoes would end.

"Indeed," said Tom, making a low bow no courtier could fault, "you may count me always a friend of the country of Princess Alaïs."

"Well . . . well, then, what do you bring us, fellow? You come from our cousin King John?" At last Philippe was acknowledging the lions of England emblazoned on Tom's tunic.

"No, Your Majesty. My letters are from Queen Eleanor at Fontrevault."

"Queen Eleanor? What could she want?" The king moved to the hearth, edged out his mastiff, who was warming his bones there, and kicked the cinders back into the fire. "Unless it's further business about the wedding. She's been unusually silent on the topic for some time. I thought she was leaving all the preparations to our court here in Paris."

"Thanks to you, Tom, for your good service." I held out my right hand for the letter, and immediately Tom opened his leather pouch and transferred the scroll with its familiar blue-wax seal to me. I made no move to break the seal. Instead I stuffed the small parchment into my left pocket.

"But why is she writing to you?" Philippe muttered absently as he took his own letter and broke the seal, still standing by the hearth. "No doubt further directives on the wedding," he grumbled. "She cannot resist managing things." He shook the scroll open and scanned the script. We waited.

"God's good bones, sister, do you know what she's doing?" After a moment Philippe burst into a rip of laughter, causing the hound to look up yet again. "Old Eleanor. What a queen! She'll put us all to shame in our own old age. This almost makes me like her!" And he flapped the scroll in my general direction.

"What piques your interest, brother?" I gathered myself to rise from my comfortable cushions, much more curious to read my own letter than hear about my brother's. A feeling was creeping over me, that kind of knowing I occasionally experience just before a shift occurs in my world. I could sense Eleanor's letter, palpable against my leg.

"She is on the way to Castile to fetch her granddaughter for the wedding with little Louis." He crowed. "Oh, to have her spirit at her age!"

"What?" My efforts were momentarily arrested. "How could she? She has more than eighty summers." I pushed myself upward using my right hand on the firm oak of the chair's arm.

He was still reading, shaking his head as he moved to the long cypress table at the side of the room. He tossed the scroll down and picked up the large silver pitcher that displayed his personal royal insignia. Dark Bordeaux splashed as he filled two goblets, and then he paused. After the space of a breath, he poured a third.

"Who knows? Probably she'll be carried in a litter, at least over the mountains." He handed me a goblet, still chortling. I had no choice but to accept, impatient as I was to be gone. "But I wouldn't put it past her to ride partway herself, keeping up with her knights, no doubt." He gave Tom the other silver goblet.

"The wonder is that she's doing it at all." He raised his glass high. "Here, Tom of Caedwyd, drink a toast with the Capet family to the fortitude of your mistress, Queen Eleanor, and to the wedding soon to come that will unite both our houses, the English and the French." He paused, then added softly, "And end this endless war."

Tom, who had been standing to the side with a grave expression and folded arms since delivering his letters, raised his cup as graciously as if he drank toasts daily with the king of France. What he made of my brother's levity, one could not say. His long, honest face was impassive and pleasant, as I always remembered it except for the day of the accident with the falcon.

"What will Jean Pierre and his men make of this? You sent them to escort the Princess Blanche to Paris. They must be in Castile by now." I had toasted the queen with a swallow of wine before setting my goblet on the table.

"That's the wonderful part." Philippe was nearly dancing with delight. He picked up the scroll again and waved it around his head. "Jean Pierre will be so put out. He'll have to wait, of course, once the Spanish court hears Eleanor is coming. A royal escort. Her own grandmother. He could hardly leave before she arrives." Philippe tossed the scroll into the air and laughed like a boy when it bounced off the head of his hunting hound. "He's become so pompous since his father died and he inherited the family title. Cooling his heels in Castile while he waits for Queen Eleanor will be the perfect lesson."

I had to struggle to keep my composure. If Eleanor only knew that she was assisting my brother in a small revenge on his child-hood rival, she would have pulled her thin, well-shaped lips back in that ironic smile that came so easily to her. Pleasing Philippe, her first husband's son and the bane of her own young princes in war, was not anything she had ever mentioned to me as a priority.

"Brother, I have enjoyed our conversation. Let me think more on what you have said. Perhaps we can talk on the morrow." I moved toward the door, but Philippe moved even more quickly, blocking my way.

"Princess," he said, bending over my right hand with courtly grace, an odd, formal gesture to make to one's sister, but so typical of him in his better moments. "A good even to you. We will speak further of your desire to visit our sister in Troyes. And, Alaïs,"—he hesitated for just a fraction of a moment, almost embarrassed—"do not take too much to heart the gossip of the court. They mean you no harm."

I nodded, oddly touched, and again made ready to leave. Then I remembered Tom, but before I could speak, Philippe was already issuing instructions to his guard to find a bed and dinner for "our welcome guest."

I did not look at Tom, but he stopped me by speaking low as I passed. "My lady, will there be an answer to the queen?"

"*Certes,*" I said. "Come to my chambers tomorrow, before the noon hour. You will have your answer then."

2

The Letter

I moved slowly down the broad, damp stone hall toward my own chambers, careful not to excite the interest of the few courtiers and ladies who passed, bowing. Philippe was wrong, as usual, when he said the court wished me no harm. I was the target of words that came like arrows from every side. The French court resented my outspoken ways and my influence with my brother, the king. And some, because of my deformed left hand, saw me as no more than a witch, with powers they did not understand. I overheard one short, fat, overdressed little toad say once that I made interpretations of dreams and foretold the future. Which was nonsense—well, for the most part.

Turning a corner, I collided with the queen's newest maiden, the raven-haired daughter of the Duc de Berry. I couldn't recall her name, but her wild, uncontrollable bush of dark, curly hair made her stand out among the other young women-in-waiting. She was carrying a bolt of new pale samite, which was so tall in her arms that it completely shielded her face. As a consequence, when she rounded the corner like a young colt, she galloped into me. I nearly toppled backward, only catching myself against the wall at the last minute. The girl dropped her burden.

"*Tiens, tiens,*" I scolded, recovering my balance.

"*Excusez-moi,* my lady Alaïs," she said, making a neat curtsy, as if that made up for nearly knocking me over. "But it is the cloth for my new gown. The queen says we must begin the dresses now or they will never be finished in time for the wedding." She retrieved her burden, flashed a brilliant smile, and darted off, her vision once again obscured. The wedding, the wedding! Always this wedding.

I was happy to obtain the refuge of my room, where no young women besotted with wedding gowns could career into me at leisure. Mimi and Justine were there, sitting on the floor before the fire. They were so deep in their game of cards they had not noticed that the fire was no longer drawing, and I nearly choked on the musky smell of trapped smoke. They scurried to help, but I waved them out and tended to the draft myself. Then I flung myself into a chair and pulled off my veil. Loosing my braids, I ran my fingers through my hair and allowed currents of rest to flow through me.

My room was the smallest of the royal apartments, but I treasured it. I had surrounded myself with things I loved. Tapestries woven in Toulouse, images of fruits and strange animals worked in burgundy and gold, covered my walls and floors. Manuscripts rolled and bound, some crisp with age, some sent from monasteries as far away as Iona, filled one whole oak table, and on another— and for this I did love Philippe—lay as much parchment for drawing and as much charcoal as I desired. I could flee into my drawing whenever I chose.

Now the fire danced in the open draft, and the flames cast light and shadows on the walls. The oil torches set in the recesses near the chair combined with the firelight and candles to give me enough light for reading. Awkwardly I used my good hand to pull Queen Eleanor's letter from my left side pocket.

At my request all my gowns had pockets sewn into the left side. My left hand had been withered from birth. I kept it hidden as often as I could. And yet it was part of me, so I must accept it, accept a part of me that had no feeling. I had learned to live with it, if not to love it. And, anyway, the pocket had other uses. It could conceal various small items that came to me while in the public rooms: items that were, like Eleanor's letter, private.

I shook open the scroll after I slid my thumbnail under the wax seal. As I did so, a little piece of paper fluttered to the ground. It seemed at first glance to be a diagram of some sort. I retrieved it and set it aside. Then I proceeded to examine the careful writing before me.

Queen Eleanor had not written to me in the seven years I had been back at my brother's court. But the elongated, spidery hand in front of me, the hand I had learned to read as a child at her knee, was unmistakably hers. Even the uncertain night's light did not interfere with my understanding as I carefully made my way through the several heart-stopping pages.

As I read, my fingers out of old habit toyed with the jeweled pendant that hung on a thin silk cord around my neck. Richard's betrothal gift to me. It had once been Eleanor's.

To Alaïs, daughter of my own heart
From Eleanor, by the Grace of God Duchess of the Aquitaine
and once Queen of England and Lady of All the British Isles:

We have not corresponded for some time. I will be direct with
you now and not waste our time on recriminations for past events.

I write to ask you to favor me with an errand, one which will

*not take much of your time but is of the utmost importance.
There are certain letters that are hidden at Canterbury Abbey, in
the cathedral. These are my letters, written to Archbishop Becket
many decades ago, in the days when he and the king were
estranged. They are my property.*

I put the letter down. It was a curious opening. And I was
amused remembering Eleanor's habit of always referring to Henry
of England, her second husband, as "the king," as if there were
only one king. But whenever she referred to her first husband, my
father, she would call him by his full name and title: King Louis of
France, as if he—unlike Henry—needed further identification.
Then I read on, and all amusement faded.

*I want you to retrieve these letters for me. A friend hid them
years ago, so they would not fall into the wrong hands. They rest
behind the altar where Becket was slain. I enclose a diagram to
show you exactly the place. Retrieving them will be a simple
matter.*

*You are the only one who can do this. You can travel to
England without exciting suspicion, especially under the guise of
making a pilgrimage to the martyr's tomb. You are of French
royal blood, formerly of the English king's household. Even with
a small escort, you would not be harmed by the English nor held
back by the Normans. You can traverse both sides of the Channel
safely.*

*I am certain that you still love England, for the sake of our
family, if for no other reason. For the sake of Henry, and
Richard, if not for my own. Upon these few letters hangs the fate
of that kingdom. The Knights Templar are intriguing against*

John's throne. They claim he has unfairly pressed the abbeys to
help him pay his debts.

I stopped again, anger rising within me. John had always gouged his subjects, especially the abbeys. Everyone at court knew he was in great need of silver, and to him the abbeys sat across the land like fat little pigeons, ready for the plucking. He needed money for the mounting costs of recovering Eire. If only he had behaved in the first place, when Henry sent him there years ago, Ireland might still be linked to Britain. Now his mother wanted me to provide his bail. I returned to her words, shaking my head.

If John's enemies find these letters, they will use them to
destroy the king's—and my own—reputation with the good
people of England.

If there is a rebellion against John, a civil war would most
likely follow, and once again we'll see suffering and destruction in
England. I cannot allow civil war if it is in my power to prevent
it. Aide-moi maintenant.

I know you may be tempted to disregard my request. But if
you help me, your reward will be great. I have certain information
in my possession, information about a child born many years ago.
This child disappeared and was supposed dead. I think you were
interested in the welfare of this boy. If you want the information
I have, I will most willingly give it to you. But first you must
help me in this crucial business of the letters.

I have been told that your anger with me over the past
continues. That you blame me for preventing your marriage to
Richard. I swear to you on the tears of Christ that I had no part
in those events that occurred after Henry separated us and

imprisoned me. Please believe me when I tell you that it was not myself who prevented your marriage to our son, Richard.

I call you now to your responsibilities as my daughter. I will reward you well if you help me. If you choose not to help, your punishment will be your own unquiet conscience.

Eleanor R.

I reread the letter, my hand trembling as if with the palsy. I was torn between anger and shock, like a rag shaken in the teeth of a lion. Gone was my cool head. The lines blurred fiercely as I reread the script. How long had she known about the child? Why had she never told me? And how dare she of all people use my child's fate as a carrot to lure me to her witless task?

I picked up the silver wine goblet next to my chair and hurled it against the wall, watching the red liquid run down the tapestried wall like blood, feeling my wrath ooze from me. And then I rested my head on the back of the chair, giving up my spirit to whatever feelings came.

I slept poorly that night. My dreams were all of the Plantagenet family. They were on a tournament field. Eleanor, tall, regal, straight-backed and porcelain-skinned as when she was young. Richard, her favored son, tall, auburn-haired like his mother, and beautifully formed, with burgeoning shoulders on his slender, adolescent figure. And of course there was Henry, large, broad-shouldered, gruff, in rough, stained clothes and smelling of horses and the outdoors. In the sheer mass of his figure and his blunt, aggressive features, his power overshadowed the others. They faded from my presence, one by one. All except Henry.

The sun, already high in the sky, sent a ray across my face. I stirred. Returning to this world, my thoughts flew immediately to the child. What was it that Eleanor could tell me that I did not already know? What gem of information could she offer that would change the past? Or the future? The child was dead.

I sat up suddenly. What if, by some incredible chance, the child had survived? If there was any possibility at all . . . if Eleanor had such news, it was my right to have it. And have it I would!

I moved now with purpose but also with a heavy head, albeit one cooler than was the case the night before. My two timid maids, after tentatively peeking inward to the chamber, advanced slowly toward my bed and helped me rise and dress. They chattered as they brought me cheese and bread and wine for my morning meal. I answered pleasantly enough, but all the while I was considering Eleanor's strange request. While I waited for Tom of Caedwyd to appear, I riffled absently through a few of the new manuscripts that had come in from Córdoba. It was from Eleanor that I had learned to love the poetry of the Arabs in Hispania.

Then I began walking, restlessly, my fingers searching the golden jeweled pendant I wore. I felt the cool cut of the ruby set deep within it and the gold filigree of the setting. I could make out, too, the fine engraving on the back. Duke William had brought the jewel back from his captivity in Córdoba. It found its way to his granddaughter Eleanor, then to Richard, and then to me. The engraving was one line of Arabic poetry from the great poet Ibn al-Faridh: DEATH THROUGH LOVE IS LIFE. In a way the intensity of the sentiment, its many-layered meaning, reminded me more of Eleanor than of Richard.

A scratch at the door interrupted my reverie and alerted my maids to the arrival of the courier. They scurried to admit him. Tom had to bend his frame to enter, and I could see that Mimi and Justine were impressed by his height and by the mysterious shuttered eye unadorned by any patch.

After I dismissed my maids, I gave Tom my hand to kiss. Then

I walked over to the table that contained my beloved manuscripts and, half sitting against it, folded my arms and regarded him well. Tom remained where I had left him, waiting.

"You've come for my answer."

"Yes, Your Grace." Tom was a perfect king's man. Neither obsequious nor lacking in respect, he simply stood, tall as a lance and just as quiet. He spoke now in the king's English, no trace of his Celtic origins.

"Do you know what this letter contains?" I asked.

"As to its general contents, yes. As to its particulars, I have not read it." Tom had the kind of face and demeanor that led one to believe he truly had not broken that royal seal to satisfy his curiosity. But then he had no need to do so if Eleanor had explained the contents to him.

"I understand that your mistress Queen Eleanor is on her way to Hispania right now, to fetch the Princess Blanche for the wedding here in Paris."

"That is true."

"Since she is gone, who will receive my answer to this request?" I prodded him, partly in jest.

A ghost of a smile flickered across his lower face.

"If you agree to the task that the queen has set for you, there is no need for a reply. I am instructed to accompany you to England."

"And if I choose not to undertake this unusual and"—I lifted my brows—"somewhat dangerous task? Who gets that report?"

"In that case I return to Fontrevault Abbey and report to the Abbess Charlotte."

"My aunt Charlotte? Is she a party to this?" I had no need to pretend surprise.

"I do not know. I only know that Queen Eleanor said if you refused her request, I should inform the abbess." He coughed here, hesitating. "My lady, as you know, Queen Eleanor has been a guest at Fontrevault Abbey for nearly five winters. During that time the queen and your aunt have become . . . quite close."

"I see." I paced to the window and opened the shutters, looking down on the Seine below. Boatmen, ordinary people bundled in dark cloaks and red scarves, were polling their barges toward the palace docks and calling to one another. Across the river on the right bank, groups gathered on corners near the food stalls as the noon hour approached. The sight of Paris on a common day, going about its business, centered me. In a way it reduced the agitation that had been building since I'd read Eleanor's letter the night before. I found then the courage to ask my next question.

"I suspect that you do not know the nature of the information your mistress has promised me when I finish her task." I tried to sound casual, but I could feel my face flush. "Therefore I suppose there is no purpose in asking you for some . . . that is, . . . any indication . . . of what the queen knows?" I stumbled through it, but it had to be asked.

I knew I was presuming on our old friendship. I was taking a risk, but I felt beyond humiliation. If he had given the slightest indication of yielding, of telling me the fate of the child, the fate that Eleanor already knew, I would have thrown myself at his feet to beg.

"Your Grace." Tom stared at the rushes on the floor, his voice grave, his own cheeks reddening. Then he raised his eyes to mine. "I know only that the queen seems quite beside herself over this situation that threatens the throne of her son. She desperately wants to retrieve her letters before they can be used to wreak further mischief in this wrangle. And because I serve her"—here he paused as if his script required elaboration—"as I serve you"—his look was unwavering—"I have pledged myself to assist in any way I can."

His candor made me ashamed. I suddenly saw myself in the reflection of his eyes and glanced away.

He paused, and for a long time we said nothing. Then he added,

"No one knows better than I how painful that . . . event . . . many years ago was for you. If I had answers I could give you, I would have done so then."

"So if I go to Canterbury, you go with me?" I shifted slightly and began sorting the manuscripts on the table, to hide my emotion from his unbearably sympathetic eyes.

"Yes, Your Grace."

"Well, then." I turned back to him. "Prepare yourself, good Tom, for we leave for Canterbury at dawn on the morrow."

His broad face broke into a smile so honest and relieved that I had to smile back. Truly, I was amused to see he had expected me to refuse. He clasped his hands behind his back, and his shoulders seemed to lift.

"I'll have to tell my brother, and I expect he will press a few knights on us for safekeeping."

He nodded crisply, still grinning. Then, without further ado, he asked leave to go. I gave it to him gladly, for I had much to think about.

In truth, I had surprised myself. When the interview began, I was by no means certain that I would give an assent to this bizarre scheme. I did not react well to the coercion Eleanor was using. And yet if she did have information about the child, I must have it. If the price was doing her bidding and—worse—opening those old wounds that had been long closed, so be it.

I rang for my servants. By the time they appeared, I had already begun the note that would be taken to my brother, requesting permission for the journey. I had to call upon all my diplomatic skills to give a convincing explanation of what I was about to do, and why. And of course I did not, exactly, tell the full story.

·3·

Tales of the Deaths of Children

We rode hard out of the Île de la Cité at dawn the next morning, Tom and I and the escort of three knights that Philippe had pressed upon us. We paused before the bridge over the Seine, Tom examining the river for boats. I turned to take a last look at the cluster of gray stone that formed the buildings called home to the Paris court. As I did so, I noted three figures on horseback some distance behind us on the road. They were well mounted, with swords catching the early light, and so must be knights, but they had no other identification. They each wore the same nondescript gray cloak, and their hoods were raised. They pulled up their horses when we did, and I was disquieted for a moment. They seemed to turn sideways as I looked. Odd, too, that such a small party rode alone at dawn.

Perhaps Philippe had provided an unannounced escort for us, not trusting our safety to such small numbers. We would see. I spurred my horse forward, and Tom and my other knights followed.

The wind was up as we crossed the bridge, and a fine mist hit our faces as we headed southwest on the royal road. The sounds of the masons working on Sully's great cathedral behind our backs followed us. More than thirty years had passed since my father had commissioned this enormous church. They said it was to be named after Our Lady, that it would be a great monument to her motherhood of God's Son. But I didn't think we would see it completed in my lifetime. When Sully spoke of his church as a spiritual quest, I knew that meant it would take a long time to build and cost France a lot of silver.

My brother Philippe walked in the footprints of my father. He was always beginning excessive public works, like that *donjon* on the right bank he called the Louvre. He even talked of moving our court to live there. These massive projects, the cathedral and the Louvre, came dearly and were a sore point with the nobles, who had other plans for the wealth of France. More horses and more armor, no doubt.

I had my own thoughts on the matter. The wealth of France's nobles might better be spent to feed the peasants and protect widows and children than in outfitting every castle owner for the next grinding siege. But my brother and the men around him were not interested in such talk.

We were a motley group of travelers that morn. Sir Owain of Caedwyd, my dear friend Tom, was my special guardian on this trip. Since Eleanor had given him the assignment, I knew he would hover over me until we were safely back in Paris. And since he was Welsh, cousin to the great Llewelyn Fawr, he was a guardian to be valued. Marcel and Étienne, both liege men who had served me during the time after Henry's death when Eleanor had confined me at Rouen, were faithful to the core. Marcel played a lute so sweetly, it lifted my heart. And I was touched when Philippe pressed Roland, his current most-favored knight, on me for this journey. Roland was one of the most impressive riders and swordsmen I had ever seen in tourneys. I knew by this gift how much Philippe desired my safety.

Roland, he of the innocent face and the billows of black curls on his head, he who was so young he scarcely had any hair to remove from his face, had no connection to me, as had the others. He was Philippe's knight through and through. I later decided that he was persuaded to undertake this journey because of his obsession with the crusades. Étienne, a grisly old-timer, had served my father, King Louis, on the second crusade. Roland was tempted by the possibility of evenings with Étienne, telling tales of knightly valor in the Holy Land as we sat around the campfires.

By late afternoon of the second day, we were in sight of the port. Even though dusk approached, we had hoped to make the journey across the Channel immediately, since we had money enough to pay the price for special service. But as we neared the huts on the outskirts of town, we could see that the sky promised trouble. Mountains of darkening clouds were forming in the north. Old Tom shook his head.

"Thou'rt not thinking still of crossing yet today?" He looked my way as we paused on a slight rise overlooking the town. Our horses were tired and pawed the ground, making impatient noises. I noticed, as our journey progressed, that Tom had fallen intermittently into Celtic speech and his old habit of addressing me in the familiar. As if I were still the child he had known decades before. I did not reprove him. "The Channel sky must have looked just this way the night the *White Ship* went down."

"Mm. And all of England's hopes sunk, too," I murmured, thinking of that night long before I was born when the only son of the first King Henry died at sea. Because of that death, England had endured years of civil war. The death of any king's child was, in every event, significant. But some deaths were, perforce, more significant than others. And who would know this better than I?

"No," I said, looking heavenward. "I was not thinking of crossing under that sky. Only a fool would brave those storm-laden clouds. Whatever Queen Eleanor wants, it can wait for another day. Canterbury Cathedral isn't going to move."

Roland said nothing, but I noticed a smile forming on his broad mouth. No doubt the thought of a bed at an inn with a cheery hearth appealed to his youthful soul more than did a soaking on the uncertain waters of the stormy Channel.

And so we found such an inn, not difficult in a town with as brisk a harbor trade as Havre. We entered under the newly painted sign of the Boar's Head Inn, complete with a somewhat frightening picture of the boar snarling in an unseemly way for a place of hospitality. I was—truth to tell—as glad as Roland to be heading to a warm dinner and a bed of any sort, be it only clean.

A short, smiling man met us at the door and immediately inspired my confidence. He was fat, indicating that the food was good, and his apron was clean. These signs boded well for the hot meal and clean bed I desired.

The innkeeper surveyed us from head to toe and then offered the ledger in which we were to write our names by the dim light of a candle. Tom and Roland could write, of course, and I wrote names for the others. The names were false, but, like all experienced innkeepers, our host asked no questions. Our heavy travel cloaks and good horses told him we had silver, and that satisfied his only concern.

I was pleased when I saw my small chamber. Blue muslin curtains had been hung in the window, and fresh water for washing was set in the basin; these were niceties I had not expected in a town that serviced mostly sailors.

After a good dinner of (what else?) roast boar served in a

large, noisy public room, our small party arranged itself around the inn's commons, choosing feathered cushions in front of the snapping fire. The expected storm hammered the roof of the inn, and we congratulated ourselves on the wise decision we had taken at nightfall.

We had already been plied with the best wine the Loire Valley had sent to this city, and now we were moving on, taking up our busy host's recommendation of his cellar stock of Armagnac. I was sitting with my back against several of the pillows, while Roland was sprawled beside me and Tom sat next to him, cross-legged, partially facing us across the corner of the hearth. The other guests had moved to the back of the room for what appeared to be a rousing game of dice, and Marcel and Étienne had joined them willingly.

I noted Tom's fatigue in the fire's light, signaled by the drooping of his good eyelid. Roland, however, with the typical insensitivity of the young, paid no heed to this sign. He only knew he wanted more tales from the old knight.

When there was a pause, I took pity on Tom and steered the conversation elsewhere: "Where were you born, Roland?"

"In south Brittany, near Quimper. Where you can smell the sea all the day through." His face seized with a sudden look of longing so poignant that I had to hold back from placing my hand on his arm.

"How did you come into my brother's service in Paris?"

"My father died when I was ten. For a time I was squire to Count Geoffrey's chief guard. When Count Geoffrey died, my mother sent me to her brother in Paris. I came to the attention of the captain of the guards for my swordsmanship and was promoted into the service of the king." He paused. "My mum was afraid there would be trouble in Brittany at the time, and she wanted me away."

"Trouble? Of what sort?"

"There were rumors that Count Arthur, Geoffrey's son, was too demanding of his uncle John, king of England. After his mother the countess died the next year, there was no one to protect young Arthur." Roland looked beyond me, as if drawing on memory lurking in the shadows of our common room.

"John has no children," I said, munching an apple I had picked from the common bowl on the table. "Neither did Richard. So Arthur was the only heir to the throne of England if anything happened to John."

Roland nodded, frowning. But he didn't speak.

"And did good King John come to visit his nephew Arthur to offer his condolences on the death of the young count's mother?" I prompted.

Roland turned suddenly and looked at me straight on. "How did you know?" he asked, his face carrying that expression of true surprise that only the young and inexperienced can summon successfully.

"Ah. A lucky guess." I tossed the core of the apple into the fire, where it sizzled briefly before curling into ashes.

"King John stayed in Rennes for some weeks . . . to offer Arthur his protection, it was said, now that both his father and mother were gone. But after about a fortnight, he left without warning. The castle steward told the foresters who were hunting daily for the king's dinner, 'No need for more venison for King John. He's back to England.' "

Roland chewed his inner lip, and for a moment I thought he would not continue. But then he did.

"It was rumored that Count Arthur had displeased his uncle by being too forward and demanding about his patrimony. He thought he would rule Brittany after Count Geoffrey's death, even though he was so young. But his uncle wanted to appoint a regent for the land. The servants said that the king and the young count quarreled loudly one night, and as a result Arthur was confined to the dungeon in the bowels of his own castle. When Count Arthur hadn't been seen for some days, there was grumbling in the village, loose talk of storming the castle to see if he was all right."

Roland reached for another tankard of ale, which a buxom serving wench had set before him. Tom and I sat very still. A kind of sadness swirled around our corner of the tavern. "People were worried, you see. The young count—he was still a lad of only fourteen summers—had always been known for his social ways. He loved to walk about and talk to his father's subjects." He gave me here a look of such blinding innocence I had to close down all expression in my own face, lest I betray my own cynicism. For I already knew well the end of the tale.

"But then folks thought the better of it," he continued. "What chance would the townspeople have against the armed guards of the king of England? After that, as I said, the king left suddenly, and the young count was not seen again. It was said he died of a fever, still in the dungeon." Roland paused and took a long drink of ale from the cup that he cradled absently in his hand. "They said he was buried by his servants. His grave is unmarked. The villagers thought that dark deeds were done, but no one could prove anything. And, anyway, who would they turn to? The line is ended, and King John has appointed someone to govern Brittany for him."

I watched the profile of my young friend in the rising and falling light of the fire. His full lips were pressed, his throat working.

"Is your mother still living?" I asked in the silence that followed.

"No, she passed over. It has been two years now." His voice altered with the memory. "I never saw her after my last visit, when she told me the story of young Count Arthur."

"Now, let's see: Arthur would be eighteen summers if he were still alive. What year were you born, Roland?"

My question caught him by surprise. "I? I have twenty winters this year."

I noticed a movement by Tom of Caedwyd, shifting as if to rise.

"Your Grace, it grows late. I do not think further talk tonight will add to our strength tomorrow. And we have a ride after Dover still ahead of us."

"Why, Tom," I said, "does it make you uncomfortable that I reflect on the birth year of our young knight?" I forced a smile.

"No, Your Grace. Not exactly uncomfortable. But I've learned in life that certain things in the past are best left dead and buried there."

"An unfortunate choice of words," I said, sharp and quick. Tom pulled back as if stung. Roland shot out of his own private reverie. "What are you talking about?"

"Tom is concerned that I'm going to remember a young lad I knew who was born in the same year as you and who died soon after. And he is sore afraid that, in remembering this young lad, I will become womanish, which is to say maudlin and weepy. Is that not so, Tom?" I baited him without mercy, my breath short, a stone in my chest.

"Your Grace, you know I . . ." Tom, flustered, broke off.

"You what?" I was relentless.

"I know your feelings. I would do anything if all that was done could be undone. But it cannot. The *baban* is gone." His words at the end were so quiet they were almost imperceptible. As if a soft rain of words could wash away the memory of a child.

"What is he talking about?" Roland repeated. Completely absorbed in our exchange, he had forgotten his poor, dead mother and the mysterious death of his young Count Arthur.

"He's becoming sentimental, remembering a time when we were both younger and were brought together around . . . an unfortunate experience. There was a child at court, at King Henry's court," I amended watching Tom wince, "who was quite loved."

"And?" Roland spread his hands upward, tilting his head.

"And the child died and was taken away." I tried to say it without any feeling at all, just to show Tom, but found my voice dropping into a whisper, as if it obeyed something stronger than my own will.

"But who was the child, and why did it matter?" A flash of anger showed. "Many children die and are taken away, or disappear altogether in war, and even their mothers don't know what's become of them. It's devilish hard for anyone to grow up at all in these times." He sounded so personally offended that it almost drew a smile from me.

But the nut of what he said startled both Tom and me, and our eyes locked. His flat statement had pulled me out of the vortex of feeling that threatened to overwhelm me and put me quickly back in the present.

I rose from the cushions in front of the fire, aided by the hand Tom reached out to me. "You are absolutely right, Sir Roland. With all of the war that has gone on in France and England these eighty years, it's a wonder any of us are left at all to tell of it. And that's the thought I will carry with me to my chamber. It grows late. Tom has the right of it. We must to bed if we leave at dawn."

I picked up the candle on the table, touching Tom's hand for the barest moment. In turning, my eye caught a commotion at the far end of the public room, near the door, which had suddenly been thrown open. The gale, gathering outside for hours, was now in full force. It washed into the room with the ferocity of a mad lion.

But it was not the storm that widened my eyes. A group of men, heavily cloaked against the rain and withal soaked by it, flooded into the room. They were obviously noble, for even in their dire, wet straits, they were accompanied by a page who carried the coat of arms of the group's leader. The entire band of a dozen men passed quickly through the commons area and disappeared into a room off to the side. The double oak doors, which had swung wide for them, closed almost as soon as they had opened. But just before the page holding the soaked banner disappeared from sight, I caught a good look at the insignia.

"Good Christ's bones," I murmured, rather to myself.

"What ken ye?" Tom was at my elbow, alert and present, the emotional exchange of the past minutes now forgotten.

"That's the coat of arms of my uncle Robert's house," I said, still blinking.

"The Duke of Orléans?" Tom breathed inward sharply. "What's he doing in this place? And on such a night as this?"

"He'll probably ask me the same," I said, gazing at the closed doors. "I'd best have a good story ready." I leaned toward Tom. "My father's brother is no man's fool."

·4·

An East-West Encounter

You'll not be talking to him?" Tom's bushy eyebrows flew up.

"Mais certes." I turned to him. "What, as you put it so concisely, is he doing in this place? And on such a night, indeed! I think we should know, don't you? It may even have some bearing on our journey for Queen Eleanor. Either these knights have just come from Dover or they plan to travel there. Why make such a perilous journey in this storm? They must have urgent business. And what was the Duke of Orléans doing in England at all?"

"I'll go with you, then," Tom said with resolution. But his reservations were etched on his face in an accumulation of new worry lines. He was not looking forward to explaining to the Duke of Orléans why his royal niece was sitting in the public rooms of an inn in a rough sea town with only himself and three other knights for protection and two of those worthy men not even present, distracted at the moment by the gaming circle at the far end of the room.

"Tom." I pressed back a smile as I laid my hand on his arm. "Trust me. It is better that I meet my good uncle alone. I think I can carry it off." His crestfallen look overlaid his worry lines, giving his dear face an almost comical look. I added, "Never fear. I will tell him that you are here and I am under your protection while I travel. But until I know what he does here with these men, I do not want to put you in an awkward place."

Roland, who was standing a bit apart, still thinking, no doubt on our conversation about survival, had missed Tom's and my exchange. He moved toward me with alacrity when I beckoned, a frown and pursed lips signaling his return to the present.

"I bid you good night, Sir Roland. We leave early in the morning, if there is a clear sky. I hope to be at Canterbury by sundown two days hence."

And without further word, leaving Tom to explain, I walked away from both of them toward the oak doors. I do not know what I would have done if the doors had been barred. It would have been a magnificent embarrassment for me to have to seek help in gaining entrance to the room that had absorbed my uncle and his party. Fortunately for my fine sense of drama, they opened easily, and I passed through them as if I were an archangel.

Inside the room the innkeeper had already made the ducal group comfortable. A generous fire blazed in the hearth, and the men clustered around it noisily, warming their hands as menservants passed among them with goblets of mulled burgundy. I could smell the spice in the air, along with the wet wool of discarded cloaks.

Duke Robert stood to the side of the group. I took in his position before I moved forward. He was in front of a table with papers spread out and conferring with two men, whose heads were bent to listen. He stood out in the group not only by the colors he wore but by the straight Capet back that caused him to rise above other men in his height.

I had entered with some flair, flinging wide the doors. Otherwise what was the point? If I had crept in like a mouse, it would have taken some time to be noticed. This way, when the doors banged the walls behind me, I had the attention of the entire group.

"Who comes thus?" My uncle Robert's head lifted at the noise. He was ever a dramatic man himself. "We sent for no women servants."

I walked directly toward him, stopping on the far side of the table. In my travel clothes, and without the customary veil of the court, I suppose I looked every inch the servant. I leaned across the table, propping myself on my hands and thrusting my face forward. I thought he could not fail to recognize me when he saw my face.

Unfortunately, he did not. "What do you want, woman, to enter our private quarters in this manner?"

"Uncle, do you not know me?" I stood back, shaking my head with impatience. He strained to see. I had forgotten his growing nearsightedness.

"*Princesse* Alaïs?"

"Yes. You surprise me, Uncle. I am your only surviving niece. I would have thought you would recognize me."

"Alaïs!" He came around the table now, his momentary irritation vanishing, as I knew it would. He had ever been fond of me, since I was a child.

He embraced me before speaking again, and I must say I felt for a moment the safety of the power of my house, which in my present guise was denied me, at least in public.

"What are you doing in this godforsaken place?" He held me at arm's length to look at me. "Why are you in these common clothes? Whom are you traveling with? How did you find me?" So like my peripatetic uncle Robert.

"Softly, Uncle! I cannot answer all at once."

He led me to a chair by the fire, a much more comfortable abode than I had left in the public room. But then, the innkeeper did not know me as a *princesse* of France.

"And I will ask you the same," I continued. "What do you here in this obscure inn with so few men and on such a dark night?"

"We have just come from England." My eyebrows raised before I could think, and he noticed. He waved his hand vaguely in the direction of the Channel. "I had ordinary business there. And this inn is not obscure if one is traveling the Channel. Indeed, it is all that is open in this village on this stormy night."

"But why cross the Channel on such a night? Surely no business is worth that risk?" I appeared to jest. In truth, I did wonder what business of my father's brother was so compelling.

"I have come from Canterbury," he said, as if more information was called for. "I had to confer there and now must make haste back to Blois. There is another important meeting tomorrow, and I—" He broke off, seemingly aware that he was saying more than needed.

"But what of you?" As if he suddenly bethought himself of my situation. "Where is your entourage? Where are your servants?"

"Oh, Uncle." I invoked the smile that always pleased him, since I was a small child. "I fancy a swifter and more private way of moving. An entourage may get one private rooms,"—I gestured about us—"but for a woman it entails too much bowing and scraping, and too little freedom."

"You always did have a reckless streak in you," my uncle commented, not without a note of grudging admiration. "But what is your purpose in all this freedom?"

"Oddly enough, Uncle, I go to Canterbury, whence you have just come." I left a space for elaboration from my uncle, but he did not take the opportunity.

"Canterbury? How odd. What is your business in that grim place?"

I assumed the proper air of piety. "I make a pilgrimage to the martyr's tomb."

At this my uncle threw his head back and laughed heartily.

"Uncle!" I said, alarmed. If this was the response from my uncle, how would my pilgrimage story be received at Canterbury?

"You hated Becket. You are notorious for saying in public you never thought he was a saint at all. Everyone knows that."

He leaned forward, his elbows on his knees, light from the crackling fire playing across his face. It caught a heavy black onyx jewel embedded in a ring on the hand that he raised to his face, to prop his chin. "What is the true reason for your journey?"

I considered my options. They were not many. I decided quickly to tell the truth . . . well, a version of the truth.

"I have agreed to undertake an errand for old Queen Eleanor," I said.

"At Canterbury?" Duke Robert's hooded eyes opened a little wider. "Whatever for?"

How had I fallen into this trap? I was either faint with fatigue or not half as clever as I thought myself.

"She has need of some letters that are stored there," I mumbled, casting about in my own mind as I spoke for some safer topic. "Were you meeting with the abbot?" I asked this last partly in desperation to turn the conversation but also thinking to pick up some clues that would allow me to make my arrival at Canterbury more plausible.

"No, I had other business," he said tersely. "And Hugh Walter is not there at the present time." A frown creased his wide forehead and narrowed his almond-shaped Capet eyes. The mention of his own business had distracted him from mine, at least for the moment.

"Is he not?" My voice registered my true surprise. I had expected that Abbot Hugh Walter, a diplomat of the first order, would welcome me. He had many ties to the royal houses of both England and France.

"He is in Rome, pleading the abbeys' case against King John."

"Ah, yes. I have heard John is creating trouble by pressing the abbeys. But what can you expect from a man who murdered his own nephew?"

"Alaïs, have a care!" My uncle's tone was sharp. "You may say that here in the privacy of our room, but do not think for a moment you can say such things with impunity on the other side of the water."

I tried to look properly contrite, but he shook his head. "Heed me, niece. A sharp wit may amuse, but if it is recklessly used, it can snap back on the user, like a whip."

I paused a moment before speaking. "So if Hugh Walter is in Rome, who is in charge at the abbey?"

"Someone I think you once knew when you were a child at Henry and Eleanor's court. You must recall a lad called William of Caen, also raised there."

"William of Caen?" My eyes popped open. "William of Caen, that young prig who had his lessons with us royal children? The favorite of King Henry? We couldn't stand the sight of him."

Duke Robert flashed a look of unaccustomed humor. "The very same. I thought you might remember."

"He has risen in the world if he is running Canterbury Abbey," I said. "We called him William Orphan when we were young. He was insufferable. Always prepared for our tutors—"

"No doubt he was," the duke interrupted. "He has a reputation for brilliance, although I understand he was a little mite when he was young."

"Yes, that's it exactly." I laughed. "A mite. I remember him as a skinny lad, always ducking and blushing. He was always apologizing when he knew his lessons and the princes didn't. And King

Henry was always holding him up as an example to his sons, which didn't help him one bit with them when the king wasn't around." I caught myself. "Of course, we were all children then. I suppose we could be excused for our unkindness. Children are dreadful."

"It's quite a different matter now, Alaïs." The duke's tone was suddenly serious. "If you are going to stay at Canterbury, you will have to deal with Prior William. Take care. In his way, William is every bit as weighty as Abbot Hugh . . . in his way," he repeated.

Suddenly the doors I had entered a short time earlier were flung open again. What a busy inn for an out-of-the-way-place, I thought. But I was startled when I saw my uncle not only attending the distraction but rising.

"Who . . . ?" But my question was voiced to the air as my uncle left me to stride forward, arms outstretched, toward his newest visitor. I struggled to see the face through the dim torchlight and caught a startling glimpse of a slight figure robed—no, rather I should say swathed—in white fabric from head to toe. Three men, in pale robes, clustered around him, and when my uncle reached the little group, he embraced the man in white and bowed low to the others.

They engaged in intense conversation for long moments as I watched, uncertain of how to proceed. Just when it seemed my uncle had forgotten me altogether, he turned and led the white-robed figure to me. I rose, although protocol did not demand it. Something about these men was different.

"Alaïs, permit me to make you acquainted with my longtime friend and teacher, Averroës of Córdoba. Master Averroës, this is my niece, Alaïs, daughter of my late brother King Louis and Constance of Castile, your countrywoman."

The man bowed low to me, and I returned the gesture. I seemed to be under the sway of a feeling such as animals experience, that causes movement without thought or plan. When I stood again, I saw that the master was my height and looking directly into my eyes. His own were deep-set, dark pools in a face of leather that bespoke a lifetime in the blazing sun.

"Master Averroës," I echoed, of a sudden recalling the name Eleanor had often invoked when teaching us. The Arab master of philosophy and medicine, who knew as much astronomy as he did language, here in this cold, sodden port city of the northern border! And meeting, not by accident it appeared, with my very own uncle.

I bowed again to the master and to each of his men in turn. I then received their homage.

"Indeed, a pleasure to meet the *princesse* who carries the blood of the royal houses of France and Castile." The voice was parched and thin, like desert air or leaves underfoot in late autumn. He must be ancient now, I mused, and he smiled as if he could see into my thoughts.

"You are not rain-soaked, Master," I offered, noting with interest the dry robes of all of the new arrivals. "It is fortunate that you are not in the elements this evening."

"Indeed so," the master said, his quick eyes catching the flickering light. Almost, I might have thought, he was entertained. "You have a gift of observing what is around you. Not everyone can claim that gift." He paused. "I have been in this place for two days. I must needs travel tomorrow, but they say the storm will clear before morning."

"Alaïs, you must excuse us. Master Averroës and I have some letters to exchange," my uncle said in his direct manner.

The master waited, saying nothing but continuing to look at me with an unwavering gaze. I could think of no excuse, diplomatic or otherwise, to prolong the exchange, given my uncle's thinly masked impatience. Surprisingly, it was the master himself who delayed my departure. His eyes had moved to the pendant I wore around my neck, now fully revealed because I had shed my cloak and the wrap that had kept me warm in the public room. My gown came over my shoulders in the new fashion with a deep cut down the center. I knew that the pendant rested between my throat and my breast.

"That is a remarkable jeweled piece you are wearing," he said unexpectedly. "May I see it more closely?" He motioned a page to come nearer with a torch.

"Yes, of course, Master." I moved forward so that I was standing in front of him. I could smell his sweet breath, which reminded me of the figs my mother used to receive as gifts from her own mother in faraway Castile.

"You must excuse me. I do not see as well as in former times," he said in his sere voice, and he bent over the jewel. He lifted it by its cord and turned it in his hand, being careful all the while not to touch my skin. I could feel the warmth of his breath, though, and I made an effort to hold myself absolutely still, looking over his bent head.

I saw my uncle watching us. He had moved back and slightly behind the master. His eyes met mine, and he seemed to be signaling me in some way, but I could not divine what message he wanted to convey.

"This is a jewel created by Omar Ibn al-Faridh of Toledo, is it not?" the master asked when at last he straightened. "He worked for the caliph in Córdoba when I lived there as a young man, many years ago."

"I believe you are correct." I was still ramrod straight and breathing carefully. "Ibn al-Faridh was a great poet and a master jeweler as well."

"You know our culture well, for a northerner." He smiled. Was he trifling with me, or was it a compliment? "How did you come by this? Was it in your mother's family?"

"No, it came as a betrothal gift from Richard Coeur de Lion. His mother was given it by her grandfather, who brought it back from his captivity in your land."

"Ah, yes, the famous Duke William of Aquitaine." The master

paused, his expression inscrutable. "He spent some time in Seville after he was captured in *Outremer*. He was a great favorite of al-Mu'tamid. He must have been given the jewel as a farewell present." He spoke as if Duke William had paid a social visit to southern Hispania.

"I had no idea this jewel is so well known," I said, and I could not keep a frown from forming. I did not care for notoriety of any sort.

"I remember Eleanor wore that pendant on the day she and Louis were married," my uncle offered, as if to break a rising tension.

"Did she so?" I murmured as I pulled my wrap around my bosom and flung one end over my shoulder. A page scrambled to pick up the cloak that had slipped to the floor. "It was a gift from Eleanor to her favored son, Richard. And then from him to me," I said. And then, for the benefit of the master, who seemed far too interested in my jewel, I added, "It never leaves me."

My words filled the air for a long moment. We all seemed frozen in private thought. It was the master himself who turned to my uncle and said softly, "I believe you have documents for me." He executed yet another elaborate bow in my direction. "Forgive these old men who must forgo your charming company to do our business."

"It has been my pleasure to make your acquaintance, Master," and again I bowed. It was not obligation but a recognition of his great learning and his ancient eyes that moved me. "Perhaps one day I may come to Toledo and visit the school that you and Gerard of Cremona have created."

"Ah, you know about that? We would welcome you most gladly," he said, speaking in English heavily inflected with the music of the Arabic language.

"Alaïs, will I see you in the morn?" My uncle came forward and took me by the elbow to steer me toward the door. "We could perhaps break bread together before you board ship."

"No, Uncle, my party must move swiftly tomorrow. My men have arranged a passage at dawn, if the storm has passed. We must waste no time."

"Ah, I regret that we cannot spend more time together. You must come to Blois at the first opportunity."

I smiled at that sally. "I must, if I am to see you. You never come to Paris now."

"Philippe can manage without his uncle's counsel. And I find myself extremely harried these days."

I wanted to ask him why he should be so busy when he was well past the age where he had to gather troops and lead battles. But I could sense an impatience to return to his conversation with Averroës.

After he formally embraced me, bending his tall frame to mine to brush each of my cheeks, he did an odd thing. He gently pulled my dead hand from out of my left pocket and pressed his lips to it. This embarrassed me. I am intensely private about my hand and rarely expose it. If it had been anyone but my uncle Robert, my bile would have risen. Then he withdrew a step and regarded me with his deep gaze.

"You look much like your mother, Alaïs. You have her coal-black hair and green eyes. It is a great pleasure for me to see you, and to see you well."

I was so startled by Duke Robert's sudden change of mood that I fear my mouth gaped. Then he continued.

"But, niece, take a warning. Please have a care about your person. Do not expose your jewels in these public houses. Thieves lurk everywhere."

I began to form a rejoinder when his mood slid yet again and became quite military.

"I shall order two of my men to see you to your room."

"Uncle, be sensible!" I said, finally voicing my exasperation. "I have come safely all the way from Paris with four good men, and I can certainly see myself to my room in this inn without assistance from the army of the Duke of Orléans."

He began to protest but then saw that I was serious and shook his head, speaking with a chuckle. "All right. And I see you are right to trust them. Is that not your man waiting over there?" He pointed across the room as the large doors swung open. There was Roland, propped up against the wall, his head drooping. It snapped up at the sound of the doors, and he hurried to my side.

"Good-bye then, Uncle. And Godspeed," I said, murmuring inwardly that I would give much to know where God would speed him next, and for what purpose.

"That was a long conversation," Roland said, falling into step beside me.

"You took it well," I joked. "I see you are finally growing tired."

"Tom said if I could not wait, then he would do it, but he was already nodding when the three of us sat by the fire, so I packed him off to bed."

There was a silence. I dared not laugh. As we made our way to the stairwell leading to our cramped but whitewashed rooms, we passed a small group of men who sat at an oak table in the corner with trenchers of ox stew and goblets of red wine.

I would have passed them by, intent as I was to lay my head on a pillow, but their garb caught my eye. Although there was a roaring fire in the grate and the place was warm with the sweat of the men shouting and gaming in the opposite corner, these men still wore their cloaks and hoods even as they dined.

As I passed, one turned to talk to his mate, and his hood fell back momentarily. In the torchlight I saw the outline of a high forehead, a strong nose broken at one time, and full lips. As if aware of being observed, the man made a quick gesture to pull the hood forward.

I didn't pause but took note of all. There were three of them, and I bethought myself of the three mounted men I had seen on the Île de la Cité as we rode out from my brother's Paris castle.

My mind was still on these men as I entered my chamber, drawing the heavy bolt behind me. A wall torch still flickered, and for a moment I stood perfectly still. There was something in the room, some scent that was not familiar. A musky scent of male sweat.

I lifted high the tallow candle I was carrying and swung the light into all the corners. Everything seemed as I had left it. The basin half full of washing water, my travel sack on the floor near the bed, my cloak tossed across the chair in one corner.

Then I saw it. My small casket of jewels lay inside the leather fold of my travel sack. I always packed this casket at the bottom, as I rarely pulled out jewels when I journeyed, unless I needed them to exchange for silver. The casket was less likely to fall out and get lost if it were tucked away safely under my clothes.

So someone had removed this casket and examined it. He must have been in a hurry to be so careless in replacing the item. Or he was an inept thief who didn't know how to forestall suspicion.

I stooped and picked it up. The small oval box had been a gift from Eleanor's daughter Joanna when I returned to the court at Paris, and I treasured it for that reason. Also the fanciful design of the colorful gemstones on the lid pleased me. I noticed now they were untouched, though they would have been easy enough to pry off. The small lock that held the lid to the box had been twisted and broken, however. Setting the casket on the rough oak side table, I flicked open the lid, expecting to see an empty box. To my surprise, the few jewels I had brought with me lay peacefully on the bottom: the jewels to twine in my hair (should I ever reach civilization again!), a necklace that Philippe had given me, a brooch that was a favorite, a ring that was my mother's, all nestled against the scarlet velvet lining.

I snapped the lid shut and surveyed the room again, but nothing seemed amiss. A quick check of my leather sack showed my few clothes slightly rumpled but all accounted for.

My next act was to throw open the shutters of the window. I felt violated, and I wanted the strange scent gone from my space. I leaned over the sill and looked out onto the harbor, breathing deeply. The rain had abated finally. With the passing of the clouds, the moon had made a delayed appearance. The boats bobbing in the water seemed peacefully oblivious to the recent storm. But my soul was puzzled and very unquiet.

·5·

Canterbury Ghosts

J knew I should not sleep well that night, but I burrowed under the pile of wool blankets the inn provided with some hope that after the buzz of the events of the evening inside my head diminished, I should receive some surcease in the arms of Morpheus. Alas, it was not to be. But it was not the unsettling meeting with the master nor the mysterious intrusion into my chamber that distracted me. It was the cloudy memory of a long-ago scene with William of Caen that overtook me, almost as if it were summoned.

This kind of imaging has never frightened me. I consider such visitations a gift. As an artist, and one who often draws what is not yet visible, I am not afraid of visions. It matters little whether they be memories of events or scenes of the future. But this night images from my past well nigh overwhelmed me.

I supposed it was triggered by my uncle's news that William of Caen was acting prior at Canterbury. As I closed my eyes, the picture of

William of Caen backed onto the stage of my mind. He was just as he had been as a child, short and slight. His face, when he turned toward me, was still covered with a blush so severe it looked like a rash.

I saw him cowering on the field outside of Caen, having watched King Louis's soldiers impale his English father on a spear before his very eyes. He was discovered, it was said, when the knights made a last pass through the field after the battle noise had faded. Of course I was not there. Being only a child myself, I was kept at the castle with Queen Eleanor and her daughters, but now I could see it all: the frightened little boy huddled by his dead father, the tall, commanding William Marshal, Henry's chief knight, impulsively scooping him up into his saddle as he cantered by.

And with the face of that little boy came tumbling the memories of my school days with my sister, Marguerite, and the children of Henry and Eleanor. Especially the princes.

Since the orphan lad didn't know—or was too terrified to tell—his given name, he was named for his savior William Marshal, and the great man became the little boy's patron at court, sort of his *beau-père*. Young William was a terribly bright lad, well mannered beyond his years (some thought), and at the top of his form with the tutors William Marshal provided. Soon even King Harry noticed him and took him into his own household. He began having his lessons with us, and that is when his troubles began.

What drove the young princes wild was William Orphan's constant humility, so different from their own bold approach to life. William never volunteered an answer but was always ready when the masters called upon him. He never came to the Latin lessons without his reading, as the rest did. And when he got a right answer, he seemed more embarrassed than the princes when they had no answer.

The princes' annoyance reached a pinnacle one fine summer afternoon when Master Clement pointed out to the king how good William was at his studies and not very diplomatically compared

Richard's and Geoffrey's indifferent performances to that of the orphan. King Henry summoned all of the young princes before him, even John, who was too young to be in school yet, to inform them that William's example was the one to follow. "By God's hair!" he bellowed. (I wasn't there, but later Geoffrey did his usual absolutely accurate rendition of his father's famous rage.) "How can an orphan outperform the sons of a king?" He paused (Geoffrey said), and his sons, lined up before him, hands clasped behind their backs and legs straight apart, waited; then he answered his own question in an even louder voice: "Because they are lazy, arrogant, and stupid." And he walked down the line and slapped each one lightly across each cheek. Not exactly a knighting.

Geoffrey was all for beating up the little runt after that, but Henry Court Mantel dissuaded him. Prince Henry was the eldest son and had just a touch more common sense than the others. He had learned from an early age that just a bit of restraint helped avoid an even greater punishment in that chaotic household. He did not want to provoke his father's wrath yet again, especially over that pipsqueak. But they all agreed one fateful night, when we met in the barn under the moonlight, that William Orphan was a dreadful creature and should be taught a lesson. I stood in the corner listening and hated William, too, on behalf of my stepbrothers, whom I adored.

I could still summon William's voice from the incident that happened the next day. Young William had taken the prize in Latin, hanging his head shyly as he always did when he won. The young princes were sorely put out. They lured him to the barn to play, then blindfolded him and, turning him till he was dizzy, pushed him from one to the other while he screamed in fear. I cheered my heroes on from a safe distance.

William Marshal himself happened to be passing and heard the screams. He stuck his head in the door and put a stop to the teasing with one intimidating bark. The young princes fell back in chagrin, and the marshal himself whipped the blindfold off the beleaguered boy. Then he stalked out of the barn without a word, and the young princes dispersed just as quickly. I was rooted in the corner, where I had fled when the marshal appeared.

William Orphan stood in the middle of the barn turning about with a slightly dazed air. When he finally stood still and saw me, I held my breath. Silence draped over us, like a heavy fog. He stared at me, and his eyes locked with mine. His look was not so much blaming as quizzing me, and somehow that embarrassed me more. At that moment I wished I could say I was sorry, but instead I simply ran past him and out into the open.

That night at supper, the king was angry. We knew that William Marshal would report the incident. Nevertheless, when the king called young William to him and asked for an account of the bullying scene, we all became very quiet. Although we could see his skinny legs shaking beneath his tunic, to William Orphan's credit he would not give evidence against his tormentors. He said in his high child's voice, "It was only a game, Your Grace. The princes meant no harm." Henry said to his shamefaced sons, "This young orphan knows more about the kingly gesture than you do." There was no need for a slap on the cheek this time. The burning, quiet words of the king were enough.

After these events marched through my mind, I began to search for other images in my quest for sleep. But I kept seeing only the scrawny little boy bravely facing the king. And I knew I must draw him one day. Finally even he faded.

The last thought I had before sleep overtook me was an odd one. There must be more to the history of my jeweled pendant than I knew, to have it attract the attention of Master Averroës. Where could I find more information on the inscription? But then I knew: Was I not headed for the center of all learning in England, Canterbury Abbey? Of course! Prior William could send me to the best scholar on Islam at the abbey. Perhaps there was a monk who would know why the work of Ibn al-Faridh was so compelling. Because I was becoming increasingly certain that the master was not the only person interested in my jewel. Someone else had sought it in my chamber this very eve, and been sorely disappointed.

There were no strangers in evidence the next morning when our small party gathered at the appointed hour at the inn's hostelry. I tried to put the disturbing incidents of the night before out of my mind, but they kept picking at me like impatient insects. For some obscure reason, I forbore to mention either the encounter with Averroës or the ransacked chamber to Tom. Perhaps prompted by a concern for his quiet mind.

When we reached Canterbury two days later, the sun was settling into the trees, leaving that complicated rosy-yellow smear against the western sky that spring evenings sometimes offer in Kent. The color put me in mind of some dimly remembered feeling from my youth, some formless yearning. I paused to study the sky as if it were a work by a friendly artist.

My companions pulled alongside my horse. Tom, sensing my mood, waited. Roland spoke, looking upward. "Rain tomorrow, there's no doubt." He turned to me. "My father was raised by a fisherman off the south coast of Brittany. He taught me how to read the sky at sunset when I was only seven summers."

I sighed. I didn't want to discourage the lad, but I wondered when it was that young men ever got the hang of the blessing of silence at moments like these. I looked over at Tom and saw that he followed my thoughts. He grinned. Our sharp exchange at the Boar's Head Inn had been forgotten, and I was grateful.

Within the hour we cantered up to the imposing gates of the

town. The high stone wall extended nearly as far as we could see, but the iron gates that tied it together were more formidable by far. The gates were composed of high vertical spikes that were attached to two equally long horizontal spikes, and all could swing open only if someone inside undid the huge lock. But as I gazed through the guesthouse window inside the gate, I saw that the porter appeared to be dozing on his chair. He did not look as if he had any particular interest in our small cluster of dusty travelers.

"Ho, porter, we come as pilgrims to visit the tomb of the martyr!" Tom shouted through the gates, with impressive authority. "The Lady Alaïs is a princess of France and wishes entrance to the abbey."

With that the porter came alive, jumping from his chair. He emerged from his little house, rattling his keys.

"Sorry, sir knight. Sorry, milady. Prior William knows of your coming. Brother Dermott, the abbey's hosteler, is even now on his way to receive you." He gestured up the hill.

A tall, brown-robed figure could be seen hurrying down the worn path from the looming cathedral, the cord around his waist flapping. He was struggling to hold his cowl forward against the wind that had come up with the sunset. "I'll wager this is Brother Dermott," Tom offered dryly, shading his eyes with his hand.

I turned my attention to the scene around me. A large clump of stone buildings stood directly uphill from the road leading in from the gate: the cathedral and the abbey cloisters. Between us and the cathedral complex, there lay a broad dirt commons filled with the busyness of town life. Tradesmen had set up their stalls ringing the inside of the town walls. A huge market was just being dismantled, and voices still bantered on the dusk air. Men and women called to one another across space filled with little children, a cacophony of pleasant, human discourse. Two horsemen cantered by, their saddlebags bulging with the fruits of their afternoon's efforts and another old cart laden with one farmer's goods waited to be let out of the town gates. The rich smell of roasted birds that had fed many a customer this day still hung over all. I suddenly bethought myself of my own hunger.

The grand cathedral on the rise of land dominated the scene, surveying the surrounds like the haughty noblewoman that she was. Augustine's cathedral. Becket's cathedral. Seven hundred years old. Seat of all ecclesial power in England, greater even than York. And attached to her sides, like extended arms, were the long, windowless, rectangular stone buildings of the abbey. I had been to Canterbury. I knew that on the other side of those blind walls lived an entirely different world: quiet cloister walks, herb gardens, grass and bushes and contemplative silence. So different from the busy town that lay before us.

"Welcome, welcome, noble knights." Brother Dermott was huffing as he reached us. "Princess Alaïs of France, the abbey welcomes you especially, on your pilgrimage to the martyr Becket's tomb. Prior William has instructed that I bring you to him upon your arrival—after, of course, you have been shown your room and refreshed yourself." He was a long, thin monk, ascetic-looking for a hosteler.

"How is it Prior William knew of our coming?" I was puzzled. Who would have sent couriers? Philippe? It seemed unlikely. Queen Eleanor herself? Brother Dermott chose not to hear my question.

"Indeed, my lady, your aunt, Abbess Charlotte of Fontrevault, also awaits your coming." Now I was genuinely startled.

"Charlotte! Here? And they expect us?"

"Prior William has arranged for the knights to stay in the village at the Lion's Paw Inn, Your Grace." Brother Dermott seemed skilled socially beyond his station, and this news was imparted with a combination of courtesy and firmness that brooked no resistance.

I turned to him to protest, but before I could speak, he cleared his throat. "Ah, in recent years, since the death of the archbishop, armed knights are not allowed to stay overnight in the abbey."

"You mean I am to stay without the protection of my knights?" I was outraged. And of a sudden, for the first time on this remarkable journey, I felt a cold finger of fear.

I collected myself immediately. It has always been my practice to heed feelings of fear but not to be overcome by them. Besides, the martyr's death. How could I protest? "I understand," I said.

Tom appeared even more unsettled by this news than I. He handed my horse to the brother groom who came forward for the reins, conferred for a moment with the other knights, and then turned to me.

"Please, do not concern yourselves," I said, before he could speak. "I have nothing to fear in this abbey. Prior William will guarantee my safety. And after all, my aunt Charlotte is here. There is no need for worry."

"How long will Your Grace remain with us?" Brother Dermott asked as the grooms pulled my dusty bags from the horse's back.

"Three days at the most," I replied. "Good Tom, you and the knights go to the Lion's Paw and wait there. I will surely send a message day after tomorrow. I will pray at the martyr's tomb in vigil tomorrow evening. I expect we will leave the following day, but I will send word when I am certain."

Tom took both my hands in his and looked down at me with his good eye. "Princess, if you should need assistance, send this ring with a messenger. No written word will be necessary." And, pulling off his glove, he removed a ring from his gnarled finger. It took some tugging, but it finally released, and he pressed it into my hand. A flood of warmth rose in me when I looked down, for I saw the royal lion of England engraved in the setting. This was one of Henry's rings, given in the early days of his friendship with Tom. No doubt an impulsive gesture, generous, so typical of Henry at his best.

I looked up to protest, but something in Tom's face stopped me. My fingers closed around the ring.

"I will see you day after next," I said to all, putting forth more confidence than I felt. Something about these events gnawed at me as I turned to follow Brother Dermott, who had slung my travel sack over his shoulder and was already hurrying off.

It had been many years since I had visited Canterbury. As Brother Dermott led me to my quarters through the great hall and down the outer cloister walks, I saw again the intricate carvings that had been chiseled everywhere. In the stone all along the side walls and in the capitals of every column surrounding the courtyard garden, everywhere we looked, we saw exceptional miniature scenes, little dramas of the faith.

Brother Dermott, although taciturn at first, proved a storehouse of knowledge on these scenes when questioned. He could describe every picture to me, explaining even the smallest figures: This overhead was the dialogue of devil and angel over a monk's soul; that one showed two monks in prayer; a larger carving in the stone wall was the scene of the Blessed Mother's assumption into heaven. It was the whole of the Christian belief system chiseled in stone and set in the cloister walk, a daily reminder of heavenly choices. I was seized by a desire to return and examine every scene in this sweet corridor. Such formidable, unquestioning faith that produced these stories! How I envied it. Did William himself have such faith now? Or was he only the cynical custodian of these good monks?

I was to be settled in a small freestanding guesthouse in the close between the main monastery buildings and the great cathedral. After we left the cloister walk, Brother Dermott fell silent once again. I tried to draw him out on the history of the abbey, but his replies to my questions were brief, almost monosyllabic. An awkward silence grew as we paced along the path.

"The abbey seems to be thriving under Prior William," I finally ventured as we made our way down a winding path through a small herb garden.

"*Oui, madame,*" the brother replied, gesturing for me to follow him as he took a right turn at the northwest corner. This stone path was much narrower than the cloister walk, so I was forced to drop back slightly behind him to avoid the spring mud on either side. Brother Dermott spoke to me now in nearly flawless French, turning his head slightly so that his words would drift over his shoulder. "*Prieur Guillaume est un bon prieur, certes. Mais, la seule raison pour laquelle il est le chef maintenant est l'absence de l'abbé Hugh Walter. C'est Hugh Walter, lui-même, qui a fondé cette communauté, vraiment. Abbé Hugh est le chef.*"

"You speak French! Are you Norman, then?" I didn't bother to conceal my confusion. "Your English is excellent. In fact, I would have sworn at first you were a Lincoln man." I was walking directly behind him now, as he led the way across the cathedral close.

"Aye, and so you would have the right of it." He reverted to his native English with surprising ease. "Born and bred in Lincolnshire, I was. And how is it that you, a royal princess of France, know a Lincoln man's speech?" he asked, his head turning toward me. I came alongside him as the path suddenly broadened, and when his cowl slipped back, I saw by the light of the setting sun his long, narrow face dominated by his black eyebrows. I noticed with surprise that his left earlobe was missing. He pulled his cowl forward quickly.

"I passed my childhood years at the court of King Harry and Queen Eleanor," I replied. "When we were in England, the king insisted that we speak English. When we were in Normandy or Anjou, it was always French." I was bemused. Brothers in service to an abbey do not ordinarily address a guest princess with such directness. Brother Dermott seemed singularly at ease. If all the monks were like this, no one would be awed by the French royal house. I might pass my time here under no particular notice.

After a pause I spoke. "And if you truly are from Lincoln, how is it you also speak the French tongue so easily?"

"I spent some years on a crusade to the Holy Land. There were many Frankish knights there also. We shared boredom, and battle, and the occasional game of dice."

I waited.

"That was long ago." His voice was oddly deep and steady, the voice of a much heavier man. There was another silence. "In these times we all play many roles," he added. A cryptic comment at best.

"Exactly when," I asked, "were you on crusade?" I glanced sideways. From what I had seen of his weather-beaten cheeks, he might be any age. Could he be old enough to have made the crusade at the time of my father and Queen Eleanor? But no, there had been no English knights on that crusade. It was all French folly. In those days the English were still immersed in the civil war Henry's mother, Mathilda, had started. This monk was my age perhaps, but surely not a generation older.

"I made the last crusade to *Outremer* with King Richard in '91," he said.

"Ah, with Richard," I replied, clenching my fists against the lurch of my heart. I only hoped he did not hear my quick intake of breath. We finished our short walk in silence, and passing through a thicket of gorse bushes already blooming yellow in defiance of the raw English spring, we came to the door of the guesthouse.

Brother Dermott fumbled with the large ring of keys on his rope belt, found one that looked right to him, and inserted this into the rusty keyhole. He turned it this way, then that, twice before we could hear metal slip inside. The heavy oak yielded to the light push of his free hand. I had observed his labored process with some trepidation, since my fatigue would not allow me to stand much longer. I sighed with relief when the door swung inward and the room opened to my view.

Brother Dermott gestured for me to enter and gently handed me my leather travel sack as I passed. Then he bowed in silence and turned to leave. He was forbidden by Benedict's Rule to step over the threshold of a woman's chamber, even to be hospitable enough to show her the quarters. Suddenly he turned back, as if he had forgotten the most important message. "If you please, I will return within the hour. Prior William is—"

"I know, I know, Prior William is impatient to see me." I finished his predictable sentence and, smiling still, closed the door firmly.

In truth, I was glad to be rid of the good brother. I had been more affected than I would have thought possible by Brother Dermott's casual reference to the crusades. The mere name of Richard was still enough to undo my composure. I was glad to be surrounded by the solitude of the little guesthouse, where someone with kind intentions had preceded me. Warm water was in the pitcher and a fire recently laid danced in the grate.

The hut was spare, only a rude chamber with a small privy attached, but it lacked no necessity for my comfort. A narrow bed was shoved against the wall, its rough Brabant wool cover peeking out from under the furs, the latter undoubtedly added for the comfort of a princess of France. Two chairs in the corner opposite the fire faced each other, as if a priest might be summoned at any moment to hear confession and absolve the tired traveler who stayed here. But torches lit the corner in a friendly way, and the chairs had cushions that looked comfortable. This unrepentant pilgrim was grateful.

In the center of the wall facing the door hung a cross with Our Savior on it. The wood was old, and the rough figure had real hair falling over the sacred brow. Putting hair on images was an innovation from Hispania, one I looked on as rather morbid. But the image as a whole touched me. It presented a wordless reminder of the salvation available through the sacrifice of another. I placed the travel sack I carried on the floor and lowered myself gingerly into one of the chairs, contemplating this sign.

I became intensely aware that I was in the shadow of the great cathedral, the very house of God eternal. A calm feeling invaded my bones, a feeling akin to peace. This was a foreign state for me. When had I last experienced such serenity? The French court with its intrigues receded. Queen Eleanor and her demands seemed far away. For the blink of an eye I desired to let go of everything and remain just here for the rest of my life.

A creak in the walls caused me to look upward to see if the roof would hold against the wind, and I saw with surprise that the rough beams that crisscrossed the ceiling had carvings on them. As I raised my candle to examine them, I found that I could read their inscriptions. They were lines from the Psalms: THE LORD IS MY SHEPHERD, read the one directly over my head. And next to it: I SHALL NOT WANT. And on the next beam: REMEMBER THY COMPASSION AND THY LOYAL LOVE; DO NOT DWELL ON MY SINS, THE SINS OF MY YOUTH.

Ah, yes. The sins of my youth. The journey along the cloister walks had brought memories of my last visit to Canterbury and forced my thoughts back to my youth and King Henry. Henry, the source of my young joy and of my current sorrow and fear.

But the memory of Henry that rose unbidden was earlier than the Canterbury visit. It was the time when he first touched my heart. The scene remains etched in my mind and haunts me always, for it shaped my future and my life.

The day, I remembered, was one of those changeable days during Eastertide when the air capriciously becomes warm and sweet and the world occasionally seems altogether right.

The whole court was at Angers enjoying the first days of being outside without cloak and gloves. I was not a child any longer, and the games of the royal children were beginning to bore me. On this early

May day, I was high up in the castle on a stone window seat staring out onto the countryside, trying to draw with my charcoal the enclosed courtyard with the sloping green hills behind it. I was unaware of anyone near until I felt a presence behind me. I looked up and was surprised to see the king, peering over my shoulder at what I had drawn.

It was unusual for King Henry to be in the halls alone. Always when I saw him, he had three or four men striding with him while he spit out rapid-fire orders or comments in that staccato voice.

I was so startled that I dropped the charcoal on the stones, and it broke. He paid it no heed.

"Not bad, not bad for a child, " he murmured. Then he straightened up slightly and looked down at my upturned face, as if surprised.

"Well, little Alaïs Capet. What are you doing here alone? Why aren't you at your lessons or outside with the others?" He waved his hand toward the opening. We could hear the shouts of the boys. "Don't my children include you in their games?"

"No, don't be angry, sire. I mean, yes, they do include me. But the boys are sometimes rough—without meaning to be, I'm sure. They're only boys, after all. And I do so love to draw."

He leaned over me again, this time taking the parchments from under my hand and raising them to the light. He squinted as he held them nearer to his eyes, looking at first one, then the next. "That's very good, child. You've captured something there." His stubby finger tapped the second sheet as his gaze went quickly from the paper to out the window and back again. "It's not altogether accurate, though. You see the gate is farther forward than you have it, and I don't see these"—his hand brushed the parchment—"things or animals or whatever it is that you've drawn here. But still, on balance, quite good."

"There aren't any animals there now, of course," I said, gathering my patience. "It's May. They're all in the pasture. But if I only drew what was there, there would be no imagination, only a cleverness with my hands and eyes. That's what my father, King Louis, told me. He taught me that word—'imagination'—to explain to me the pictures I see in my head. Those are the pictures I draw."

"Imagination? What imagination? What's that?" The king's voice always grew a knife edge when he didn't understand something. "Imagination is what's false. It's what's not there at all. What would happen if I ran my kingdom on imagination, eh?"

I sighed. "I don't know about that, sire. But when you close your eyes at night, don't you ever see pictures of things that are stored inside you? Like your mother's face in a summer cloud? Or your brothers when they were young running through the fields?"

I paused. The king was watching my face. I was babbling, I thought, and he would be in a rage soon. I fell silent.

But he only shook his head and picked up my other drawings. One was a fox that I had drawn from a memory of the previous winter, another a face that he recognized. "That's Richard," he said, jabbing his finger, obviously pleased with himself. Then he came upon another picture full of dense lines.

"What's this?" He sounded irritated again. "I don't see anything here. What are all these lines?"

"Our tutor is reading to us in Latin. That's Julius Caesar's army, fighting the Gauls. Or what I think the fight might have looked like, from the inside of the battle."

"Hmm." The king frowned, straining.

"Look." I took the drawing from him. "Hold it here. Look at the whole thing. Don't try to pick out figures. Just imagine how it was in the fight—all those men, wounded, falling, so scared, the clash of steel and cries of men over everything. That's what I was trying to show. The image of my feelings if I had been there." I stopped. In my efforts to find the words to explain what I'd drawn, I had forgotten it was the king I addressed. I felt a flush rise. "Sire," I added, standing to curtsy.

He straightened and stared at me with those sharp gray eyes that nailed me to the spot. "How old are you now, Alaïs Capet?"

"Twelve summers," I stammered. "Almost thirteen."

"Your lessons are going well?"

"Yes, Your Grace." I was standing tall now, but still he must bend downward to me. I could have reached up and touched his well-trimmed beard at that moment if I had desired it.

"And you have enough charcoal and parchment to draw as much as you like?"

"Oh, yes. The tutors are very generous." I paused. "They know that I always study my lessons better if I have parchment to draw upon afterward."

"Good." I thought I saw a light in his eye before he turned away and stalked off as abruptly as he had come. He muttered, over his shoulder and loud enough for me to hear, "Imagination. Hah! Louis has imagination, all right. He imagines he owns half my kingdom."

His words brought a smile to my face. I knew I should resent what he said about my father, but I had learned that King Henry never said anything truly harsh about King Louis. And I was so pleased that he was getting the sense of the word "imagination."

The Canterbury wind rattled the guesthouse door, and my moment of reverie passed. Whatever I remembered about Henry, whatever I had once felt for him, was far in the past. All that mattered now was to find the child, if he lived, before someone discovered that he was the son of a king.

After I washed, changed my linen, and braided and tied up my hair, I put on a clean, simple robe of newly worsted dark green wool, the color of the deep English forest in summer. King Henry's favorite color, and so mine to this day. I belted it loosely and stretched out on the bed.

I reached inside my travel sack and drew out the thin parchment, Eleanor's letter, and cradled within it, the diagram of the altar of Becket's Chapel in Canterbury. I unrolled it slowly to prevent cracking, skimmed it for sense, and then reread it yet again with some wonder. The light from the oil lamp on the desk and the torches and candles scattered around the room were more than adequate. Eleanor's script on the paper was as tall and elegant as she herself had been when she was young.

This reading of the letter did not bring on the wrath I had felt only days earlier. Instead I marveled somewhat dispassionately at the queen's effrontery in daring to use the fate of my child to draw me here. Then I had to laugh out loud, for here I was, and here I would stay until I possessed the letters. Her ploy had been utterly successful.

Next I turned my attention to the diagram of the altar that would lead me to the letters. I had barely scanned it earlier. Now I saw that the diagram appeared to constitute a map of sorts, showing the altar on the side of the great cathedral where Becket was murdered, the very spot where he fell marked by an X.

My attention was directed by means of an arrow to a small inset in the lower corner that looked—upon closer examination—to be the back of the altar. The stones were sketched in and marked numerically. The stone I sought was inked in and circled. It couldn't have been marked more clearly.

Directions were written in a crabbed hand across the bottom of the diagram. The hand was certainly not Eleanor's elegant script. I wondered briefly who had drawn the map for her.

I was to count nine stones down from the top of the altar on the left side (as I faced it while standing behind) and two in toward the center. In that place I would find a stone that was slightly different in color, a sort of pale rust or rose as opposed to the common gray of the others. This was a stone with a strange design carved on its surface. This stone would be loose. When I removed this stone, I would find behind it a small space hollowed out of the altar. There rested the packet of letters I sought.

If the rosy stone had been tightened, I must pry it out, so a white cutter's chisel would come in handy. Tom had suggested this when I told him details of my mission. Ever resourceful, he had secured a chisel for me when we stopped to change horses in a village near Havre. The tool rested in my purse now, under my hand, and I could feel its hard outline through the thin leather.

I placed the letter and its diagram in my purse and drew out the chisel to inspect it. As I turned it in my hand, I tried to focus my thoughts on the coming meeting with Prior William and my aunt Charlotte. Many questions clamored for my attention. There seemed to be much more to this situation than Eleanor's letter had led me to believe.

For one thing: What was the Abbess Charlotte doing here? She must have known that Eleanor's request would send me to this place. Her current visit to the abbey seemed too coincidental. Tom of Caedwyd's comment echoed in my head: Queen Eleanor and the Abbess Charlotte had become "quite close" since the queen had retired to Fontrevault. There must be a game here. But what was it?

Then there was my uncle Robert's remark on the prior: "It's quite a different matter now, Alaïs. . . . In his way William is every bit as weighty as Abbot Hugh . . . in his way." It almost sounded like a veiled warning. But about what?

I was still turning over events, looking for clues in all that had happened so far, when there was a light tap on the door. Before I rose to open it, I slipped the chisel into my small travel purse, which hung across my chest by a thin gold rope. Then I straightened the braids of my hair, took a deep breath, and moved to open the door to greet Brother Dermott, he of the missing earlobe. I had no answers, but I felt sure that the questions—and the evening to come—would eventually prove entertaining.

.6.

Evening Supper
with the Prior and
the Abbess

Brother Dermott stood in the doorway with a lantern. I was surprised to see that darkness had fallen completely in the short while since he had left me.

"So Prior William awaits me?" I asked, throwing my cloak over my shoulders. "Odd, that he would have known of my coming." This remark raised no response from my laconic companion. I lapsed into silence myself.

Spring in England, I thought, as the keen wind coming through the open door pierced my chest. God's sweet blood itself would freeze here in this chill season.

Finally he spoke, saying only, "The prior has set a supper for you. He will see you in his private chambers." The companionship of our earlier exchange appeared to be forgotten. Brother Dermott showed no inclination for further conversation, and I had to hurry to match his stride as we crossed the abbey herb garden and moved toward the cloister walk.

I had forgotten where the abbot's rooms were in Canterbury. Though Henry and I had been Hugh Walter's guests for dinner on my last visit, twenty years earlier, the sands of time had dulled that experience. Memory is like an old parchment on which the writing has faded so much that a scribe can use the scroll again. So I must follow Brother Dermott's lead, he gliding like a black-robed ghost along the passages and I wandering a little behind, moving reluctantly toward the interview with William of Caen. I found my palms moistening as we walked, even though the night air had a chill clip to it. When we came at last to a large iron door with a huge stone angel kneeling beside it offering blessed water in a stone shell, Brother Dermott paused only briefly before giving one soft tap.

A muffled voice barked, and Brother Dermott swung wide the door. I saw first a large chamber remarkably lit with torches, candles, and oil lamps, so bright it was almost daylight; next I saw another tall black-robed monk standing directly across the room. His hands were clasped behind his back. He was dictating or speaking to a young clerk who sat at a table on the opposite side of the fire, writing furiously.

The younger man had auburn hair so burnished in the light that it looked as if it were on fire. The older man was as dark as the other was fair, and he was unmistakably the William of my childhood memory. Yet he was quite different.

The monk paused in midsentence as his gaze moved from the young secretary to me. The younger man continued to write for a moment after the voice stopped and then he looked up. Without turning his face from me, William made a brushing gesture with his hand, and the fresh-faced redhead scrambled to gather his papers and quills. He bowed and scuttled from the room, though not without a certain grace allowed him by his long legs.

William's expression gave nothing away. He simply stared, as if he had not been expecting me at all. I looked full at him across the room. I saw that though he was still somewhat lean in the body, his height and broad shoulders gave him the appearance of force. Ice-blue eyes, so unusual with that black hair, held mine as he advanced.

Two thoughts skittered into my head like mice: First, Prior William seemed not quite so physically unappealing as I remembered, and then, rapidly, it also occurred to me that it would be difficult to dissemble in front of those eyes. They had the quality of the eagle about them.

He moved toward me reluctantly, it seemed. I was surprised when he embraced me, but it turned out to be that dry, formal embrace Norman nobles use with each other to assure themselves that neither is holding a sword. His cheek grazed mine on either side, and then he withdrew, his arms dropping. It was nothing personal.

"Welcome, Princess. I'm delighted that you're here." His voice was unexpectedly deep and full. What had I expected? The voice of a child? I shook the cobwebs from inside my head. Speaking over my shoulder, the prior instructed Brother Dermott, still hovering at the door, "Please tell the abbess that the princess has arrived. And tell the steward to see to our supper. I'm certain our kinswoman is hungry after such a long journey." Then to me: "I believe that the abbess will join us shortly."

I heard the latch catch behind me and knew that we were alone. I, who moments earlier had reams of questions, now could think of not one comment. I let the prior slip the cloak from my shoulders, which he did with practiced ease. Where did a cloistered monk learn such courtesy with women? I wondered.

"It's been many years," I said, immediately feeling foolish at the banal statement. "How has your life gone since last we met, William?" Not much better on the second try.

"I'm older, for certain." His laughter was unexpected, and it made me smile as well. At least our awkwardness was mutual. "But you look well . . ." His voice faded.

"Despite?" I could have bitten my tongue. Why was I always so ready with the rapier of my words? He might not even remember my failed betrothal.

"Rather, I should say, because of . . . the intervening years since last we met," he replied gallantly.

The prior gestured toward one of the large carved chairs arranged at the far end of the room. I saw that there were three fireplaces, which gave the room warmth and light. In the center was a round table, already set for our repast with fresh white linen.

I took my place in the chair he indicated and found that it was made comfortable by many soft cushions. A small, low table between the chairs held a decanter and two glasses within easy reach.

William waited until I settled myself, and then he took the opposite chair, watching me. In his black robe, hood resting across his shoulders, he might be any simple monk of the order: a vintner perhaps, or a cook. Why, then, did I feel so disconcerted?

"So what brings you to Canterbury in this crisp spring air, *Princesse?*" William finally spoke.

"I thought you would know that," I parried.

"I?" He looked genuinely puzzled. "How would I know?"

"You knew of my coming. Since the journey was spontaneous— uh, in a way—I can't imagine how you knew. But you did. Your hosteler said you expected us. A week past, I myself didn't know I would come here." I was smiling, but I fixed my gaze on him. I was intent on getting information before the abbess joined us. "So I assumed you would also know my purpose."

"Ah, I see." His pleasant expression was bland. "As to my knowledge of your coming, I'm afraid there is no mystery about that. A half-dead courier arrived from Paris yesterday with the news from your brother that you were coming soon, accompanied by several knights. The king said you would explain your purpose yourself but that I was to prepare hospitality and assure him of your safety while you are here."

The prior couldn't have been smoother. And it made sense. Perhaps.

"My purpose is no mystery either, Prior William. I have undertaken a visit, a pilgrimage really, to the martyr's tomb. I want to do penance for my sins." I met his eyes again. "Something I know you will respect, given your close association for so many years with the saintly archbishop."

Prior William's handsome features flew upward in surprise. "You remember that I was the chancellor's clerk."

"Indeed," I noted. "With the chancellor and later, when he had risen in the world, the archbishop. And after that, I recall, King Henry's secretary. Was it not at Henry's court we last met, nearly twenty years ago?"

A sudden event forestalled his reply, which was just as well. I had taken a risk mentioning Henry's court. That could open up the conversation to any number of recollections, most of which I would willingly forgo. But I'd said it to establish that we had an adult connection. Our childhood seemed very far away.

There was a rush of air as the door opened with barely a knock. William rose easily. I followed suit thoughtlessly. It was wise, for, without any warning at all, my aunt Charlotte shot into the room with the speed of an arrow.

The abbess of Fontrevault needed no introduction, nor was she likely to tolerate any. She brushed past Brother Dermott, who probably had attempted the knock, and headed straight in my direction. Before I had even a good look at her, she enveloped me in her embrace. I nearly smothered.

Then she held me at arm's length. "*Princesse* Alaïs, cherished daughter of my dear, dead brother Louis. You look wonderful." I was afraid she would once again clasp me strongly to her bosom, but instead she stood back and surveyed me.

"But you have changed, *ma chérie*. I remember you as a girl, long-legged and gawky as a young colt. Now"—she raised her elegant hands as if in blessing—"you are a woman."

"Bonsoir, chère tante Charlotte," I replied, retreating slightly, eager to put one of the prior's tall chairs between myself and my aunt's enthusiasm.

I may have appeared altogether different, but my aunt Charlotte had not changed one whit since last I had seen her twenty years earlier. She still looked magnificent. She was tall, straight-backed, and bold. Although slender, she gave the impression of being very large. This was accomplished by her extravagant gestures, her booming voice, and her astonishing clothes. She refused to wear a religious habit and dressed instead in the finest wools and furs. In the summer she was known to wear silks from head to toe. The abbess was one of those women who filled any room she entered. And afterward everyone wondered how she did it.

Her one concession to religious life was to minimize the jewels she displayed, it was said. But this evening there was no evidence of such reticence. Her fingers glistened in the reflected light of the many torches and candles. The twinkling, jeweled clasp on her cloak reeked of royalty. I was glad I had left most of my own jewels in their casket for the evening, for I could not compete with her! I fingered my modest Arab pendant, as if to protect it from comparison with its newly arrived cousins.

"And what a beautiful woman you have become," my aunt was saying. She bestowed her glorious smile on me. "Please, come sit beside me and tell me everything that has happened to you since last we met."

She nodded briefly to William and then sought her chair, opening the brilliant brooch and dropping her cloak. Brother Dermott, who had observed her entrance with evident amusement, rescued it before it hit the floor.

My aunt caught me glancing from her to the prior and laughed, a kind of throaty, infectious sound.

"Oh, do not fear for my manners. The prior and I have already greeted each other. In truth, we have just spent the entire afternoon conferring. I am not ignoring him by paying attention to you. I am just eager to hear all your story."

"I have a better idea," William said, offering my just-seated aunt his hand. "The princess must be tired after her journey. Let us all to table, and the servants will bring our dinner."

Even Charlotte, who appeared to operate on a trajectory of her own, could not refuse Prior William in his own chambers. And so the three of us awkwardly made our way to the table, jostling one another as we arranged ourselves.

"Please, across from each other." William made a gracious gesture to the two chairs. "I'll sit here at the head." It was clear he was used to commanding.

As if by magic, the large double doors at the end of the room opened and servants appeared with steaming platters of poached lamprey and shrimps, followed by equally attractive platters of poultry and meat and deep flagons of rich red wine. William chose for us, deferring occasionally to my aunt's interjections. This process took some time, during which they both ignored me. It gave me a chance to study William, which I did with interest.

His mature face was long, with a deeply chiseled look to his bones. I saw little of the whey-faced orphan I remembered. Only the strong bend of the nose (had one of the Plantagenet princes broken it for him when he was young?), the prominent cheekbones with hollows beneath them, and the piercing quality of those deep-set eyes seemed the same.

His brow was bereft of the shock of black hair I recalled constantly falling forward into his child's eyes. His hair, though still thick, was now laced with gray, and it swept back from his face with a certain authority. The fierce, dark eyebrows seemed permanently knit in a subtle frown, which lent him overall a skeptical attitude. A line carved his face on each side from under his cheekbones to the corners of his mouth, giving him a look of natural severity that only deepened when he smiled. And smile he did, as my aunt and he parried over the menu.

I was rather more tired than hungry, so I was pleased when William waved off the last of the servants and the turmoil of their service died down.

"Alaïs, tell me how goes it now that you have been back at Paris for—can it be?—five years already," Charlotte asked while she appeared to focus on the pheasant breast in front of her.

"Seven," I mumbled, savoring the taste of a small *chèvre* covered in herbs on the rich brown abbey bread.

"Yes, of course, how time does slip off. Rather like wealth. How is your dear brother? He stopped to see me only last year when he was passing Fontrevault. But I haven't seen you for . . ." She paused. "And tell me again, why are you here at Canterbury?"

I peered across the table at her. With the candles flickering between us, it was difficult to determine her expression. She must know of Eleanor's letter. Tom of Caedwyd had said she and Eleanor were close since Eleanor had moved to Fontrevault. But her features reflected only mild curiosity.

"I was just explaining to the prior as you arrived, Aunt. I decided to make a pilgrimage to Becket's tomb."

"*Vraiment?*" My aunt had a way of using inflection that vastly extended the meaning of a single word. "Whatever for?"

"Abbess, please," said Prior William, feigning offense. "It's not such an outrageous intention. Many people make pilgrimages here. Becket still is revered as a holy man."

"So I understand. The people all come, do they not! The peasants come because they believe. The nobility come to be in vogue." Charlotte turned her large brown almond-shaped eyes in William's direction. "You knew him well, Prior. Do you think he was a holy man? Do you seriously think he deserves all of this adulation?"

"In some ways, toward the end of his life, I think he began to embrace holiness." William took his time answering, breaking his bread slowly between his strong fingers. "In his earlier years, perhaps not. But—if you recall your Plato—what is important is the ideal, not the actuality. If any one of us can call others to greater holiness after our death, who is to speak against it? And given our lives of imperfection"—he flashed a look in my direction and winked—"who of us is fit to cast the first stone against Becket?"

"Nonsense." Charlotte speared a fish with her Italian fork and nibbled at it. "If he hadn't been killed by those hotheaded knights of Henry's, he would be remembered in the chronicles as an ecclesiastical troublemaker. He nearly wrecked a kingdom with his pride."

"I was just asking the princess the purpose of her visit when you arrived." William had decided to move the conversation along. He was, after all, prior of Becket's abbey. Yet, withal, he seemed reluctant to embrace the role of defender of its hero.

"As a matter of fact, there is a definite purpose for my visit at this time." Suddenly I was inspired. "It's been nearly twenty years since King Henry and I were here. He came then to do penance for Becket's murder. I thought I would come to renew that penance in his name, as well as do penance for my own misdeeds. It is in honor of King Henry that I make this visit."

Both heads snapped up in surprise.

"I thought Henry denied responsibility for Becket's death," Charlotte said. "I heard him say so himself, on more than one occasion. In fact, that is the only reason we allowed him to be buried at Fontrevault Abbey."

That and a substantial endowment, I'd wager, I thought. But I said only, "Henry did not believe he was responsible for Becket's murder. Those knights of his who crossed the Channel were rogues. He never ordered that killing. They misinterpreted his words." I took a swallow of wine to calm my rising voice.

"Imagine the scene," I continued. "The happy Plantagenet family keeping Christmas at Bures, feasting and laughing, when suddenly the whole contingent of English bishops trails in, led by an angry Roger of York. They told the entire court their astonishing tale. It seems when Becket arrived back in England, he had immediately excommunicated them all. That had been no part of his agreement with Henry to end his exile. The bishops demanded immediate redress from the king. Henry flew into a fury. But he never told his knights to kill. I was only a child, but I witnessed the scene. He did not order the killing."

"Still, it was Henry's knights who did the deed." William passed a silver platter of herbed greens to my aunt.

"Yes, but you know he would never have touched Becket. Above all else, Henry was too skilled a politician. He knew that if Becket were martyred, it would make more trouble for him in England than ever Becket could make if he were alive." I licked the almond cream from my spoon, feeling quieter now. "And the last thing he wanted was the satisfaction of seeing Becket made a martyr, after all he did to polarize the kingdom."

"*Peut-être tu as raison,*" the abbess said, looking thoughtful. "So why do you think he did the penance here all those years ago?" She was looking at me, but it was William who answered.

"He needed to placate the people. Becket's popularity was growing, the myth of the saint was spreading. And Henry was considered guilty of the murder by most people. So a few years later, he agreed to abase himself here and allowed the monks to apply the discipline, in penance for whatever role his thoughtless words had played."

The abbess wiped her fingers daintily on her napkin. "That corresponds with what I was told at the time," she offered.

"And being King Henry"—I shook my head—"when he came to atone, he held nothing back. I could draw for you the picture right now if I had charcoal in my hand. I was here. I will not forget the scene."

They were silent.

I closed my eyes. "Picture Henry, naked, stretched on the floor of Becket's still-bloodstained chapel. A long ribbon of courtiers and monks winds down the center of the cathedral and curls around the side aisles. Solemn faces, expressionless as always in ritual punishment, as if no one of them is responsible for his action. You can hear the echo of lashes as the monks, one by one, pass by, each savoring his one stroke of the silk-corded discipline on the bare back of the prostrate king."

I paused, aware of our common breath. "It was an early spring night like this one, and the whish of the whip was echoed by the April wind whistling outside. I remember standing stiff as a rock, my cheeks scarlet, as Henry's daughter Joanna pressed her fingers into my arm. We kept each other from fainting."

I was surprised to hear a quaver in my voice. Charlotte looked down, turning the handle of her fork over and over.

"So"—I assumed a blithe tone—"I thought I would come here in memory of the king and do penance as he did. And also penance for my own sins, not as famous as the King Henry's but still a burden to me."

William looked at me for a long moment. I thought he was going to say something kind, but instead he remarked, "I certainly hope you're not going to cast yourself naked on the floor of Becket's chapel and wait for the lash."

I was startled by his flippancy. I closed my eyes briefly and saw again that image I had just described. In the background, among the courtiers, perhaps there had been a tall, dark-haired cleric watching with pain, as I had watched, the difficult scene. When I opened my eyes, William had turned to my aunt to respond to a question I had not heard. I forced my attention to their conversation.

"And Aunt Charlotte"—I took my turn at our question game at the first opening—"what brings *you* to Canterbury in this cold spring weather? Surely this is not the most opportune moment to visit Kent for you either." I was determined to quell the mysterious feelings aroused by the memory of Henry's penance and of all the events of that fateful year. "And I believe I am safe in assuming that *you* did not come to revere the martyr's tomb."

The abbess's expression was momentarily comical, but she recovered admirably. "I have business with Prior William. There is a plan to hold a convocation of abbots and abbesses in all of England and Normandy within the year, to discuss certain problems. Although Fontrevault is not a Benedictine abbey, we have been invited to participate. Prior William and I are conferring on arrangements."

William caught the *moue* my aunt had made when I teased her about praying at Becket's tomb.

"What occasioned that look, Abbess?" he asked as he applied garlic sauce to the pork with gusto.

"My niece considers me too secular, I think," she replied, with no hint of irritation. "She sees my love of finery and imagines that I have little piety. I'll wager—"

"No, not exactly, Aunt," I broke in. "It's just that I know your history, and no part of it includes prostration before anyone, with or without clothes."

William chuckled. After a draft of wine, he applied his *serviette* to his lips with an elegant gesture. "That's very interesting." He glanced my way. "Tell me more about your aunt. I had no idea her past had such color."

I sallied forth, aware that my aunt might not want her colleague to hear her story. But I thought it added to her cachet and could not help but make William hold her in even higher regard.

"My grandfather, King Louis, he who was called le Gros, made an early marriage for Aunt Charlotte to a count in a southern province." I looked at the abbess across from me. Impossible to read her expression. "Correct me if this is not true. But it is the story my father told my brother not long before he died."

"Go on," said Charlotte, now shaking with silent laughter.

"The marriage turned out to be an unfortunate affair. The count was given to drinking Armagnac spirits for weeks at a time, shut up in a tower with his favored mistress. He would emerge from the tower periodically to harry and beat his royal wife, then retire again to his favorite pastimes. Not surprisingly, they had no children—or at least none that survived." I glanced again at my aunt. Perhaps I was too cavalier with these painful events. But she seemed unruffled.

She even took up the story. "Eventually the dreadful man died. The count's son from a previous marriage took over his father's *château* and, it was said, the mistress and tower as well. I was sent back to Paris posthaste and with little ceremony, like a rejected package."

"Charlotte returned to Paris a stronger woman than she had left," I stated. "She announced to her father that if his plans for her included another marriage, she wanted none of it. When he tried to arrange other marriage contracts for her and brought forth suitors, she produced prodigious tantrums, screamed and tore her hair, and so frightened the nobles, old and young, that they all fled. After a time the word in France and Normandy, and as far down as

Gascony, was to avoid overtures from King Louis about marriage with his daughter—at all costs."

"Oh, no, surely not as far as Gascony," she murmured, easing her plate away from her.

"Finally, in desperation," I continued, "my grandfather endowed the abbey at Fontrevault with enough money to buy the seat of the abbess. He told Charlotte to go there and run it, and not to come to court again unless he summoned her."

At that the abbess laughed out loud, a hearty sound for such a refined woman.

"Is this true?" The prior raised his fork in question to our companion.

"Close enough," she admitted. "I would have embroidered the story somewhat. It sounds dull in the telling."

"I am astonished," William said, looking not at all astonished. "It was clearly the Paris court's loss, Abbess," he said, signaling for the servants. "I will show proper respect from this point. Such a forceful will should inspire only awe."

"Speaking of forceful wills," I interjected, "I understand there is trouble here in England with King John's use of coercion against the abbeys."

A swift look passed between my companions. It was William who answered. "What sort of trouble?"

"I'm not sure. I simply heard rumors that John is pressing the abbeys for silver and that there is resentment building here on the island and in Rome with his current policies."

"We hear the same rumors, although Canterbury has been spared his importuning," William said, leaning back in his chair. His long body seemed restless after sitting for a period of time. "That must be another benefit of having the martyr's tomb here. Even King John does not want to disturb the ghost of the archbishop and raise the specter of another fight between church and state, one that might well lead to another episcopal murder." He turned toward the abbess. "But others, especially the Benedictine abbeys in the north, have been pressed. And they are not happy."

I wondered if the proposed convocation of the heads of the large monasteries across the north country had anything to do with John's campaign.

"And, of course, John could always turn in this direction." He spoke as if to himself.

Suddenly I recalled my thought to find an Islamic scholar at this abbey, who could tell me more about Ibn al-Faridh.

"Prior William, I have another errand, besides the prayers I wish to say at the martyr's altar. You must have many scholars here who have traveled or studied in the south."

He tilted his head and frowned. "Ye-es, there are a few who have been for some years in Italy. But travel is dangerous of late, if one is not a knight on crusade with an army alongside. So we have been restricting our scholars. What is it you seek?"

"I'd like to talk with someone who knows Arab poetry, one who could tell me something about this jewel and its history." I fingered the pendant lightly.

"It's a handsome piece. I noticed it earlier. It appears quite rare." At the mention of jewels, my aunt became interested, leaning forward to look more closely.

"I believe so, too. The man who made it was a poet as well as a jewelsmith. There is one line of a poem on the back of this, and I would like to know more about the entire work." I made every effort to appear nonchalant. I had no intentions of telling my companions of the intense interest expressed by Master Averroës in my gem nor of the strange sack of my chamber in Havre.

William rose and went to his writing table, there to make a note on an open parchment. "I think the man you want is Father Alcuin. He spent many years in the Benedictine abbey in Sicily, near Cefalù.

He speaks Arabic and can probably quote the poem you want." He grinned. "He also speaks English and French, so you won't have to guess what he is telling you. I'll have Dermott take you to him tomorrow, sometime before the dinner hour."

He didn't return to the table but extended his arms to the cushioned chairs near the fire. "Abbess, Princess, please let us remove ourselves to the hearth. Sitting too long at table is difficult for me."

But I found myself quite suddenly without energy to sustain further conversation. I mumbled my excuses and prepared instead to depart, looking around for my cloak. William reached the bell pull to call for Brother Dermott, but the abbess forestalled him.

"I can walk with my niece, William. My guesthouse is next to hers, and I will see her safely home." I wondered if I had enough strength left to endure a private exchange with Charlotte.

A servant brother had just presented the prior with my cloak, and he was casually placing it around my shoulders when suddenly I remembered my vigil and turned to face him. We were now quite close, and I was forced to look up.

"Prior, I nearly forgot. It is proper that I ask for your formal permission for my vigil of penance at Becket's altar tomorrow even. I intend to keep watch through the night, alone. I hope you will agree."

"At Becket's altar, did you say?" He moved slightly away from me and leaned against the wall on one shoulder. "Why not the tomb? You perhaps do not know that we moved his body after the great fire. It is no longer buried under the altar." He chuckled. "It's quite a grand tomb."

"I'm certain it is, but I prefer the altar. It has a more direct connection to my past." I gathered the collar of the cloak about me. "As I have explained this evening."

He glanced over my shoulder at my aunt and then shrugged. "Yes, if you insist. In memory of Becket—and Henry, too—I give you permission. Though I warn you, it will be a cold vigil. Your bones might resist. None of us is a child, as we once were." There was an air of impudence about his tone that did not sit well with me.

"Prior, speak for yourself. I feel quite up to the challenge, despite what you consider my advanced years."

He only laughed and brushed his lips to my hand, like any courtier. He did the same to the abbess, and then he lifted a small lantern from its wall hanging. But my aunt protested. She said that there was no need for him to see us down the stone stairs; she was quite capable of finding her way out as she had already found her way in. She took the lantern from him smartly, and we gathered our cloaks about us.

When I turned back for one last look before the door closed, I caught the prior still standing with his hand on the ornate hearth mantel, watching us thoughtfully and without a trace of any smile.

Our cloaks flew out behind us like falcons' wings as we moved quickly along the darkened cloister walk. The abbess had the lantern in one hand and the other on my elbow in an iron grip. I was not certain if it was for her aid in walking or to bind us more closely in conversation. There was a footfall behind us, and I slowed, would have turned, but with her hand she pressured me on.

"The prior will have sent us an escort, despite my protests," she said, as if she could read my very thoughts. "He has a mind of his own. And he wants to be sure of our safety. Should he misplace two women of the royal house of France, he would have a lot to answer for."

"Misplace?"

"A jest, niece. I meant if anything untoward should happen to us here."

"But we are in Canterbury's walls. Are we not safe here?"

"One would suppose. But Becket thought the same thing, and you see what can befall you when you have a false sense of security. Now, tell me, what are you really doing here?"

I pondered the question for a moment, then decided. Let her reveal her hand first. How did I know what Eleanor had confided in her?

"For exactly the reason I told you and the prior. I am here to do penance at Becket's tomb, in memory of Henry and for myself."

She was silent a moment. I felt as though we were in a duel, each pausing to size up the other between thrusts, each basing our next remark on our opponent's last point.

"I think it's a bad idea."

"What? Doing penance?"

"Oh, not that exactly. I'm generally in favor of doing penance for those who feel a need for it. No, I think keeping a vigil inside the cathedral tomorrow night is a bad idea."

"Why so?" I was feeling comfortable. If my responses were kept to a minimum, my aunt would have the burden in this exchange.

"Mm . . . the great church is drafty at night. And it's dark. You'll be alone. And even if we are inside the cathedral close, there is always the possibility of rogue monks or thieves. No, you definitely should not undertake this mad all-night vigil." We entered now the paths through the herb garden, and our skirts brushed the low plants on either side. I could still hear soft footfalls behind us.

"My advice is to say some prayers in daylight at the martyr's tomb tomorrow. And call an end to your pilgrimage. You don't have enough sins in your past to justify this atonement scheme."

"My thanks, Aunt," I said, highly amused. "If you run your Fontrevault Abbey with such human concern, I trust it prospers."

We had reached my door. She stopped and turned to me, her face flickering in the uneven light. "I am only half in jest, niece. These are uncertain times. We must all beware. Why take unnecessary chances?"

"Then come with me," I said. "We'll keep the vigil together."

I said this to tease her. She was half again as old as I, her magnificent raven hair now disappearing under gray wings at her temples. Besides, she did not revere Becket, and the prior knew it. She would never consent to accompany me on my night vigil. But I threw the gauntlet down to end the duel.

The moon was nearly full, and its light covered the ground around us like cream. It stopped only at the invisible line of the shadow of the great cathedral from which we had just emerged. As my aunt faced me, the moonlight fell on her features.

"I think your mission is futile," she said, her lively voice suddenly toneless. In the white light, her grave expression reminded me of a death mask on an ancient tomb. "You are taking a serious risk for nothing."

She took her free hand and bent my head to hers, kissing my lips briefly. "I leave tomorrow early. I am sorry not to speak with you further now. Perhaps we will meet soon again in France. I would like to know you better. But, oh, my dear, be careful." And then, before I could respond, she whipped away, my unvoiced questions trailing after her like her beautiful, rustling, silk-lined cloak.

Still puzzling, I opened the door. The first thing that met my eyes was the fire, which had been well tended and blazed heartily. And then I scanned the rest of the room and had to hold a hand to my mouth to stifle the cry that came. All my belongings had been tossed into the center of the room, the travel sack emptied, the furs from my bed—all heaped onto a huge pile. Even the cushions from the chair had been added, giving the immediate impression of a preparation for a huge bonfire.

Sweet Jesu, dear God, I prayed, for once King Henry's oaths failing me. For an instant I thought of calling out to my aunt, who had just moved on to her own guesthouse. But I caught myself and instead stepped quickly into the room, closing the door and shooting the bolt. I must reflect, I said to myself. I must not act, not yet.

I moved to the chair next to the fire, now bereft of its cushion, and sat down. It was not the pile of goods that stunned me; it was the implication of a bonfire, a sacrificial fire. I knew stories from my father's court, even stories that had drifted into England's court, about the heretics that had been burned in Lyons, in Flanders years earlier. Was this some kind of message? Who was following me, and why was he—or they—threatening in this way?

After some time I moved to straighten the room, beginning with the chair and the bedcovers. As I put away the things on the top of the pile, I saw that my clothes had been pulled hither and thither and that the jewel casket was once again toppled and askew, on the floor at the bottom.

I picked it up but had no need this time to raise the lid to know that it would now be empty. As it was, I set it down carefully on the small table next to the bed and looked at it.

I was not a fool. If those who had disturbed my room now wished me harm, so be it. But they could not have been the same as the men who had entered my room at Havre. At Havre all the jewels could have been taken, but they were not. The thieves were searching for something special, something they did not find. But here the jewels *were* gone, and a great fuss had been made to distract me.

It did not require a canon lawyer to arrive at the conclusion that these were not the same thieves. I bethought myself as I slowly continued to restore the chamber that the first set of thieves had sought something they did not find, while the second had found something they did not seek. The muscles around my shoulders were beginning to soften, and I was aware that my fears were receding like a chastened tiger. Whoever had been in my room had been here to deliver a message, perhaps to frighten me. The jewels were merely a bonus for them. But I did not think they would return.

7

An Enlightening Interview

J heard Mass early the next morning in Becket's Chapel, as it had come to be called since his murder. Brother Dermott came for me before dawn, for it was the custom in this abbey for the monks to say their Masses at the various altars of the cathedral immediately after Matins. I decided not to report the theft of the previous evening to the hosteler. In truth, until I knew those whom I could trust in this abbey, I would tell nothing. And I knew that if William heard that my chamber had been ransacked, it would be the end of any permission to keep my vigil this evening and retrieve Eleanor's letters.

Mass was not an event I felt compelled to attend. My faith was in an uncertain state, and I had been avoiding rituals lately whenever I could without causing scandal. But William's hospitality and my alleged purpose in visiting the abbey demanded a show of piety. And, anyway, on a practical level, I had a need to see the

chapel where I would spend my vigil so that I would be better prepared to carry out my task.

Brother Dermott led me silently along the cloister walks and
into the massive church. The air inside was sharp, noticeably colder than outside, as if the cathedral insisted on holding fast the night
while outside the day was creeping in. Many torches lined the walls,
and wrought-iron holders as tall as a man held giant candles. They
stood like silent soldiers up and down the aisles and all around the
altars; stillness and gloom prevailed.

Monks were stationed at the many side altars, already murmuring the Latin of their required daily Masses, creating a soft, eerie
cloud of sound that rose and fell around the church. As we moved
into the nave, I saw three monks at the central high altar, concele-
brating a Mass that was already in progress. They wore the white
vestments of Eastertide; the gold thread running through them
flashed as they moved. I wished heartily for my charcoal. If I only
had paint, these men would look like three large goldfinches on my
parchment.

I assumed that one of these monks was William. He would have
the right, as prior, to celebrate Mass at the high altar in the absence
of the abbot. But then I noticed a solitary figure sitting in the ornate
chair off to the side, near the choir stalls. Alone, unattended, and
not in Eastertide vestments, but in the plain black robe of the order.
The cowl was pushed back, and the upturned face, revealed in full,
was blank of all expression. It was the face of Prior William.

I puzzled over this as I dutifully followed Brother Dermott to
the side altar—called simply "the altar of the archbishop"—which
would be the site of my vigil that evening. There Mass was already
in progress.

The archbishop's chapel was small, a sort of alcove off to the
side of the nave of the larger church. It contained a modest altar
and individual wooden prayer seats with kneelers, what the monks

called a *prie-dieu*, for a handful of the faithful. The altar stood out from behind the wall, just as Eleanor's map had indicated. A row of twenty kneelers crossed in front of the altar, and I had noticed about the same number of rows extending behind me. If I were kneeling just here, I thought, on the end of the first row, it would be a simple matter to slip behind the altar, loose the stone, retrieve the letters, and return to my place. The whole thing could be done in minutes.

My attention returned to the present. The priest was beginning to distribute communion to the little group gathered in our corner. He was a young monk, tired-looking. I took communion, so as not to draw attention to myself in this crowd of faithful, although whether my soul was in a state of grace could be debated. When all had been served, the priest turned and faced us. He opened his arms. "Go in peace. *Ite missa est,*" he intoned in the familiar Latin.

As if on cue, Brother Dermott appeared at my elbow. "We leave now. You have time to rest. Then the prior has instructed me to take you to Father Alcuin. We will find him in the abbey's library."

Brother Dermott and I joined the orderly procession of monks leaving the great cathedral by the side door, which allowed a narrow tunnel of light to flood down the aisle. We moved through it in silence. As we came closer to the door, the monks noticed us and stood aside to let us pass. I pulled my veil more closely over my lowered head. The cathedral had that effect on me, or perhaps it was the monks.

On my return to the guesthouse, I found that the fire in the grate had been restored once again. But this time I had no evidence of malign visitors. The room seemed almost welcoming after the dank, shadowy cathedral, although I could not shed a vague sense of unease still. It was due, no doubt, to the astonishing and unpleasant surprise of the previous evening. Even though I did not yet feel completely safe, I was very tired. I crawled under the furs on my simple bed and slept without dreams for several hours.

I was awakened by the knock on my door, the signal that Brother Dermott had come for me again. I wound my plaits around my head, smoothed my wool gown, and made myself ready. Brother Dermott waited patiently outside the door as I placed my veil. After a terse greeting, we walked silently in the direction of the chapter house. I was struck by the fact the each time he fetched me, Brother Dermott appeared more removed. And the challenge of introducing conversation in the face of such withdrawal was too much, even for my courtly skills.

We passed by the chapter house and through the great hall, then down a long indoor corridor that led to a stairwell. He preceded me up these, gesturing for silence, rather unnecessarily, I thought.

When we came to the top of the stairs, we were in a huge room containing many tables and shelves. Several monks were working at long tables, carefully copying manuscripts. Others stood at higher tables, engaged in similar work. As we passed between them, I could see that some were working at calligraphy while others seemed to be drawing the elaborate artistic schema around the first letters of the chapters. A few looked up, but most kept to their work.

At the head of the scriptorium—for that is clearly where we were—sat a large, dour-looking figure, full of face and bald as a babe. He glanced up occasionally from his own reading to scan the room and assure himself that all were assiduously employed. On one of these movements, he sighted Brother Dermott and myself, threading our way between the desks toward him. He did not appear particularly pleased to see us.

"Father Alcuin, Prior William requests that you provide information to our guest, Princess Alaïs of France, on the subject of a certain Arab poet." The two monks exchanged bows, and Brother

Dermott turned to me. "I'll return for you in less than an hour," he said.

Father Alcuin had risen at our approach, and he made a substantial bow in my direction. "Please," he said, indicating a chair on the opposite side of his table. "How can I help you?"

"I seek information on the Arab poet Omar Ibn al-Faridh. This pendant, which has been in my possession for years, has an inscription on the back that contains a line of his poetry. The object seems suddenly to have become of interest to others, and I would like to know why." I noted that I now had the monk's attention. "Prior William tells me you have studied at the abbeys of the Tyrrhenian Sea area, and I thought you might know the history of the Arab poet who made it."

"May I see it?"

I shook my head. "I am sorry, but it never leaves my person. I can tell you the inscription. It is from a longer poem. The inscription says 'Death through love is life.' "

The monk frowned, then nodded slowly. He seemed burdened by his weight and years. "I know the poem, but I must get the full text, so I do not make a mistake." He moved ponderously, disappearing through a door into another room that opened behind his desk, which appeared to contain shelves of books and scrolls. I was glad I had not entrusted to him the jewel, for what would I do if he walked away with it?

He was back shortly, breathless, carrying two scrolls and a book. "I had forgotten that I brought two of these home from Sicily. You may be interested to see a copy of the poem in the poet's own handwriting." And he shoved one of the scrolls across the table to me.

I opened it with trepidation, only to find that the poem was written entirely in Arabic script, and I could read not a word. I looked up to see Father Alcuin grinning at his little joke.

I smiled as well. "Do you have a translation, Father?" I asked in a pleasant voice.

"Yes, I do." For a moment I thought he would refuse the translation until I let him hold the pendant, but then he flashed again an elfish grin. After glancing at the scroll open in front of him, he recited, with eyes closed:

> *The repose of love is a weariness; its onset, a sickness; its end, death.*
> *For me, however, death through love is life; I give thanks to my Beloved that she has held it out to me.*
> *Whoever does not die of his love is unable to live by it.*

"That's beautiful, but I'm not sure that I understand it," I admitted.

"Are you familiar with the Arab mystics?"

I shook my head to indicate I had never heard of them.

"Ibn al-Faridh was the leader of a group of Arab poets who were obsessed with platonic longing after the ideal." He paused and grimaced as if an unsavory idea had occurred to him. "You *have* read Plato?" He fixed a beady eye on me.

"Yes, in my studies when I was young." He was visibly relieved.

"Many of these men were writing when I was in Hispania, in my youth also." He acknowledged me with a nod, as if we had something in common. "But their writings were often misunderstood by their own people. Indeed, al-Hallaj and Suhrawardi, two of the leading poets of my time, were put to death while I was in Sicily because the symbolism they used was unacceptable in Islamic tradition. They were accused of a subtle Manichaeanism, a duality between good and evil. What they really sought was to write of human love as an illustration of divine love, as if it were the union of man with the divine, or with the soul."

"A mystical union?"

"Yes, that's exactly right."

"It sounds somewhat like the poetic traditions of the troubadours in the south."

"That is not surprising," he said, rounding his lips in thought. "If I recall correctly, William of Aquitaine was inspired by the Arabs he came in contact with while in captivity. He was the first of our Provençal troubadours."

"So you follow Provençal poets as well as Arabs?" I was more and more intrigued. Strains of the poems I had learned at Eleanor's court in Poitiers were drifting into my head. "It was William who brought this pendant back from his stay in Seville, generations ago. It came to me through his granddaughter, my stepmother."

Suddenly, on impulse, my trust having increased during this exchange, I loosed the cord around my neck and handed my jewel across the table.

"Father Alcuin, forgive my earlier reticence. I would like you to examine my pendant. Perhaps there is something there that I cannot see. Can you think of why it has value today, why someone would want it?"

He reached a pudgy hand across the oak and took my offering. He looked first carefully at the filigree setting, then turned it over to examine the inscription. As he did so, his tongue ran along his upper lip, almost as if he could taste something delectable.

"Yes, there is no doubt it is the work of al-Faridh. He was not only court poet but master jeweler to the caliph of Toledo before Alfonse took the city, and later to the caliph of Córdoba." He looked up at me. "This would be valuable for many reasons, not the least of which is that al-Faridh has been dead for over a hundred years."

"But I thought you just said he belongs to a group of Arab poets who write mystical love poetry, that some were still writing when you were a student."

"Indeed, he was their founder. He was the first. The others have come much later and are still writing or only recently dead."

"So one reason this jewel is of interest is that there will never be another; its maker can make no more."

"Well put," the monk said, rubbing his beardless face with his soft left hand. "You know your Aristotle as well." He held the jewel up to the light with his right one and looked at it again. "Another could be just its intrinsic value. I am no jewel master, but even I can see that the amount of gold in the setting is worth nearly the price of the ruby it holds."

"Is there anything else?"

"Look here," he said, laying it on the heavy wood. "See the pattern in the filigree?"

I leaned over the table, peering. In truth, though I had often fingered the delicate gold setting, I had never looked closely at it. "It is in a pattern of arabesque, which the Arabs consider symbolic of the search for spiritual clarity. This is a very spiritual piece." He leaned back in his chair.

"So someone who knows its true value might also seek it for its spiritual significance." I was thoughtful as I picked it up from its resting place and fastened it again around my neck.

"Have you reason to believe someone wants this jewel now?"

I paused. I was beginning to like this monk, but I still feared to trust anyone with the story of the recent attempts at theft that had been visited upon me. I knew not who could be involved.

"I . . . it has recently caught the attention of some and made me wonder as to the cause," I said, relieved to be able to tell a partial truth.

He raised his shoulders and lifted his opened hands upward. "So it could be gold, or it could be God."

I was amused, thinking this monk could best me in a contest of aphorisms. Then I added, "Or it could be something else."

"Which would be?" He looked genuinely puzzled.

"Leverage," I said. "Trading power, with someone who has something else that is wanted."

He pursed his lips again. "Ah, yes, I see. . . . You may have something there. I think you should—"

I was never to know what he thought I should do, because at that moment Brother Dermott appeared from behind Father Alcuin, having come up the back stairs. He appeared rather out of breath.

"Your Grace, I am sorry to be late. I was to have you at the refectory before the start of dinner, but I was delayed. Father Alcuin, you are to come, too. Prior William wants you at his head table this very afternoon."

And that announcement, carrying as it did the full weight of the prior's authority, ended our exchange. For although the three of us walked together hurriedly through the cloister walks, neither Father Alcuin nor I raised the topic of the pendant again.

8

A Curious Luncheon

A clear bell sounded as our little party entered the immense dining hall. A sea of black and brown robes greeted my eyes. The black robes, the monks, were seated at tables arranged in the middle of the hall. The brown garb of the servant brothers circled in the outside tables, making an interesting border of color.

In the very center was a long polished cedar table positioned on risers, slightly higher than the others. The table was ringed with monks, and Prior William sat at its head. I expected William to preside over the community, since he was the abbot's replacement. Still, it surprised me to see him in the midst of his men in this way, as if surrounded by a small feudal army all dressed in their lord's colors. It seemed incongruous with his solitary state at Mass only hours earlier.

The monks, who had been standing in silence, all sat down at the bell's sound, and a low murmur began. As I passed through the hall to the high table, the noise increased. I was glad I had dressed in a subdued black gown, with only a simple veil of light cream over my hair. I felt I almost blended with the monks, except for the veil, of course.

William rose as he saw me approach. Brother Dermott helped me take the single high step up, and I faced the prior. I was again surprised by his height.

"Your Grace," he said, bowing to greet me, as if we had not been in rather intimate conversation not twelve hours earlier. I responded with equal formality. I had been well trained at Eleanor's court.

"Father Prior, greetings," I said as he bent over my hand and then used it to guide me to take the seat on his right. I marveled again at his courtly manners. They could not have been more perfect had he been raised by Eleanor herself. He threw me a strange glance, as if he read my thoughts.

"Fathers, Brothers." William raised his voice and extended his arms. The hall fell silent. "Please welcome the Lady Alaïs, princess of the royal house of France." His public voice was surprisingly resonant. There was a pause, and then all the black and brown robes rose in unison and bowed. "She is our guest these few days. She has come on a pilgrimage to do honor at the martyr's tomb."

Then William motioned me to sit, and he did likewise, as did all at his table. As if on cue, all the benches in the hall scraped the floor as two hundred dark robes resumed their places.

William introduced the monks around the table, calling each by his religious name. There was Father Basil, Father Anselm, and next to him Brother Francis, the youngest man at table and the only one who wore the brown habit. Then Father Raynulf and Father Rheinhart. Father Alcuin had also taken his place among them. I soon lost track of names. They were twelve or fourteen in number, too many to remember.

I noticed with some curiosity that two or three bore the same type of marks I had seen on Brother Dermott. One was missing several fingers, and the other had a scar along his face. Yet a third monk came in late and made his way to our table limping, as if he had a wound on his leg that would never fully heal. This monk, a tall, broad-shouldered man who looked as fit (except for his limp) as if he might have been a knight once, mumbled something in Prior William's ear and then took the one seat that had been vacant at the table. Perhaps many of these men had sought the peace and tranquillity of the monastic life after adventures on crusades or in border wars.

"Do you not keep silence during meals?" I asked William, as a babble filled the hall. The monks had resumed discourse with one another, which rose like the Channel on a rough day. "What about reading from Scripture?" As a small child, I had spent more than one interminable Sunday at St. Denis before I was sent from Paris.

"Not on feast days. It is not required," William said. "There is still a reading after prayers at the opening of the meal, and we keep silence during that. But, with impeccable timing, you managed to miss both prayers and reading." Uncertain how to respond, I cast an inquiring look in his direction. He leaned toward me.

"My recollection of you," he murmured, speaking with his head close to mine, "from our time together at the court of King Henry, is that you had a positive aversion to holy liturgy. I remember that you created false illness one year so as to avoid the long service on Holy Saturday eve." A tremor danced around the corners of his lips.

I did not know whether to be offended or amused. Was the prior of Canterbury having a jest? Or was the remark intended to be a reprimand on my Christian lapses? The only certain thing was that this William was altogether unlike the shy youth of my childhood memories. I decided that it would be best not to take offense.

"Not fair, Prior. Brother Dermott was late in fetching me from the interview with Father Alcuin." I gestured with my head in his direction. "You cannot blame me for the abbey's scheduling problems."

This rejoinder brought another good-natured laugh.

Suddenly a plate was set before me by a serving brother. It was a riot of salad, herbs and radishes and lettuces all jumbled together. "I'm impressed, Prior William, to see parsley and fresh chickweed and lettuces at this time of year. And the fennel looks fresh as well." I could scarcely wait until he had given a signal to eat, so accustomed had I become in the past few days to the hard bread and tough beef stew of the traveler.

When all at the table had been served, William raised his fork to the other monks as a signal to begin. Then he looked my way and responded, "Princess, this is Canterbury, after all. What we can't buy and keep, we grow here even in the winter, in covered gardens."

I pondered without comment the vast resources of Mother Church. Her larder seemed as bountiful as that of the Paris court. William turned to talk with the monk on his other side, a rough-looking man with a Roman nose and shoulders that could challenge a bull. He seemed vaguely familiar, but I could not place where I had seen him nor whom he put me in mind of. The monk on my right was engaged in some kind of theological debate with another across the table, citing Peter Abelard twice that I heard. I withdrew into myself and mused on how I would draw this strange ensemble of men, if I but had the charcoal in my hand.

We had scarcely begun to eat the salad when a second dish was set in front of the prior and then passed to me. One after another the platters appeared: pork pie, chicken smothered in a sauce replete with mushrooms and brightened with a red coriander dust, grilled bream with a pale accompaniment that proved to have a ginger bite to it, a large cut of honest red beef (that English staple that the French court spurned), spiced meatballs that had been sautéed with nuts, and finally a large platter of *mouton,* undisguised.

While I was grateful for the first dishes, I soon tired of both the amount of food and the variety. When I shook my head at the *mouton,* William noticed and turned casually back my way.

"What, not hungry, Princess? And after such a long journey, too." It rankled me to have him comment on my habits. It seemed overly familiar.

"Your hospitality is quite overwhelming, Father Prior. There is more food here than a mere woman can manage." I couldn't resist going further. "The venerable fathers must fast often to warrant this kind of feast on a saint's day."

"Mm, yes. Many days pass with little food," he said, unruffled. "It is a delight to see the men enjoy themselves. The regular work schedule is suspended for today, you know. Mass, of course, took longer."

"I noticed," I murmured.

"And we are never such depraved gluttons as the legendary monks of St. Swithin's. When I was secretary to King Henry, they appealed to him to rescind an order their bishops had placed suppressing three of their usual number of courses at table."

"Did they so?" I did not recall hearing this story.

"Yes, but they made a huge mistake. They did not count on offending against the royal prerogatives. Henry asked how many courses the poor deprived monks had at a meal, and the answer was ten. He immediately flew into a royal rage at this great number and demanded they reduce their courses to fewer than those served at his own royal table."

I felt a great ball of laughter gathering within me. William's eyes were shining, but he maintained a grave expression. "They never complained to him again. Please, at least try this delicacy," he

said without a pause. "It's a specialty of our abbey." He motioned
with his hand, and before I could protest, a serving brother had
placed two large spoonfuls of some congealed, lumpy white sauce
on my plate.

"What, pray, is it?" I eyed the stuff as if it were still alive. I had
never fancied all those thick sauces my brother found so appealing.

"Such a favorite of the community on meatless days that we
order it on feasts, too. They call it Welsh partridge. The Welsh prefer it, we are told. One of our brothers in the kitchen has family
there."

"Is it game, then, smothered under all that sauce?"

"No, no. It's bread. It just looks as though it might be game.
And with all the cheese sauce on it, it could be anything." He
cocked his head and raised his finger, as if making a point to his student monks. "Try it. You may find it quite appealing."

I tasted a small bit of the gluey stuff, immediately laying down
my fork. At least they had forks. Thank God for Italian ingenuity.
Ties with Rome were useful in many ways. Canterbury was certain
to be the local outlet of inventions from the south, with all that ecclesial intercourse.

"You are still intent on holding your vigil at Thomas's shrine
this night?" William's tone remained casual, so the sharp change
of topic took me by surprise. He signaled the servant brother
who stood behind me to fill my goblet and then took a draft of his
own ale.

"Yes, of course." I took one more taste of the cheese mess to
hide my surprise. "It's the reason for my visit. But, Prior William,
I remind you once again," I spoke with painstaking patience, "I will
stay at the very altar of his execution. Not at the tomb."

"Princess, I have given more thought to this request of yours,"
he said, propping one elbow on the table to rest his chin in his hand
and turning his face toward me. "You will be alone all night. The

cathedral will be cold. There is no one present between Compline and Matins. I am concerned somewhat for your safety if you insist on going forward with this . . . adventure." He paused.

I frowned. "You seemed to have changed your position since our conversation of last evening."

He made a noncommittal noise in response.

"You need not concern yourself with my weal." I put a breezy note into my voice, feigning an ease I did not feel. "A pilgrim must accept such conditions. What is the point of penance if it doesn't create some discomfort?" I took a draft of the dark wine and waited. We were speaking in low voices, but even so I noticed that his gaze moved around the table to be certain no one was listening.

"Are you deliberately not hearing me, Princess?" His voice hardened. "I advise against your plan."

I glanced sideways at him, while appearing to be absorbed in dabbing my lips with my linen.

"That's odd. My aunt had exactly the same arguments, and the very same advice, for me last evening," I murmured. "Have you discussed this with her, by chance?"

"I think it's a mistake, especially tonight," he said, ignoring my question. He was looking down the long head table as he spoke.

I followed his lead but saw only a monk and the brown-robed brother engaged in an intense exchange. It seemed to be about the food, as one gestured to the fish on the other's plate. Father Anselm and . . . what was his name? Ah, yes. Brother Francis. An odd pair: Father Anselm with a long, scholar's face, his bony finger tapping on the table in front of him, making some point to his companion; Brother Francis as young as his companion was old, peach down barely brushing his soft cheeks, listening intently. What was such a young man doing at the prior's table? He could not be twenty summers. And a brother at that.

Of a sudden I recognized the boy by his reddish hair. He was the young man who had been taking dictation when I arrived at William's chambers the previous evening, William's young secretary. Then, as if by some invisible transfer of my thoughts, the youth looked up and saw me watching him. His curious gray eyes with sandy lashes, visible even from this distance, met mine. I started. I had seen this young man before, in some other context, but it was impossible to place where. Even the diamond shape of his face, the outline of his head seemed familiar. I waited for a picture to form in my mind, some clue to tell me the source of this mysterious feeling. But nothing came. After a time the young brother turned back to his neighbor. At that very moment I realized William was speaking rapidly, close to my ear, reclaiming my attention.

"You may be aware that the shrine has a troubled history. There are many who come here to pray at the martyr's tomb, but others come who have motives less pure." At his words I turned full to look at him, only to find him still watching his young secretary, even while speaking to me. "I have reason to believe we may soon have a visit from the latter group. I would be distraught if that visit occurred tonight, or if any harm should befall you because of it."

"Prior William, why should I fear anything? Do you tell me that a *princesse* of France raised by the royal house of England has anything to fear? In an English cathedral?" I paused. As soon as the words had left my mouth, the specter of the fallen Becket rose before my eyes. Chastened by the image, I continued, but in a more subdued voice. "Has the peace of the kingdom broken down so far under John that even royal persons must fear for life in the very churches of God? Or"—now I watched his face closely—"should I have a fear particular to *this* church?"

William leaned back in his high oak chair, working his shoulders absently for a moment, before signaling the head serving brother. Plates of tarts and sweets were now set before us and the awful cheese stuff taken away, God be praised. But I found that my appetite had totally disappeared.

"I would say that the fear is not just particular to this cathedral. Rather, particular to this cathedral, to this time, to this person. To you."

"Are you telling me someone means me harm?" I kept my voice level, but I could hear the hard tones of Henry at his most intense creeping in. "Tell me what you know, Prior. I am not a child to be protected from knowledge about my own well-being."

"After you left last night, I had a visit from two knights, men I trust well. They had just come from London. They claimed that John is on his way to Canterbury to pay a visit to the martyr's tomb, or so he says." William shook his head, one corner of his mouth pulled back in irony. "The last time John paid his respects to the martyr is beyond the memory of anyone in this abbey. I fear that his visit has other than sacred purposes and that it bodes ill for someone, church sanctuary or no."

"What is the source of this information?" I sounded like King Henry quizzing his lieutenants.

"As you know, there is trouble between John and the great barons as well as John and the abbeys. The barons' leadership is friendly to Canterbury." William put two small berry tarts into his mouth before he answered. He was expert. The only stain from the berries lay on his fingers, like small blots of blood. He wiped his hands fastidiously on the linen. "The knights who arrived in such haste last night were sent by Baron Simon."

"Hah. There is no surprise in the barons' rebellion. It's about time they woke up. John couldn't govern a peat bog. He is an incompetent. Always has been since he was a child." I toyed with the sweet cake the servants had placed on my plate. Sugar spilled over my fingers. I raised it up, then put it down without a taste.

"It is a pure shame that he is the only one left of all the Angevin eaglets," I continued. William leaned toward me. "He is the least able to hold the royal kingdom together. It is ironic, John's being king now, at the end of it all. You must remember that at one time his brothers called him 'Lackland,' because they all had a patrimony from their father and he had none."

"Yes, well, Lackland may be having the last laugh. They are all gone, and he is still here, isn't he? And he governs all of it— Henry's Normandy and Brittany and England, Wales and Ireland, and Eleanor's Aquitaine. He won't be able to hold it, certainly not the French lands. And the Irish hate him." William drank long from his cup, then slammed it down with finality. "But for now he is king."

A brief silence fell on the men at our table.

"It's true, as you say, Princess. We have both mead and wine on feast days," he said, raising his voice. "Other days it's only wine. And sometimes, I regret to say, not the best wine." After the space of a cat's breath, the buzz of talk rose again.

I was puzzled. "Why would John make trouble here at the tomb of the martyr of Canterbury? His father did penance here at least three times. Even Richard honored the shrine. And you know his lack of sentimentality."

As I spoke, I struggled to keep my expression serene. I wondered briefly how much William remembered of my ill-fated betrothal to Richard. Would he have any idea, cleric that he was, of unrequited love? Now, there was an interesting thought. I observed his face more closely. No, not likely. War or abbey management, power perhaps. But not love.

"John may have changed. What if he truly does come to do homage to Becket?" I ventured.

"To venerate the tomb is not, I think, John's purpose." William's tone was as dry as eggshells underfoot.

"No? What then?" I broke with his gaze to shake my head, signaling no at the offer of more hot pastries despite the fragrant apple oozing out from them.

"You." He brushed the crumbs from between his hands and pushed the remains of his meal from him, turning his face fully toward me. "You, Princess, are the object of his errand here."

"Fiddle." I snapped my fingers. William watched my face. "John is terrified of me. Remember, we were raised together, like brother and sister."

"That argument is worthless." He tossed his *serviette* aside. "I knew many brothers and sisters who were capable of killing each other as children or even later." A pause. "Some did."

I shook my head. "Let me tell you a story. John is six or seven years younger than I—I forget exactly, but something like that. Anyway, one summer day when I was about twelve, he tried to bait me. He called me a name, said something bad about my father being the spineless king of France. We were all in the barn with the horses. His older brothers were getting ready to hunt and paid us no heed. I was above in the loft, and John was taunting me from below. I took a sack of open oats and dumped it on him. John nearly suffocated. His brothers well nigh fell off their horses laughing. John never liked me after that, but he always left me alone."

I rubbed my brow, oddly moved by the memory of that long-ago afternoon. But I didn't want to show a bright eye to William. Emotion was not a sign of strength for women. "He seemed like a spoiled baby to me. He was always so . . ."

"Ineffectual?" William supplied.

"Yes, I guess we could say that. I would have said feckless." I had to laugh. "Poor John. Poor little Lackland." But then I remembered the story of young Count Arthur's end, and I ceased laughing.

"Princess"—William's voice took on a certain urgency—"I trust my sources explicitly. They tell me that you have something John wants, some information. He heard you were coming here, and he seems determined to confront you. I don't know precisely why, but the situation is serious."

Our conversation was brought to an abrupt end when a high, clear bell rang out three times. The monks around the hall rose and bowed their heads for a common prayer of thanksgiving. Our table joined. William's arm brushed mine as we stood.

"*Pater noster qui es in caelis . . .*" The prior's strong voice intoned the prayer as effortlessly as if he'd had nothing else on his mind throughout the entire meal. It filled the hall. I was aware of the bulk of his body next to mine and found it hard to concentrate on the prayer. The rhythmic rise and fall of the Latin chant as the monks rendered their brief thanksgiving should have been comforting, but my heart was unquiet.

When the last echo had faded and the monks had resumed their normal silence, Prior William turned to face me, as if our conversation had never been interrupted. This time he spoke in a whisper.

"I think you should heed this warning. Make your reverence to the martyr while there are still folk about the cathedral, best between Vespers and Compline, at the martyr's tomb—"

"Altar," I interrupted.

"Tomb, altar, anywhere you like. But do not keep an all-night vigil alone in the cathedral." His hand chopped the air as he warned me. "A whole net of ears covers the country. My information is sound. You are in danger."

For one brief moment, I paused. What if his informers spoke true? But then I remembered Eleanor's letter and thought of the child. No, this task, even if dangerous, was worth the risk. And besides, I had no intention of spending the entire night at Becket's altar. I'd have the letters and be gone ere the midnight bells tolled. If John meant me ill, he'd have to be speedy about it.

"Do you forbid my vigil, then, as prior?" I challenged William.

He looked at me, his mouth and the creases running down

his face tightening. I thought he would refuse on the spot, officially dismissing my plan. But he only said, "By God's true cross, you are a determined woman. No, I do not forbid it. I advise against it."

"This vigil is important to me. It's about Henry . . . and his penance," I lied, assuming an apologetic look, which in no way fooled him. "I need to do this to honor Henry's memory as well." William's expression at that moment was intense but unfathomable, and I felt ashamed for my pretense.

But there was no further opportunity for exchange. Even as I spoke, the monks at the end of the table began to file out. I saw the young redheaded brother bound off the dais rather quickly and accidentally jostle one of the older monks. This provoked a startled reaction, and the older monk murmured something to the young clerk, who dropped his head and fell into line behind him.

William and I passed last from the dais. He stepped down first, then offered his hand to me. Again it was done with the elegance of a courtier. When we were on the stone floor, his table formed two rows of a human guard, and we passed between them.

The rest of the room waited as the prior's table processed toward the huge double oak doors. The monks were now silent, as in the church. This time I could hear a mild rustle of habits and sandals as they followed behind us, no doubt in their interminable, efficient order.

A quick glance over my shoulder yielded the same scene I had witnessed in the cathedral that morning: flocks of dark, hooded birds, wings at their sides, now gliding silently over stones in some predetermined arrangement. I wished to draw this scene. In charcoal, on parchment, I was certain I would see it as revealing a great, hidden truth of faith.

Just at the moment of our exit, a brown-robed brother catapulted into the dining area, nearly colliding with the prior. His cowl askew, his cheeks flushed, he barely apologized. He was shorter than I, no more than a youth. And he was clearly in distress.

"Prior, Prior, you must come at once. Something terrible has happened."

William looked stern. "Collect yourself, Brother Hadrian. Nothing can be this important."

"Oh, but it is, Prior, it is. In the herb garden, near the guest-house. Someone has died. You must come."

William, his face grim, turned to follow the youth immediately, waving to three of his monks to follow him. They were close behind, but so was the rest of the group that had been within earshot of the boy's annoucement. The entire body of monks cascaded like a vast dark wave, along the cloister walks, through the great hall and along the route Brother Dermott and I had taken so frequently in the past day.

I joined the monks. Even Brother Dermott appeared to have forgotten about me, so I moved along with everyone else. And after all, they were going to the garden of my guesthouse. What else would William expect me to do? Wander the monastery grounds?

And I must confess to a growing sense of unease. While no one had yet said that the death near the guesthouse was unnatural, my conscience was troubled. It occurred to me now that I should have reported the theft of my jewels. Perhaps someone had died because I had been too careful to guard my own secrets.

We turned the last corner and began to cross the small gardens that separated the guesthouse from the abbey buildings. I saw nothing at first, so I slipped through the monks who crowded in front of me to find William's tall frame. As I came up next to him, he turned to me. I looked on the ground and could not hold back a small cry. For the person who lay on the ground, clearly dead, wore the pale wool gown of the men from the south who had been with my uncle at the Boar's Head Inn.

9

Sailing into Darkness

A t first I had the wild thought that it was Master Averroës himself, but then one of the monks drew back the hood and I saw a different Arab face, bronzed but much younger, and with a small beard. It was not clear how he had died, but from the position of his body, it was obvious he had been taken by surprise.

"Princess?" William asked, fixing his eagle's eye on me. "Do you know anything about this?"

I shook my head, still not able to find words, my hand seeking his arm to steady myself. After clearing my throat, I was able to say, "I saw this man, or some dressed as he is, not three nights ago in Havre, at the Boar's Head Inn. They had some business with the Duke of Orléans, my uncle Robert. Our meeting was accidental. He introduced me to them." I paused. "Master Averroës was with them."

"Master Averroës?" William's eyes widened. Then he turned to the monks nearest him.

"Take this man to the infirmary. I do not doubt that he is dead, but I want the apothecary to look at him closely. We need to know if he died of natural causes or, if not, what killed him."

William turned back to me as the monks began to pick up the man, his pale wool robe now stained with the earth of the herbal garden and the blue gentian flowers he had crushed in his fall.

"You understand what this means," William said to me.

"No all-night vigil," I said, my voice flat, for the first time unable to come up with a witty rejoinder.

"Indeed," he said curtly. "This incident is too near your quarters for my comfort. But I cannot move you into the abbey. You will have a guard through the night. If you need anything, let him know."

"I will do that. But, Prior"—he stopped at my words—"have I your permission to attend Compline at the least? With Brother Dermott as my guide."

"Granted," he said shortly, and left.

Brother Dermott appeared again at my elbow. I hadn't seen the signal that brought him there, but for once I was grateful. He paced with me to my guesthouse and opened the door.

I half expected to see everything in disarray again, but that was not the case. All was as I had left it this morning, yet everything was changed.

"Someone will be here soon, to stand guard for your security," Brother Dermott said. "And I will return at the hour of Compline to take you to the prayers."

I nodded without speaking, and when he had left, I shot the bolt on the inside. I sat in the chair by the window and looked out. I could see the spot in the garden where the body had fallen, early plant shoots pressed to earth in its outline. And I had no idea what to do next.

By dusk I had constructed a plan to retrieve the letters, given my new situation. I would ask Brother Dermott to leave me for an hour after Compline. After all, William had denied me only the all-night vigil, not the opportunity to reverence the martyr alone. With Dermott outside, or at least in the back of the cathedral in the shadows, I knew I could move the stone and retrieve the letters quickly.

An evening supper was brought to my guesthouse, but I could do no more than pick at the breads on the tray. I sampled the wine but found I had no taste for it. I occupied myself with my drawing and my thoughts until the light in my guesthouse faded entirely.

When the bells rang for Compline, I put on warm woolen wraps for my legs and folded a wool scarf around my shoulders under my cloak, should I need a covering for my head in that dank cathedral. I dreaded the bone-soaking cold more than the loneliness of the vigil, but I could think of no other way to get the hidden letters.

Brother Dermott arrived soon after to escort me to evening prayers. As we walked through the night air, I told him of my desire to stay and pray alone for an hour at the tomb of the martyr, since I had now been forbidden my all-night watch. After a moment of thought, he agreed to leave me alone for a short time for prayer and contemplation. I wondered what William would say to this if he heard, but I was happy to take what I could get from Brother Dermott.

I asked him about the result of the apothecary's examination of the man from the south. He said, "He found no trace of foul play. He thinks that perhaps his heart gave out. But no one knows what he was doing in the abbey at all, nor how he got past the porter at the town gates. No one saw him before his death, yet his clothing clearly marks him as a stranger." Dermott shook his head. "It is a mystery."

"Will Prior William be at Compline this even?" I was already preparing myself for interference from William in my revised plan, should he discover it.

"No, Prior William has left for London on urgent business. He won't return until tomorrow nightfall."

I was oddly disconcerted at this piece of news. Now I would not see William again, as I was determined to leave this abbey early in the morn. Somehow our brief encounter after all these years seemed incomplete.

Brother Dermott accompanied me into the darkened cathedral. It was mysterious to be in a church at night, especially one so cavernous. The candles carried by the monks cast sporadic light in the recesses of the side altars. The drafts caused wavering shadows as the monks made their orderly procession into their choir stalls. The chanting began. First the clear voice of the cantor rang out like an alto bell, then the musical rumble of the monks as they answered one another, like dueling choirs of black-robed angels. I marked the beauty of the chant, all simple, all rational, a sea of musical worship filled with light. In spite of all this, I was possessed of a dark foreboding.

Dermott escorted me to a place of honor in the nave near the choir. I knew he would return at the end of the prayer and lead me to the martyr's altar. As the last strains of plainsong fell and the echo from the cathedral's stone walls likewise drifted off, one by one the monks filed out with their candles. Brother Dermott appeared at my side with, wonder of wonders, two torches. He handed one to me and motioned me to follow.

When we arrived at Becket's Chapel, he lit the tall tallow candles in the holders on the altar from the torch fire he carried. He placed several more candles beside me on the stone steps, as if provisioning me for a long journey. Then he placed both of the torches we carried in the sconces on the wall.

I had brought a small pillow for my knees, and he smiled slightly when I pulled it out from under my cloak. It struck me that Brother Dermott might be close to my age and have aches of his own. I grinned at him amiably. Still, even after I was settled kneeling on the *prie-dieu,* he seemed to linger. Finally I asked, "Yes, Brother? What is it?"

He demurred. "If you should want for anything, Your Grace, I leave this bell for you. Just ring it. Someone will hear. There's a fearsome echo in this church. And a warden monk is always sleeping in the passageway between the church and the cloister. I'll return within the hour."

"Thank you, Brother. I'm right grateful for your thought." I truly was touched, although my impatience for him to be gone was mounting. I wanted to get to my task before my time disappeared. "I will await your return."

"Yes, Your Grace." He bowed and jammed his hands into the sleeves of his habit, in that way monks have. Then he faded noiselessly away, leaving me to marvel how a Lincoln man could speak so smoothly when he chose, almost like a Parisian courtier. It must have been Richard's influence.

The great cathedral had darkened now, except for the pool of light in my small chapel area. It had much the same feel at the end of Maundy Thursday when the pomp and ceremony of the bishops' washing of feet was over. As a child I always feared the moment when we faithful, putting on our shoes again and taking up our staffs, departed. Our footsteps echoed mournfully as one by one the torches and candles were doused to signify the end of Christ's life.

I knew I had to wait until all likelihood of being discovered had passed before I could begin. It was difficult. I was known for my patience when I was young, but the habit had departed. Perhaps the uncertainties of living with Henry and Eleanor had left their mark on me. I wanted now to accomplish my task as quickly as possible. But I knew if some stray monk should chance on me while I was loosening the bricks behind the altar, I should have much to explain. Pilgrim indeed! And while William might wink should he hear such a tale, there was no telling who else was in the abbey. The memory of my eyes meeting those of the young brother at the end of the table at lunch still unsettled me. Could he be connected to John?

My hip began to pain me again. I could scarcely wait for my task to be accomplished and thought with longing of my cozy guesthouse.

I tried to call up pictures from my childhood. There were such marvels that came to mind from time to time. Riding hard in Normandy, across the plains south of Rouen. Christmas in Chinon Castle, with Henry and Eleanor getting along for once and a goose larger than any I had ever seen brought into the hall for our Christmas dinner. Languid summers in Poitiers, where we all read and wrote to our hearts' ease, taking delight in each other's *poésie*. Richard was always the best. He knew how to put into words what we others thought. He had his mother's gift that way. I fingered my pendant, the only thing I still carried with me from those magical years. The shadow of Henry's wrath hovered over us, but I was too young to know it fully. It was only later that I learned.

Memories flitted through my mind like fireflies. Had I my charcoal with me in this cold cathedral, I could not have drawn one picture from my musings. Not one image stayed in my head, only the feeling of those times. Wind on my face, freedom, joy in a celebration, quiet happiness of being near my first love.

I caught myself as I nearly fell forward. I must have been asleep on my knees. Surely now it was late enough for me to act. I listened for a long moment. There was not a sound, not even the small scurrying of a cathedral mouse. I could proceed to search for the packet without fear of discovery.

My last feelings, just before the hands seized me, were of my cold limbs. My last memory before darkness was of a trivial nature. I recall noticing the torches lining the cathedral walls and the leaping shadows that sprang from their fire to perform a macabre dance as if for my entertainment. They reminded me of a traveling dance troupe from Venice I once saw, tall, thin figures garbed in black cloaks and doublets, rising and falling like shafts of dark water in rhythm. The cold gusts of air feeding the torches seemed to increase as I watched, as if doors had opened somewhere. I should have been warned, but instead I paid no attention.

So engaged was I in that arduous task of rising that I failed to hear the slight sound behind me that would have signaled my fate. Instead I was taken completely by surprise. The only thing I felt was a strong arm around my neck, another around my waist and— before I could cry out—I smelled the thick, sweet scent of a mandrake-soaked cloth. Unforgiving hands clapped it against my face, and all went dark.

BOOK II

The Heart's Search

10

Old Sarum Tower

I seemed to be struggling upward with a heavy heart. I could see far below, into a valley. There was snow, a whiteness that was nearly blinding. Then I found what I sought. A small child, a dot of red on the snow, using a pine bough to stave off howling animals that surrounded him.

There was no one to help, no other sign of color on the ground below. I was the only one. Would I give up this loved child to these wolves? I knew I was wounded, but I stretched my wings wide. I felt the power of the black wingspan as the cold air invaded my lungs, and I knew I could do this thing. If only I had the sight in both my eyes again, as once I did. If only the snow were not so white. I circled twice and made ready to dive.

But someone held me back. There were hands on me, and a shaking that was not caused by the wind. I resisted and fell back into my dreams, but the flight was ended. The snow and the child had faded.

Now it was summer. I knew because I could smell the scent. I could feel the summer breeze, and before me young Richard sprang over a low wall. He had the start of a fuzzy red beard on his chin, and we were surrounded by the garden flowers of Poitou. He stood gazing down at me. The flower scent was powerful, unusual. A bee, or many bees, were buzzing around us, creating a sound that grew in my ears. The sunlight fashioned a halo around his head. The aura expanded. Light was taking over.

"*Princesse* Alaïs, can you hear me?" A voice reached me from afar. It seemed to be a woman calling.

"*Princesse*, I think you are waking now. Can you hear me? Can you open your eyes?"

Something in the voice caught at me, like the siren calling Odysseus. I could not refuse. I began a movement toward the voice, leaving behind first the images, then the buzzing, moving always toward the voice, which seemed to be in the light. I felt now as if I were coming up from a deep well. Only the smell, those unusual flowers, followed, a trailing, bittersweet fog.

"Please open your eyes if you can hear me."

I had been summoned. I did as I was bidden, for some reason seeming to have no will of my own. The sight that met my eyes was a small face quite close to my own, with wide brown eyes, a pert nose, and the dark skin of a woman from the South of France. In the background low voices murmured.

I closed my eyes, hoping the rich, sweet, familiar scent that hung around me still would subside before I became sick.

Then I opened them again, slowly. The face no longer hovered over me, but a woman's voice spoke. "I think she is finally coming 'round."

"It's about time." A man spoke from across the room. I could hear his impatience. The voice had a familiar ring, but the identity was just out of reach. The murmuring stopped.

The canopy over me wavered. My unsteady gaze traveled around the heavily curtained bed hung with wine-colored velvet pulled back and tied at each corner. Through the wide triangle between the curtains, I saw a room of whiteness. The ceiling was white, the walls coming down from it were white, and a white light filled the room. There must be many wall openings to allow such light. My head throbbed, but gently. Little by little the bright light became bearable. Forms and shapes attached themselves to voices.

My right elbow pressed into the bed, I began the considerable task of raising my body to better see where I was. As I attempted to steady myself, I heard a rustle and felt a small but strong arm slip under my shoulders. I was surprised that someone wished me well enough for that gesture. For I did not imagine for a moment, even in my confused state, that I was among friends.

When I had attained a sitting position, I had to fight another wave of blurred lines, but then my vision began to clear. Someone placed pillows behind my back and adjusted the fur rugs over my lap.

I tried to make sense of the present. I seemed to be in layers of clothing, more than I had need of, even though the air in the room was chill and the wind whistled outside the narrow openings in the wall. The maroon wool cloak lined in fox that lay around my shoulders and the spring-green wool gown under it were my own. In the grate a fire burned. I could feel wool wraps around my legs and wondered briefly why I would be wearing such extra clothing. I had no memory of putting these things on nor indeed of anything that had happened to bring me here.

Then I surveyed the room, or what I could see of it. It appeared to be a large rectangle made entirely of whitewashed stone, with my bed at one end and a large table up against the wall at the other. The stones were clean and smooth. I focused on the intricate way they had been arranged, as if each had been specially cut and polished for its particular place. The room gave the impression of spaciousness, although I judged that it was in truth no larger than the dressing room of my apartments in Paris. Many long, slender openings in the wall allowed light to come in, but the openings were situated in such a way that I knew I was in a fortress. The place seemed familiar. Had I been here before? Or just dreamed it?

"Is she awake enough to answer questions?" The importunate man spoke again. There was a strange, regular noise, like a cork popping from a bottle.

My eyes drifted across the room to the source of the voice. I squinted to improve my vision. A slender, dark-haired man sat at the far table, playing with a jewel-handled dagger. He flipped it over, the jewels glinting in the morning light. There was another popping sound as the point stuck in the table. The jewels swayed. When he looked my way and saw me watching, he stood up and jerked the dagger from the table, jamming it into his belt as he came across the room. A small white terrier followed this lanky form, happily wagging its stunted tail.

"Oh, no." The words slipped out as he came near. "Not you."

He was older now, and leaner than I remembered him, but it was unmistakably John Plantagenet, he whom his brothers had called Lackland. The strong chin jutting forward clearly marked him a Plantagenet, while the insistent eyebrows, growing into a perpetual frown in the middle of his forehead, and his small eyes set him apart from his handsome brothers.

"Alaïs Capet, you will show this king of England more respect than you have shown the others." In four quick strides, he was at my side. "I am not my father in his dotage, nor my lovesick brother Richard, for you to address me with such insolence." With one angry movement, he yanked the bed curtains down, revealing me to the entire room. I looked past him and saw that there were four or five knights with him, all hanging back against the walls. Silently they watched their king.

My eyes came to rest on the pretty woman whose face I had seen on waking. Now she sat next to the bed, her hands loosely folded in her lap, a look of mildly questioning interest on her face. It was she who had helped me to sit upright and placed the pillows behind me. Once the curtains were drawn back, we could see each other fully. This must be John's new queen, Isabelle.

I returned to John. He stood, hands on his hips, looking down at me. My gaze scored him from head to foot. "You've acquired a new tailor since last I saw you," I said. "You must have come into silver recently."

I could see his brown eyes turn black, as they always did when he began a tantrum. One of the knights snorted and quickly covered it with a cough.

"I warn you, Alex," John said, calling me by the English version of my name. He grabbed my arm, twisting the skin on it, an old child's trick to hurt without leaving bruise marks. "If I were you, I'd watch my words."

"If I were you, I'd take the same advice." I pulled my arm away as his fingers relaxed slightly. "I am not without the means to avenge wrongs done to me." In his face I saw a flicker of the old fear that he used to show whenever I called his bluff as a child. But, being John, he pressed on with mindless courage.

"Sister, dear, you haven't asked me what I want with you." He leaned over me, his forearms jammed on either side of my body, his garlic-laden breath dusting my face.

"No doubt you'll tell me when you're ready." I folded my arms across my chest and rubbed the sore spot. I held his eyes without flinching.

As John tried to stare me down, he was betrayed by that old nervous tic in his right eye. It had always given his gaze a certain instability. As if he could read my thoughts, he flung himself away from me and paced back across the room. Several of the knights leaning against the wall shifted as John passed. Twice he turned his head to look at me, as if I were a bad dream that might disappear if he were lucky. Suddenly I had a vision of John in a meadow, a green meadow, walking to a makeshift table in the sunlight, turning around, just like this, looking back at a ring of murmuring men as if uncertain what to do. His confusion touched me. I shook my head slightly to clear the image.

"Do not dare to shake your head at me, Princess," he bellowed from across the room.

"All right, John." I spread my hands in an exaggerated gesture. "You win. I'll play your game. What is it that you want from me?"

He came toward me. "That's better," he said. "Now, tell me straight: Where are the letters you were trying to steal at Canterbury?"

"What are you talking about? I wasn't trying to steal any letters. I was keeping a vigil at the altar of the martyr Becket. I was in the sanctuary of the church, John. Which you have violated." I stabbed my finger forward in the air to make my points. "And not only the sanctuary of the cathedral but the very altar of the martyr. You should fear for your eternal salvation, King John." I lowered my voice to a stage whisper.

"Bosh. I care not a fig for salvation." He snapped his finger on the word "fig." "When I'm ready, I'll have gold to bribe a bishop for my ticket into heaven." He was standing again in front of my bed, his voice loud enough to impress his knights.

"Be careful, John," I warned. "The bishop may cooperate, but God may not get the message. And I doubt the bishop will want to accompany you to clarify things."

The knights stopped fidgeting in the background and moved as one slightly closer to our scene. They sensed that battle was joined. They would likely lay bets if they didn't think the king would notice.

"Where have you brought me, John?" I asked quietly as he moved closer.

"You are in the keep at Old Sarum." So I *had* been here before! Well did I remember it. "This is the tower where King Henry kept my mother captive for sixteen long years. I thought you might enjoy the surroundings, since you were so close to her." Honey dripped from his words.

As John intended (was he really as simple as I had thought? Mayhap I had underestimated him), the name of his father brought my thoughts into focus. My sharp intake of breath betrayed me.

"I'm not in the mood to trade family memories with you," I muttered. The waves of nausea were starting again deep in my body. "And anyway, what did you care for your mother? Your father was the one who raised you. You didn't care a fig, as you are so fond of saying, for your mother *or* her captivity."

"I cared more for my mother than you, who took to his bed so easily once she was his prisoner," he hissed, leaning over me once again. I turned my face away.

"God's blood, John. Don't add hypocrisy to your blasphemy. Do you think I have no memory? I heard your raucous laughter at supper the night we returned to Clarendon Palace, after he locked your mother here in this very tower. I lost the stepmother of all my childhood years that day. My betrothed, your brother Richard, had just declared war on his father. I cried myself to sleep that night." I turned my face back to look at him. "Even your father was somber. But you—you drank and laughed all night with the king's men."

John's face paled, and he clasped his hands behind his back. I closed my eyes to escape the sight of him. But before either of us could continue, nature intervened. Suddenly billows rose from my deepest insides. "I need a basin. I'm sick."

Isabelle suddenly sprang to life. "Ho!" she shouted at the knights. "Call the servants from the next room. Now!" Even in my extreme distress, I could tell that she was used to being obeyed. The knights departed swiftly, *en masse*. In minutes the servants were there with basins and water. Afterward I lay back on the cushions as they wiped my brow. Then, on some secret signal from Isabelle, they scattered as quickly as they had come, taking their basins and their comforting, cool cloths.

Isabelle stood next to John at the side of the bed. I saw her casual glance graze my withered hand. I quickly slid it under the bedcovers.

"Why were you trying to steal my mother's letters from Canterbury when my knights found you?" John was standing with feet apart, a hand on his sword, in the same threatening way he used to stand as a young man when he tried to intimidate the servants. "What is in those letters that you want?"

"I already told you, I was praying at the tomb of the martyr." It was difficult to talk through my raw throat. I could feel sweat beading my brow.

"How amusing. But it won't work, Alex. I know what you are up to."

"You've been misinformed, John." Despite my weak state, I was determined not to let this man bully me. "I was making a pilgrimage."

"You're a liar, Alex, as you were wont to be when it suited your convenience."

"Or someone else has lied to you and you have been made a gull again, as *you* were wont always to be."

The little white dog chose that moment to bark. John's reaction was swift and brutal. He turned and administered a vicious kick. The animal flew across the room and landed in an inert mass of curly white fur. It did not move.

"Christ above, John," I whispered. "It was just a dumb animal."

When his face turned back to mine a moment later, a smile spread across it. "You may want to reconsider cooperating with me, sister. I've always had such a bad temper." The tic in his eye returned.

I looked at Isabelle, who sat beside the bed once again. She had tented her fingers, and they tapped noiselessly against each other. Her face registered no emotion.

I bit my lip and thought for a long moment of the danger facing me before I replied. "Perhaps Philippe understands fraternal love better than you do, John. What do you know of such things? I wonder what your brother Geoffrey would say about your notion of familial devotion if he were here. Or young Arthur."

"You are not one to talk about loyalty," John snapped.

"I have never betrayed those I loved."

"What about my mother?"

"What about your father?" I countered in a whisper only he could hear. "Your beloved father who raised you?" His face contracted as if a hearth pot of hot soup had been overturned on him.

"You dare not—" He caught himself, but I saw instantly my advantage. I could hide my feelings about the past, but John could not.

"I dare not speak of your father?" I baited him. "Just because you betrayed him doesn't mean that I did. And"—I pushed myself up on my elbow toward him—"just because you failed to please him doesn't mean I failed."

His hand shot out before Isabelle could act and caught my cheek in a slap that was more like a punch. It knocked me back against the pillows. I could feel the stinging imprint of John's seal ring on my face. My eyes were filled instantly, but it was small payment for the satisfaction I felt. I had found the touchstone. For John it was always jealousy.

The king turned away from me, his hand pressing his brow, and he moved out of my line of vision. I could hear the knights' low voices, talking to cover their embarrassment. Isabelle continued to observe John solemnly from her chair. Eventually her crisp voice broke the silence.

"John, if your goal is to get information from Alaïs, I don't think you are going about it in quite the right way."

I struggled to sit up again and turned to face her. She was not two sword lengths away from me. When her clear, slightly elevated voice had rung out, the murmuring knights fell silent.

"I don't think we've been properly introduced," I said. "I am the *Princesse* Alaïs of France. You must be the new queen of England." I gestured to John, aware of the rising welt on my cheek. "You must forgive our little family fights."

"I am Isabelle of Angoulême," she said. "And I know well enough who you are." She pinched her mouth for a moment, and then, unexpectedly, her thin lips curled upward in amusement. "You won't provoke me, Alaïs Capet. John may revert to childish actions around you, but you have no such power over me."

"Then, since we seem to be the only adults involved here, perhaps you and I can manage the situation. Can you explain why I have been brought here?"

She had just opened her mouth to answer when John reappeared at the foot of the bed, this time with a goblet of Armagnac. I could smell the brandy on his breath from where I lay.

"I'll give you one more chance," he blurted out after a deep draft, leaning on the carved bedpost. "You can tell me what you know, or you can resign yourself to starving in a damp tower in England."

"John, follow my thoughts, please, if you can." I spoke with immense care. "Suppose I did go to Canterbury to find your mother's letters. It's obvious I thought they were there. If I didn't have them on my person when your men took me, I didn't get them. Why think you I would know where they are now?"

"Because these letters are of more concern to you than to me. You want them as much as I do. And I know you, Alex. You will do anything to get what you want."

His voice had the winter feel of Henry's when he was crossed. For the first time in this exchange, his words gave me pause. I recalled my drugged vision of the little boy in the snow, and I could feel my heartbeat hasten. I had to proceed carefully.

"I do not have a care about your mother's letters to Becket," I said, feigning exasperation. "What is it about your family, that you all think I want to be involved in your intrigues? Why could I possibly want to put my hands on some musty old letters to the archbishop, written when I was barely a tot? I tell you I know nothing of them. Now, let me out of this absurd tower." I struggled to put my feet over the edge of the high bed and stand to face John.

As I heaved myself to my feet, the room reeled and his face receded. I backed my leg against the bed to keep from falling. Suddenly Isabelle was there to support me. She gently pressed me to a sitting position on the edge of the bed and sat down beside me. My strength dissolving, I allowed it.

"Will you stop this bickering?" She spoke firmly, as if we were children. "If you are both interested in recovering the letters, should we not try to find them? Working together, as family ought to do?"

I quelled my astonishment and looked at her. I was not quite able to match her firm, rational tone when I spoke. "Of course. You are quite right, Isabelle. As a family. Now, can you explain why these letters to Becket are so almighty important?"

John made an aggressive noise, but Isabelle simply turned her back on him and faced me. She was silent for a moment, as if considering some decision. Then she began to speak in a low, comforting voice, as if I were a hysterical child. "It is thought that Eleanor wrote some letters years ago—important, personal letters. Letters to Thomas à Becket, as you say, and written at a time when Henry and the archbishop were quarreling."

"I know this," I said, gently easing aside her arm, which still encircled my waist with an alarming familiarity. I replaced it on her lap. "Eleanor told me. She is afraid the letters will be used to embarrass John, raising all the old rumors of Becket and the queen's intriguing behind Henry's back. Possibly raising issues of John's parentage."

I thought I might have gone too far, but then I saw that John, in his relentless pacing, was out of earshot.

"Ah, but there is more. It's true that certain of these letters may have been addressed to Becket and may prove momentarily embarrassing. But it is rumored there are others of the queen's letters bundled with them, letters written later, while she was imprisoned here at Old Sarum." Isabelle gestured. "Letters written in this very room, I understand, but never sent. Letters she entrusted to a monk to hide for her."

"Go on," I said. She had my attention at last. Two sets of letters. It seems Eleanor had omitted crucial information when she had pressed me to undertake this search.

"We . . . are not certain of the subject of these later letters, nor to whom they were addressed." Isabelle cast a look over her shoulder at John, who watched her morosely, swilling his brandy. "They couldn't have been to Becket, because he was long dead by then. We have information that some of these letters may contain vital information, proof in the queen's own hand of the existence of a rival claimant to the throne. And whoever has possession of these letters—Queen Eleanor, the Knights Templar, John, or you . . ." Her voice trailed off.

"Has the power," I said, looking into the distance.

"Exactly so. And if the letters fall into the hands of the Templars, they could use them to force John—" She stopped abruptly.

"Force John to do what?"

"Oh." She brushed the air with her hand. "Make certain concessions."

"Minor concessions, such as giving up the throne?" I just couldn't restrain myself.

Isabelle glanced sharply in my direction. "Such as giving the powerful abbeys relief from the taxes they owe the crown," she snapped. "Such as making the king of England their private pawn."

But I was losing myself, despite the interest I had in this conversation. My eyes were heavy again, and I ached to sleep. "If such letters were written when she was captive here at Old Sarum, how could she ever have thought they would find their way out into the world? The queen was under heavy guard."

"It's not at all clear the letters were even sent when they were written," Isabelle said. "At first Eleanor was quite shut off from the world. Later, though, she had much more opportunity. Henry was soft of heart where Eleanor was concerned, and he granted her most of what she wanted in the end."

"Except, of course, her greatest desire. Her liberty," I pointed out. Nevertheless, I knew that what the English queen said was true.

Isabelle took no notice, as she continued. "If she had been unable to send these letters, she may have decided they represented a danger to her if they were found. She may have decided to have them hidden on the outside. They could have been smuggled out in any number of ways. She ordered cloth for new dresses, doubtless sent things back to merchants. The pipe rolls show many such transactions, so we know there were merchants in and out of Old Sarum constantly."

Isabelle, still sitting companionably beside me, bent her head toward me so that I became aware of the musky scent that her body gave off, like an attractive animal. I thought I might be sick again from the sweetness. "There were many avenues through which to distribute treasonous correspondence," she murmured. "We just don't know what happened—"

"Isabelle," John cut in. He had repositioned himself once again at the table against the far wall.

"It's right, John, for Alex to know the truth about the letters. I don't think Eleanor has been completely candid with her."

And those, I thought grimly, may be the truest words spoken by any of us today.

"Isabelle, dear Isabelle, could you help me rest against the pillow. I do feel faint. John, what did your men use on me? That dreadful mandrake root, I suppose. Pity it's so easily available in England. They say its effects last for days." As the buzzing returned, the room seemed to grow smaller. "I'm afraid I can talk no longer in the present moment."

I sank back against the pillows as Isabelle rose and lifted my legs onto the bed, remembering as I did that there were herbs in my small purse that might do well for me. I was beginning to experience a dreadful thirst. Hang the risk of poison. I was forced to ask for water.

"Isabelle, please, water, if you would, from the hearth pot. I have need of something to still my head." I paused, fighting the nausea rising within me again. When it had passed, I steadied my voice. "What are the supposed contents of this second set of letters?"

The king and queen exchanged a long look as Isabelle rose. "They may contain merely personal news, or mayhap Queen Eleanor's opinions of state matters." Isabelle's nonchalant voice belied her next words as she bent over the fire to take water from the kettle. "But we have been told the Templars believe that these letters contain information confirming a rival claimant to the kingship of England. Information that could topple John's throne."

I wanted to say that the throne would stand, it was John who would topple, but the time for any levity had long since passed.

I pulled my purse out from under the coverlet and undid the

binding. The small packet of herbs was still intact, inside a cheese-cloth with a drawstring. I took several of the longer leaves out and soaked them in the steaming pewter cup Isabelle handed me.

"What are you drinking?" John left his chair and shot across the room, nearly knocking the cup from my hand in his effort to peer into it.

"Not poison, if that's what you fear," I took a long draft of the tea, watching him over the rim of the cup.

"I believe that you know where my mother's letters are." John's voice was intense but not loud. "I know that my mother told you where to look. And I think you know why the Templars want those letters also."

"John, she's your mother." The light that had filled the room was lessening, time itself was moving, and we three in this room spent our time in witless exchanges. "Why don't you send to ask her what instructions she gave me? And while you are at it, ask her what these many letters contain, words that could be turned on you now. Surely she wouldn't deny your request. She always loved you so."

John knocked the cup from my hand, and I watched it skitter across the room. It came to rest beside the body of the little white dog.

"Alaïs, the game is over. You can rot in this tower, for all I care." I thought he would strike me, but he only stood looking down at me, his jaw working before he spoke again. "I know that those letters are proof you had a bastard child with my father. My mother knew it, and she wrote about it." His lips tightened grimly. "And I think you know where that child is now."

Checkmate.

I had to swallow twice to keep from making any noise at all. I summoned all my guardian spirits to hold my body still. I looked at him, saying nothing.

Still watching me, he lifted his arm in a half wave to his wife.

"Isabelle, we leave." He picked up his wife's ermine cloak, which had slipped to the floor, and tossed it to her without even looking at her.

"But—"

"I said now." He leaned over me once again, his face close enough for me to see the pores on his nose. "Think this over, Alex. You are our guest here and remain here at our pleasure. For the time being, we will see that you have wood for your fire and food and drink. But our patience may grow short." He suddenly dropped his royal persona. "I want those letters in my possession, and, by God's blood, you'll not get in my way. You know something about this, and I'll have your knowledge before long." His eyes narrowed like a whippet's in sunlight. "Or you'll pay a heavy price, *princesse* or no."

He stopped by the door and threw over his shoulder, "I'll leave you the dog for company."

Isabelle was standing next to John as he finished. Something close to sympathy fluttered across her face as she looked down on me, merely the brush of a bird's wing. I thought for a moment she would speak, but she gathered her skirts and followed him out. I closed my eyes and slid down into the warmth of the bed.

Christ above. Only one thing could cause such an uproar. The child had lived after all. Eleanor, John, the Templars—everyone knew it but me. Only now I knew also. John had just told me. And now I must reconsider all my plans.

I had just seen John revealed as he truly was: a dangerous man, and unstable. I thought of his bizarre smile after he had kicked the little terrier. Not a man in control of himself. Not a man to trust at all. And he wanted desperately to know the whereabouts of my child, a son who would now be a grown man. A son who posed a danger to the man who had not hesitated to kill his own nephew, young Arthur.

The drugs captured me once again, and I drifted off to dream of many little boys lost in the great hall of an unknown castle, all running around trying to find their mothers. Small white dogs snapped at their heels.

Much later I woke to find that someone had lit a fire in the small hearth. Wood was laid by it, and in the glow I could see a tray of food. The body of the dog was gone.

It took me some minutes to adjust my eyes to the dim light, still longer to realize that my head no longer felt like a large drum. And the roiling stomach I had experienced all through the conversation with John and Isabelle had disappeared.

I raised my stiff body awkwardly from the bed. I was still wearing the woolen leggings I had put on to fend off the cold in the cathedral, and I was warm and uncomfortable. I slipped off the cloak and divested myself of my shift, which had been drenched with sweat. I was glad to be free of it. The leggings came next, and I put my gown back on.

I padded to the fire, feeling lighter of heart. The tray held simple enough food: two shepherd's pies, still agreeably warm, some bread and ale. The smell of the meal made water start in my mouth, and I settled myself quickly as near to the blaze as I could. I discovered I was ravenous. As I chewed, I thought. I had to lay my plans. And I still knew not those I could trust.

Not Eleanor, who had withheld the truth of the letters from me. Not John, nor Isabelle, who would stop at nothing to secure the throne. Not the faceless Knights Templar, who wanted my son only to use as a pawn in their power game.

The image of William rose before me, but I pushed the thought away. He was in London on important abbey business. He might not even know of my abduction. And, even if he were of good will toward me, which was by no means certain, how could he help, with only a bunch of monks for assistants?

The fire was settling now, and I threw another piece of the small woodpile onto it. Outside, the wind made a terrible noise. It reminded me of something. The howling of wild animals or perhaps the angry sea. I remember what Eleanor once told me. She swore that when she was captive in this very tower, she could hear the sea when the wind was up, even this far inland. Of course, that was impossible. She must have imagined it.

Eleanor. I stared into the fire. What did she write when she was kept in this tower so long ago? She knew about my child. And she wrote of it to others. I buried my head in my hands, but then I bethought myself of the child. I would find a way out of this tower, and I would find that child. I would make certain, no matter the cost, of his safety. No matter the cost to anyone.

11

Entertainments
in the Keep

I soon crawled back to bed and fell into a fitful sleep. When next I opened my eyes, light again filled the room. Eleanor's room. For the first time, I was alone in daylight, and I had the leisure to ponder my last visit here. It had been more than twenty-odd summers since Henry swooped down on Eleanor's court at Poitiers chasing his rebellious sons. When he finished closing the court, he dragged Eleanor back to England, and he brought me along with her.

Our family was taken entirely by surprise one damp spring afternoon when the king descended on us. We had only an hour's warning. A messenger, soaked with rain, had blown into the courtyard like a battered bird with the news that Henry was not ten leagues away, riding hard with an army at his back. And he was in a fury. The king had discovered that Eleanor and his sons were plotting with my father, King Louis, behind his back. He was riding for blood.

There was just enough time for Richard and Geoffrey to dash to the stables and throw themselves on two horses. They rode out in a panic, desperate to escape the wrath of their father. Eleanor watched them go, shading her fine hazel eyes against the sun. Then she pulled me by the hand so that I fairly flew into the great hall after her. If I close my eyes, I can still see her and hear her words winging around in my memory.

"Come, Alaïs. We will dress as men, and follow Richard. We still have an hour's start, if we go now."

"But what is happening?" I bleated like a lost lamb. "What will become of us?" She only said she would explain later, as we dashed to her chambers. We threw on the clothes of our pages, brought quickly at her sharp command.

It was too late. Even as we pulled cloaks from her armoire, we heard the hoofbeats of the king's company. I trailed the queen to the parapet to look down below at the great sweaty fuss of the personal guard of the king of England. They rode into our courtyard with Henry at their head, still spurring his horse. William Marshal rode at his side.

We had a rough crossing back to England. The Channel waters were whipped by high winds, but the king was in such a rush that he refused to wait for the weather to shift. We were crossing anyway, he shouted, flying into one of his famous rages. His men complied.

He wanted Eleanor, we discovered, safely locked away in Old Sarum tower. Her days of intrigue against him were over. He wanted to slam the door on her for good.

The day we arrived at Sarum, the weather had finally broken, and a watery English sun covered our caravan. Because the family had spent so much time in Normandy while I was growing up, I was not familiar with the Plantagenets' English castles. William Marshal explained Sarum's history to me as we rode up the hill toward the tower. King Henry had never favored Sarum and had rarely stayed there. It had been a fortified keep a hundred years earlier, built for strength, not comfort, by King William, he who was called the Conqueror.

The original building was the keep itself, containing a royal bedchamber, receiving rooms, and a vestibule with a small chapel over it. Later Bishop Roger of Salisbury, who built the great cathedral, had attached more comfortable royal apartments, a large receiving hall, two more chapels, and the great kitchen.

As William Marshal recounted this history, I noticed Eleanor just in front of us. She appeared to be lost in thoughts of her own, not turning around once. William Marshal had been assigned the queen's personal guardian on this journey, but it was her choice to ride alone. The king was far ahead with his high knights, and many others rode behind us.

When we reached the crest of the hill, we could see masons laying a stone wall that coiled like a serpent around Sarum. It appeared the wall would encompass the entire settlement, including Bishop Roger's great cathedral that sprawled to the north of the royal buildings.

Eleanor must have jerked her reins when the wall came in sight, for her horse suddenly shied and bucked. William Marshal spurred his own mount to come even with her and placed his hand on her bridle to steady the animal. He leaned close to her and spoke low. Her shoulders, which had remained firm through all of this ordeal, slipped slightly, as if she released a long-held breath. And for the remainder of the climb to Sarum, her head was down. He left her and returned to my side.

"Perhaps the queen would be glad of my company," I suggested when he was again in earshot. "Shall I ride with her?"

"Aye, she will need your company right enough, but for now she must be alone." He sighed. "It was left to me to tell her—she will be lodged in the keep, not in the royal apartments."

"In the keep? The king is going to make her stay in the old keep?" I was astonished. "I've heard that's practically a dungeon."

"*Non, non.*" He reverted momentarily to the Norman French he so often spoke with the king. "*La tour est très haute. Il y a beaucoup de lumière à l'intérieur.*" Then he caught himself. "It's been made comfortable enough, I understand. But still . . ." His voice drifted off as he searched the landscape ahead of us.

"William Marshal, how long will the queen have to stay there? What is this quarrel between the king and queen about?"

He shook his head and said nothing. I looked into his face and could read only sadness, etched in lines that crossed his forehead and sprang from the corners of his kind eyes. I remember wondering how old he was and how much more sadness he would see.

William Marshal led the queen up the tower stairs to her rooms, and I trudged behind, with the maidservants bringing up the rear. The rest of the cavalcade had ridden on, leaving only a few knights to accompany the marshal. They followed us.

The maids chattered behind us as we silently climbed the circular stairs to the upper chambers. Even their voices stilled eventually. Then the only sounds were our echoing footsteps and our guards' swords striking the sides of the narrow stairwell.

Although high in the tower, the room was white and clean. Indeed, a fire burned in the grate, and the queen's accustomed furs covered the beds. There were provisions made for her two maids in an anteroom, and much of her wardrobe had been assembled from her English castles. It was clear that someone had made an effort to see to her comfort. But still, a reigning queen of England imprisoned in a castle keep!

It was only after the queen was settled in a high-backed chair, sipping the broth the servants had prepared and staring out the narrow window, that William Marshal beckoned me away. In the tower stairwell, placing his hand under my chin and tilting my face up toward his, he told me I must make ready to go. I was not to be allowed to stay with the queen. I must instead go to Clarendon Palace, where the king was lodged. It was the king's order.

When we came back into the room, Eleanor had been watching the fire. She raised her head. "He's taking Alaïs, isn't he?" Her tone was bitter. "This is the final insult."

William Marshal's hand fell to the queen's shoulder, but she shook it off and turned away from us. She refused even to embrace me, although I had done nothing to hurt her. I resisted crying in front of the queen, but I couldn't stop the tears from running down my face as William and I descended the tower stairs. I had no illusions about the future. I was fifteen years of age, and I had already lost two mothers. Life held bleak promise.

Now it was years later, and I was back at Sarum. This time it was I who was in the keep and John who had brought me here. William Marshal, I mused, faithful to the queen, but above all faithful to the king. How I wished he were here to advise me. I had heard he was now Earl of Pembroke, lifted to the nobility by Richard before he died. William Marshal still in the service of the Plantagenet kings. I wondered how he was dealing with John. The thought nearly brought a smile.

The sun was warming the room, so I threw back the bedcovers and stretched like a great cat. I felt better than I had since my abduction, and suddenly I had a need to move around. The spare chamber contained minimal furniture: the bed, the chair Isabelle had used in the interview of the day before, the table and chair John had favored in the far side of the room. Then I saw something I had missed the previous day. I rose from the bed, albeit a bit unsteadily, and walked over to a small, elegant writing desk.

On closer inspection I saw that it was beautifully carved in the Italian fashion, with small legs that ended in little claws. The dark oak top had been so smoothed and oiled at one time that a writer's quill would fly over parchment without a snag.

Suddenly I remembered where I had seen the desk before. It once rested in Eleanor's bedchamber at the ducal palace in Poitiers. Her private rooms were a favored place of mine in those years. On many a sunny morning like this, I would run into her chamber without announcement to find her settled at this little desk, writing her verses or reading a letter just delivered by some breathless courier.

Eleanor adored words, and writing was her particular joy, especially after she and the king parted. It seemed she was always writing something that must be finished before she could be persuaded to come sit in on our Courts of Love, our gentle assizes where the knights would compete for our favor through poetry rather than swords.

King Harry must have ordered the desk to be brought over by ship at Eleanor's request. As Isabelle had reminded me, the king had softened toward the queen in later years. She must have persuaded him to bring her this dear table. I had heard some rumors that writing and reading poetry were her main diversions in those years of captivity.

Someone had recently wiped the top of the desk free of dust, but the legs had been overlooked. Whoever had received John's order to prepare the chamber for me must have been in a hurry. A blanket of cobwebs stretched from one leg to another underneath, and my foot broke through it as I pulled the small chair forward to sit at the desk.

A clatter on the stairs interrupted my thoughts. I turned quickly, my hand going to the purse with its sharp tool. Then I steadied myself. I stood, not wanting to call attention to the desk.

A short, burly man entered the room, followed by a large hound. He wore the lions of England on his tunic. A beard well trimmed, his dark hair cut short, and the sword at his side indicated a businesslike approach to his job. The dog stood next to him, no less commanding.

"Your Grace." A bow, the minimal courtesy. "Robert of Warwick, at your service."

"Are you so?" I raised my eyebrows.

He continued as if he hadn't heard. "I have the assignment of your safekeeping while you are King John's guest here. If you have need of anything, hang this red wool cloth out the opening. I will always have two men stationed below, watching."

"Very kind," I said dryly.

"You will have food brought to you in the morning and again at night. The king sends wishes for your safety and your health."

"I'm sure," I murmured. "And what does the king want from me in return?"

"He has said to me that when you are ready to give him the information he seeks, he will be glad to see you."

"The king resides here then, at Sarum?" I remembered the royal apartments next door and hoped the water still poured into the royal bedchamber when the spring rains came. Henry had been drenched more than once when he slept there, cursing Bishop Roger and his architect every time.

"The king has left Sarum for the time being. He is lodging at Clarendon. He has given me command of his men here. If you want to send him a message, he is less than a half day's ride." Robert of Warwick continued to talk as if reading a royal proclamation, without any emotion whatsoever.

"Is there no maid to serve me?" Suddenly it seemed ominous that only men and dogs surrounded me.

"No, Your Grace. This is a garrison now. There are no women here."

"Then I have another request. I'd like some drawing materials."

"We have no pens and parchment here. We're soldiers." He assumed a dogged look.

I turned away. I did not want to encourage him further. If he became insolent, I had no recourse.

"One more thing, my lady," the man added. I waited. "King John urges you to honor his request for information before he loses his patience."

"And did the king give some indication of when that unhappy event might occur?"

"He said he would expect you would send for him within the week."

"Otherwise what?" I turned to look at him.

For the first time, the man seemed to hesitate.

"Well, come on. Out with it."

"He, uh, didn't say directly." Robert of Warwick stared at a point on the wall behind my left shoulder.

I shook my head and made my way back to the bed. I was hungry and needed drink, but I was too annoyed to raise the subject with this lout. I sat down heavily.

"There is no message for the king."

Robert of Warwick stood still until I looked up at him. "Go on, man. It's not your problem." He bowed stiffly, somewhat lower than the perfunctory bob he had made on his arrival, and left without another word.

I swung my feet over the side of the bed, lay back, and rested, thinking again of my years at Poitiers. The wind was always gentle there, never the damp, cutting weather of England. How was it we had come to the south, after years of knocking around in the Plantagenets' castles in cold England and damp Normandy? I remembered suddenly. I was only twelve summers when Richard's sister Joanna came dashing into my chamber one morning.

"Alaïs, make ready. We are to start for the south tomorrow with Queen Eleanor."

"What? Have they had another quarrel?"

"No, it's nothing like that. They called Richard and Geoffrey in this morning and said we were all to depart in haste. The king has decreed that the queen must establish a court at Poitiers to quell the rebellious Gascognes. The king says he is tired of their antics and they are the queen's subjects anyway. We're all to go with her, and we'll stay for a long time. 'As long as it takes to straighten them out,' the king said when Richard asked."

"Poitiers. In the south," I murmured. Perhaps, I remember thinking, if we were all to go, Richard might finally pay attention to me. We *were* to be married one day, although the king and queen would not say when. Just that week my sister, Marguerite, who was living at court again, had been in my chamber when I undressed for bed. She noticed the slight swelling in my chest, which she pointed out to me. She said I was becoming a woman. When I pressed her for details, she said our nurse Francesca would explain what came next.

Four years later, when King Henry descended on us like the furies, the swelling in my chest had flowered. And my hopes were coming true. Finally Richard was taking notice of me—when he had time, that is. He was mightily occupied in those years with his hunting and his fighting and his *poésie*.

Despite his youth, Richard seemed to want to learn how to govern, for Henry had agreed that he would inherit the Aquitaine. He was an eager student. He would spend hours locked with his mother and her counselors in the privy chambers of the ducal palace, looking at maps or reading correspondence. He talked earnestly with his tutors or closeted himself with the couriers the king sent with alarming frequency.

But slowly things changed. Richard began to absent himself

from Eleanor's court a great deal, riding out often late at night and back days later when least expected. I can still hear his voice as I lay in my bedchamber watching the reflection of the torches play on the ceiling. He would summon the grooms as he rode in late at night, calling for help with the horses. "Ho, grooms. *Ecoutez. Aidez-moi, immédiatement! Vite, vite!*"

Oh, he could be gentle, and he was sometimes. And always polite. Everlastingly polite. Bending over my hand, bowing like the courtier his mother had trained him to be.

Sometimes in the evening, when our meal was done, the entire court would sit outside the palace, in the sweet scented gardens dotted warmly by our many torches. Richard would read his *sirventes*, those poems he had composed while he had been traveling, and we would all listen. At the end he would bow to me—to me, *Princesse* Alaïs, his future bride. And once, when we were alone . . . but it does no good to remember.

If I had not resigned myself so many years ago to my fate, I could bring myself to cry for lost hopes. But of what use is that maudlin pursuit?

I thought about the rooms in the ducal palace at Poitiers. My own chamber, that of my sister, Marguerite, and her husband (until the king wrote that he wanted his son Henry posthaste back in London), the queen's antechamber and bedchamber, hung with the green and blue Toulouse tapestries she so admired. And the writing desk.

Suddenly a half memory inspired me and I started to sit up. The movement sent a shot of pain up the back of my neck. The after-effects of mandrake. I quietly cursed John.

With more care I tried again and this time was able to rise. Through the openings in the walls I could see that the sun had circled the chamber. I must have dozed. It was now well into the afternoon. Since it was early spring it would be dark in a few more hours. I moved toward the desk.

A recollection of Eleanor seated at this desk years ago formed. This same desk. And the picture of her talking to me: "Come here, young Alaïs. I shall show you a great secret. This is a very special desk."

I sat again on the chair and pulled the top of the desk toward me. It opened as I remembered, making a writing ledge. The inside was as dusty as the legs had been before my feet crushed the webs. I ran my finger along the inside, pulled it out, and saw a neat row of dust along my index finger.

I pulled out the drawer, placed three fingers of my right hand along the inside wall of the desk frame, and pressed, repeating this as I moved along the length of the desk. Suddenly I heard the slight sound of a spring. The side gave way, falling outward, and I felt a hollow of some significant space under my fingers. I let out a breath of satisfaction.

I explored this area, my fingers edging as far as they could stretch. I wasn't certain what I expected to find, but an excitement began to course through me. What if . . . ?

And I was rewarded. A torn edge of parchment touched my searching fingers. I wiggled them, trying to coax the page closer, to capture it. But a sudden noise distracted me.

I quickly pushed the sidepiece up until I heard it snap into place, replaced the drawer, and then sat with my hands folded upon the top of the desk. There was a faint shuffle just outside the door that led to the tower stairs.

I was looking out the small aperture near the desk, turning slowly, when I heard the noise of someone on the threshold.

There, outlined in the golden afternoon light, breathing heavily from her climb, was the lovely Queen Isabelle. I didn't have to feign surprise.

12

A Joust with
Isabelle

I thought good Robert of Warwick told me John had departed this fortress."

She stood in the doorway, poised for a dramatic entrance and doubtless pleased to see me look so startled. She appeared changed, though I couldn't quite place the difference. Perhaps her eyes, rimmed now with dark half-moons, small pouches of fluid under them marring her high, aristocratic cheekbones. I did not rise.

"And so he has." Despite her deep breathing, she appeared insouciant as she entered my chamber without an invitation. "The king left at sunset last evening. He was in a terrible temper." She strolled across the room and seated herself in the chair John had favored on their earlier visit. She crossed her arms and leaned casually forward on the table. Gradually her rapid breathing eased, while a slight dew formed on her upper lip. "I spent the night in the royal apartments next door," she added.

"Please sit down." Now I rose, curtsied,

and gestured to the chair she had already taken. She only smiled. "And as long as you're here, why not ask the guards to bring in some bread and wine? It's getting late in the day."

"In fact, I have already done so," she said. "They still keep a fine cellar here, and I thought good wine might aid our conversation." Isabelle seemed to have several persons at her disposal. The one who just spoke was the chatelaine, the *grande dame*, thoughtful and bountiful.

"And what is our topic to be?" I was put in mind of Isabelle's southern roots. The Aquitaine produced poets and diplomats and florid speechmakers. They never liked straight talk as the plain-speaking English did. If Isabelle controlled it, this could be an interminable interview.

"I don't know why you're pouting," she said. "I thought you'd be glad of the company."

I did not want Isabelle asking questions about the writing desk so I crossed to the table, where she sat, taking the chair opposite her.

"Did John depart so quickly that he left his queen behind?" I deliberately made it sound like an oversight.

"John never sleeps at Sarum." She was unruffled. "He prefers Clarendon. He says his own father would never stay here after he brought Queen Eleanor to this place."

"And you? Why are you still here if John is gone?"

"I wanted to talk with you one last time."

"You stayed behind on my account? How touching." I felt drug fatigue creep back into my bones. "Just a friendly talk *entre nous*." I leaned my head against the high back of the heavy chair. The late-afternoon western light was casting golden shafts across the floor through the wall slits.

"Isabelle," I began, putting my fingers to my temples to ward off the ache I felt return just behind my eyes, "I appreciate your position. If I were married to John, I'd do what he ordered, as you do. He is unreliable, given to fits of temper, crafty, and dangerous."

"You have no—"

"Oh, yes, I do." I sat forward and slapped my open hand on the table. "They almost forced me to marry that . . . marry John, once. When Richard was captured by the Hoenstauffen crowd on the way home from the crusades. My brother was intriguing with John to steal England from Richard while he was away. Did you know they offered to pay Leopold and the emperor one thousand silver marks for every month they kept Richard captive? Just so they could carve up his kingdom." I leaned forward on my right elbow. "John himself came to the castle at Rouen where Eleanor confined me after King Henry died, and gloated over the fact that he would soon wed me, and that our son would rule over both England and France."

"And how did—"

"I spit on him. He was rude and lascivious, and he deserved it. I said I'd see us both in hell first." At this Isabelle's reserve wavered. Her eyes widened. "Anyway, Richard came home and took back his crown, and John skittered away like a wounded lapdog."

I jabbed my finger in her general direction. "Richard forgave him, but John was always faithless. At the end of King Henry's life, John—the favored son, mind you—was the only one who continued to intrigue against his father." My tone softened. "I wouldn't trust your John, if I were you. He'll do the same to you, if it serves any expedient end."

Isabelle sat silent as a rock. The only movement in her face was that of her brown eyes snapping at me.

"Now, as to the purpose of this conversation." I became suddenly brisk. "You want to know about the letters. I know no more about these phantom letters—either set—than I knew yesterday. I can tell you no more now than I could then."

I broke off as we heard a shuffling on the stairs, clearly the step of a woman. So Robert of Warwick had lied when he said there were no servant women in this place! More intimidation.

"Place the tray there." Isabelle gestured toward the table when the girl entered. I noticed the heavy hips, the blunt facial features, the hostile look the girl cast at her mistress as she complied. Probably a local peasant girl pressed into service. I wished I had my charcoal and parchment to draw her face. What a picture of naked resentment. Isabelle watched the girl go, waiting until she disappeared through the door before speaking again.

"John thinks otherwise. He thinks you know more than you have told." She turned to face me. "You have all but admitted that his mother sent you to Canterbury. You can hardly deny that it was to collect the letters. And"—she paused, spreading her hands as if to denote her helplessness in the face of overwhelming evidence — "he knows that you would never, ever, in this lifetime, make any pilgrimage to pray at Becket's tomb."

"Apparently everyone knows that." I pressed my lips against the urge to laugh. "I'll make you a bargain, Isabelle." The sight of the food was distracting. I absently wondered if Isabelle were the hostess, or if it was my responsibility to begin the meal. "If you promise to bring me charcoal and parchment so that I can draw, I'll tell you what I know."

"Charcoal?" Her voice rose. "How strange. Why not a better bargain? Your freedom, for example, in exchange for your information?"

"I try not to make witless bargains." I poured the wine into two heavy earthenware cups and handed one across to Isabelle. "You have no authority to free me. But I'm certain you could manage the charcoal if you chose."

She raised her goblet to me. "Well said. John told me you were no fool."

"I'm sorry I don't know you well enough yet to return the compliment. Will you send for drawing materials?"

"Yes. You have my word on it," she said, purring like a cat. I scanned her face. I could do a lovely portrait of that face, I thought, despite the thin lips. With the full sun on it, perhaps in a garden or by the sea. Yes, by the sea. She would make a long sea journey one day. "Now, tell me what you know," she continued, unaware of my distance from her.

I sighed as I moved my attention back to the newly laid tray. Awkward as always with the use of only one hand, I broke off a piece of the brown bread and laid it in front of me. Peeking under the white kitchen cloth, I discovered boiled fruit and scooped some into a small bowl.

"There is one other condition." I spoke while managing the bread and without looking her way. "You must tell me why John thinks I know where the child is."

She was clearly startled. "Alaïs, you must not pay too much attention to what John says when he is in the grip of anger."

I waved away her comment with the knife I had just picked up. "Tell me why he thinks I know the whereabouts of his rival, and I'll tell you in turn what I do know." I used the knife to cut the cheese and then put it on the bread, all with my good hand. Isabelle watched me with a detached curiosity.

She hesitated, weighing the options like turnips. "I can tell you this," she finally said, her two hands now expertly gathering her own food. "This rumor that a rival claimant to the throne exists is a dangerous one. Whether legitimate or no, if such a man exists—and he is a man by this time—he will attract followers. He may become a rallying point for activities against the king. Indeed, that has already come to pass. The Templars have got wind of this young man's existence, and we know they are about to threaten John with him."

"You did not answer my question."

"John thinks you may have known the whereabouts of the child all these years."

So much for what John knows, I thought. I determined to change the flow of our talk. "But, Isabelle, how could anyone oppose John now? Even Eleanor supports him. All his lawful brothers are dead: William, Henry Court Mantel, Geoffrey, and Richard. Even Arthur is dead." With satisfaction, I watched her wince. So she did have some suspicion of John's dark deeds. A picture of John, in the late night, unable to sleep, finding solace in Isabelle's slim arms passed before me.

"Arthur was no real threat to John. But he seems to have disappeared anyway in that castle in Brittany where his uncle king had locked him up. Now there is no one to stand between John and England." I threw a questioning look her way. "Mayhap his own folly has alienated some. But he is surely the last of Eleanor and Henry's sons with a clear right to the throne."

Isabelle shifted her position, turning sideways so I could not see her face clearly. "John's position is fragile. He believes if the youth appears, things will become even more difficult for him. He knows not where it would end."

"Curious. I can't imagine Eleanor writing any letters that would harm any of her sons, even John." I paused, then said wickedly, "So tell me: Why doesn't John just ask Eleanor what the letters reveal?"

"He has," Isabelle rejoined, picking at her food with a silver fork. I was ravenously gulping my portion. "Eleanor will tell him nothing. She claims there were no letters at all written at Old Sarum. But his sources tell him otherwise. He flew into a rage when he had her reply. You saw him yesterday when you brought the subject up."

Yes, out of control, I thought.

"She doesn't much like John, does she? He doesn't know why."

"Of course he does." I took a long draft of wine, carefully blotting my lips with the *serviette*. "First of all, she didn't want him when he was born, and he knows that. She and King Henry were already estranged. So she left him to be raised by Henry, who then spoiled him to spite Eleanor. John's revenge on everyone was to behave badly all 'round. How could anyone like him? Sorry," I added, but when I looked up Isabelle only met my eyes with a mildly reproving look. In truth, what did I expect? After all, he'd given her a crown. How could she do otherwise than support him?

"Now you must keep your part of the bargain." Isabelle spoke suddenly, her tone firm, her gaze direct. The woman narrowed her cat's eyes, searching my face. "What did Eleanor promise you in return for retrieving her letters?"

"I went because I was bored at the French court," I announced, dipping my fingers in the bowl of water the servant had placed with our food. I carefully twisted the linen between them. My left hand remained in my lap. "Everyone is obsessed with the coming royal wedding. I was eager for the excuse to get free."

"Do you tell me that it was only a whim sent you to England in this cold spring weather?" Her mocking laughter ricocheted around the room. "Come now! I know that Eleanor promised you something!"

I solemnly shook my head and held up one hand, as if taking an oath. "Just an adventure."

Isabelle watched me with a thoughtful expression on her pretty face. Then, all at once she became coy, plucking her skirts. She spoke hesitantly. "The second set of letters—we think they may include letters written by Eleanor to your father."

"King Louis?" I was jolted, in spite of myself. "Surely after Eleanor's divorce from him there was no correspondence between them. He was exceedingly bitter about her quick marriage to Henry. Everyone knew that." All the servants in the kitchen at Chinon knew it, I recalled.

"Yes, he was especially bitter when Henry went off and took the English throne the following year." Isabelle flashed a look my way, but I busied myself pouring more wine. "We do know that after the early years with Henry, Eleanor went back to intriguing against him with Louis. Her letters undoubtedly would be treasonous, if for no other reason than that they were addressed to Henry's prime enemy."

I was quiet for a moment. Before my inner eyes floated my father's face when last I had seen it. I was with Henry when the two kings had their final meeting in this life. My father's face was crumpled with the strain of age. He was strangely formal, as if my association with Henry had separated us in some unforgivable and final way.

I found myself staring out one of the openings in the wall, as if I could find answers in the air beyond. Dusk was approaching, and the rolling mists hid the spring-green valley below.

Isabelle's tone was honeyed as she continued. "Eleanor was expert at treason. John says the entire family was savage."

I grew weary of this conversation and weary of Isabelle.

"I'm certain John thinks of his family as savage, with all the fighting among sons and father. But John participated fully and with less honor than any of them, switching sides at every opportunity. He was the best loved of his father." I saw the image of Henry, old and ill and wounded, lying in a drafty castle in northern France. When he looked at the list of those against him, John's name was at the top. They said when he saw that, he turned his face to the wall and cried. "He broke his father's heart at the end."

"You sound bitter. I thought you cared not for this family." She had a needle in her, this English queen.

"I loved the old king," I said, letting down my guard for one moment. "Despite everything. He died alone and friendless, Richard and Geoffrey and John victorious, his queen imprisoned. Only the old bastard son of his youth, Geoffrey, and William Marshal were with him at the end. Even the servants deserted, stripping his dead body and stealing his belongings before they ran off like rats to join his pursuers. A sad end for a great king."

"If you cared for him so much, why weren't you there with him?"

"Because I was in England at the time, by the king's orders. I could help no one." I touched the linen to my lips again to hide my emotion. "Now I find that I am very tired, and I would like to be alone." I stood and brushed the crumbs that had gathered in my green wool lap. "Yes, Eleanor sent me to Canterbury. I owed her a favor from long ago, so I agreed to retrieve her letters. But as you know, I was not successful. I know nothing of any letters to my father and nothing on the whereabouts of the infant son of Henry and myself. I thought he was dead."

I spoke to her over my shoulder. "Tell John that even the dreariness of my brother's court is preferable to the tower at Old Sarum. Tell him I would like a safe conduct and some servants to help me make my way back to Paris." I walked across the room with some effort, catching the white stone wall with my hand at one point.

"I'll tell him," she said rising, pulling her cloak about her. "I don't know if he'll believe me."

"God's breath, why should he not?" My patience snapped. "All of these things happened years ago. They have nothing to do with me now. I can't see how John thinks I can harm him."

"Alaïs." Suddenly Isabelle was at my side in one quick move, her hand staying my arm. "There is another way you can help. And you should take it. If those letters to Louis are found, it will embarrass Eleanor more than I can say. It is your chance to get back at Eleanor for all she has done to you in life."

I whirled on her. "Do not presume—"

"It is rumored you have the gift of second sight. Use it to help us find the missing youth."

"How dare you ask me to use my powers for such a vain effort!" I jerked my arm from her grasp.

"The throne of England is at stake," she persisted, like a dogged robin pulling at a worm in the ground. "You owe the Plantagenets something. They were your family. You could not want to see the throne of England pass from them."

"To my son? The son of King Henry?"

"Your son is not the lawful king."

Now it was my turn to lay a hand on her, and I did so with the iron strength of my good right hand. I held her wrist and twisted it quickly behind her with all the fear I felt within myself. She let out a sharp cry like a caught animal and then began to whimper, close to tears. I loosed the pressure on her arm slightly, keeping her wrist still enclosed with my fingers.

"Go back to John and give him this message: Not for you, not for him, not for the godforsaken Knights Templar, nor for anyone else in this wretched world would I ever give up my son." I dropped her arm and watched her gather her cloak around her. She cast a baleful look in my direction, but my face was set in stone. I heard her footsteps on the stairwell grow faint.

She left me alone with one chilling thought. There was not much time. The wolves were closing in. I must find the child before they did. As always in a time of worry, my fingers crept to my throat to seek reassurance from my talisman. But my throat was bare. The pendant was gone. It had been stolen while I was groggy with the mandrake. And there was no doubt who had it now: Isabelle.

13

Out of the Keep
and Back
on the Road

Torn as I was between dread and anger, it was some time before the drugs finally overpowered me once more and I slept. Even then I drifted in and out, and when I woke finally, I was surprised to find that my head had cleared. Light from the rising moon filtered in and lay in careless ribbons across the floor. Most of the chamber rested in shadow, but I could make out the dim outlines of the writing desk and the chairs Isabelle and I had occupied. The fire had gone out completely. I wagered with myself there was no tray of food brought in as before. John and Isabelle were going to let me languish here as I had languished in Rouen. As if, somehow, I could be browbeaten into submission.

I thought of the jewel and how many people seemed intent on possessing it, and I still had no clues as to why. Then I remembered my discovery of the writing desk just before Isabelle's visit. I crept from the bed and began to make my way quietly across the room. Although I could hear no sound, I did not want to give the guards any signal that I was stirring.

I bumped into the chair and was able to drag it over to the writing desk. After I sat, I located the top of the desk, and opened it carefully. The room vacillated between light and dark as the moon played hide-and-seek through the narrow slits. I pulled out the drawer, as before, found the spring, and the side dropped. My fingertips explored carefully and finally located the rough edge of the parchment. The cache I had discovered appeared to be several flat papers stretched out under the thin piece of wood that separated the hidden part from the rest of the drawer.

They felt dry to my touch. It took some time to figure out how to retrieve them without damage. They seemed to be more fragile than parchment. Perhaps they were this new paper that had come from the south, made from wood pulp and not skins at all. When we were at Poitiers, Eleanor had been fascinated with the new paper, though she was able to obtain only a few sheets at a time from the queen of Navarre. I remembered that paper tore more easily than parchment and fingered these sheets carefully.

Someone had taken care that these papers would not be easily removed, even if the false drawer were discovered. Whoever had hidden them could not know the task would be made even more difficult because I could use only one hand. I worked my fingers gradually around the edges of the false bottom and discovered that the left side could be raised higher than the right, leaving a small opening through which I could slide the papers. With care I did so, using my left hand as a prop and extracting the layers one by one with my live hand. One, two, three, four—that seemed to be all. Then I felt a fifth and teased it out. I didn't want any of them to drift to the floor, to be discovered in the morning by whoever brought my food, if any should come.

A slight noise behind the wall that ran opposite the bed distracted me. By now the room was completely dark. The noise, at first like the sound of a small field animal, grew louder and more complex. As I watched with astonishment, the entire stone wall opposite the bed began to move. I hurriedly snapped up the false side of the desk, replaced the drawer, and managed to roll the letters. Stuffing them into the top of my gown, I moved away from the desk.

An entire section of the wall swung open, just missing the oak table by two feet. Lights glimmered in the cavity now yawning where the wall had been. Several men entered noiselessly, the lead carrying a torch. He swung it around the room until it discovered me, standing behind the chair Isabelle had occupied the night before.

"This must be the chamber," said the last one to enter. "Desolate place this, with no fire on this bitter May evening. Ho!" He raised his voice slightly when he saw me. "Princess Alaïs. Is that yourself?"

"Yes, of course it is the Princess Alaïs. Who else would be here in the tower? King John?" Despite my pleasure at seeing someone who approached as a friend, I felt owlish with surprise. I began moving toward the arc of light cast by the torches. "The question is, who are *you*? And why are you here?"

"Earl Graham of Chester, Your Grace." The flaxen-haired young man in front of me managed a bow, passing his torch to his short companion. Even in the dim light, I could see that his skin was as fair as his hair. But of course: The earls Chester came from the north, not yet much contaminated with dark-haired Normans' blood.

"I'm here in your service. That is to say, I've been sent to get you out of here."

"Earl Chester. I thought you were older," I said, squinting at him. A memory of the Earl of Chester from years earlier ran through my head. He was a bearded and bent, grayer version of the lad in front of me. Same large ears, same round, open blue eyes.

"You must remember my grandfather, Your Grace. He spoke to me often of meeting you when you were with King Henry." The young man paused, then bowed again. "He said you were the fairest of all the young princesses."

"Did he so? That must have sent Eleanor's daughters into a spin." His words brought a smile despite my efforts to be stern. "What are you doing in this place? And with such an unorthodox entry."

"Not so unorthodox, Your Grace. We came up through an old passage that hooks into the secret tunnel to the treasury. It's thought the wall was false from the time the tower was built, but no one knows for certain."

"But how did you know about it?"

"Oh, we have many sources of information."

"That's a comfort," I replied, nettled. "What about the guards? Was there no danger of being seen?"

"King John always has a tendency to leave fewer guards than he needs. There are only four here, and they are occupied with a game of hazards in the vestibule of the postern tower. They won't trouble us. They seem to be well along in their ale cups." He smiled briefly. "Nevertheless, we should not tarry. We must be on the road. There is always chance in these situations."

"I'm ready," I said, pulling my cloak quickly from the bed. I glanced at the leg wrappings and shift I had shed earlier, then stepped over them. "I came to this place with precious little, and I'm happy to leave with even less." My hand brushed against the front of my gown where the papers crinkled, then around my bare throat. As an afterthought, I slung the small travel sack, still holding the chisel and my small Book of Psalms, over my shoulder.

"Then follow me." His tone was commanding, I noted with amusement. "We'll go back down the passage through the treasury.

It's a bit tricky out the other end, since there is no formal passage to the outside. We have to drop down a bit at the end."

I grimaced. I could already hear my hip creak with the effort that would be required to make a jump to the ground. But I put a good face on it and followed the young earl down the steep passageway. His three knights, who had remained wordless, followed behind, pulling shut the piece of wall they had opened. I could see from this side that the wall door was plainly marked, although there was no evidence from the other side that a passage existed. I wondered if Henry had cut that door and built the passageway. If he did, it might have been to pay Eleanor private visits when she was here. I blinked at the thought. If that were true, it cast a whole new light on the relationship of their later years.

Moving down the small passage was not difficult, nor was the drop at the last, which was shorter than I had feared. The knights had pulled several large stones over to boost themselves up, and these had to be pulled back so that I would drop onto the softer ground.

Eight more men stood watch, several on horseback, and they moved with a collective rustle when we started dropping out of the passageway.

After I had landed and been helped to my feet, I was happily surprised to see Tom of Caedwyd and Roland and Étienne, who came immediately to my side. My men greeted me warmly, and Tom, looking somehow older than when we had parted at Canterbury, asked me if I were unharmed. When I reported that I was all right, they said no more.

"And Marcel?" I whispered as we made ready to mount.

"Dispatched back to Paris by Prior William when he heard about the abduction," Tom said. "He sent word from London that one of us should return to the French court, to tell your brother what had befallen you . . . and all about the rescue plan," he added hastily, no doubt in response to the alarm leaping to my face. The last thing I needed was Philippe tearing across the Channel to confront John over me. Then I heard what Tom had just said.

"Prior William." In truth, I was as startled as I sounded. "God's bones, now I see. Prior William ordered you to Old Sarum." Roland waited patiently at my horse's side, and I placed my foot in his hand.

The young earl, who was on his horse first after being the last one out of the chute, was having trouble controlling his feisty mount. But when he heard my words, he turned my way and said, "Of course. I thought you knew."

With that, everyone mounted swiftly, and we were off without another word, while the guards in the postern tower on the other side of the keep apparently never looked up from their game of hazards. I had no idea of our destination. Under ordinary circumstances I would have demanded information before setting out. But no matter now: I had a good horse under me, and I believed I was among friends. And I was eager to show my back to Old Sarum.

We seemed to be heading north and slightly east. Large forms loomed through the fog rising off the still-cool land as the predawn light began to glow. The mounds could have been anything—groups of waiting warriors or unfriendly houses—but they turned out to be only stands of large pines emerging from the night. We were making good time, and it was with surprise I saw in the first rays of the rising sun the ancient, giant white stone horse of Wiltshire plastered against the hills ahead. Thank the stars for the goddess who inspired that stone formation, for now I knew where I was, and with that, suddenly, I had a sense of safety for the first time in days.

We'll stop soon, Your Grace." The young earl was looking a bit ragged as he pulled back from the front of our small group to ride with me. But of course he had ridden all night, whereas it had been but a few hours for me.

"And what is our destination?"

"The manor of a knight we trust," he replied. "We'll rest there for a time. We have a conference there later today." He made a vague gesture with his hand.

"And for me? Will I be given safe passage back to France?"

The earl was about to reply when one of the rear guards rode up unexpectedly.

"What is it?"

"A single rider, quite far off. I can't make him out, and there is quite a cluster of knights a distance behind him. He seems to be trying to catch up with us."

"What colors does he show?"

"None, my lord," the knight replied.

The earl's face broke into a broad grin. "Tell the archers to hold their fire. I know this man. We won't slow down for him. Let's see if he can catch us."

"You have not answered my question." I was not accustomed to being ignored. "Will I have passage back to Paris?"

"I cannot say how events will unfold, but you will know soon enough. The place we seek is not far now." And the earl departed my side without further ceremony, urging his men on as if we were in some kind of race.

"I'm certain they'll arrange your passage to France, Your Grace." Tom, riding on my other side and grinning, had read my thoughts. "There must be a reason he can't say now. I know it's not just because you are a woman."

With that, I reached over and lightly lashed his horse, which gave a satisfying leap forward, almost unseating my old friend. But I smiled, too, for my heart was growing lighter.

A large estate settled against the rolling hills came into view as we rounded a bend in the road. We saw first the walls and then the several stories of a great stone manor, built in the modern style of a long, rectangular building. Italian glass stained many colors had been set into some of the windows, signaling a prosperous owner. Smoke curled upward from the chimneys, and I suddenly longed for a clean bed with a warming brick.

Beyond the manor house, we could see stables where liverymen and boys already rushed about. I was tired from the ride and felt as if I would fall from my horse at any minute. Never in the future, I resolved, would I even break the seal on any letter from Eleanor R., much less undertake any requested mission. When we finally rode to a halt in a courtyard, Tom helped me down from my sweaty horse, and I was glad to lean on him. For, truth to tell, I could not have stood on my own.

The owner of the manor received us graciously, standing in the vestibule of his grand house. He introduced himself to me only as Baron Roger. He was formally dressed in a longer tunic, cloak, and riding boots, despite the early-dawn hour. He was a tall man with a soft face, older than myself, with jowls that fell gently over his collar. His tired look came mostly from the black rings around his eyes that, coupled with the shape of his face, gave him an air of quiet resignation. He reminded me of Philippe's hunting hound. His wife stood by his side, a small round, pretty woman, much younger than Sir Roger. She wore a delightful gown of rust with a slash of white, to match the barbette and wimple wound around her throat and head. I envied her youth and good looks and the high color in her cheeks. But for myself, if I had youth at that moment, I would have traded it without thought for a dry, warm bed.

The earl and Baron Roger greeted each other formally, as if they had met somewhere a long time ago. The earl presented me simply as "the Princess Alaïs," saying it with the English inflection. Baron Roger bowed low, as did his wife, Lady Margaret. I tried to appear gracious, but fatigue was pressing on me.

Then, from the very road behind us, the single figure who had trailed us for several miles burst through the gates. The Earl of Chester sprang forward, catching the man in an embrace as he slid from his horse. "Victory, victory! You could not catch us!" the earl was shouting. "You owe me a pound of silver!" The man laughed, pummeled the young earl on the back, and made many protests about his intentions. As they talked, the rest of the stranger's retinue rode hard into the courtyard.

There was mayhem for some minutes as greetings were exchanged all around. As I watched the busy scene wondering whether Tom would catch me if I dropped over, the leader of the newcomers began threading through the general hubbub of knights. He stopped to have a word with Sir Roger and then made his way toward me. The man was dressed even more richly than the baron, his cape trimmed with fox fur as good as the one I wore. But it was his face that astonished me as he drew near. It was Prior William! And from the look of his elegant clothes and jeweled sword, he was far in every way from Canterbury and his monk's robes.

He moved as when I had first seen him at Canterbury, intentionally and swiftly toward me. I thought perhaps I was seeing a vision in my fatigue, but when he kissed my hand, I could feel on my skin his mouth and face still cold from the night air.

"Good day to you, Prior William," I said, quelling my astonishment.

"*Princesse.*" He smiled. "Welcome. Sir Roger and his wife stand ready to make you safe and give you rest from your hard journey."

He waved to a line of servants who had suddenly materialized from the house, gathered hastily outside the entryway of the great hall. They appeared to be looking to William for orders, which he seemed inclined to give.

"Servants. Here! Attend the princess. She requires a warm bed, dry clothes. She needs hot water to wash. Be quick!"

"Prior William," I said, recovering myself, "anyone would think this was your house to hear you ordering the servants about."

"Would they, *Princesse?*" he shot back, obviously amused. He had discarded his head covering and donned a felt wool hat, which he pushed to a jaunty angle while the other hand rested on his sword.

"But what are you doing here in knight's clothes? And if you're here, who is minding Canterbury for Hugh Walter?" I could feel shooting pains begin in my legs from the long ride. "Surely the monks' chapter needs a chief?"

His face lightened at that. "You need not be concerned for the monks of Canterbury, although it is touching. Hugh Walter has returned from Rome and resumed his abbot's chair. He's given me leave from Canterbury for several weeks."

"What for?"

"To put certain affairs in order." There was a fleeting wry ghost of a smile that dented his face and threw the deep vertical lines into relief. "The cathedral and its monastery have many interests in the outer world. I must attend to some of them this week."

"Why are you not in monk's clothing?" I began with more questions, but he shook his head.

"We'll meet again after you've had your rest," he said. "Save your questions until then. Ah, and here is your old friend Tom of Caedwyd." He drew Tom to us with a familiar gesture. I was about to remind him that he'd denied Tom entrance just days ago at the gates of Canterbury, but I had no chance. "Tom will see you to your chambers."

A flock of servants suddenly surrounded us. William began to drift off, responding to a knight who seemed to have urgent business. I caught his arm as he turned away.

"Am I safe here from John's long reach?"

"No one is ever altogether safe from the king," he murmured, bending his head toward mine. "But you may rest here for now without fear." He followed my glance to Étienne and Roland. "Your knights will be well cared for. And you will see them later today."

"Unlike Canterbury?" I asked.

"*Princesse*." He swept his hand in a grand gesture. "Did you not notice? This is all unlike Canterbury." And he turned away to confer with the earl, who had by now joined the knight in seeking his attention.

Tom saw my exhausted state and put an arm around me for support, and I was grateful. Suddenly I bethought myself of Henry's ring, still on my third finger. I slipped it from my hand and pressed it into his palm. "Thanks for your trust, Tom. This ring has never left my finger since you gave it me. I could not send for you at Canterbury when I needed your help."

"I know what happened, Princess. I only wish I could have been there to prevent it."

Handing the ring to Tom put me in mind of my treasure, which I had lost. That misbegotten bitch, Isabelle! I must have made a noise, for Tom looked at me, startled. "My lady?"

I sighed. "It's nothing, Tom. Only I had a keepsake—like your ring—and it was taken from me while I was drugged."

"Those whoresons," Tom said before he caught himself. "Your pardon, my lady, But when I think what they did, how they took you by force and drug and held you prisoner—and then to rob you as well—it passes understanding. They say it was King John who arranged it all. But why would they take the keepsake?"

"I do not know why," I muttered. "Unless it be just the habitual venality of the house of England."

"Come, Princess, you need to rest," Tom said, perhaps feeling me sag against his arm. He might well have added, *Before the next crisis occurs.*

.14.

The Safe House

Some hours later, rested and washed, I sat in a new crimson wool robe that had been carefully laid on my bed while I was sleeping. Finally I had some leisure to observe my surroundings. My chamber gave the impression of being quite large, but that may have been because it was sparsely furnished. What furnishings there were appeared rich indeed. The chairs scattered about held deep cushions with needlework as beautifully fashioned as those of Eleanor's court. The rich threads of deep red and blue-green against the cream background were of the kind found only in the South of France.

The tapestries with scenes of maidens and hunters and unicorns covering the walls were finely made as well. And the house, recently built, had the new-style casement windows with tiny panes of real glass stained with color and molded together. I roused myself to move toward the windows that lined one whole wall of this rectangular room. I unhooked the small latch on one and pushed it open, then another. Fresh country air flooded in. Even though a soft rain fell, the room seemed to brighten when the outside light entered.

It appeared to be midafternoon. I had slept for hours. Below, the courtyard was silent, except for a few servants who were unloading a wagon that had just pulled inside the gates. Beyond the wall encircling the yard stretched two roads, rolling off into the distance over gentle hills. The misty rain obscured my view but was greening the hills even as I watched. I leaned out and lifted my face, and the fresh, wet feeling seemed to wake me from my lethargy.

Only then did I recall the letters I had found in Old Sarum. The thought caused me to turn quickly from the window. I had carefully stowed the packet under the featherbeds before I'd drifted off to sleep, sure that they would be safe from discovery if I were sleeping on top of them.

I was almost surprised to find them in the same place, slightly more creased than before but none the worse for wear. I carried them toward the light, placing them on a long table under the windows. To see better, I opened another glass casement and sat down to examine my cache.

Alas, even in the added light, I could not discover the contents of these papers. Five pages covered with the queen's fine script were in my grasp. But they would reveal no secrets.

For Eleanor, crafty witch, had written in code. Oh, they were her letters, all right. She could not disguise the broad, flowing hand I'd known since I was a child. But these letters might as well have been written in Arabic. She had switched symbols and transposed letters until my head ached for looking at it. The words were gibberish.

My fingers played with the edges of the letters, as if worrying them would yield more clues. The whole thing was exceedingly strange. One would expect to find letters in her desk that had been addressed to her, but here instead were these in her own hand.

First there was the mystery of their provenance. She must have written them with the expectation of communicating with someone outside her tower prison. But why were they never sent? Did she change her mind? Or could she not find a courier trusted enough to convey them, someone who would carry them to her secret correspondents instead of heading directly to King Henry? Perhaps she could not take that risk. For who knew whose life might be threatened by things hidden under that flowing script?

And then the mystery of their fate. Someone had flattened them and hidden them under the false bottom of her drawer. No doubt Eleanor herself, or someone she trusted with the secret of the desk. But why? A curious puzzle.

A peremptory knock startled me out of my reverie. Before I had time to sweep the letters from the table, and without my leave, the door opened. I was about to protest when I saw that it was William of Caen. For the second time that day, he took me by surprise. My open mouth snapped shut.

It would be difficult for a man of William's size and bearing to "slip" anywhere, so I cannot say he slipped into the room. But he moved like quicksilver immediately after the brief knock. It was clear he did not intend to be seen entering my chamber. I rose from my chair.

"Prior William! Uh, Sir William," I amended, remembering the greetings of his comrades this very morn. He crossed the room to me, unbuckling his sword and tossing it on a low, wide bench next to the wall.

"*Princesse.* You are safe now." He grasped my elbows. All the *bonhomie* of his early-morning greeting was now absent. His face registered only concern. I was unsettled to see fatigue lines in his brow and darkness around his eyes in the light from the open windows. There was a shadow of a beard on his face, before so smooth-shaven. "I regret that you had to suffer this experience. John will answer for it."

"I'm quite well, considering," I said, forcing cheer into my voice. "I told you at Canterbury that John is afraid of me. He would never hurt me."

William dropped his hands from my arms and shook his head. He made no attempt to conceal his impatience. "Must you always show that bravado?" He flashed a trace of a sad smile. "Will you always be that frightened child new to the Plantagenet court, keeping up a front? Can you never say what you truly feel?"

I was startled. The ground under my feet shifted slightly, as if William were the one with second sight. Then I surprised myself.

"If it gives you satisfaction, then, here is the truth of it: I *was* afraid when I awoke at Old Sarum. And after my interviews with John and his queen, I was more so. You were right about John. He may be a fool, but he is a dangerous one. I think he might well have let me starve in Eleanor's tower if I had not been rescued."

I looked into William's eyes and saw reflected there the morning's warm embrace in the courtyard with the Earl of Chester. "You sent the earl, didn't you? How did you know where I was?"

He turned slightly away from me, moving toward the large stone fireplace. I followed, stepping in front of him.

"You knew that John planned to take me from Canterbury," I continued, tracking the logic. "You allowed him to abduct me! And then you sent the Earl of Chester to the rescue."

"What did John want from you that forced him to such a radical act?" William edged gently around me and knelt on the stones. He began to fiddle with the kindling in the hearth. His expression was conveniently hidden from my eyes.

"I thought *you* might know, since you seem to know everything else." I instantly bit my lip in regret. He said nothing, laying stick upon stick in a methodical way that only increased my impatience.

"Information!" I finally threw up my hands and walked away. "He wanted information. Only John would think it necessary to undertake such drama to get information. Why couldn't he just ask me? We could have had a civil conversation right there at Becket's altar." As soon as the words had left my mouth, I knew it was an absurd statement. It didn't deserve a rejoinder.

Rumbles filtered in through the windows, shouts of men and the hooves of horses. William rose, frowning. He moved with his peculiar, quick grace to the open windows and scanned the courtyard below.

"Information about what?" He threw these words over his shoulder. We were like two people on a ship's deck, our voices divided by the winds.

"John badgered me for a long time at Sarum. He claims I know the whereabouts of some old letters." I joined him at the window and followed his gaze. Below us the courtyard was a stir of horses and men, with more pouring in through the gates. A large party of apparent importance was arriving. Beyond the manor house spread the lush fields of Wiltshire, alive with peasants pulling in the greens for our dinner. The rain had ceased, and a multicolored rainbow framed the tall stone gates.

"Why all the fuss?" I asked, annoyed at the distraction.

"William Marshal has arrived," he said, continuing his observation of the courtyard but still addressing me. "What information did John want from you?" He was relentless. "Was it about the letters you thought were behind the altar at Canterbury?"

"William Marshal! Here?" Then the full import of what he had just revealed struck me.

"You knew my true purpose at Canterbury all along!" His recalcitrance at the supper with my aunt, his warning at luncheon the following day were now explained. "And you knew that John was after the letters. You allowed the abduction."

He shook his head, turning back from the window, his face now composed. "I couldn't tell you what I knew. Nor could I let you know that the papers you sought were no longer in the cathedral."

"No longer . . . Why not?"

"You may recall that I tried to persuade you not to keep that futile vigil, even before we found the Arab dead and I outright forbade it," he said as he moved away, picking up an inkwell from the desk and examining it from several angles before continuing. "I had information that John was nearby, and I suspected he had an idea of your true mission at Canterbury. I knew he wanted to get either the letters or you—or possibly both." He put the distraction down and turned toward me, the table between us. "But you must tell me how he questioned you. I need to know the extent of his knowledge in order to deal with him."

Prior William would deal with King John? Had the world gone entirely mad? I sank again into a beautifully furnished chair and pondered my response. He stopped pacing and threw himself into the chair opposite me, frowning, waiting.

"John has his own impeccable sources of information. He knew that his mother had sent me to Canterbury." I paused, seeing again in my mind that impatient, scowling man flipping his dagger into the oak table. "He seems to know more about the letters than I do. As do you." I squinted at William across the space between us. The long body was relaxed now, his legs extended and the fierce lines in the face arranged in an expression of patience.

"But I don't think it was only the letters to Becket that John was after," I continued. "It's true, he wants the Becket letters to keep from being embarrassed by old scandals raked up against Eleanor in this uncertain time. But that's not his real quest. John wants information about a supposed by-blow of King Henry—a bastard he said was born in secret and hidden from everyone. He thinks I know where this child is."

"And do you?" William looked grave.

"I told John nothing."

"Did he threaten you?"

"He bullied me. When that wasn't successful, Isabelle came alone on the second day to cajole the answers out of me."

"And what did you tell her?" His quiet manner had a calming effect.

"That I know of no such child. That if there ever was such a child, it is surely long dead, since I have never heard of its whereabouts. And that if there is such a child, it is of no concern to me." Our eyes locked as if they were lances on the tourney field. I wondered if he found a clue to my true conversation with Isabelle in my eyes.

A door slammed somewhere near my chamber. I heard several footsteps in the hall and a shout in another part of the house. William gave no sign that he noticed. A cool breeze was now coming in through all the open windows. I reached for a shawl for my shoulders.

"I did learn something interesting from Isabelle," I continued, breaking the silence. He merely raised his brows. "Eleanor herself refused John's entreaty to help him recover the Becket letters before his enemies found them, and she has also refused to help him locate the child—the alleged child," I amended hastily.

"Who would be a man now, if he had lived," William added softly. "And knowledge of that young man would be invaluable to the right people for the right reasons."

"Or the wrong people for the wrong reasons," I echoed. "So there is a rift between mother and son, even while she is working to save his throne." I wanted him off the trail of the child.

"Eleanor doesn't trust John," William said in a matter-of-fact voice. "Do you, *Princesse*?"

"I don't think I trust anyone, Prior. Not one of the players on the stage at the present."

"I know what you told John. But what do you truly think? Do you think there was such a child?" The question startled me, more for the curt tone than anything else. There was something mildly challenging about his manner.

"How would I know of such a thing?" I tried to keep my voice even.

"Oh, come, Alaïs. You lived with Henry and Eleanor all the years of your childhood and youth. It's certain you would hear court gossip." He paused and stood up, moving casually back to the fireplace. He was speaking to me almost absentmindedly. "Surely these servants could light the hearth fires earlier on damp spring evenings," he muttered, kneeling in front of his earlier work and striking flint.

I waited. He continued in a steady voice, concentrating his attention on the flame that flickered up. "You couldn't have been that close to the king and queen without knowing if there was another son, an unacknowledged son, that had been born somewhere, at some time. And after Eleanor was imprisoned, you were the king's mistress. Surely you would have been privy to such information then."

I heard, astonished, the words "the king's mistress" tossed off as if they were a scattering of rice. But they entered me like arrows. Some primitive sound, a groan of woe, rose right out of me, and then my throat closed as if a python had my neck.

"The king's mistress? Do you say I was the king's mistress? Well, you would know, wouldn't you?" I spit the words out. "You were there with us at court at Winchester, Henry's clerk. You must have heard the gossip about Henry and me. You probably enjoyed it. Would you like to hear my feelings? Would you like to know how a fifteen-year-old girl felt when her stepfather took her? When she saw the hope of her betrothal shattered? Would you like to know how it feels when dreams of a lifetime crash to earth in a bed-chamber in the middle of the night?"

My voice rose on each question, bouncing off the walls of the room. But I seemed helpless to stop the flow of words directed toward the man who had just touched this dark place in me.

"Or are you merely interested in the details, like all the others at court?" I was nearly shouting now. "The dirty bed linen, the sly glances of the maids when they brought the bath in the morning. Do you want a description of the eyes and whispers that followed me everywhere once people knew that the king was making nightly visits to my chambers?" I flung myself from the chair, lost in my rage. "What is it exactly that you want to know, Prior William?"

I flew at him, pummeling his chest as hard as I could with my one hand in a fist, then reaching to scratch his face, that face in which I read every courtier's smirk of two decades earlier.

He caught my wrist and held it, but that only increased my frustration. I let out a long scream, a wail that had been building inside me all these years, and he was forced to put his hand over my mouth. He got my nose, too, so that I couldn't breathe, and that stopped the noise. When I ceased struggling, he released me.

I was sobbing and could not stop, and I could hear nothing, not even my own heart beating.

I shook within his grasp as he led me to the bed and was helpless as he gently pressed me to sit. He sat beside me this time, his arm around my shoulder, talking quietly. Then his hand came up to stroke my hair while he murmured as if to a distraught child.

As I came back into possession of my body, it gradually ceased heaving, and as that noise subsided, I could hear what William was saying to me, as if through a waterfall or from a great distance. "Please forgive me, Alaïs. I was crude in my search for information. I did not mean to provoke those memories."

Then he stopped stroking and simply put his hand around on the side of my head, pressing it into his shoulder. He stopped speaking after that.

I didn't stir for a long time, more because I could not bring myself to look at his face than for any other reason. I was ashamed of my loss of self and so mortified that another had seen me show the hurt I had covered for so long. I was shocked, too, that feelings I'd thought were put to rest had leaped up in me so readily, like a fire that had been lurking in the ashes of a hearth.

Finally I pulled away and, without looking at him, made my way to the table, on which servants had laid cloths and water. I dashed cold water onto my face and toweled it. Only then could I turn to William, who still sat on the bed watching me warily, as if expecting another outburst.

"Enough," I said. "It is finished."

Then William said, in a voice so quiet I hardly recognized it, "Alaïs, forgive me, but I must ask you one final question." He spoke now in our native French, and I was startled to hear him use the familiar *tu*, as if our relationship had now been irretrievably altered. "Do John and Isabelle think this child exists?"

"Yes, they seem to believe it. Isabelle asked me if I knew that the Templars were involved in trying to use this bastard child of Henry's to unseat John."

"Did she?" William murmured, looking past me out the open window again, his intelligent face inscrutable once more, his ice-blue eyes distant.

"I don't know what any of it means," I said, and I threw the towel down on the desk. As I did so, I spied the letters I had been examining earlier. I had forgotten about them in the distraction of William's visit. I eased around the desk, sank into the chair, and placed my forearm over the papers. I should have guessed that no gesture escaped William's sharp eye.

"What, then, are those papers you seek to hide?" His voice had a slight edge. For one brief moment, I considered lying, and then I decided that would not serve. Anyway, the letters were no good to me, in code as they were. I couldn't decipher them.

I let out a long breath. "I found these letters in Eleanor's desk at Old Sarum. They were written in her hand, but they seem to be in some kind of code. I don't know what they contain." I gestured with my right hand. "I thought they might provide a clue to this antic chase I've made."

"Interesting," William said, rising from the edge of the bed, now all business. "Found in Old Sarum, right under John's nose and by his very prisoner." He made a small, amused sound as he walked over to the desk and sat down opposite me. I pushed the letters to his side of the table. He thumbed rapidly through the pages, glancing at the headings of each as if he could decipher the code right there. Presently his eyes narrowed, and something like a low whistle escaped his lips.

He picked them up, the five pages that seemed to be four letters, and shuffled quickly through them, then folded them in half and tucked them inside his doublet.

"William," I protested, not bothering to hide my irritation. "What are you doing? These are my letters."

"I'm sorry, Princess," he said, pulling them out. He spoke again in English and seemed imperceptibly more formal now. "I seem to be singularly lacking in diplomacy today. It's true. They are your letters. I saw that I could decode them for you, so I made to take them. But I will do so only if you allow it." He carefully placed the letters back on the desk, but I wasn't fooled.

"How can you decode them? Do you count ciphers among the skills you learned in Becket's service?"

"It's not important how. But I can do it or have it done. It's up to you." He turned again and began the pacing I now found so familiar. "Tell me how you found these letters. Are you certain they are Eleanor's?"

"Who else's? They are in her hand. I know it well. And they were hidden deep in her desk," I said. "What are you suggesting?"

"That someone left the letters there for you to find, knowing you would be imprisoned there."

I shook my head. "I recognized the desk from our family years in Poitiers. She must have talked Henry into having it brought over for her."

"And how is it you came to find the letters, if they were hidden so deep?"

"When I recognized the desk, I remembered that Eleanor had shown me the spring when I was a child, as a kind of secret between us. No one could know about that false bottom without being shown."

"Will you let me take them?" He leaned forward across the desk, propping himself on his folded forearms. I became aware that my nose was running and rummaged in my pocket for a linen square.

"Who else will see them?" It was probably red, too.

"Perhaps one or two others; I promise that is all. They will travel no farther."

"You'll return these very letters to me?"

"Most assuredly. Along with the translation." He paused, then said, "And soon, at that. I don't think this code will be difficult to break."

I handed them over to him—what choice did I have, after all?—saying, "Answer me this in return: Are these the letters both John and I thought were behind the altar at Canterbury?"

He took my papers and replaced them in his doublet, this time quite deliberately, all the while shaking his head. "I don't think so. For years certain mysterious letters were rumored to be hidden behind Becket's altar at Canterbury. But I myself had a thorough search made last year, and we found nothing. If there are letters from Eleanor to Becket, they must be very old," he added. "Becket's been dead these thirty years."

He had risen and was buckling on his sword as he spoke. "I know nothing of the whereabouts of such papers. If such correspondence exists, it was written when Becket was in exile, and Henry would have been furious if he had known. Imagine, his queen corresponding with his disgraced archbishop. I can understand why she wants the letters back." He shook his head. "Eleanor is a complicated, gifted woman, but I must say she has brought most of her troubles in life on herself. So headstrong."

"God's sweet feet, you men are all alike. You don't want strong women around. You'd all be happy to have puling, sniveling wives for queens, like milksops. As long as they are pretty."

For the first time that afternoon, William laughed the laugh I'd heard at Canterbury, the laugh of a man certain of himself, caught totally by surprise. It was a huge guffaw, chased by chuckles that echoed till I had to smile myself, reluctant though I was. When he saw that, he came 'round the table and reached down to my right hand to pull me to my feet. I allowed it.

"That description doesn't fit Eleanor, and, by God's blood, it misses the mark on your own self as well." His gaze swept over me in a familiar way and came to rest on my face. For the third time that day, he caused my breath to stop.

"Alaïs, I want you to come to dinner this evening." He continued to hold my hand as he spoke. "I know you sent word to Roger that you were too tired to come, but it's important that you do. I want you to talk and laugh and be your strong self in public, even if you excuse yourself early. You must make an appearance."

I was shaking my head, but he pressed on, finally dropping my hand to raise his own.

"Hear me out. Richard Glanville will be here. He is John's man to the bones, and I want to flaunt you in front of him. John needs to understand that you are under my protection. I don't think that was clear to him before."

"Under the protection of a bunch of monks?" Either my expression or my words made William laugh again, a short, terse bark this time.

"Well said. Yes. Believe me when I say that *this* group of monks can take care of you." He gave me a long look that puzzled me. Then he turned away with that abrupt change in mood I was learning to expect.

"I'll see you at dinner, although I will pay you no special attention. Tomorrow you leave for France. Be ready by the midmorn." He was on his way to the door.

"What?" I stepped forward. "I thought I would rest here for some days."

"No. You're going to a demesne near the Vienne—"

"Another of your houses?" I did not take kindly to having decisions made for me.

"—where one of my friends has a large house," he continued. "It's a pastoral estate but most comfortable. You'll be safe there for a time. Later, when things have been resolved, you may be able to return safely to Philippe's court."

"A sorry fate, for all that," I muttered. William, with his hand already on the door latch, turned on hearing me.

"You're not happy there," he stated, more to himself than to me.

"Ah, well. Happiness is a state of mind. Mayhap I only imagine myself to be unhappy."

He only said, in a cryptic way, "I'll see you at dinner." Then, with a mischievous nod, "Be certain to wash your face again before you come down. The tears do stain." And before I could pitch the inkwell at him, he had closed the door behind him.

I threw myself onto the bed. A mixture of feelings overwhelmed me. A tremendous sense of sadness mingled with something else, something so deep I didn't know what to name it. Perhaps it was only the release of feelings long pressed down like dried flower petals inside me.

At what point in the many scenes we had just played had William called me simply "Alaïs"? At what point had he used the familiar *tu*, erasing the barriers of time and station between us? And what possessed him to give me that final, impudent instruction?

Shaking my head, I rose again and went over to inspect the clothes the servants had carried in while I slept. I could disobey William, of course, and not attend the dinner. But I had a feeling even more would be made clear to me in the course of this evening. I recalled that William Marshal had arrived this afternoon, and I looked forward to seeing him. Also, I was seized with a sudden irresistible desire to meet Richard Glanville, King John's right-hand man.

As to being flaunted, I must remember to tell William that I belonged to no man and therefore was not available for flaunting. Yes, I would do that—but probably not until he had given me back the translations of Eleanor's letters.

15

The Dinner Party

They were all gathered in the great hall when I descended the grand staircase. I could see them through the wide entrance. There were far more than I had expected, above forty knights and a scattering of well-dressed ladies. By the quality and cut of their clothes, I could tell the knights that had ridden in with William and Chester from the shire's gentry. The local squires, those county landowners who were rarely at court, wore good-enough wools. Their doublets and tunics, however, were of sober black and dark green, whereas I could spot William's group by their elegance and flair. The wool of the knights' garments was finer and the colors brighter. Some of them wore a similar gold chain with a heavy medallion, and they seemed, as a group, leaner and more seasoned than the county folk.

I was glad that I had chosen well from the gowns that had been brought to my chamber. The deep claret-colored cut-velvet gown was

an improvement over the once-favored green wool that I had worn
night and day since my abduction. I had been only too glad to shed
that robe. In truth, I never wanted to lay eyes on it again.

Miraculously, the velvet fit as perfectly as if someone had delivered it from my own apartments in Paris. From the shoulders trailed
a train of the same velvet trimmed in ermine. I had piled my hair
high on my head with the help of the maidservant, and she had
found pearls and gems to twine through it. I wore my hair uncovered, which was my right as a *princesse royale*. Around my neck I
had arranged a slender rope of wrought silver strung with rubies,
which had been delivered by a servant just before I left my room.
Its provenance remained a mystery.

The great hall was brightly lit. At the far end was an open
hearth, with a huge boar roasting on a spit turned by the servants.
Although most of the food would be made in the kitchens elsewhere
in the house and brought to the great hall, it was the mark of afflu-
ence still to have a portion of the food roasting in front of the
guests. Especially when it was such a magnificent beast as this one.

Tables to accommodate the guests had been spread with fine
linen, and the servants were already circulating, filling the wine
goblets before the guests had even taken their seats.

Baron Roger came over to me as soon as he saw me in the doorway and led me through the milling throng to the high table. The
head steward struck a gong next to the fireplace, and all the company drifted toward the tables.

I was pleased that dinner was called. I dreaded common talk with
strangers. As a princess in my own court, I was usually able to avoid
such shallow encounters, but here I was more vulnerable. As I moved
behind Baron Roger, I became aware that Sir William was standing
at the head of the table, deeply engaged in conversation with another
knight, a short, heavy fellow. Baron Roger motioned to a seat that
was to be mine, but Sir William stood in front of it. I waited.

"Ah, my lady." Sir William broke off his conversation when he noticed me. "Permit me to say you look ravishing this evening. May I present to you Sir Richard Glanville, Knight Hospitaller and special envoy of King John." I nodded coolly. Sir Richard had a broad, bony head and an expression of superiority, aided by his long nose and prim lips. After he had brushed my hand with those dry lips, I treated him to my most dazzling smile. William, observing, glowed with approval.

"Sir Richard, this is the *Princesse* Alaïs of France, our honored guest." Glanville's face reddened. So he knew my name. "I leave her in your keeping for the evening."

"Your Grace," Sir Richard said, inclining his head toward the seats next to Lady Margaret. "I believe these are intended for us. Please." He assisted me into a chair and then sat down, arranging his bulk with great care and satisfying himself that the *serviette* at his place was clean.

I greeted Baron Roger's wife, who was seated to my left. I knew Margaret Howard's family, a powerful northern clan, and had just begun to ask about her father's health when Sir Richard claimed my attention. He did this most adroitly, taking the opportunity when the steward asked Lady Margaret a question.

"Your Grace is visiting England for"—his raspy voice lifted— "pleasure?"

I smiled like a snake. "I have business here."

"Here? In Wiltshire?" He blinked.

"Yes. Wiltshire, of course. It's beautiful country, *n'est-ce pas?*" The company was seated. The servants began to lay the first course, a tender kid on silver plate, before the guests. "And very important to the crown. Why, only yesterday King John himself was in Salisbury, so near to us."

The face flushed again as he made a sort of grunt. Now the servants came between us, and I seized the chance to turn back to Lady Margaret.

"Are there children, Lady Margaret?"

"Oh, la, yes, Your Grace." Her eyes twinkled with the intelligence women sometimes flash when they are asked about their special realm. "Four sons and two daughters. All grown now. Two of the boys in King John's service and our eldest son, Roger, to be knighted soon."

I couldn't help but smile. "You must be very proud," I said. I didn't offer that young Roger had my private sympathy.

As we talked, my attention was drawn to a spirited discussion halfway down our table. I recognized the two men involved. The larger, smooth-faced, round-jowled man in a dark wool tunic was, to my surprise, Father Alcuin, the librarian from Canterbury. He was engaged in a heated but good-natured debate with a familiar-looking young man who was none other than William's clerk, Francis. I marked the expression on his pale, freckled, cherubic face, which was at once lively and thoughtful and somehow old beyond its years.

He was no longer dressed in the brown brother's robe of the abbey but now wore a good woolen tunic, like the others. He was clothed in the sober colors of the Wiltshire men, wore no gold medallions, yet something about him, his bearing and natural grace perhaps, marked him as a knight and a part of William's company.

A voice in my ear like a sword sawing against metal cut into my thoughts.

"Your Grace, I see you recognize Sir William's young clerk."

I was caught unawares and turned swiftly to Sir Richard. How dare this man observe me? My face must have registered my thought. "I mean no disrespect, my lady," he added hastily. "I simply saw your glance. The young clerk was taking his orders in the foyer from Sir William when I entered the manor tonight."

"I don't know him," I lied. "I've not seen him before. I only heard his laughter, and that drew my notice."

"Your Grace, I have a question for you, just to satisfy my curiosity." Sir Richard apparently had collected himself and thought of another way to hold my attention.

"Yes, Sir Richard?" I found that my appetite had fled, and I allowed the servant to take away the silver plate with my roast kid untouched.

His voice was artless, as if he asked about the weather. "How is it you knew that King John was in Wiltshire this fortnight?"

"Why, I saw him myself," I said, putting on a cheerful countenance. "King John is my kinsman, you must know. It would be a natural thing that we should meet. And Queen Isabelle as well."

His mouth dropped, but he recovered and made a smile out of the gesture.

"But now I hear he has moved north," I continued, nodding to the servant who appeared over my shoulder with yet another dish. "Is that not so?"

Like a willing circus bear, the knight responded. "That is secret information, Your Grace. I'm sorry, but I cannot discuss the king's whereabouts."

"Nonsense. There's no great secret about where King John goes or what he does." I raised my voice slightly and gestured around the table with the partridge leg in my hand. "Why, the king held me prisoner at Sarum within this fortnight, and I'll wager half the company here knows of it."

Sir Richard began to choke on the food he was eating. I thought he would fall into a fit, so red did he become. I beckoned to the servants for more wine.

I noticed William, sitting on the other side of Sir Roger, looking at me with reproof.

This entire tableau was interrupted by a dramatic event. The doors of the hall swung open, and in strode a tall man in knightly garb. He was well known to the crowd, for the din abated as people turned to stare at him. He entered alone but with the presence of a man who needed no escort to demand respect. He, unlike most of the others, was wearing his sword. A low murmur seemed to follow him as he made his way toward our end of the great table.

I confess that my eyes are dimming, and it is often difficult for me to see faces at a distance, but I knew immediately who it was.

I rose in my chair as he came closer to me. By God's hair, I thought happily, it was indeed William Marshal. Though he had aged, I knew his figure and face as well as I knew my own brother's. And my heart was glad to see him.

He went straightaway to Baron Roger, bowed with perfunctory grace, and exchanged brief comments with Sir William. Then he moved toward me, and I met him halfway with my arms outstretched.

"*Princesse*," he said formally. But he embraced me within his strong arms as if I were his own daughter.

"How are you, old friend?" I asked, feeling a mist in my eyes. "I saw your company ride in today. I wondered when you would join us." He held me at arm's length, and I could see that his noble face was grizzled with age. He wore a short beard now, and that changed his appearance. There were lines around his eyes and thinning hair where before there had been fullness. But still his vigor seemed to emanate from him like a halo in a saint's picture.

Suddenly the choleric Sir Richard, who had also risen, was inserting himself between us. "Earl Marshal," he said, bowing.

"Sir Richard," William Marshal said, with a nod and frost on his voice. Then he turned with his arm around my shoulders and guided me slightly away with such grace that Sir Richard scarcely knew he had been slighted.

"Lady Alaïs, I did not intend to be late this evening. William of Caen told me when I arrived this afternoon that you would be here.

He said you would be tired and might not stay long at dinner. Before you slip away this evening, I need to have a word with you alone."

"Of course, Sir William. Or must I now call you Lord Earl?" I teased. He shook his head, but he was smiling. "I was so glad for you when I heard Richard had given you Pembroke's title."

"Such formality is not necessary between old friends." His gaze shifted behind me to Sir Richard's back. "Have a care what you say to that knight," he said in a low voice. "I know John's rash actions. Glanville is John's eyes and ears, and he is sent here to sniff around. Be prudent."

"I shall indeed," I murmured.

"Immediately the party disperses, meet me in the back of the hall. There are several alcoves, and I believe we can talk undisturbed there. I have information you must know."

I nodded and drifted back to my chair. I was curious about the urgency in the marshal's voice. It was going to be twice as difficult now to sustain any conversation with Sir Richard.

After many more courses and toasts, Sir Roger and Lady Margaret rose and signaled the end of the dinner. I, too, stood and bade Sir Richard Godspeed. I heard with relief his plans to leave at dawn, delighted that I would not have to encounter him the next day, even by chance, in the hallways of the manor.

I gave my thanks to Lady Margaret and made my way to a place in the back of the great hall. There I found the marshal examining one of the hall's huge tapestries, the one with the unicorn at bay and the hounds raging at it, teeth bared and jaws dripping. He turned when he sensed my presence.

"This has always been my favorite of the unicorn scenes."

I was surprised. "I thought you would have preferred some that were less bloody," I said.

"This scene is a good reminder of the fortunes of war. If a man forgets what it feels like to be brought to bay by enemies, he is in danger from that point to the end of his life."

We paced together to a small alcove and sat easily on the cushioned benches, half hidden by velvet hangings from the view of those who remained in the great hall still talking. He gazed across the crowd, as if looking for someone.

"I hope Lady Pembroke is well," I said.

"Indeed she is. Only the recent birth of our daughter prevented her from accompanying me here." He chuckled. "Imagine. A child again at my age." Then he turned back to me. "But what of yourself, Alaïs? Are you well? I was concerned when I heard of John's rash abduction of you. He shall hear from me about this, you may depend on it."

"I survived the experience, with only my dignity damaged. But it was stupid of him. It was the act of a desperate man. Are you in his service now?" I remembered the last time I had seen William Marshal. It was ten years earlier, just after King Henry had died. Queen Eleanor would have no one but the marshal accompany her back to Fontrevault to bury the king. Then he came briefly to Rouen, where she had already interned me.

"Yes, I serve John," he remarked, looking down briefly and then back to meet my eyes. "You know, Princess, I serve the house of Plantagenet, not the man. I was faithful to old King Henry, to the young king when I was with him, and then to Richard. John has asked me for help, and, even though he is"—here he paused and sighed—"not quite the man his father was, nor his elder brothers, he has a call on my loyalty."

"John is a fool," I said.

"Hush, Alaïs. Such talk is treason." William Marshal glanced around. "And not only unwise but simplistic," he added, bringing color to my own cheeks.

"You may be right." I marveled at how William Marshal, in his dignity, still had the power to make me feel ashamed of a slighting remark about John that I knew he entirely deserved. "But John forced me through an ordeal that I'll not soon forgive. He acted in bad faith, and he will regret it."

"Perhaps." He ran his fingers through his graying hair. "His actions were foolish beyond measure, but John is beside himself. He has been persuaded—"

"I know," I cut in. "He thinks there is a bastard of Henry's somewhere who threatens his throne." I was amazed at how easily I tossed off this phrase and how little the ever-present knot in my stomach tightened. "Truly, William Marshal, even if there were such a person, we both know it matters not. No bastard will ever rule England."

"Don't rush to judgment, Princess." William frowned at me, and, as ever, it had the effect of slowing down my tongue. "Remember that William the Conqueror was a bastard."

"But that was years ago."

He held up his hand. "And as well consider this: John is the last of Henry's direct descendants. Arthur has died in a Brittany dungeon."

"We all know who was responsible for that."

"And John is childless so far. There is no other son of any Plantagenet living." William Marshal continued. "England would surely not take one of the daughters as ruler. The memory of the civil war Mathilda created is too fresh. And besides, the Plantagenet daughters are all married elsewhere. Why would they come home? So that leaves the possibility—if anything ever happened to John—of an illegitimate son of Henry's ruling England. If one had ever survived. And could be found." These last words seemed to be afterthoughts.

"So what are you telling me?" I parried. "That John has reason to fear for his throne should a bastard of Henry's have survived?"

"Yes." He nodded in my direction. "I don't excuse his behavior to you, his kinswoman. But there is a true threat that he must meet."

"From what quarter?"

"The Knights Templar are upset with John."

"So I've heard." I paused. "And with good reason, I understand."

"There are various reasons for their anger. But the Templars have enormous, hidden strength here in England." He glanced around again, a careful man. "They may use it to unseat John. All that's lacking is a real-life, in-the-flesh candidate of royal blood to replace him."

"And John, at least, thinks the Templars have found one."

The marshal nodded. "I don't think it will come to that. I have the confidence of the Templars as well as the king. I have been trying to mediate their disagreement. John has given the good knights reason to want him off the throne. They are considering their course of action. But they haven't made a decision yet."

"Do you think the Knights Templar would kill a king?" I watched his face.

"I'm not saying that at all." William Marshal spoke with the deliberation of a canon lawyer. "I am only trying to give you a context for what is happening. You have somehow been caught up in a complex intrigue, Alaïs. You should get away from England."

"Oh, I fully intend to do that. I'm to leave for France tomorrow."

"Under some protection? Because it would not be wise for you to travel alone."

"I can scarcely bear the thought that I need protection in England. I was supposed to be queen of this land once." I couldn't keep the bitter note from my voice. William Marshal laid a hand on my shoulder, and I was moved by his sense of my loss.

"Nevertheless, how will you travel?" he persisted.

"Prior William—Sir William—has promised me aid returning to France. He seems to have"—I paused, searching—"connections."

It sounded odd in the telling, more mysterious than I had previously considered.

"Alaïs, I want to tell you something." William Marshal leaned forward and glanced out the alcove to his left and right. Apparently he was satisfied, for he leaned his back against the tapestried wall behind us, stretching his legs as only a man will who has been on his horse more hours of his life than on the ground. "I want you to listen carefully. You only need to know this information. You need not act on it."

I leaned toward him, for I could scarce catch his words, so low had his voice dropped.

"Do you remember when Henry did penance at Avranches in '72 for the murder of Becket? Two years before he made his public display at Canterbury?"

"I heard some story. Of course, none of us were at Avranches when it occurred. We children were at Eleanor's court at Poitiers in those years. But I remember Eleanor telling some version of those events to Richard and Geoffrey." I was curious. "Why do you ask?"

"Listen well. I was there, at Avranches. It was right before the king assigned me to watch over Henry Court Mantel. At Avranches, Henry agreed to a number of actions as part of his penance for being the indirect cause of Becket's death. One was to send ten knights to join the Templars in the Holy Land."

"Oh, yes." I laughed, my head sinking back against the cushions. "And another was to take the cross and go himself, but he later got out of that by founding three abbeys. I remember it well. Henry once told me he never had any intention of going to the Holy Land. He said it was beastly hot there, and he never could tolerate the heat."

William smiled.

"And he thought it the greatest waste of English manhood to go off batting about the Holy Land on a useless mission, getting oneself killed by infidels far more valiant than the Christians, and all for the pope's politics. I still hear the echo of his voice shouting one night at Oxford, after drinking too much good English ale, 'England is my holy land. There will I spend myself.' "

At this William laughed aloud. He had known King Henry well. He knew all his warts and faults, and still, none had loved him as much.

"He prevented Richard from going as well at that time," I added. "To take the cross was Richard's fondest dream."

"Yes, well, Richard eventually had his fill of the Holy Land." William Marshal had little romance left in his soul. "But did you mark what I said just now? You seemed to be in a dream."

"I'm sorry. What is it you said?"

"One of the ten knights King Henry sent to the Holy Land was your friend William of Caen, recently acting prior of Canterbury."

It took a moment for me to grasp this piece of news.

"What?" I felt stupid.

"One last time, Princess." William Marshal's voice assumed an urgency. "Heed my words. One of the young knights promised to the Templars in the Holy Land at Avranches was Henry's young clerk, William of Caen. He who is standing over there near the hearth with young Chester as we speak. He who was my namesake."

"Are you telling me Prior William is a Templar, not a monk of Canterbury?"

"Yes. And I'm telling you that you appear to have fallen into the middle of a developing storm here in England between the king and the Knights. The Templars are powerful men, and I don't want you to be used as a pawn by either party."

"If William is not a monk of Canterbury, what was he doing there as prior?"

"The Templars have deep connections with Canterbury. Some

say Hugh Walter himself is a Templar, although I doubt it. He has always seemed to me a quintessential Benedictine. But I know for a fact that William was never ordained a priest, and when he is at Canterbury now, it is usually because the Templars and Hugh Walter want him there."

I recalled the Mass over which William did not preside and understood now what I saw then.

"But William has offered to help me get back to France. Should I not trust him?"

"I am certain William means you no harm. But be aware that he has other allegiances. He may not always make decisions that place your interests first." He paused. "My information is that he holds high office with the Templars in England and Normandy."

I considered this statement with a sinking heart. The letters in code I had given Prior William earlier that evening flashed before my eyes. No wonder at all that he had contacts who could decipher them. I could feel my hands becoming damp. What information did they contain that the Knights Templar might use to find my son?

"Alaïs." William moved closer to me and I noticed the stiffness of the old warrior's body as he did so. "I don't believe that the Templars are evil or unsafe. It's just that they have consolidated enormous power in recent years. And if they decide John is unworthy to rule England, they can bring him down. You'd best stay out of this quarrel."

I listened to these words as I looked straight ahead, watching through the velvet curtains while that very same William of Caen worked his way steadily through the vibrant colors of the crowd toward our alcove. His strong face with its prominent nose and deep lines exuded social grace at the moment. He was nodding and passing pleasantries to all, but he was moving inexorably toward me. It was not a casual course he took, I noted, despite his frequent stops. Of a sudden I had a new view on my childhood acquaintance. Well,

well, a warrior monk, not a child of the rule of St. Benedict after all. And his motives for helping me, it now seemed, were not just for the sake of childhood friendship.

"William Marshal. I say my good-byes now. We may not meet in the morning."

Sir William, as I was now to think of him, was speaking as he entered the alcove. The older man rose, and the two embraced. As they parted, I could see a hint of softening pass over the younger man's chiseled face. Then he turned my way, bowing briefly, speaking as if we had not seen each other in intimate circumstances that very afternoon. "Princess, I trust that your stay in this house goes well, and that your evening has been a pleasant one."

"Sir William. Thanks for your kind thoughts. Sir Richard Glanville and I had a lively talk, as you supposed we might."

"I noticed. He almost had my sympathy by the end of it." He spoke with not a trace of irony. "But you must grow tired. You nearly didn't come to the feast at all, so burdened with fatigue were you when I saw you this afternoon. Shall I have someone see you to your chamber?"

"Thank you, Sir William, but I believe I can find my way to the sleeping chambers in this manor without assistance."

I embraced William Marshal heartily, pressing my cheek against his shoulder, for who knew when we would meet again or whether I would see him anymore in this life?

"Give my regards to John," I said mischievously, "and tell him I am well, no thanks to him. And take care for yourself." I turned once more to look at him when I reached the center of the great hall, wishing I had taken the opportunity when we were alone to ask him the one question I had not the courage to ask. Years ago, when Henry and Eleanor's eldest son, Henry Court Mantel, expelled the marshal in anger from his traveling court in Normandy, were the rumors true? Had William Marshal possessed my sister Marguerite's heart, even for a short period? Now perhaps I would never know.

I mounted the staircase feeling weary. Despite my bravado in front of William of Caen, I was hard put to find the chamber assigned to me in the dim torchlight. After a wrong turn, I retraced my steps and reached a door I recognized by the bronze lion knocker. I entered and closed the door behind me on the demands of the world. I was weary to death. And I was sore confused.

16

Across the Channel and Heading South

I woke before dawn in a sweat. There had been a dream, an odd set of scenes in which so many of those who had peopled my past years appeared, but in roles so bizarre I could only wonder.

I reached back into the mists of my sleep, burrowing deeper into my pillow, as if that could retrieve the fading scenes. There had been a kind of rectangle as a backdrop, and we were in a kitchen of sorts. A huge fire burned in the grate, and there were kettles hanging over it, with soups or stews boiling.

Henry was ranging through the kitchen in his customary way, his leonine head thrust out, his hands behind his back. He wore the rough hunting clothes he favored all his life, and he was laughing hard as he peered in the pots, then moving on, pacing, coming 'round again. Eleanor sat by the fire writing something, while the women around her were polishing swords. Richard and Geoffrey as young boys were off to the side, rolling on the ground, locked either in play or mortal combat. Marguerite, my sister, was doing a slow dance on the other side of the hearth, while her husband, Henry Court Mantel, leaned on the mantel, looking useless. Almost a ghost, so faint a figure was he.

Then in the dream, Eleanor called me to her. I came running from somewhere all out of breath and stood before her. Suddenly she rose and slapped me hard across the face. Henry stopped his incessant pacing and in one minute had come to my side. I thought he would strike his queen, and I held his arm. But he only shook me off. Then he pulled Eleanor to him and began to dance with her, and they moved away from me.

I woke again. All was dark about me. I had a profound sense of loss. It was true. I had lost both of them, and all of their children. I had lost my own sister, Marguerite. She had disowned me when I became Henry's mistress, viewing it as a threat to her own husband and the children they might have. But it was a futile fear, for young Henry died even before his father and before there were any children from the marriage. And after that, Marguerite was married off to a German prince. I was alone now.

Against my will, scenes came again, but this time, because I was awake, the pain of remembrance was exquisite. I remembered Henry, shouting at Eleanor as he rode to the front of the caravan that led us out of that beautiful place, Poitiers, "You will regret what you have done, woman! Turning a man's sons against him is unnatural. I will strip you of what is dearest to you!" And she, furious, berating him in front of his men. And I, only fifteen, watching, stunned at the powerful anger of the two people I loved most, next to Richard.

Then followed another scene, the inevitable one. After Eleanor had been locked away at Old Sarum's tower and I was resigned to a life in Henry's household, such as it was when he was not moving, I was sitting by the fire one night late. We were staying at Laxton, an old Norman keep in the north, one of Henry's favorites but never one of mine. It was solid and grim, a soldier's fortress, with little comfort to recommend it. I longed for almost any of his other castles—Chinon, Rouen, Oxford; even Winchester was better than this.

I was drawing in charcoal that night. At least I always had drawing supplies, a kindness I knew was taken at the king's direction. And because I was only fifteen, I had two ladies in waiting to assist me, who went everywhere with us when the court moved. They sat near me now, Ragnhild's lined face bent over her needlework, her fingers nimble despite her age. And Annette, across from me, with her plain broad face lit by the fire, stared into space. Her sewing lay neglected in her lap as she entertained her own daydreams. Alas, that was all we had in Norfolk that bitter autumn.

The king came pacing past the fire, on his way back from his usual nightly inspection of the keep's guard. He stopped some steps from me and stood in silence, watching all three of us. I was aware of him but wanted to finish the figure I was making. Finally I looked up.

"Your Grace?" I asked.

He did not respond but continued staring at me.

"Do you want me?" I asked again.

"Yes," he said. I waited, but that was all. He turned and walked away.

I was afraid I had offended him, and it cast me down. He truly was good to me, and I knew he was sad at what had befallen his family. He loved the queen, although he could not live with her. And when his sons turned on him, he blamed her, although I knew it was as much their impatience and greed that caused the wars as anything the queen had done. Henry, Richard, and Geoffrey wanted their share of the kingdom, and the king kept it all to himself and doled out meager resources to the young men. The king was like that, always in control, and blind as well, not seeing the consequences of his approach.

Other times in these long nights, the king would ask me to read to him, and I often read the lovely poetry of the south, as I remembered Eleanor reading to him when we children were young. Although the king could read well enough himself, he often said he loved to hear women's voices reading poetry.

But on this night he asked for nothing; he simply turned and walked away.

I sighed and put up my drawing materials. I bade my women good night and went to my chamber. I slipped off my gown and hung it up and was standing in my shift when the door opened and the king came in without warning.

He had never entered my chamber since the years when I was a child and he would sometimes burst into the nurseries seeking the queen. Now he and I faced each other. My known world hung for a moment in space, then fell apart as he came for me.

He swung me up easily and carried me to the bed, where he laid me gently down. He wore no sword, only a tunic and hose and his cape held by a jewel at the neck. He unclasped it and tossed the garment onto the bed beside me. He said, gazing down at me, "You look stricken, like a wounded doe. How can I take you if you look so?"

I said, "You are my father," my heart beating in my ears like the hooves of running horses.

He said, "You are mistaken. Louis is your father, always and still."

I said, "It is only because you hate the queen that you want me."

He said, "No. If it were so, I couldn't take you, because it would also harm you. It is you. It is your coal hair and your dark skin and your green eyes." He leaned forward over me, bracing himself on his strong, short arms, so close over me I could feel the whisper of his warm breath.

He frowned, as if bent on solving a powerful problem, and shook his head. "No, neither is that true. It's only . . . I want you because you see things none of the rest of us sees." He smiled, a rueful flicker. "And with that gift you possess the world. Whilst I only have these disorderly kingdoms."

A sound of some kind escaped me, but I made no move away, no turning under him. I think if I had, he would have left me alone. But I lay still, watching. Then I stretched my arms upward in a gesture I could never undo, and he came down to meet me.

When his arms went around me to begin lovemaking, I welcomed them. The inexpressible sweetness of the skin of his face, that face I knew so well but had never tasted, astonished me. And the gentleness of his rough hands, callused from holding reins and swinging a sword and hunting, melted my heart. I felt my whole body become water, and in my trust he entered me.

Now it was more than twenty years later, and what I remembered was not a dream. I was here, in Baron Roger's house in Wiltshire, and alone. I turned my face into the pillow and began to moan softly, wishing I had tears to replace the sound.

My own voice prevented me from hearing a soft tap on the door. It was persistent and eventually worked its way into my realm. I drew myself up from my half-addled state, whether from remembered desire or shame or longing, I could not say.

The dying embers in my hearth gave off an uncertain light. I called out for the servant to enter, hoping it was someone with a pan of hot coals. When I sat up, the cold night air was like a blast, so I burrowed again into the pillow and the furs covering the bed.

"Put the coals on the fire and leave," I said in the direction of the dark figure.

"Alaïs." William's voice came strong, but at a low pitch. He was moving toward the bed. "There's been a change of plans."

I sat up again. "What are you doing here?" I remembered I was annoyed with him because of the evening before but couldn't quite get the details straight. Too much dream and memory had intervened.

"You're leaving now." He took a taper to the fire and coaxed it to catch, then began to light the wall torches. He pulled a heavy cloak from the large wooden wardrobe near the bed and flung it onto the bed. "Get up and make haste to be ready. Take no clothes with you. They will be provided. And you must travel lightly."

I knew I should be angry at his improper intrusion into my private chambers, but somehow it seemed natural, as if he were my older brother rousing me for a family journey.

"You said midday." I got out of bed and padded to the stained-glass windows but could not make out if it were dawn or still dark outside. "You said we would leave at midday." I felt stubborn as a child.

"Forget what I said. I've had news that compels us to change our plans." He turned on his heel to leave.

Of a sudden I remembered the information I'd acquired the previous evening. The Knights Templar and the several identities of Prior William. But I sensed now was no time to address these mysteries. He would never pause to give even a cursory explanation. He was operating in his commercial mode: a man with business to do and no time to tarry.

"I'll await you in the lower hall. Please come immediately." And he was gone, closing the door firmly, as was his practice. Everything William did was firm, I thought. Pity he didn't have more indecision. He might enjoy more of life's many possibilities.

I grumbled to myself as I moved around the chamber, bumping into things in the dim light. No suitable fire. No water with which to wash. I put on the clothes I had been given on my arrival the day before (marvelous how well they fit), took the small bag I carried with my stonecutting weapon and the Book of Psalms Eleanor had given me many years earlier, and, carrying the heavy cloak, prepared to leave. Before I closed the door, I cast a longing look toward the garderobe that held the beautiful velvet gown I had so enjoyed just hours earlier. Then I made my way down the staircase still possessed by the shadows of the preceding night.

Yet another surprise awaited me in the lower hall. There stood Tom of Caedwyd, Roland, and Étienne. I had not seen them since our arrival the day before. Tom looked tired, and Roland, as usual, impatient, but they greeted me right gladly.

Then my young deliverer, the Earl of Chester, appeared, dressed for travel. He came into the room with Prior William, who was talking earnestly, his hand clapped upon the shoulder of the younger man.

"*Princesse*," William said as they approached. He gave a formal half bow. Graham of Chester made a deeper bow and took my hand to his lips. I remembered how much I liked this young man's manners. I must recommend to Roland that he take this young noble as his mentor in the ways of *politesse*.

I saw that William was not in travel clothes. A suspicion seized me. "You are not going with us?" I tried to keep the concern out of my voice.

"The earl will ride with you to France," I heard William say, smooth as butter. "He has instructions to take you to a safe place near Chinon. I have business myself in London. I'll be along later. Oh, by the by, we believe that a small band of knights will be an advantage. We're sending half a dozen knights and a few other men to accompany you. That guard, together with your own— Ah, here they come." He broke off and hailed the men who had just entered the hall.

I frowned. "I don't need all this protection, William. My men and I managed to get across the Channel once. Surely we four could do it again."

The words were scarcely out of my mouth when I saw among the new men William's clerk. That angelic face, diamond-shaped with high noble cheekbones yet sprinkled with freckles like any adolescent with rusty hair, troubled me. Even in its youth, the face held a haunting familiarity.

"William," I said, catching at his sleeve as the men milled about us, putting on cloaks and talking loudly to one another as men do when they are about to set out on an adventure.

"No, Alaïs, you will not ride alone with your men." William didn't look up, occupied as he was with reading a message one of the servants had just handed him.

"No, no. It's not that." I moved toward him, bending my head slightly so as not to be heard by the others. He turned for the moment, hand still in the air signaling another servant across the foyer, and leaned down. For just a moment, we were suspended in space, our cheeks nearly touching, my hand still on his arm. "Who is the young monk or knight or whatever he is? The auburn-haired one in the Lincoln-green cloak."

Like a spring his whole body lifted away from mine. He merely shook his head, looking down, and murmured, "Just a young brother of Canterbury, François by name, loaned to me by Hugh Walter for the business of the moment." I stared at him. "He's just my clerk, *Princesse*."

"But he reminds me of someone. Who were his people?" My hand didn't release him.

"No one you would know." William was already turning away, though he was too polite to shake loose from my hand. Then he turned back and added, as an afterthought, "You only think he looks familiar because you saw him at Canterbury. He sat at my table at the noon meal the day of your vigil." Then he gently drew away from my hand and busied himself in conversation with Earl Graham a few feet away, leaving me still standing with my head bent as if to hear more, as if to prolong the moment when I thought William would tell me something that would clear my sight and memory around this youth.

I shook the cobwebs from my head and threw on my own heavy black travel cloak. We all stepped into the chill air to find our horses saddled and pawing the ground fitfully, held in place by the manor's servants. Baron Roger was nowhere to be seen.

Tom was suddenly by my side, holding my stirrup. I swung up and, on impulse, threw my leg over the horse. It was always easier to ride like a man. I heard Tom chuckle softly.

And then we were off to France.

I was not looking for company when the earl fell in beside me. We had been traveling no longer than an hour. I was not particularly easy with the young lord—he was too intense for my taste—but he seemed to be making an effort to be amiable. We chatted for some time about his family, and then I asked about our companions. He became suddenly very reticent.

"The knights are connected to Sir William." He waved his hand vaguely. "Most of them were with him years ago in the Holy Land. The others are from your household in Paris, are they not? They rode with us from Canterbury two days ago."

I was not to be distracted. "Do the knights belong to William's household? Or are they attached in some way to Canterbury? And there are more than just the knights. I thought I recognized Father Alcuin, the librarian at Canterbury, among them."

"Most of the knights are attached to William's household. A few, like myself, join him from time to time. I believe that Father Alcuin is riding with us because he is destined for an abbey in the south. Some correspondence, I believe, must be delivered." The young earl was looking around as if to find something he'd temporarily misplaced. "I never know with William. He has so many connections. Excuse me, but I must check our lead knights. I'll return soon." And he applied his spurs and moved forward. He rode like the wind, I'll say that for him, when he wanted to get away from questions. I thought he must also be very good in battle. But he was a poor dissembler in conversation, and I could tell that his nonchalant air was assumed. He was not going to give me any information worth having. Soon I was too taken up with the hard riding to worry more about the mysterious young clerk.

I did resolve, though, to find some time for conversation alone with Father Alcuin. For one thing, I wanted to know about the Arab found dead in the herb garden near the guesthouse where I stayed. And I knew he might be helpful with more information on the Arab poets. I had not forgotten my quest to find the reason for such interest in my jewel, just because it no longer hung around my neck. Indeed, my curiosity was now all the more intense.

That night we had comfortable beds at an inn near the waterfront. We would sail the next morning, and everyone was glad for an early dinner. We had a private room with two tables and a great feast. The innkeeper did his best to please us, and I had a sneaking suspicion that he knew the earl, perhaps from earlier crossings to France. Where *was* the money coming from for all of this lavish feast, I wondered, as course after course was placed in front of us: The rabbit, the mutton, the fine breads and good stews and platters of legumes seemed endless.

Roland—who became uncharacteristically jovial with the wine— Tom, Earl Graham, and I sat at the small table nearest the fire. It had been laid with white linen in honor, I supposed, of the lady present. I was hoping that Father Alcuin would sit with us and that I would have a chance to explore further the elements surrounding my Arab jewel. But word had been sent that he was indisposed and preferred to dine alone in his room that eve.

I noticed the young auburn-haired knight with his companions at the other end of the room. As the seemingly endless meal drew to a close, I rose as if to ease my legs.

Roland, who sat next to me, began to lift himself out of his chair, but I shook my head. He must be under instructions not to let me walk alone, I thought, as he was dogging my every step. But at this moment I had no need of his service. I was not going out the door of the inn, but only to sit at the other table. I had decided to take the direct approach. Since neither William nor the earl would tell me about the background of the familiar-looking François, I would put my questions to the young man himself.

He was sitting quietly, his eyes lowered in thought, while around him his comrades were laughing at some joke. The laughter subsided as I approached the table, but I signaled for them to continue their conversation. After a brief rise and respectful head duckings all around, they did just that, although their merriment was more subdued. I sat in the vacant bench on the end, the young man to my right. We formed a small, sober island there, in the midst of the merriment. He had glanced up at me as he made his obligatory rise and then sat again, looking at his empty plate. Whether from shyness or an intense sense of privacy, he did not invite conversation.

"Were you not at Canterbury when I visited recently?" I asked. He looked up.

"Yes, I was there." He produced a sudden, generous smile. "I remember you well. We don't often have royal guests, and scarcely ever French ones . . . and never before a true French princess." His eyes flashed my way for a moment but were quickly lowered again. "I was in Prior William's chambers when you and the lady abbess came to dine with him."

"I remember," I said softly. Then I couldn't resist adding: "But Canterbury has had a visit from a true French *princesse* before. This very *princesse* visited the abbey with Henry of England many years ago." He looked up, tilting his head expectantly toward me. "But that was before you were born, I believe."

He smiled, twirling a goblet between his hands before he lifted it to his lips. His eyes watched me over the rim, as if he were the cat and I were the field mouse. It was a most adult look, and so disconcerted me.

"Your name, I've been told, is François."

He nodded. My question had caught him midway as he took a long draft of ale, so for the moment he was relieved of the obligation to speak. Then he said, "I prefer the English Francis, but I answer to both."

"And have you been at Canterbury long?"

He smiled again, putting down his flagon. "I am personal secretary to Sir William of Caen, who has been prior pro tem of Canterbury while Abbot Hugh Walter was in Rome. I may enter the novitiate at Canterbury and make a church career, but that hasn't been decided yet."

"Decided by whom? You or the abbey?"

"Not either one." He sought refuge in another draft of ale. "It is Sir William's decision." After a moment he added, "I am attached to his household."

"Ah," was all I said. No need to comment on the impatience in his voice or the slight pause again over William's title. His eyes met mine.

"And *your* wishes for the future?"

He shrugged. "As I said, it is not my decision. I will do what I am ordered."

After a moment of silence, I tried another tack.

"You travel with Sir William, then, wherever he goes?" He bit his lip. I could see that my aggressive pursuit threatened his need for privacy. Nothing was decided about this young man's life, and he was impatient. Only his respect for his elders and my royal station held him captive to my questioning. With his pale cheeks dotted now with the red of the ale and his auburn hair above, he was like a bright butterfly pinned by my attention. He squirmed slightly, still smiling in that distant, maddening way only the young can manage.

"Most of the time." His voice was softer than I expected in a grown man. His eyes met mine, however, without any sign of timidity.

Indeed, after engaging the youth for a few minutes of conversation, I found myself revising my earlier conclusions about him quite rapidly. Far from an adolescent, this young man was well into adulthood. He had nearly twenty years at the least. And far from the shy young monk he appeared to be at a distance, he was articulate and easy in his dialogue, and very careful.

Our conversation took a more public turn. Upon another question about his studies, he opened like a flower. I discovered he had a love of the Greeks; as well did I. He had studied philosophy at the University of Paris and debated with the masters, he said, without perceptible modesty. He had never seen the great Abelard, of course; he was too young. But he had been taught by men who had been taught by the master. And I could see he had somehow acquired what I understood to be Abelard's greatest gift in public discourse: style.

He was well versed in Arabic, too, and knew all the great poets of that tongue. As the subject shifted to poetry, his eyes lit and his face became animated, a half smile leaping frequently to his lips, his russet eyebrows lifting as he expounded. I asked him if he had ever heard of Ibn al-Faridh, to which question he replied by quoting the entire poem that contained the line inscribed on my lost pendant. If only I still had it. François went on to wax eloquent on the life of the great poet and the favor he enjoyed from the caliphs of Toledo and then Córdoba until the end of his days.

It was no trouble at all to appear a proper audience for this lad, for I was familiar with all of the *chansons de geste* that he knew by his heart and also many of the great troubadours he quoted. He knew de Ventadour, de Born (the perfidious bastard), and he could even quote from Richard's own *sirventes*, which won my heart in an instant.

Needing little encouragement, he soon switched to English tales, recounting the exploits of ancient Saxon heroes. He had somewhere heard all the Arthurian legends and began to tell them. The conversation around us tapered off, as the young man's fellow knights began to listen to his storytelling. He warmed to his audience, rising and gesturing as he acted out the encounter between Sir Gawain and the Green Knight, a story that had just come out of the court at Champagne. I felt as if I were watching a very skilled performance. He continued, his speeches punctuated with applause and cries of "More! More!" from his comrades and the thumping of metal scabbards on the floor. Indeed, I joined in these cries, so entertaining was this young man. With the story of the hapless cuckold husband of Nottingham, he had us laughing until the tears came.

Our merriment grew so loud that the innkeeper appeared and begged us to soften our shouts so other guests could sleep. And that announcement brought Earl Graham, who had joined us for the storytelling, to his feet, suddenly recalling his duties as our captain. He ordered us all to bed, the better to be ready for the last length of our voyage early the next morning.

It was only later, when I lay abed with many thoughts crowding my head, that I recalled the dexterity with which the young François had turned my initial questions into an opportunity for himself to entertain us while, incidentally, deflecting any more inquiries from me. Neatly done, young clerk, I thought. But why? And then, gradually, William's face moved before me. There must have been orders, directions given to all the knights who rode with me. Thwarted again by William.

The day had been long, and despite my will, it wasn't many minutes later that I felt my senses lift from me.

Our Channel voyage was uneventful, and after one last night near the water, we began the journey south with fresh horses. Truth to tell, my heart was more at rest now that we were back on Norman soil.

We traveled hard the next day, taking little rest. Father Alcuin had appeared briefly when we broke our fast, but he was pale and seemed preoccupied. Roland never left my side until I was mounted, so I had no time to address my questions to the monk. I was growing worried that an opportunity had not presented itself for a private conversation. If he was indeed on some mission for the abbey in the south, he might depart our company at any time to take a different road.

Sometime after our midday meal, we came upon a small stream. We had to follow it for a while to find a place that could be forded. When I saw this, I felt in my travel sack for the chisel I had brought with me to Canterbury. It had been sharpened to a fine edge, and I pulled it out, careful not to be seen. I quickly began working on the leather thongs that held my saddle to my horse. Within a short time, I had severed the main tie, and my saddle began to slip.

I easily slid to the ground, being both agile and prepared, and the entire party was forced to call a halt. Tom rode up to me as the others waited, and he gave me a quizzical look as he examined the frayed part.

"We shall have to stop for a bit so I can repair this," he called to Earl Graham.

"Fine," the earl said, riding over. "Just so you are not harmed, *Princesse*," he added with genuine concern.

"Do not trouble, yourself, Earl. I am unharmed and, truth to tell, glad of a respite."

"I am sorry we have pushed so hard," he said. "I want badly to get to Montjoie's by nightfall. But perhaps a short rest will refresh everyone."

As Tom worked on the saddle, I saw Father Alcuin leave the others and move toward the stream. Blessing my good fortune, I followed, taking care not to appear too deliberate. The large man was kneeling by the water scooping up handfuls when I came upon him from behind. He jumped when I spoke his name.

"I'm sorry, Father. I did not mean to startle you," I said hastily, feeling some guilt to see that the water had splashed down the front of his tunic.

"It's not a problem, *Princesse*," he said, brushing himself off. "I was thinking of other things when you spoke."

I sat beside him, spreading my cloak first so as not to become damp from the moss covering the ground.

"We were interrupted at Canterbury in our conversation, and I was forced to a hasty departure from the abbey later that night. But I think I would like your further opinion on some things."

"I'm glad to help, if I can," he said.

"First, I would like to inquire about the Arab man found dead in the abbey's herb garden. What did the apothecary say was the cause of his death?"

"The prior later spoke to the entire community about this incident. He said that the stranger's death was a natural one, a failure of the heart, I believe they said. They could find no evidence of poison nor marks of strangulation, no wound of any kind on his person." He looked out over the stream. "He was quite elderly."

"Did they know who he was or why he was there?"

Father Alcuin seemed to pause for a brief second, and then he answered rather firmly. "The monks were not given any information except that the man appeared to have entered the town gates the day of the market, the same day you arrived. He may have entered hiding in one of the farmers' carts, as the porter monk had no knowledge of him. He had no papers or correspondence on him that would identify him. I believe that the prior's council had a long discussion about where to bury him, since they thought it not proper—nor respectful of him—to bury him in Christian ground."

I pondered this matter for some moments, until his voice interrupted my thoughts. "Were there other questions, Your Grace?"

"Yes. Regarding Master Averroës."

"Master Averroës? The famous scholar?"

"You know him, do you not?"

"I have never met him. But who does not know of him? He is the greatest translator of our age. Without him we would never have had the Aristotelian texts that have now been put into Latin. He is without peer in our lifetime. But surely he is very old now."

"Indeed, he is ancient. Can you tell me: Has he visited Canterbury of late?"

"Master Averroës?" Father Alcuin appeared to make a genuine effort to consider. "No, not ever to my knowledge. And unless it were a secret meeting, I would no doubt have been involved, since I am one of only three monks in our community who speak and read Arabic. Translators are always useful in such meetings," he added, as if he had presumed with his assertion.

"Can you think of any reason why the master would forsake his warm country and come north to our brisk season?" I probed, while, out of the corner of my eye, I saw that the earl was gathering the knights around the horses. In a moment Tom would come for us.

Father Alcuin frowned. "Master Averroës is known as a man of peace. About five years past, the caliph of Egypt enjoyed a major victory in the Mediterranean Sea over the Christians of Hispania, and a number of Christian knights were captured. There are rumors that the caliph was willing to ransom these knights. If by some remote chance Master Averroës were in the north for any reason, it may connect to those negotiations."

Tom was at my elbow now, and Father Alcuin made a great show of rising to his feet. "I cannot tell you more," he whispered, as if to confirm my sense that this conversation was best held in confidence. And, in truth, I felt the very same.

I allowed Tom to take my hand and help me up the riverbank. And he, seasoned agent of kings and queens, asked no questions. Indeed, he was silent, as if to give me space to think.

We mounted then and set out again, the earl seeming to have gained even more strength from our brief respite, as he led us on a hard ride. But I had much to ponder. It was now becoming clear that my jewel had value far greater than I had imagined or, for that matter, than Richard and Eleanor had imagined. And that Master Averroës should come north for ransom negotiations could well connect to the widespread interest in my pendant. But I still puzzled: How was my uncle involved in all this? And what connection could be made to the dead man in the abbey garden outside my guesthouse?

We rode the last ten leagues quickly, down through Chinon on the Vienne River, past the castle that housed so many of my childhood memories, through the marketplace in the center of town, and across the bridge that still spanned the river, the same bridge I had ridden with young Henry and Marguerite and Richard when we raced horses as children.

We traveled the road along the south side of the river for some miles and then turned off to move *en masse* along a road cut through the fields of wheat, a road so white and perfect, lightened by the sun that also beat down upon the golden wheat on either side of us, that I thought I must somehow be riding through heaven. It was a perfect day on the edge of spring.

I could see the manor of the Norman Chevalier Armand Montjoie, for I had been informed by Earl Chester that this man would be our host well before we came within shouting distance of the place. The building sat on a small hill that seemed to rise straight up out of the flat field land we rode across. The manor was a tall, broad, powerful clean piece of work in white stone. Totally without frills, it was so like the Angevin personality I knew as King Henry of England. How fitting that this edifice was the home of one of his liege men.

As we approached the manor, my fatigue began to recede. I felt a ripple within me, a strange sense of elation, almost as if I were coming close to touching something important. But what, exactly, it was eluded me. Mayhap, I thought, it is only a temporary feeling of well-being, naturally connected to a return to the place of my childhood. Or mayhap the memory of the ugly incident with John was dispelled by the sun. Whatever it was, I welcomed the feeling as a harbinger of hope.

17

A Minor Adventure

O ur little party of knights and travelers—we made only a dozen in all, counting myself— made our way down the wide entrance road lined with stately cypress trees. We were cantering two and three abreast, talking and laughing as we came, so that at first we scarcely noticed the silent party assembled in front of the entrance.

We sobered somewhat on seeing the small group dressed in black that awaited us. A man and his dame and three or four servants stood watching. There was something odd about them; they seemed to be less a group than a tableau of several individuals thrown accidentally together for the occasion. They neither talked nor looked at one another as we came toward them. The man at the center held the lead of a large hound that was sitting on his haunches and surveying us as we approached.

"Well," said young François, who had ridden up to my side when we entered the long

drive of the estate, "our welcoming party looks rather somber."
And I could not but agree.

The man who greeted us was a far cry from the urbane Sir
Roger who had gathered us into his manor in Wiltshire as if we
were King John himself with all his court. This man announced
himself Thibault, our faithful servant, and made the obligatory
bow, but I sensed a small resentment blooming under his well-cut
doublet. This was not an assignment he had undertaken gladly.

He was not, he said, Armand Montjoie but Sir Armand's steward, Thibault of Limoges. Sir Armand was away on business, but
Thibault and his wife, Petronella—he indicated her with a swift
motion of his head—would do their best to make us comfortable in
their master's absence.

As he made this speech, civil enough but not warm, the others
nodded in agreement. Suddenly the woman by his side came to life
at the sound of her name. She had black hair and blue eyes and a
perfectly round face, round as the apples that dotted her cheeks. I
saw her eyes sparkle as I came closer. She wore the shirred, bulky
peasant clothes of the country, but on her slim figure the muslin
dirndl skirt and brightly embroidered blouse only enhanced her
charms. She curtsied in the French manner and then raised her eyes
to mine without coyness. Although she did not speak a word, we
had a communication between us of the kind only women can create in silence.

And then the moment passed, and Steward Thibault reclaimed
my attention. He swept us into the house and up the stairs to our
quarters with formidable efficiency. Earl Graham, being a good
sort, made a foray at conversation to put the man at ease. It must
have been with an effort, however, for when I glanced at his face as
we arrived at my door, I saw the marks of fatigue etched thereon
and knew that the earl had found the ride as tiring as I myself had.

The day was so glorious it beckoned me, but I knew that my

first chore was to settle my few belongings and wash the dust from my body, despite my fatigue. Fresh clothes and water for washing had been brought for me. I could see that the garments were French country clothes made of rough muslin, gathered skirts and a bodice, not the beautiful wools given to me in Wiltshire. These clothes were not exactly my style, but there you are: The trip had been long, and the gown I wore could doubtless stand on its own with acquired grit, so I shed it.

After refreshing myself, I opened the shutters, leaned on the deep window casement, and looked down the road that spilled away from the *château*. Questions chattered in my head, despite my best efforts to think only of the sun warming my arms. How long would I stay in this place? Was Eleanor back at Fontrevault by now? Why had I let William coerce me into coming here? Would Earl Graham attempt to stop me if I tried to leave? William had said, "Later, when things are resolved, you may be able to return safely to Philippe's court." What things needed to be resolved?

I then pondered the loss of my Arab jewel. The exchanges at the inn on the subject of the great poet and my conversation with Father Alcuin on the riverbank had brought back a sense of loss over the keepsake. And I puzzled over the jewel. I remembered the search of my room at Havre, and again at Canterbury. Someone, or perhaps more than one person, had been looking for the jewel.

These were not random attempts at theft, nor did I any longer believe that it was the gold and ruby in the pendant that made it desirable. Something else was going on.

I watched the ribbon of road unwind beneath me. I could see it curl down the gentle hill, to the crossroads. One branch continued toward the river and the bridges to Chinon, the way we had come. The other wound its way through the fields toward Fontrevault.

I made a decision in that sudden way of my own. If William did not come within the week, bringing back my letters and their translation, I would leave this place. I'd leave it by night if necessary, and I would take myself to the left at the crossroads in the fields. I would return to Fontrevault and confront Eleanor with or without evidence. I would wring from her the true reason for my errand, the trap she sent me into at Canterbury—for I'd no doubt she had known that John would find me there—and demand as payment for my troubles the truth about the child.

That left one week in which to rest. I eyed my ridiculous new clothes. The worst part was the lack of pockets for my withered hand. I rested my arm on the windowsill now, my hand before me, a useless claw, a private sorrow. The feeling gone from the wrist down. I did not even have a glove to cover it. Sighing, I turned into the room and saw with surprise something I had not seen earlier: Someone had left vellum and charcoal on one of the wooden chests in the corner of the room.

It occurred to me, not for the first time, that life could have been much more miserable if it were my right hand that had withered in my mother's womb rather than my left.

I drew all afternoon, creating sheet after sheet of scenes and events of the past weeks. When I finished those, I drew the faces of Prior William, Earl Graham, the mysterious young François, King John, and his beautiful wife with the thin mouth. I drew the phlegmatic Baron Roger, the apoplectic Richard Glanville, the fine, noble aging face of William Marshal.

Then I began to draw faces from the past: Eleanor when she was young; my sister, Marguerite, and her husband, young Henry; Richard in his teens with his marvelous reddish blond hair flowing. It was as if there was an outpouring from the center of me, some release from memories I did not even know I still held. As I began to fill the last sheet of vellum, the head of King Henry took shape, and I felt tears flowing down my face.

I stopped as the sun was beginning to fade, having used all the vellum and worn the charcoal down to its nub. I discovered then, when finally I paused, that a crashing ache in my head had formed while I was working. I stumbled to the bed, hoping to still the mallet beating inside by lying down. When a servant scratched at the door, I barely lifted my head to respond. I sent him downstairs with my excuses to the others for dinner. I could not say, however, what I knew to be true: The world of my soul was too crowded, and the pain had spilled over into my body. From then on, and for some time, I could scarcely distinguish light from dark. My main companions were the shades of my past, their images swirling in the hollow chamber of my mind.

At the end of the second day, the throbbing eased and the pain began to recede. I had been dimly aware that Earl Graham had stopped to see me, as had the faithful but still-distant Steward Thibault, followed by his wife, the pleasant Petronella, whose aprons smelled always of freshly baked bread, making soothing sounds. They had provided powders, but I had refused them and requested only heated water in which to dissolve the herbs I still carried myself. Finally, on the third day and after a day of my own treatment, I could bear to look at the light. I was returning to myself.

For the first time in recent weeks, I truly wished for another woman for company. I had not been well served by women in my life: starting with my own mother and then, as things turned out, by Queen Eleanor, by the waiting women at my brother's court, and more recently by Isabelle, who'd tried to manipulate me for John. Yet now I longed for Marguerite, the sister of my childhood, or my nurse Francesca. Anyone to talk to but these tiresome knights. I might even rise for dinner tonight, I thought, if I knew women would be there.

Even as I was thinking these thoughts, lying on the large bed watching the sun's setting rays play on the wall tapestry, a gentle scratch came again to the door. This time, without a wait for my leave, it opened.

It was Mistress Petronella, she of the cherubic face and perfect cheeks and bobbing curtsy. I had noticed her beauty in the melee of our arrival, but now the sun caught her full, lively face as she stood quietly inside the door, and I saw she was intelligent-looking as well.

"What is it?" I asked, my voice cracking like a dried board.

"Is there anything Your Grace desires?" she asked, without much deference in her voice this time, at least none that I could distinguish.

I sat up and leaned on one elbow, the better to see her. I listened for the pain in my head with the movement, but none came. I said, on impulse, "Yes. I would like my clothes. And a cloak, if you please." I swung my legs over the side of the bed and sat upright. Still no pain. I was weak, but I was free.

"Your Grace is feeling better. Will you come to dinner?"

"No. Please make my excuses to Earl Graham and the other knights. But I am going out to take the air."

"I'll tell the earl. He said to be sure to let him know when you felt better."

"Don't, under any circumstances, tell the earl I feel better," I said sharply. "Just get my clothes and a cloak and tell them all I'm still too ill to join them for dinner."

"But, Your Grace—"

"Come here, Mistress Thibault." The young woman came closer, hands clasped behind her back, eyes straight on to mine. She still retained that interesting air of independence in her demeanor. Clearly, she was not cowed by my station. "I sorely desire fresh air. I think it will improve my condition. But I don't want to trouble anyone with my whims. I prefer to be alone. Do you understand?" The village idiot would have understood.

She nodded, smiling.

"Do you know who I am?"

She tossed her head. The gesture could have been interpreted as affirmation or sauciness.

"If you help me, I'll reward you with silver. If you do not do as I ask, it will not go well with you." Vague threats were often much more powerful than real ones, I had discovered at court. Real threats had defined limits, but vague threats played on the imagination. The field was infinite for each person.

"Yes, Your Grace." She provided me with one more of her interminable curtsies, bobbing her head slightly. I had the distinct impression she was hiding a broadening smile. Then, going to the large wooden wardrobe against the far wall, she opened the door. I could have done as much, I suppose, without her. The spate of illness had addled my brain.

"Clothes have been placed here for you. They are the clothes you are used to wearing. We . . . it took some time for us to get these, so at first you were given some of my own things." She frowned slightly. "We were not prepared for your arrival. We had only just opened the house ourselves that morning. You were earlier than we expected."

"It is your things I require to wear now," I said, puzzled by her words. The house unoccupied before we came? The servants newly planted here for our benefit? "Or, better still, the clothes of one of the menservants."

She looked astonished at my request. I repeated myself, speaking slowly in her native Norman tongue.

"I would like the clothes a manservant would wear," I paused to see if she understood. "Can you bring me such clothes now?"

"*Oui, un moment, madame,*" she said, suddenly seeing I was in earnest.

"Are the knights at table yet?" I crossed the room to the chest as I spoke. One of my knees gave way, causing me to stumble, but she was following close behind and neatly caught my elbow. I continued on my way, determined to regain my balance. With each step I felt stronger.

"Not quite, my lady. They are waiting, out of *politesse*, I believe, to know if you will join them."

"Then go down and tell them I am still too ill to dine and wish to be left alone tonight. After they have gone in to dinner, I shall take the night air alone. I command that you do not tell the knights below I have gone out. Do you understand?"

"Yes, Your Grace." An impish look flooded her face. "I do understand perfectly."

"Good. Then bring me the clothes I have requested, even if you have to thieve them. And a cloak of some kind as well." She turned to go, and I added, "And be quick about it."

"Yes, Your Grace."

I stopped her one last time. "But only after you have assured my knights that I will not be joining them for dinner. And make certain you are not seen bringing me the clothes."

She darted out the door, and I felt certain I had an accomplice who would keep my confidence.

I was impatient to be off and lost no time once she returned. Outside, the moon was already rising as the last glow of day was fading. The white ball hung in the clear south sky and boded well for my adventure. The night air refreshed me, and after a few minutes, my initial queasiness began to dissipate.

I headed straight for the stables, staying close to the line of trees that ringed the road. The subdued sound of male voices floated out from the courtyard behind the house, where the knights were no doubt taking the air before dinner. The drone of their male talk was punctuated occasionally by claps of laughter.

Fortune was my friend this evening. No stray servant loitered at the stable door. The livery servants were likely at supper in the kitchen. I picked the smallest of the horses of our pack, the dappled palfrey I had ridden from Calaïs, and led her silently out of the stables. She came along sweetly now, rested, ready for my adventure. When I was far enough from the manor so that no sound reached me, I mounted and soon broke into a canter. At the fork in the road, I took the right turn to Chinon.

I knew it was the week for the fair, for I had seen the preparations even as we rode through the town a few days earlier. There was a stage set up in the center of the market, which meant entertainment. Torches were placed all around on pikes, and people were gathering already for the evening festivities as I made my way across the bridge. I looked up at the sky dotted with stars in the deepening dusk, and I felt glad. Then I was lost in the jostling good spirits of the townspeople and forced to dismount and lead my horse into the town square, so great was the collecting crowd.

Dressed as I was in tunic and hose, with a short cape tossed across my shoulders and a felt cap hiding my long braids, no one took any notice of me. I was passing as a servant, or perhaps a squire. Although my knees were still a bit weak, the cool air was bracing, and I felt better with each passing hour. I was feeling free as a child. And how fitting that it was here, in the shadow of the castle I had loved most growing up, that it should be so.

I stopped at a booth and stood in line to buy a small roasted hen, which I tore into with gusto, licking my fingers like any peasant. Then I found the wine booth and satisfied my thirst with some dreadful village vintage. After that I made my way toward the center of the square, where benches were crowded around the stage. Whatever was happening there, it was drawing great gusts of laughter from the throng.

I settled myself on a bench toward the back, where a lucky chance provided a space so that I could see through to the stage. The platform on which the performance was offered was high enough to allow a short person a clear view. I began to listen.

At once I recognized the play. It was the dialogue between the drunk and the fool, beloved of French country crowds and often performed at court for amusement from what Philippe called—always with a sigh—the peasant offerings. The farce had entertained us royal children as well when we were in Normandy or Anjou. Now I had to smile again, in spite of myself, as the fool whacked the drunk on the head and he fell down, only to trip the fool as he turned to the audience for his bow. No philosophy here, no thought: just a rendering of the stupid human condition.

Soon the two *bouffons* exited the stage, and the crowd grew quiet. Most knew what was to follow, for the playbill had been posted.

Two cowled figures mounted the stage. One wore a white robe, the other black, and I saw we were to be entertained by that old pair of inseparables, the Body and the Soul.

The figure in white took the lead in the exchange: "Do you not realize how your intemperance endangers your eternal life?" he thundered from under the safety of his voluminous hood. But the abstract spirituality of the white one was no match for the earthiness and vitality of the Body. This fellow, dressed completely in black with his hood sheltering his face so we could not see his expression, was easily the crowd's favorite. He had all the witty lines, some I suspected made up on the spot, and soon the cheering for him was interrupting the Soul's ponderous responses. It was as if this serious dialogue on eternal matters had been infected by the levity of the fool and the drunk that preceded it.

I myself was laughing so hard that my sides were shaking. The actors were improvising marvelously on the traditional arguments, creating comedy that warmed the villagers. No wonder the bishops railed against the theater. Laughter was probably the greatest danger to orthodoxy. Just underneath all of our assumed piety was this layer of irreverence. How delightful to have it erupt among us on this star-marked night. And good for the actors!

"But what assurance can you give me that if I give up my neighbor's wife now, there will be any future reward? Will my own wife stop nagging me?" the black-hooded figure called out in a clear, young voice. The audience roared again, but my attention was caught for another reason. The actor's voice had a familiar ring.

"He's good, isn't he?" said an even more familiar voice close to my left ear. I started, turning quickly. William's keen eyes were watching the stage, even as he spoke to me. He was crouching behind me, having to bend his tall frame slightly to put his head close to mine.

"What are you doing here?" I nearly fell off the bench, but he steadied me with a strong hand in the middle of my back.

"Following you. What else would I be doing at a county fair watching nonsense on a stage under a full moon?" he said, clipping his words in a martial way. Around us, people were straining to hear the actors. They hissed in our direction for silence.

"When did you . . . ?" I began.

He put his elbow under my arm and half pulled me from the bench, drawing me firmly toward the edges of the standing crowd, which parted reluctantly to let us through. Conquering the impulse to resist, I moved with him as one.

When we arrived at the crowd's edge, he did not release my arm but tightened his grip as he bent his face close to mine.

"Now to answer all your questions at once and get it over: I arrived this afternoon. I didn't send to your room because I understood that you were not well. I didn't want to disturb you until you felt better, foolish fellow that I am. So much for *courtoisie*. But the steward's young wife came to us as we were going in to supper and reported that you had escaped on a lark of your own."

"God's teeth!" I said ruefully. "Buying another man's servant is fool's work."

"And that little message forced me to forgo the fire and an early bed and chase back across this rotting river to find you." He stopped. "And to your next question, as yet unasked, the answer is yes, I have broken the code on your purloined letters. You may have the translation tonight."

"Mother of God!" I had almost forgotten the letters. In my glee, I clapped his arm with my good hand. "I'm very glad for it. But can they wait until the Body and Soul finish their debate? When you arrived, the Body was winning the encounter handily, and that pleased me no end. If his advantage holds, my conduct in the future may be affected."

"You can't be serious!" His heavy brows lifted. "You of all people? *You* love the stage?" He started to laugh aloud. People near us turned with rude comments, which he happily ignored.

"I love the stage, I love crowds, I love the open air, and I love game hens cooked on a spit," I said, licking the grease that lingered on the tips of the fingers of my right hand, feeling the sensuous movement of my tongue. "I love all the things of ordinary life, the things no one ever let me have as a child, and I love them the more because of it." I pointed to the booths with their hens trussed and turning on spits like a company of well-trained soldiers. As if on cue, a breeze blew our way, wafting the good scent of roasting garlic. "Try some, since you missed dinner at Montjoie's. I guarantee that the food will put you in a much better mood."

"No thanks." He grimaced. "Hens flavored with dust is a dinner I won't eat unless I am in the field, and even then only if I'm ravenous. I'll be treated to Thibault's best farm pigeon at dinner when I return."

"On my word, these rough hens taste better," I said, but William had already turned back toward the stage and did not hear me. The Body and Soul had finished their debate, and the hoods of the actors were tossed back as they took their bows to the cheering crowds. In the torchlight I could see the black-robed figure bow, his smile merry as the applause showed him clearly the favorite. He lifted his arms and his face upward to the light as his hood fell back. It was the diamond-shaped face of the young clerk, François.

"As soon as he joins us, we'll be off," William said, shifting his gaze from the stage to me. There was a searching quality to his look, I thought, but I might have imagined it in the dim light.

We walked away from the stage and toward one of the many passageways between the stone buildings that led out from the town square down to the river. When we reached the bridge, William paused, then turned to me and asked, without preamble: "Did you have conversation with François in your journey from Wiltshire?"

"We talked at dinner and some while riding."

"And what do you think of him?" The question seemed casual enough.

"A fine young clerk—or knight or monk, or whatever you and your men are," I answered, but then I felt his eyes still on me.

"Would you like such a man in your service?" he asked. It did not sound like a question put lightly.

I covered my surprise as best I could, and honesty made me hesitate before I replied, "William, it's not clear to me where my service would lead. I cannot say yes or no at this time, for I haven't decided whether or not I will return to Philippe's court." I thought for a minute. Perhaps I had misunderstood. "Are you offering him to me?"

"Not exactly," he replied. But then our opaque conversation was cut short, as the young man in question caught up with us, panting hard from running, his black-hooded robe slung over his shoulder. It was only then that I saw he had purloined a Benedictine habit as his costume for the morality play. He showed no surprise at seeing either of us, nodding to William first and then bowing quickly in my direction.

"You acquitted yourself well," William said to the disheveled young man, cocking one strong eyebrow quizzically. "You may have missed your calling. Mayhap you should forget aspiring to a knighthood or the church and follow the stage."

"I was surprised to get your note," the young man said, with a remarkable demonstration of *sangfroid*. "Thanks for letting me go on."

He bobbed his head in my direction, then said, "What brought you here tonight?" The question was directed to William. Apparently he had little interest in what *I* was doing at the scene. The young face had revealed no surprise when he saw me, but then I had just seen a fine demonstration of his acting ability onstage.

"Chasing after you, you young rake. What will Hugh Walter say if I tell him his best classics student spends his free time frolicking on the stage?" William reached out to ruffle the burnt auburn hair, but François ducked with expert timing. "And making a comedy out of the very serious debate between the body and soul. The church does not take her mission to save souls lightly, young man, I can promise you. You should have learned at least that in your years at Canterbury."

"You promised I wouldn't have to go back if—" François was laughing so hard he could hardly speak, but he stopped abruptly when he saw William's expression alter at his words.

"Later," William said, with that occasional and sudden curtness and change of mood that left one wondering if he ever truly relaxed for more than ten heartbeats.

"My horse is over here." François recovered gravity and gestured with his head back toward the stage, making the transition in the conversation with admirable grace. Again I thought, He has the makings of a formidable actor.

"Not anymore it isn't," William replied, continuing to lead us in the opposite direction. "It seemed sensible to have all of our horses in one place, close to the river, so that we could leave before the crowds tire of their entertainment."

I glanced over my shoulder and saw another play just beginning. We were among a handful of people leaving the square. From
the shadows now deepening around us, five more knights materialized on horses, three of them leading ours. How did he do it? I
wondered, shaking my head in the dark. It was as if he had a secret
kingdom at his beck and call. And we all mounted and rode off.

.18.

Misunderstandings

William himself saw me to my chamber. I paused with my hand on the door latch. I expected that he would want to discuss the translation of my letters, but he did not make any move to prolong our conversation or to come into my chamber. As if he read my thoughts, with that uncanny energy that flowed between us, he merely said, "We are all tired. In the morning, after we've broken our fast, we'll talk. I'll bring the letters then."

"But you lead such a mysterious and peripatetic life," I countered, with as much lightness as I could summon. "What if you get called away suddenly in the midst of the night? My letters will go with you. And there will go also the answers I believe might alter my life."

"Or might not," he said, jamming his thumbs into his belt. The hall torches shadowed his face, but they illumined mine. "Alaïs, trust that nothing will take me away from this house tonight, not before we discuss your letters." His voice was as hard as iron.

Suddenly I became aware that we were standing close together. My back was leaning against the door to my chamber, my face to William in front of me. He seemed to be blocking my way, although it was I who stood against my own door. His gaze, framed by those remarkable brows, was directly on me in that peculiar, intense way of his. I placed my hand on the latch behind me. He might enter my room if I opened the door—he already had demonstrated a penchant for entering my private chambers at will—and it would be easier to face him in my chamber than as we were now. In my own room, I could put space between us. From this intimate position, I felt oddly vulnerable.

Without warning, he stepped back and turned about without saying a *bonne nuit*. Before I could speak, he disappeared around the corner. A confusion of feelings overtook me, both release and chagrin. I pressed the latch and entered my chamber.

There was new vellum on the table next to the chest. The torches were lit, and the room was filled with wavering light. There was no chance for sleep the way I felt at that moment, so I sat to sketch. Perhaps I could capture some of the joy of the hours just past while the night scenes in the Chinon town square were still in my mind's eye. But that was not to be. I made one try after another to draw the stage, Body and Soul in their debate, even the townspeople lurking on the outskirts of the crowd, which I usually found so fertile as subjects, but the charcoal did not cooperate as it usually did.

The face of William kept interfering. Finally I gave in and sketched that face. First the face I saw on the high altar at Canterbury—uplifted, distant, arrogant—then the busy host at Baron Roger's dinner party—social, charming. Next the face of the man who embraced me when I cried in my chamber at Wiltshire, a softer face, and then the laughing, ironic face, so full of fun, so essentially human, that caught me unawares in the town square in Chinon this very evening. Finally the impassive, preoccupied face of the William who had just left me so abruptly. I sketched all, a whole parchment full of Williams, and once I had finished, I looked down with satisfaction. I almost liked him when I contemplated those pictures. Or perhaps I should say I almost liked them, for there was a collection of people on my sheet of parchment. If I did not like one, I could take another.

I threw down the charcoal, washed myself in the water that had grown cool in the pitcher, and put on my night shift. Dousing the torches seemed a task for which I was well suited at that moment. Welcome, darkness.

As I lowered my tired body onto the bed, I had a strange *déjà vu*. It had to do with feeling pinned at the door by William's presence. I had been once, when young, in just such a position with Richard. My memory took me back to Eleanor's court in Poitiers, when Richard and I were both young and ardent. The three *sirventes* he had written to me privately to announce his love had been snatched from his room impishly by his brother Geoffrey and read aloud to all Eleanor's court that evening at dinner, much to the merriment of his sisters and brothers and my own sister, Marguerite.

By this trick Richard's love for me had been declared openly. It was almost a relief. We had only to wait until my sixteenth birthday for the nuptials, for us to fulfill that promise of love. There was no question of consummating our love before then. Our parents, rulers of France and England, would have been outraged if I had come with child before the wedding. And the chance for an illegitimate heir to complicate matters was a grave one.

Nevertheless we lived, we breathed love, because we were at the courts of love. Marie of Champagne, Eleanor's daughter by my father, was mistress of our revels of love. She decreed that we would hold court to ascertain the true meaning of love. Under her direction the monk Capellanus evolved a code of love to which—Marie said—we all must pledge ourselves. To abstain from lust, to refrain from physical love for the greater glory of poetic love, to create love in words—this was our highest ideal. We were equal to the challenge. Richard and I could wait for the nuptials.

That night when Richard went with me to the door of my bedchamber, he leaned down to press his lips to mine for the first time. The palm of my good hand became moist as he grasped it, then encircled me with his arms, pinning me to him.

If he had asked to enter my room at that moment, I could not have refused. I had no will left that did not race in the direction of coming closer to him.

But it was he who pulled away and, as abruptly as William tonight, turned and left without a word.

The moon shone through the openings in the wall. I watched the shadows of the trees outside play upon the ceiling for a long time. My own shadows were the decisions I needed to make about my future. This entire wild errand was over as far as I was concerned once I had heard what the Sarum letters contained. But in this process, and quite beside the point, something else had happened.

Tonight it occurred to me that I need never go back to Paris. Why have a life at court at all? They were occupied with vanity and position, clothes and feasts. Prattle they had aplenty, but there was not one whole creative idea in all of the combined brains of the court of France.

But if not back to Paris, where then? Charlotte's invitation to come to Fontrevault still echoed, suspended somewhere in the air. I was close right now. Fontrevault was an afternoon's ride from where I slept this very evening. I could ride to the abbey and take up quarters beside the aging Eleanor, assuming she ever came back from Spain alive. That arrangement would give us plenty of time to work out our secrets and misunderstandings!

But still there seemed to be something else beckoning me. In truth, my heart was changing. My adventure tonight in the town of Chinon, where I was free as a common peasant, had been a delight. Why should I not go about as I pleased, without everyone's knowing I was a princess?

And then there was this matter of feeling, the fullness that sometimes came over me when I remembered past scenes. Was it not possible that feeling could apply to the present? Wasn't my reaction to William tonight a response of feeling? Perhaps I wasn't dead in my heart after all.

But no, that was absurd. The idea was almost unseemly. Consider, Alaïs, your age, your lightening hair, your unlucky stars in love, your aching hip, for God's sweet sake!

I amused myself with my upraised arm, tracing the shadows waving on the ceiling in a mock sketching exercise, smiling all the while, and so missed the gentle opening of the door and the first sight of the candle.

When I became aware of the flickering light and the large shadow beside it, they were near me. The man bearing the light lowered himself to sit on the edge of my bed. I raised myself on my elbow, catching with my good hand the purse with its sharp chisel, as if by habit.

"You don't need a weapon, Alaïs." William's voice cut through the darkness, with its edge of habitual irony. I pulled myself up to a sitting position against the pillows and waited, my heart sounding in the silence.

When he finally spoke again, it was a prosaic request. "I would like to light the torches." He was close to me, and for the first time since Canterbury, I was aware of his scent, a smell of strong soap and ginger and something male that was indefinable.

"Yes, if you wish," I replied, my body turning farther in the bed to face his shadowy form.

He reached out a hand and stroked my cheek with the back of it, once up, then with his palm, once down. The dim candlelight fluttered between us. I kept myself still with an effort. Then he rose and lit the torches on the wall one by one. Light, of an uncertain stability but nevertheless light, flooded the room.

He stood near the table, wearing a bloodred silk robe over his tunic and hose. I noticed it was tied with a fringed sash, Oriental style, which seemed frivolous and not in character for him. Then I had the odd thought: That robe was from the East. It was visible proof of his service as Templar.

William was looking directly at me, in an unsettling way. Gone was the haughty, impatient demeanor he wore in public like a knight's cloak. Gone was the authoritative visage of the prior, the stand-in for Hugh Walter, and gone the sociable face and political edge of Baron Roger's dinner party. Now there was just a man, the intense eyes piercing mine from under those formidable eyebrows, the hawklike nose raised.

"Come, please, and sit at the table." It sounded more like a command than a request. If the circumstances had been less peculiar, I would have argued that I should be the one to issue orders in my own chamber. But curiosity and surprise compelled me to rise and wrap myself in the robe of simple unbleached muslin that had been provided for me.

I went toward him, and we stood facing each other on either side of the table, our long sleeves dusting its edges. He placed his candle on it and lit three more, so that I could see quite well. Then he gestured, and we both sat on chairs on opposite sides of the table. It felt like the beginning of a tournament. For the first time, I noticed he was carrying a small pouch of worn leather, slung by a slim strap over his shoulder. He slipped it off and tossed it onto the table.

"I wanted to wait until morning. I don't want to do this in the middle of the night. But I can't sleep. You may as well know now."

A cold wind blew across my heart. Until this moment it had not occurred to me that I might not want to know the contents of Eleanor's letters. Finding them had buoyed me, a long reach into the past that might give me answers about my son. But now I saw the other side: The letters could contain information, news I would rather not know.

"Wait." I held his hand down with my own, as it moved to open the pouch. I wanted to delay the moment of knowing. I said the first thing that came into my mind: "You must tell me who you are."

He looked up, surprised. "You know me," he said simply.

"No." I paused, looking him full in the face. "I knew you once. But that was long ago, and we were no more than children. I don't know you now. For instance, what did you study when you were Becket's clerk?" I could see, even with the dim light, his baffled expression.

"The university course, the trivium and the quadrivium. Like all the other clerics. The Greeks, Socrates, Aristotle, Aeschylus, and Sophocles. Latin. Horace and Ovid. French. Scripture. Arabic numbers. Euclid. Celestial navigation. Much as you studied when you went with Eleanor to Poitiers. Wasn't that your course of study as you prepared to marry Richard? I heard that the school at the Poitiers court was exceptional, designed by Eleanor herself."

"Indeed, we studied most of those subjects, except for celestial navigation,"—I smiled at the thought—"for Poitiers, you may remember, was inland." I paused. "And I can tell you, we did not study Holy Scripture in Eleanor's court."

The deep vertical lines of his face relaxed in a smile. "No, remembering Eleanor, I can safely believe that. She loved not the church and its pronouncements. She always had a wicked wit about her on the subject of piety. And the church loved her no more than she loved it."

"When did we lose track of each other, you and I?" My question caught him off guard. He crossed one foot over his knee as he leaned back from the table and casually rested his forearm on the raised knee. I was aware of the length of his limbs and their elegance. His robe parted to reveal scarlet hose, and I saw the Armenian slippers trimmed in small jewels on his long foot.

After a moment, during which he gazed at the beams over the room, he said, "I was with you when we were all in Normandy, when I was very young. Then Henry gave me to Becket. When the archbishop died, Henry sent for me again. He wanted me at his court, and I was delighted to go back. I remembered our lessons when I was young. I had enjoyed being with the royal children."

I could feel myself flush even in the dark. Was he baiting me? "Did you? My recollection is that we were not kind to you."

"You did the best you could," he replied. "The young princes were beset with all the demons of childhood. They had difficult, demanding parents. And they envied me."

"Envied you?" I was astonished.

"What came easily for me, they had to work for. And they were spoiled, so work was hard. But for me, an orphan, work was necessary. I had to survive."

I saw again the scene in the barn, with the handsome princes pushing the whey-faced orphan from one to the other, and I was ashamed.

I noticed William tapping his long fingers on his knee. "But then Henry and Eleanor split apart. No sooner had I arrived at Chinon than all the children went with her to the south, you and your sister and Henry Court Mantel, Richard and Geoffrey and all the Plantagenet daughters. Even Louis sent his daughters born of Eleanor. Every royal child on this side of the Continent was there, excepting John. Henry kept his best-beloved son in England, away from Eleanor's dicey influence." He paused, then said, with an odd sort of whimsy, "Everyone was in Poitiers but John and myself. The two lost boys."

Into the pause this time, I could hear the call of crickets outside. Spring had come to northern France in the few days I had been in England.

When William spoke again, it was in his former casual voice. "The removal of Eleanor's court deprived me of most of my companions, and I was lonely. Soon after you all went to Poitiers, Henry took pity on me, and then it was that I was chosen to begin traveling with the king."

"Yes, I remember that." Coming upon the king and the young clerk in the garden at Chinon one day when I was still a girl, I watched and listened to them converse for some time before they noticed me. I remembered their familiarity, the way the king placed his hand on the clerk's shoulder, almost as if he were his own son. Then William made a pun in Latin, and Henry laughed so abruptly—that sudden, sporadic laugh of his—that the pitcher I carried slipped out of my hands and crashed to the ground. The king sprang back as if he were guilty of some misdeed, and I, cheeks red, apologized and curtsied to him.

"*Princesse*," William said now, breaking into my reverie, "what else do you want to ask? We cannot spend the night re-creating the past, pleasant though it is to do so."

"All right, only one more." I wondered if I dared, then charged ahead. "Are you a monk of Canterbury, or are you a Templar?"

"Who told you I was a Templar?" He stiffened, his hand flying to the pouch at his side.

"William Marshal told me in Wiltshire. And I have every reason to believe him."

"How so?" He stood suddenly and began that edgy walking I had noticed earlier. "You know I'm a monk of Canterbury. You have seen me there."

"I saw you there. But I also saw you at Baron Roger's, in knight's dress, charming the crowd. You arranged for me to be rescued from King John's little drama and to be brought here by those same knights. You have, I believe, arranged for the letters I found to be decoded. No mere monk of Canterbury commands such resources and travels about so freely, unless he be the abbot. And I know Hugh Walter is abbot."

William didn't answer. Instead he continued his silent pacing, punching his fists together as if that would help him to think. After a time I wondered if he would answer at all. I waited.

He was passing the chest against the wall for the second time when his eye was caught by the parchment I had filled with sketches not an hour earlier. The one large piece, with all his faces sketched from memory, lay upward. He picked it up and held it to the nearest wall torch. He seemed to regard it much longer than was necessary. I felt warmth rising to my cheeks and cursed my need to sketch every minor image that presented itself before my inner eye.

Then he replaced the parchment gently on the chest and turned to me. "My story can wait. I came here tonight to give you the translation of Eleanor's letters. I think we should look at them together. At some later time, perhaps I will tell you more of myself. But for now"—he walked back to the table and cast the leather pouch onto it—"let's to the letters."

That closed off further conversation, but what was I to do? And anyway, why did I want to hear this impossible man's story? He obviously liked women no better than he had as that stiff, arrogant child who pulled away from all who would draw him into games or tease him. I cared not, I told myself. I had only been delaying the moment when I would have to face the information in Eleanor's letters by my questions. Still, I was aware of a gentle, falling cloud of disappointment within myself.

William sat down, and pulled open the travel pouch, and pushed several sheets of paper toward me. I saw that the translations were made in Latin. Of course! They were made for William, who was, after all, an educated man. Latin would be his second language. Fortunately, I could read it as well.

He folded his arms and tilted his chair back, silent, waiting for me.

I picked up the papers and moved the candle closer to read them.

19

Letters, Lies, and Secrets

here were four letters in all. I read them through carefully, lost in wonderment after the greeting of the first one.

Date: 26 janvier, Year of Our Lord 1176

To my beloved daughter Joanna, Queen of Sicily
From your mother, Eleanor, by the Grace of God Queen of the English and Duchess of the Aquitaine:
   I bring you greetings.
   I hope this letter will find its way to you at some time, though I do not know when. We are watched here constantly. The king, your father, has placed his trusted servants here to watch me, and I do not know how I will be able to send this letter to you.
   I think often on our days at Poitiers. I hope you are happy in your new marriage.

For myself, I believe that it was precipitate of your father to arrange it for you so suddenly. But then, perhaps, nothing he does is sudden. He only makes it seem that way. Your husband is a good man, I hear. I trust you will be happy.

I have received no communication from Richard. If you have heard from him, find way to get me word. If you send a written letter, I will destroy it. If Henry finds me in communication with any of you, I will most certainly be punished. My separation from you all was a condition of his agreement to leave me alone here, in Old Sarum.

I have everything I need, except for books and my children. I languish without intellectual conversation. At least I have some writing materials, smuggled in by my maid, Bess, as she is called.

Please pray for me.

Enclosed, if you get this letter, are herbes *which you must take until you are delivered of your child. They will increase your strength afterward.*

1 novembre, *Year of Our Lord 1178*

To Joanna, dearest daughter
From your mother Eleanor, by the Wrath of God Queen of the English and Duchess of Aquitaine:

I bring you greetings if you receive this message.

It is weary here in this drafty castle. How I miss my own lands. The king, your father, has sent me many books, finally, for which I am grateful. But he still forbids me to write letters. He says my letters have always been a source of trouble for him! Foolish man. He is his own source of trouble. Always has been.

I long for company. I think of you in the gentle south and hope that your life goes well. The birth of your child should by now have come to pass. I have not yet been able to send my last letter and may not send this for some time. Still, to write brings you closer to me. When I can, I will send herbes that will help you recover from childbirth. I will continue to try.

I have a new maid, name of Kate. I think she is a spy. Bess was sent away because, I believe, your father received news that she was sympathetic to me. Indeed, I gave her the first letter I wrote you, and she tried to take it to a courier but was stopped and questioned so sharply by Gérard of Blois, whom your father has made jailer here, that she became frightened and returned the letter to me. Soon after she was sent away, and the new maid arrived.

This new one has shifty eyes. These are the eyes that read letters intended for others. She may eventually read this. Anyway, I shall keep it hidden in my writing desk until a moment arrives that is propitious for sending it. And, of course, I write it in code. You will not find it difficult to have it translated. Any educated monk can decipher this code, as I once taught you. One cannot be too careful.

I hope you enjoy motherhood. I always loved it greatly myself, when the children were young. It was only when you all grew older that I found myself lonely once again.

Your loving Mother,

Eleanor R.

24 mars, 1179

To Eleanor, Queen of Castile, and dearest daughter
From your mother, Eleanor Plantagenet
Queen of the English and
Duchess of the Aquitaine

Duchess of Normandy and Countess of Anjou:

I bring you greetings.

I do not know if you received my earlier letters. They were taken by Maurice when Henry let him return to France. He promised me on his word he would see that they were delivered to you or destroy them. I made copies, though, for I want you someday to read my words.

If you have received those letters, then you know the worst. Your father will have a new child by next summer, by one of the Capets. Yes, your playmate Alaïs has become your father's new mistress. Who could have predicted that the child I nurtured in my bosom when she could scarcely walk could grow in such a short time to produce another heir for Henry?

I am filled with anger. I suppose he coerced her. She is, I am told, his virtual prisoner. It is a calculated revenge. He told me when he placed me here, in this secured, stormy fortress so near the sea I can hear it roar on a summer's eve, that I would pay for conspiring against him.

He sees conspiracies at every turn. As if my friendship with Becket in exile were a conspiracy, when I simply tried to give the poor man comfort. He was, after all, in love with Henry, not myself.

On the other hand, I have some understanding of why he made the charge that I conspired with Louis against him those years we were in Poitiers. It's true, I did have an active correspondence with Louis, but much of it was about our daughters. You remember, both Louis's and my daughters, Marie and Alix, were with me at court. What more natural than to strike up discussion with their father Louis on their well-being? In the course of things, perhaps, we mentioned once or twice the future of your brothers and the topic of the borders of France and England. But this was always done only out of concern for all our interests in the future of these great realms. I hope you

understand. If your father pursues this course of charging me
with mischief against him, who knows what punishment he will
cook up for me, like a bad stew?

You must write to him, Eleanor, and talk sense to him. He
always listens to you. I am near to going mad in this fortress. I
miss company. I miss the discussion of ideas. I brood and lick my
wounds, like a mother wolf.

Succor me if you can.

Remember that I love you, and be strong.

Eleanor R.

14 mai, 1179

From Eleanor, Queen of the English
Duchess of the Aquitaine and Lady of the British Isles
To our son, Richard Plantagenet, Prince of England
Duke of the Aquitaine:

I send you greetings.

I hope this letter finds you well. I intend to send it once I can
ascertain which servants I can trust. Your father replaces them as
soon as they appear to show sympathy to me. He is the very devil,
that man, and so is the captain of the guards here, Gérard of
Blois, although he is pleasant enough to my face.

You have by now discerned that this letter is written in the
code we used to use when we wrote among ourselves in Poitiers.
Little did I imagine how useful that exercise would be. It's not a
difficult code, but in fact too sophisticated for Gérard of Blois to
break, God save his bones.

Oh, yes, I have everything I need, except for intelligent
conversation and friends, except for my children and servants I
can trust, except for the warm, fragrant flowered air of Poitiers,

and except for my freedom. And most difficult, except for my youth.

Your father has promised me—by courier, of course, since I haven't laid eyes on him for two years—that I may be released to keep Christmas with him this year. He has much to discuss with me, he says. I'll wager that's true.

You must know by now that the Princess Alaïs is enceinte at the court at Oxford. It is rumored that your father is much concerned about the health of the princesse and the birth of the child. Well he might be, considering that her age is only sixteen summers. Although, come to think of it, I was only sixteen myself when I married Louis. Still, hardly more than a child.

Louis will be furious when he hears. This is the child that could disrupt all his careful diplomacy. Years of planning to merge the two countries when Henry dies, with you and Philippe as joint kings, are now thrown into chaos. This child will be a child of both royal houses of France and England and, whether legitimate or not, will pose a threat to both Henry's and Louis's plans.

I can't imagine what Henry was thinking. Revenge against me, I suppose. He knew how I adored that little girl when Louis gave her to us. I was furious when I first heard news of this child, but now I feel only sadness. She is undoubtedly the latest pawn in our life's blood feud. I don't know if she even understands what has happened. What impact this will have on Henry's plans I also don't know. William Marshal was allowed to look in on me last month, ostensibly to see if I was well, and he told me that Henry is giving up plans to force the succession to John. He seems to be making peace with the idea that you are much more the king than John will ever be. I hope that is the case.

I write to you now to encourage you to make your peace with your father. He and I are growing old. Who knows how long we will live? If he dies naming John as his heir, you will have to fight your brother for England.

I don't think this new babe will be a threat to you, unless you continue to provoke your father. That might be dangerous. Who knows what he will do in a fit of temper? This is the time to fold up your tents, as my grandfather William would often quote from the Arabs. The crown of England should not be lost to pique.

I will try to find a way to send this to you. Reply only if you are certain you can trust the messenger. The one person I continue to trust is William Marshal. Although he serves the king faithfully, he still reveres me and would not break my trust. Henry knows this and allows it. Further evidence that he is growing old.

I do not know what effect Henry's relationship with Alaïs will have on your betrothal to her. You will have to deal carefully with him. He bellows in his rages and behaves badly, but he is wily like a fox in all his diplomacy. If I were you, I would force the marriage soon. The safest way for you to secure the throne, if their child survives, is for you and Alaïs to have a child also, this one legitimate. Do it for my sake, if for no other reason.

Your loving mother, Eleanor

I blanched when I came to the letter to Eleanor of Castile. I could feel the color draining from my face as I read the rest of it. But the letter to Richard undid me. I tried to assume a casual air when I tossed the letters onto the table, but any fool could see that my hand was trembling.

William was waiting for my eyes to meet his. I could feel it, but I chose instead to look away. I stared for a long time at the letters scattered on the oak writing table. I marked how, even in the candlelight, the surface of the table was scarred and marked from long

usage, as if knives had been used to write all the letters here written, rather than quills.

"It was an ordinary code," he said, to break the silence. Finally
I looked at him. "So common, schoolchildren use it. She must have
taught her own children this code for amusement. One replaces all
the vowels in words with the first consonant following that vowel."
He lifted a shoulder. "If I'd had time to look at these letters before
I turned them over, I could have made the translation myself. As it
was, I could see even when you gave these to me those names of
Eleanor's children at the top of each. I was embarrassed when my
translators called to my attention the simplicity of the device." He
spoke gently. "Did she not teach it to you also, when you were
young?"

"No, she must have used it either before or after my time with
the family. I do not know the code." I paused, and then I said,
more honestly, although to say it cost me no little pain, "No,
that's not it. She taught the code to her own children in secret, but
not to me. Proof again that she thought of me as an outsider. I
was Louis's daughter, not to be trusted." I fiddled with the tassels
on my belt, looking down, although indirectness was not my
usual practice.

"I read them, of course," he finally said.

"So now you know."

"What? That there was a child between you and Henry? Of
course I know. I knew at the time. Everyone north of the Mediterranean knew." He glanced at my face. "At the time," he added.

My eyes flew up to him. "You say this is true?"

He nodded.

"Why did you ask me at Baron Roger's manor if I knew of a
royal child? Were you but playing games with me then?"

"I wanted to see what you would tell me, how far you would
trust me, what you thought others knew. I needed any informa-

tion I could get to see why John was so disturbed that he would abduct you."

I stared at him in disbelief.

"*Princesse*. Please." William leaned forward, his head now cupped in his hand, his keen eyes boring into mine. "Did you think that this babe was some grand secret? It's not easy to keep a baby secret, even—or especially—a royal one."

"Yes, you were there," I said slowly. "I had forgotten. You were at Henry's court at the time I was with child."

"Yes. I saw you growing big all that summer, despite your clever gowns."

"I tried to hide it." My face grew warm.

"I thought then the king was using you. And I knew the consequences of this baby for your betrothal to Richard." He leaned back heavily in his chair once more, balancing it casually with his knees against the table. His arms were crossed over his chest in a martial position, reminding me of the distance between us. "I once made bold enough to address the situation with King Henry. As close as I was to him, I thought then he would kill me."

My eyes widened, but I said nothing.

"He was dictating letters to me," William continued, watching me as he told the tale. "I did all his correspondence in those years. He would trust no other. There were two guards in the room that afternoon, but at a distance from where we sat. They lounged near the door casting dice." William looked aside as he so often did when thinking or remembering, then back again. "It was warm that day. It must have been summer. I remember that I had seen you in the courtyard that morning, with one of your women. You were large with child, and your face, your lovely young face, was marked with a rash of some sort. You looked so sad, my heart went out to you. I decided on the spot that I must try to do what I could with the king.

"That afternoon the king called me in to dictate a letter to his

captain in York. When he finished, he did not dismiss me immediately. In the pause that followed, I asked him directly if he
meant to send you away now that you were with child. That perhaps he should do so, that it would be better for you and for all
the court."

"And how did he respond?" I could scarcely push the words
from my throat.

"Hah. His arm came back across my face so quickly, and with
such strength, he knocked me off my chair. Blood poured from my
mouth." William seemed to warm to his story, suddenly sitting up
at the table while the front legs of his chair clattered to the floor. His
long mouth pulled into a rueful smile. "He wore those damnable
heavy royal rings. I had forgotten about those rings. I thought I'd
lost a tooth at the least. But then I realized that the blood was coming because my teeth had clamped into my tongue."

"He could have killed you." I was in wonder at what I was hearing.

"Indeed. My face was bruised for weeks. Believe me, it was the
only time I ever broached the subject with him." He rubbed his chin
as if the memory still had power. "The guards were on me in a
minute. They thought from Henry's quick move that I had threatened the king's person. They had swords drawn, and they would
have dispatched me right there, but he motioned them off, too
angry to speak. You remember how it was when he took a rage; we
couldn't tell whether he was having a fit and we should call the sur-
geon, or whether he would rebound in a minute and strike someone
dead. But after pacing once or twice, he waved me out of the room
without speaking to me, and I didn't know when—or if—I would
be called to serve him again. I cooled my heels for some days in my
rooms in the castle, I can tell you, expecting at any time a summons
or a direction to leave the court."

"Were you afraid of him?" I fiddled absently with a corner of
one of Eleanor's letters. The story of William's defending me to

Henry was so peculiar, so moving, that I momentarily forgot about the translations.

William rose and walked to the window, pulling back the tapestries that covered the opening against the night air. A full moon rising behind him threw his Gaelic profile into relief. The hair flying back off the forehead, the bony, arrogant nose, the deeply lined face looked familiar. I felt as if I had known this face in some other life, that there was a connection with this man, only just now discovered, built into my very marrow.

"Afraid that he would harm me? Not after the first minutes. Those rages of his made him unpredictable, but you may remember he rarely killed anyone while in a rage, not anyone he truly liked. No, I wasn't afraid that he would kill me. But I did think he might send me away."

"Why? Because you dared to lecture him on his duty to me?"

That strong profile turned toward me now, and with the moonlight coming behind him, I could not read his expression. He moved slightly and leaned against the wall behind him before he answered.

"No. Because he now knew I was aware that his heart was involved with you. And that knowledge made me dangerous."

"And the others? I suppose they thought I was the king's slut."

"No one thought of you as a slut, *Princesse*. You always had too much dignity for that. But there was much shaking of heads among the king's counselors over you . . . uh, always, of course, when the king was not present."

"What do you mean?"

"By taking you openly as his mistress, Henry had put into risk his entire careful strategy to blend the English and French royal houses. Richard could never marry you after you were known to have a child by his father. And Philippe was going to be furious at the Plantagenets' treatment of his royal sister, whatever happened."

"Ah, yes," I murmured. "In the end it all comes down to politics among men, doesn't it? Even wrongs done to me were important only because they disrupted the plans of men." William said nothing. "But these letters prove that Henry achieved at least one of his goals." I flicked my finger under the top letter and ruffled it.

"Which was?"

"To drive Eleanor mad. He must have seen that she got news of the child. Else how would she know? How could she have discovered it? Henry held her incommunicado in Old Sarum for nearly fifteen years. She would not have heard unless it was his intention to tell her."

William proceeded slowly. "Part of the game of wits between Eleanor and Henry was always who could outsmart the other. They were expert chess players. I used to watch them play when I was young, sometimes long into the evening. Henry would move one way, Eleanor another; a pawn would tumble, the bishops would be captured, the knights would leap, the castles be put in jeopardy. But almost always, on the board, the king and queen would survive. There was scarcely ever a checkmate between them. They had equal skill." He paused. "They did the same in real life. In later years I don't know if they could tell the difference."

Neither of us spoke for a time. "Are you thinking Henry deliberately used you to hurt Eleanor?" he finally asked, his voice taking on an unaccustomed gentle quality.

I nodded, feeling a sense of defeat and a sudden urge to give way to tears. "What else should I think, reading these? He saw to it that she knew of the child. There was no need for her to know."

"Ah," he said softly, moving away from the wall that had supported him. "So you think these letters tell you Henry's motivation in getting you pregnant." He walked back to the high chest against the wall and poured two goblets of wine from the decanter. In the process he glanced again at the drawings I had made earlier. He brought the goblets back, set one in front of me, and took a chair on the other side of the table.

"Did you love him?"

I looked up, missing a breath. "Why do you ask?" Protesting the impudence would have been useless. We had moved beyond that.

"Because it matters now."

"I don't understand you."

He fingered the glass, then took a long draft. "Do you know what happened to your child?"

"The child died, William." His eyes flicked to mine at my use of his Christian name. I continued carefully, keeping all expression out of my voice. "The king came to me less than a fortnight after the babe was born. He said it had simply been too weak to survive, that the wet nurse had come to him sobbing. The child had died that morning in her arms. He said the babe was gone, that I must be strong and put it behind me." A taste of sorrel suffused my mouth. I recalled how I had screamed and sobbed at the news, then how they had forced me to drink a sorrel-root tea to quiet me, a root so bitter I choked, drank it until I was limp with the drug. "When I came to my senses, I did as I was told. I put the memory of my child away from me. What choice had I?" I spread my hand, palm up. "Never again did I mention the child to anyone. Nor did the king, ever again, speak of it to me."

In a while I continued, allowing the bitterness I tasted now to run through me like a river, to warm me with its effect, like a poisonous mulled wine. "After that, the king slept in my bed no longer. I believed that it was because I had produced a sickly boy. He was no longer pleased. He began to make many trips to the far corners of his kingdom, as he had done when he was married to Eleanor, suddenly rising early and rousting his household to accompany him. Nothing planned. Nothing settled. Rarely did he even dine with me. And he made many excuses to cover it all, until finally he went back to the Continent, with orders that I should stay at

Winchester. He said he would send for me, but I never saw him again." I watched my hands clasping and unclasping on the table, as if someone else directed them. "He always made certain I was in a different castle when he came to England. Sometimes they would move me on a moment's notice. He was finished with me."

The moonlight traveled across the table while we sat there, as if it were alive and part of our conversation. It filled the space as we breathed and was oddly comforting.

"Did you love him?" he repeated after a time.

"Yes, I loved him mightily." I sighed, as if giving up a burden. There did not seem any need to pretend any longer. "I loved the king. He was a man with passion. He had feelings. He showed them in a world where everyone from the queen on down took such care *not* to show feelings. Even though he had been like my father, I loved him from the time I was a child. And when I was no longer a child, and he wanted me, I loved him like a woman. Only it couldn't last."

"And what did you expect to happen then?"

"I didn't have any expectations. I went from day to day without much thought. After the queen had been imprisoned, her children scattered. The sons disappeared, and the daughters were sent to other courts, to marriages Henry had hastily arranged for them. Even my sister, Marguerite, found a way to join her husband, who was inventing ever new ways to annoy his father in Normandy. I had no one except the king to hold on to. But I still hoped all would be well when Eleanor was released. I thought I could count on her."

"As long as she didn't know about Henry and you."

"As long as she didn't know about the child."

"So you were relieved when the child died?"

"Don't be stupid," I said harshly. "I nearly went mad. It was my babe."

He sipped the wine, saying nothing. I hadn't touched mine.

"What if the child had lived?"

"I was prepared to go away with it. I suggested the plan before ever the child was born. At first Henry seemed to agree. He said the child would not be safe with the intrigues at court, but perhaps I could live in Scotland. He talked from time to time of a castle just over the border, out of reach of Eleanor and of my own jealous family. Henry's relations with William the Lion were always strong. With the king of Scotland's protection, the child and I would be safe." Finally I lifted the goblet to my parched lips. "But it was always a dream. I knew it would never come to pass."

"It certainly would have been awkward for you and the child if you had stayed and Henry had released Eleanor from Sarum to come again to live at court," William stated, with that gift for irony that occasionally laced his words and made them like spears. "What would you and Henry have done then?"

"But she didn't come out of Sarum, did she?" I said. "So there was no need to create a plan or an explanation. And why was it just now that you asked twice if I loved the king?"

He shook his head and stood so abruptly that his chair teetered backward. He steadied it with his foot. "Enough for one night. I have things to think on myself. I suggest we talk tomorrow, when we are fresh. For now, sleep beckons." He leaned over and scooped up the letters, stuffing them back into the leather pouch.

"Are you keeping those?" I protested.

"For your own well-being, *Princesse*."

"But they are mine."

"And so I shall return them to you in good time." He swung the leather strap over his shoulder. "These are not the original letters. I have those. It will do no one any good to have copies floating about." He eyed me as he moved toward the door. I rose and followed. "A word of warning, *Princesse*. Do not be so trusting. Everyone does not wish you well."

"A cryptic statement, Sir William. Please embroider it."

"Only take care. Watch about you. Trust few."

After I opened the door, unable to keep from frowning at what he had said, I extended my good hand to him. He bent over it, like the practiced courtier he was. His lips were warm, and they lingered for just a moment longer than necessary. When he rose, his eyes met mine, again with that unsettling directness. I saw with surprise the slight scar on his cheekbone, just under his left eye, the scar from Henry's ring. How strange that such a small detail can raise subtle fingers of feeling. It was the first time that I saw this brisk, strange, guarded man as vulnerable as I myself.

"So what happens next?" The words were mine; the voice seemed to belong to someone else.

"Well, we have two choices. For one, we could do as you did after your child died, simply live from now on day to day without much thought or hope."

"And the other?"

"I have information that Eleanor is back from Spain. I reckoned perhaps you and I could pay her a visit. Mayhap we can ask her about these mysteries. However did she find out about the child? And were these letters you found at Old Sarum copies or were they the undelivered originals? And why did she send you, of all people, to retrieve her ancient letters to Becket from their hiding place in Canterbury?"

"Eleanor back from Spain," I echoed. "Yes, I would like very much to see her. I have many questions of my own to ask."

"Indeed." He rested his hand on the doorframe, propping his body against it. "I might even be persuaded to give her the letters she wrote to Becket so long ago, the letters that she hoped you could bring her from Canterbury."

"You have those letters?" My voice jumped.

"Did I neglect to tell you that?" He was brazen. "I found them years ago. They have been safe with me. I thought they might be useful one day."

I stared at him, speechless.

He ducked his head, comically, as in mock fear that I might strike him, a look of pure mischief on his face. And before I could say more, he slipped through the door. I sat down, my own head spinning.

I reflected on the many surprises of Prior/Sir William and tried my best to work up anger over his deception to me on the Canterbury letters. But somehow it seemed not important enough. Instead I nursed the peculiar, new, warm feeling within me that our conversation had produced. Was the cause of this tingling the final unburdening for me, of the long-stilled love I had once felt for the father of my child? Or was it something much more in the present, concerned with the man who had just departed but whose sharp, male scent yet hung on the night air in my room?

Sleep teased me with a dance but did not settle on me until light oozed through the crack between the shutters, which I had closed against the chill night wind. And with the dim light came the rain.

20

Storms over France

When I descended the staircase the next morning, I was thoroughly out of sorts. The servant's knock on the door had come just after I had fallen into a deep sleep, or so it seemed. I mumbled from under the bedcovers, but the voice on the other side of the door responded sharply. I realized that it was William and rolled out of bed, but by the time I opened the door, he was nowhere in sight. The voice had been peremptory. He obviously wanted me to make ready with speed for the day's journey. He must have his martial-commander mask on this morning, I thought grimly, preparing myself for a long, tiring ride.

The weather matched my mood. Gone was the sun of the past few days. As I reached the lower stairs, I could feel the sharp air and see, through the open door, the mists and fog rolling in.

William stood at the bottom of the stairs, true to form, busily directing servants and knights. There seemed to be an increase in the number of men rushing in and out of the receiving hall. Of course, I thought, he must have brought his own party with him when he arrived yesterday. Slipping out for my adventures last evening and returning late, I would not have seen them.

He cast an impersonal glance my way, and the incipient smile faded on my lips. Gone was any sign of the familiar, almost teasing quality of his exit from my room last evening. Gone also the air of intimacy that overhung our entire conversation as we sat at the old wooden table in my chamber. Now he was someone else, our leader, the head of these men, arranger of safe houses, a mysterious knight/monk. Today he was in total control and out of my realm entirely. He merely gave me a curt nod and a few words.

"Break your fast now, please, *Princesse*. We leave within the hour." His tone was brusque. Without waiting for any response from me, he turned to a small circle of four knights and began speaking.

I wandered into the dining hall and experienced a household in chaos. Servants ran to and fro, packing dishes, putting linens in chests. I sat at the only place with a *serviette*, and someone suddenly materialized with bread and a cup of mulled wine. A few minutes later, some apples and a bowl of cooked grain, accompanied by warm almond milk in a pitcher, appeared at my elbow.

I ate in silence, which was in truth the only option open to me, since even the squires rushing through the room did not pause to speak to me. When I returned to my room, I saw that the servants had packed my few belongings in saddlebags that had appeared from nowhere. The room was newly made up and looked for all the world as if no one had slept in it for months.

I glanced around for the drawings I had made in my stay here and spied them next to the saddlebags, rolled carefully so as not to break the stiff vellum, and wrapped in a leather thong. Someone had taken care with my belongings, no doubt at William's direction. He seemed always to get things done right. It was almost tiresome.

The door to my chamber was standing open as I surveyed my baggage. Petronella appeared in the doorframe and lowered her head as she curtsied. When she rose, to no surprise of mine, she still gazed at the floor.

I spoke first, as I suspected she would not have the courage to start after her betrayal of my whereabouts the previous night.

"So it is Petronella, is it?" I put my hands on my hips like any common fishwife ready to deliver a round scolding. "Come back to the scene of your crime, have you?" The young woman looked up as I spoke, her features assuming a quizzical expression.

"I only tried to serve milady," she said, all innocence.

"It's true you served me right well with clothes, yester e'en, but it appears you did not do as well with my confidence. I instructed you to tell no one I was going into the village, but lo, Master William knew right where to find me when he had a mind to do it. Now, who do you suppose provided the confidential information that allowed him to find me so quick?"

"Your pardon, Your Grace. In truth, I did tell Sir William where you had gone. But you did not forbid me to tell Sir William that you had ridden into town." Although the young woman had not moved from the spot where she'd made her first curtsy, she tossed her head pertly and twirled her hand with each point, so that I thought for a minute she might break into a dance. "You only said not to tell the knights below." She pursed her lips as if to take further thought on the matter.

"And anyways"—now she raised a forefinger to make a point—"I only told Sir William because he asked me if I knew where you were. I was bound in honor not to lie to him. Sir William is in the house in place of my master, Sir Armand Montjoie. I am bound to obey my master, as my husband. So I am bound to obey him who comes in my master's place." Having delivered herself of this questionable piece of logic, Petronella seemed to take heart, for she looked at me right boldly with her round saucer eyes. I was surprised to see no pleading in them. The independence I so admired earlier now annoyed me no end. After all, I was a *princesse royale*. And who was this peasant to talk of honor? Monks running around commanding armies, peasants thinking they had honor to protect. The entire world was in disarray.

Then I saw the humor in her and, indeed, in my very own self for being so serious about such a small matter. "Well, well. I suppose you did what you thought right. There was no great harm done. And I thank you for the clothes and for the potion you brought for my *maladie*."

I had intended to dismiss her by my tone and started to turn away, but she continued to stand just inside the doorway. Suddenly I had an inspiration.

"Petronella, I will give you a chance to redeem yourself."

"How, mistress?" She eyed me carefully, as if I might be a dangerous spider.

"Sir William has some letters of mine. We were discussing them last evening, and he went off with them by mistake. They are in a leather pouch wound with a black thong, among his things. You might fetch them for me if you would." I hesitated. "No need to trouble Sir William. He's down in the courtyard organizing our journey. But I'm certain his things have not been taken down yet."

I rummaged in my pocket and brought out a silver coin, which I offered her. When she demurred, I said, "It's all right. I just want to read the letters once again. Sir William and I are traveling together, and I will return them while on the journey."

She, frowning slightly, reached out to take the silver.

"I'll wait here," I said. William's rooms were close to mine, and it took Petronella only a few minutes to retrieve my letters. When she came, she carried something else.

"*Princesse*," she said as she handed me the letters, "you will need an extra cloak for your trip to the south. This is a false spring we have had these few days. It may be very cold still, even in the Limousin." She held out the cloak, which I saw was a very fine one made of Brabant wool.

"But we're not going—" I stopped. Was I truly about to discuss my travel plans with a servant? That mandrake root John's men forced on me must have affected my mind.

"Thanks to you, then, Mistress Petronella." I took the cloak she offered and put it on. In truth, I had felt a chill from the moment I had seen the rising mists through the windows. Perhaps I should lay aside my testiness and simply be grateful. I inclined my head, and at last she seemed content to go, but only after one more elaborate curtsy.

When I joined William on the circle in front of the manor, I was pleased to see that the spotted palfrey I had ridden from Wiltshire had been made ready for me. Blankets were strapped, and even as I prepared to mount, I saw my bags placed on another horse. A servant came to place his hand for my mounting, and I swung easily up.

"Where is the rest of the party?" I asked, edging my horse near to William. Although there were many men milling about in the courtyard, I saw that only William was mounted.

"We travel lightly this time," he said, waving impatiently at a small party cantering around the corner of the mews toward us. I could make out the auburn hair of my young friend François, Roland's dark head, and another young man whose face I did not recall seeing previously.

"Where is Tom?" I asked, suddenly realizing I had not seen him since our arrival at the Montjoie mansion. "What's happened to Tom of Caedwyd?"

"Tom is gone," William responded, reining in his fiery horse with some effort. The horse was clearly in a hurry to be on its way, but William was a match for it.

"Without my leave?" I reached over and placed my hand on his bridle, to get his attention. It was a risky gesture, part presumptuous and part proprietary. We were quite close now, our horses dancing lightly in an effort not to collide. "He is loaned to my service, after all." William's head snapped my way, but he made no effort to remove my hand from his bridle. He eyes narrowed somewhat.

"*Princesse*, I sent Tom to Fontrevault." He spoke in a low voice, with some urgency, which struck me as odd. "I'm sorry I could not ask your permission first. He was the only man I could send, the only one I could be certain would get through. He will catch up with us after tomorrow, and he will be sore tired and in need of sleep by then, I'll wager."

"Why did you send him to Fontrevault?" My suspicions were rising. Recalling Petronella's words, I feared I already knew his answer. "We're not going to the abbey after all, are we?"

"Not today. By your leave, *Princesse*, we are going south to Poitou. John has men surrounding Fontrevault. He knows that you will travel there to see Eleanor, if you think she is at the abbey. He lies in wait for you."

"But . . ."

Now William did remove my hand from his reins and placed it gently back on my own horse. "However, he will be surprised. The queen isn't at the abbey as he thinks. She is in the ducal palace in Poitiers. Tom will bring us information there about the number of men at Fontrevault and whether John himself is among them. We ride south to see Eleanor. If we can make our destination this evening, and there is a hot dinner waiting, perhaps I will have time to explain all."

"But why does John want to capture me again? He had me once. He knows I know nothing."

"It's not you he's after. You just happen to be included in the party." William wheeled away from me with those words, and Roland, as if on cue, rode up beside me. I found the young clerk François on my other side, and they set me a good pace. I couldn't have lagged behind if I had desired it.

21

Against All Odds

It was long past sundown when we rode into Poitiers. Spring had come to the south. I could hear the birds coo-cooing in the trees and the heavy, seductive smell of blossoms was everywhere. Poitiers, where I had spent the brief years that bridged childhood and womanhood. Poitiers, where I had been close to Eleanor and closer still to Richard. And where Henry had been, mercifully, absent.

We had changed horses three times, stopped for bread and cheese and a flagon of ale at a rude country inn, and then, riding pell-mell onward, achieved our destination after nightfall. It was not the four-hour ride to Fontrevault I had intended to make when I rose that morning!

Although my backside was sore, I discovered, when I finally dismounted in the court-yard of some inn William had chosen just inside the city walls, that my hip no longer pained me as it had at the beginning of my long journey to Canterbury. God's throat! Was I recovering my bodily youth in all this mindless dashing about?

I was bone tired; there was no question of that. But not so tired that I had any intention of sleeping before William gave up his secrets. There was something yet to be discovered, some piece of information he had almost let go of the previous evening, in our intense conversation. I intended to discover it.

This newest dwelling was yet another surprise. From the stone mansion in Wiltshire to the stone mansion in the Loire to a stone inn in the Limousin, there were only differences of magnitude, not style.

With this house William had surprised me well. Fires burned in the grate in the hall, and the innkeeper came forward right quickly to serve our needs. Pleasant, clean maidservants appeared to direct us to pleasant, clean rooms.

But it quickly became apparent to me that, although it seemed a substantial inn, our party made up the sum total of the guests. I had noted that only two grooms came forward to lead our horses to the mews; no shouts were heard in the courtyard once we were safely indoors. In short, there was a phantomlike quality about this place that made me uneasy.

I found fresh water in my basin and so washed the dust of my travels from me. As I was drying my face, I noted the spaciousness of the room. A large bed was set against one corner, covered with furs and tapestries that seemed too rich for a simple village inn. In another corner a square table, unusually large for a chamber table, stood. I noticed that it had a linen cloth on it, candles, and those clever new forks from Italy again.

The floor, too, in this room was not covered with rushes, as one might expect. A multitude of woven rugs, of the kind Philippe had brought back from *Outremer,* made a soft carpet underfoot. When the knock on the door came, I was not surprised that William opened it before I gave permission. Nor was I particularly surprised that behind him came three servants bearing steaming bowls of hot soup, then the white bean cassoulet of the kind they are fond of in the south, followed by platters of legumes, roast birds, bread and wine and cakes. William motioned them toward the table, looking at me.

"Supper," he announced, rather unnecessarily.

"So I see."

"I thought it would be more"—he hesitated—"private to have supper in your chambers." He glanced my way with unusual delicacy.

"I didn't notice the common rooms overflowing with people."

"No, but our party makes up seven. The others would take their meal with us were we downstairs. This way we can talk."

"Is there serious news, then?" I moved to the garderobe and threw the door open. "Now, why did I suppose I would find clothes here to fit me?"

He didn't reply, but I saw a half smile twitch at the corner of his mouth.

I pulled out a wool robe much fresher than the one I wore and disappeared behind the side of the giant armoire. Tossing off one garment, I slipped the other on, reflecting once again upon how easily one may be refreshed when one is traveling.

When I reappeared, William was standing, looking at some documents. I had no idea how they had appeared.

"Come, Alaïs. Have your supper while it is hot. The servants have gone to some trouble to prepare dishes worthy of a princess."

"Other than having no information on where I am going next, being thwarted at every turn when I try to go someplace myself, having my letters purloined, having my chambers ransacked not once but twice, and being kept in the dark about King John's intentions, Queen Eleanor's intentions, and your true identity, my least complaint on this journey would be about cold food."

He didn't glance up from his reading.

I sat down, and William absentmindedly seated himself across the table once again, still reading. He paused to pour the wine, then finally put the papers down to offer me the dishes, one by one. I was struck by the ease we had now developed with each other when we were alone, almost as if we were man and wife in some small cottage taking our evening meal in the silence of our long familiarity. First the cassoulet, then the legumes, then the bowl that held something unidentifiable but which might be hare in cheese sauce. Probably from Wales.

"So now that we have achieved this much-desired privacy you speak of, suppose you tell me the rest of the story," I said, taking the dishes one by one with my good hand as he passed them.

"Starting with . . . ?" He began to tuck in to his soup.

"Starting with today." I sharpened my voice, and he looked up. "Why are we here, William? Oh, perhaps we came here because John's men have ringed Fontrevault and we can't get past them without capture. No, I forgot." I snapped my fingers, as if making a great discovery. "John doesn't want me. It's someone else in our party he seeks. Let me guess." I pulled an exaggerated grin. "I know. It's you! King John is tired of your pranks and irritated because you had me freed from Sarum. And anyway, Hugh Walter wants you back at Canterbury, not dashing around Normandy spending the order's hard-taxed money. So John wants to capture you to aid Hugh Walter!"

William shook his head, smiling faintly as if I were a dim-witted child he would humor.

"No? Then let me guess again," I continued, preferring the game I'd started to that intimate silence that had pervaded the room earlier. To complicate matters, William finally noticed when he passed me the dishes that I had to put them down in order to serve myself, since I have the use of only one hand. When he saw me place the cassoulet and begin to spoon out the beans, he quickly took the spoon from me. He served me himself, reaching across the table as if it were the most natural thing in the world. I could feel my color rising.

"Or . . . let me think. It is myself after all, isn't it? Both king and the abbot agreed you could have me. It will make less trouble if I am out of England. So you've decided to hold me here for a well-deserved ransom from my brother. No again? You are shaking your head. Then, if it isn't you and it isn't me, we must be fleeing because John is after one of our other knights." I talked faster now, my words tumbling out. "How about Roland? Could John make him a pawn in a game with the French court? No, I think not. Not Roland. He's not important enough."

"Please eat, Alaïs. You have not taken food all day." William spoke quietly, making the echo of my mindless chatter sound even sillier.

I picked up my fork and began. The food was truly savory. The southern people create the best cooking on the Continent. Eleanor always said so. Eating distracted me for a moment, and I realized how my appetite had risen as a result of the day's ride. But then the silence created discomfort, and I began again.

"So it must be another person. I have it!" I produced my most brilliant smile, with some effort. "It must be young François. He of the red hair and the scholarly background and the actor's aspirations. François, the Body of the 'Debate between the Body and the Soul.' John wants him for his court jester."

William wasn't laughing now, only staring at me.

"What, William?" I joked, taking a draft of wine and returning my attention to my plate. "Why aren't you laughing? You don't want your young clerk to be considered more valuable than you as a prize? Then, perhaps, explain to me: Who is John laying traps for now?"

After a moment of his silence, I looked up from addressing the hare to find a strange expression settled over my companion's face. I removed my wounded hand from the table, where I had carelessly placed it, to my lap and watched him. My heart raced, as ever it did when I suspected he would confront me.

"I'm going to tell you something that may be difficult for you to accept. I would prefer to give you this information in the form of a story. I don't want you to ask any questions until I am finished. That's the only way I can do this. Is that agreeable to you?"

"That sort of introduction is hardly reassuring."

"Will you stop sparring and let me tell this my way?" For the first time in this conversation, he voiced the impatience I read in his expression.

"All right," I said, suddenly willing to pay any price to end the game.

William stopped twirling his wine goblet between his thumb and his forefinger. He placed his elbows on the table and his chin on his joined hands. His eyes locked with mine.

"Last evening I told you a story, about Henry's anger when I challenged him over his behavior toward you. I didn't tell you the complete story of those years." William pushed his plate, still full, aside. "I didn't tell you what happened after we had the quarrel."

"I remember. He struck you. You had a bloody tongue, but it was because you bit it in the course of the event."

"So you *do* listen to me." But no smile appeared. "There was more of consequence that happened." A slight pause as he seemed to gather his forces. I was very still.

"About three days later, the king summoned me. He had decided on my punishment. I was to be the one to whom he would entrust his sacred errand." A pause. A draft of wine, followed by a brief throat clearing.

"He wanted me to take a child—a special child—to a place he had arranged. For safekeeping."

My heart began to throttle my ribs. I couldn't bring my hand from my lap to my goblet, though I longed for some wine.

"Of course the child was dead." I said it more to reassure myself that the world was as I had known it these many years than from any certainty that what I said was true. "It should not have been so difficult." I forced myself to speak, as if forcing my body through a narrow chink in a prison wall. "A small, inert bundle should not be so much to dispose of." The picture of the little dead white dog at Sarum flashed before my eyes.

"No, the child was not dead." He folded his hands on the table and leaned forward. I felt a vertigo. To keep my balance, I fastened on his large onyx ring glinting in the candlelight. Then my mind went blank, and it was with difficulty that I brought it back to the sound of William's voice, moving on inexorably, telling a story I could scarcely bear to hear.

"There were three of us, two knights and myself. Our errand was kept a secret from the rest of the court, except for only four of the king's counselors, who were sworn to secrecy."

"Was William Marshal among them?" I heard myself ask it and then thought how odd that I should focus on that small piece. Would I feel betrayed if he had known all these years, or would I feel grateful?

William glanced down momentarily, then up. "I think you should ask *him* that question." He had a worn look about the eyes, wrinkles at their sides I had not noticed earlier in the evening, as if the conversation itself and not the long ride were suddenly tiring him. "But you must know all four of Henry's chief ministers were absolutely trustworthy."

"It's no matter now. So many seem to have known the information I should have had, and kept it from me."

"Henry had many reasons for what he did." William took a deep breath and spoke his next lines more slowly. "The safety of the realm was at stake. He also thought the babe would not be safe from his sons."

"Oh, surely not Richard!" I exploded in spite of myself.

"Perhaps not Richard," he said gently. "But John was certainly suspect. In spite of the fact that Henry loved him, he was not blind to John's deeply flawed character."

"Yes, we've seen what John is capable of."

"And remember, since the years in Poitiers, where Eleanor conspired against him with Louis and her sons, Henry never trusted any of them. He knew that your child could become a pawn of Louis as well as those of his own house."

"Do you think he made the right decision?" I was speaking in a contained way. I'm certain I sounded like any woman of my station who could be having a casual conversation with a friend. My heartbeat was slowing, too, as if I had absorbed the news right into my blood and that blood was thickening it as we spoke.

Again that quick, downward look, so curious in a man of William's social skills and courage. It was almost a gesture of withdrawal, but then he corrected it, as before, with the direct stare right into the center of my eyes.

"Yes, best for the child, if not for you. And it was the child who was at risk, after all." William seemed to breathe easier, as if things would be all right now. The moment for me to make a scene had passed. And it was that breath, exhaled ever so slightly, that undid my careful control.

"And you took the child where?" I asked, my voice elevating with each clipped word. "To Yorkshire to the sheep farmers, to have it raised on gruel and working the fields? My son? Whilst I was told he was dead?" Anger rose in me like fire, pushing me to my feet. I looked around for something, anything, to give vent to my rage. The wineglass came to hand, and I cast it against the hearth with all my strength. The shattering glass sounded like a hundred bells. I felt my anger—indeed, perhaps my whole spirit—splinter with that sound, and I sank back into my chair.

I tried to speak, but my voice emerged in globs, like clotted blood. I don't even know where the words came from.

"You fuck . . . fucking men! All of you! How co-could you do that to a . . . to a young girl . . . ?"

He half stood and reached to put his hand on my arm, but I wrenched away from him.

"Don't touch me! Don't you dare to touch me, you bastard! You are a corps of bastards, you and the king and William Marshal and Richard and John—all of you!"

"Richard had nothing to do with this." I heard the eminently reasonable voice, and I flung myself out of my chair and across the room to the bed, where I lay sobbing as if the world had split me in two. The child had lived, and no one had told me.

He sank back into his chair and neither spoke nor moved, which was a good thing. I could do neither myself. But through the pain and rage I was feeling, one thought struggled upward in me, one thought that ran counter to the anger I was feeling, one thought I knew I must grasp, but I could scarcely turn toward it: The child had lived.

William waited. After a bit I wore down, of course, as he knew I would. I raised myself up on one elbow, to see the fire burning low. He had not replenished it.

"Get out," I said. It was not a very effective command, as my voice broke in the middle. "God's teeth! Get out before I kill you!"

"Alaïs." He planted his fist on the table hard, and the dishes jumped. "Do you want to hear the rest of the story, or do you want to continue to have a temper tantrum like a child?"

I opened my mouth to scream, a release that would still my rage for one more moment.

Suddenly he was standing over the bed, grabbing my shoulders and hauling me upward, shaking me to the core. "I'm telling you the child lives, even now! Doesn't that mean anything to you? Can't you stop your idiot's wailing long enough to understand? You have a grown son!"

I nearly swooned as he threw me back against the heaped pillows of the bed. "So if you can stop behaving like a frantic child over something that happened all those years ago, maybe you can start to enjoy something that can happen today or, to be more exact"—now he was turning away, speaking over his shoulder as he moved back toward the fire—"tomorrow, since today seems to be nearly past."

I said nothing, and he seemed to take encouragement from the silence.

"I'm going to finish the story, Alaïs." He resumed speaking as he stood now, his back to the fire, his hands clasped behind him, still watching me. "Where do you think we took the child?"

I thought back over the past weeks and saw only the face that haunted me, picked at me. The face of the young secretary, the face I knew but could not place. And like lightning it struck me with full force as another image, that of a woman long dead, rose before me.

"Mathilda?" I said in a breath that still had a sob in it.

"Mathilda," I repeated as I slowly sat up.

"Exactly," he said, rocking back on his heels, his voice as pleased as if I had just guessed an important riddle and won a golden apple.

"You took him to Mathilda. She raised him in Anjou. Of course, he has her face. The very face of his grandmother stamped right on him, that diamond face, the auburn hair, the quick tongue. Even his mannerisms are like hers." I thought of the way he'd used his hands when he talked that night during supper at the inn, his habit of tossing his head when he laughed. I did not add what we both knew:

that his mannerisms might have been like mine instead, if I'd had him near me while he grew.

But no, not the face, never the face. He did not have my face. His was a face destined to be the Empress Mathilda's face. The delicate-boned but stern face of William the Conqueror's grand-daughter, the German emperor Henry's child widow, the wife of Geoffrey of Anjou. The face of the mother-in-law Eleanor of Aquitaine could hardly bear to look on, the only woman whose presence could dominate a room even when Eleanor was in it. King Henry's mother's face.

Empress Mathilda, wife of Geoffrey of Anjou, who created a civil war that raged throughout England as she tried to wrest the crown from her cousin Stephen. That hard-as-an-awl expression now transformed into the artistic, scintillating, chameleonlike face of her grandson, my own child. François.

"But wasn't there scandal? What did people say? There was never a whisper across the Channel." I had begun to hiccup lightly, but I managed to squeeze out my words as I looked up to William.

"Of course not. She put it about that the boy was a bastard of one of Henry's younger brothers." He smiled. "They were such hellions, the only question asked was, where were the rest? Mathilda was elderly when he came to her, but indomitable. She oversaw his early education and, I believe, showed him much affection. More, perhaps, than she ever showed her own sons. In fact, it is said her last words were to ask after the child's well-being."

I rolled off the bed and limped back to the table, sinking into the chair opposite where William had been sitting. He followed and stood across from me, the fire flickering behind him. His face now fell into a shadow.

"A story very much like your own. When William Marshal brought you to Rouen," I said with incipient suspicion. "Are you . . . ?"

"Don't let your imagination run off with you." He shook his head, that habitual flicker of amusement flitting across his face. "I am no natural son of any important personage. Not even, I am sad to report, the natural son of William Marshal. Although I know some have said so. I was old enough to remember my life with my parents before they were killed." He stopped for a moment then, resumed his chair across from me, watching me now all the time. His hands now resting on the table were linked, as if to keep them still, as mine had been earlier. His eyes seemed strangely bright.

"I came home from the fields to find my house burning and Henry's soldiers tearing through the village. If William Marshal had not seen me trying to rush into our flaming cottage and pulled me up on his horse as he cantered past, I would have died also."

"And François . . . who named him?"

"Mathilda." He added, whimsically, "What would you have named him, Alaïs?"

"I would have called him Henry." A grin was begging to spread on my water-sogged face.

"Oh, *mirabile dictu!*" William threw back his head and hooted like a peasant. "That would no doubt have contributed to the child's safety all through his life! Young Henry was still living then. He would have had fits to have a bastard brother with the same name. And your father, Louis. Could you picture his face when he heard? His older daughter married to the heir of the English throne named Henry and his rebel younger daughter bearing a bastard named Henry, a by-blow of her sister's father-in-law!"

"Yes, it would have stirred everyone up, for certain. That's why I thought of it."

"It was probably when you made that suggestion that Henry decided to send the child away." He seemed to have relaxed in the past few minutes, daring even this small, if risky, jest. "If you're not going to throw any more goblets or have another fit, I suggest we get back to the business of our dinner." He gestured broadly to the feast before us.

"I find I have lost my appetite through your news. But don't let me hold you back," I said, settling deeper into my chair.

"Thank you, I won't," he said, suddenly interested in the partridge again. And he began tearing it apart, using his strong fingers to make almost delicate motions. "After all, I bring you news of life, not of death. What you had lost many years ago, you now have found. That is cause for celebration, not grief."

"It's obvious to me you never bore—nor lost—a child," I said, unwilling to let go of my tremendous resentment quite yet. "Still, you have reason on your side, if not feelings. I was forced to give up my child and all my hopes for his future."

William glanced at me again, but this time not in challenge or apprehension. Only with kindness, which I had not expected. "But he is back. Against all odds he has come back to you." He extended his hand toward mine across the table but made no attempt to touch me.

"A boy who lost his mother can understand a mother who has lost her boy," he said gently, the glimmer returning to his eyes. "I do understand. And I do not mean to make light of what happened or my own part in it. Only to say the past is done. It is the future that is important. And you have that before you, with all its choices."

"Yes, I do have choices." I began to play with my food again. As if reading my mind, he filled another glass with the red Bordeaux. As he did so, I noticed again the black onyx ring on his left hand, a curious and somewhat familiar ring. "You asked me last evening if I wanted François attached to my household?"

"You have probably discerned with that knifelike wit of yours that it is no accident that François has been of the party that has accompanied you these past few days. I wanted you to be together. If you took to each other, I hoped you might be reunited, in whatever way you liked."

"Does he . . . ?"

"He knows nothing about you, except what he has heard from others about the very difficult *Princesse* Alaïs Capet, sister of the king of France."

"Am I known to be difficult, then?"

"Across four countries. Empress Mathilda herself has—or rather had—no more prickly reputation."

I could not suppress a chuckle at that news and was rewarded by a look that created a different sort of bond between us. "You would know how difficult Mathilda was only if you had worked for Henry. She was the single person, besides Eleanor, who could drive him into towering rage when she was a thousand leagues away. A letter would do it."

He paused. Then he put his fork down to say this, giving me his full attention: "François is very much like you. When I rode into Chinon the other night, I wasn't collecting one renegade but two. He had no permission to leave the Montjoie *château*, not from Earl Graham his commander, nor from me. He was a runaway, like you. You will suit each other well if you take him on." He wiped his mouth with a *serviette*. "I would make only the suggestion that he first might be loaned to your household temporarily. You could get to know each other. Afterward you can tell him whatever you wish about yourself."

"Does Canterbury have any claim on him?"

"No more than myself. He has been attached to the monastery only as a clerk and only for his studies. He has never joined the community."

"No more a monk than yourself," I repeated softly. "Yes, well, now we come to it, don't we? The very difficult and the very mysterious William of Caen. Of the many Williams I have seen, who is the true William of Caen?"

William became reabsorbed in the task of tearing his partridge, giving it far more attention than it demanded. I continued.

"How is it you can play at being prior of Canterbury, can summon servants to open closed houses at the snap of your fingers, can commission fine dinners of many courses in a day's time, can arrange for money, for escapes, for horses, for men? How is it you have more sources of information than does the king of France, more information about the movements of the king of England than his queen mother does? Explain this to me." I paused, then added in a quiet voice, "How is it you have maintained secret possession of my son for lo these many years, and not only did I not know of it but it seems no one else knew either?"

He dipped his hands into the finger bowl, then wiped them and pushed his plate aside. He considered me for some time. I was not certain at first that he would answer my question or even treat it with respect. And although I am not in the habit of fearing men, there was a glint in his eyes that reminded me of a scimitar Philippe had brought back from Turkey: a glance that was fine, sharp, and dangerous. But then he spoke, and my fears fled.

"I made a promise. I have kept it to the best of my ability." His words were quiet but clear.

"A promise to whom? About what?" But I already knew.

"I promised Henry I would be the guardian of the child. And that if the child lived, and you lived, someday I would reunite you."

My breath and my voice failed me for the second time that night. William saw it but continued, in a voice for once lacking all irony. "As I was trying to tell you earlier, it was days after our quarrel, after I had confronted him about his relationship with you, when he called me in to tell me I was to take the babe to Anjou. The babe was not yet born, but he had settled on this plan."

"And what did the king have to say, exactly, when he called you to tell you this?" I felt a need to participate in this story, if only by asking questions.

"He said if I was so concerned about this babe, and about its mother, I could take the responsibility." A fleeting smile passed over his face. "I suppose it's no consolation to you now, but he cared deeply, for both you and the babe. He could see that the situation was impossible and the babe in great danger of becoming someone's pawn. Or worse, someone's victim. The list of suspects who might use him was long."

"But why you?"

William eased his large frame out of his chair again. I was beginning to realize that every time there was a difficult part to our conversation, I could count on William to start pacing. It was an effective technique to avoid eye contact.

"He trusted me. From the time I was a young student in his household, he had chosen me for his secretary. For what reason, I don't know."

"Well," I said, trying to be helpful, "you were terribly bright as a child. Henry liked people around who thought quickly and had the right answers." I paused. "Funny. We royal children hated you when we were small. You showed us all up at our lessons. And you were such a strange little dark-haired thin person, always ducking your head when someone spoke to you."

He had reached the far wall with his pacing and turned to come back toward me. I was aware of his height, his broad, somewhat bent shoulders, that strong face, not ducking now. I thought he might be angry, but as he came closer, I saw that he was not.

"Some children grow more slowly than others," he said thoughtfully. "I was young and shy for a long time. Henry saw what I might become. And at the end, when he gave me my assignment of the child's care, he thought I was up to it." He looked at me. "He knew also that I cared deeply for you." A heartbeat passed between us.

"Cared for me?" I forced myself now to lightness of tone, though I could feel a flush rising.

"Why else would I have had the temerity to lecture the king about his treatment of his young mistress?"

"I remember you at Oxford. I always thought I read disapproval in your eyes, for my relationship with the king."

He shook his head slowly. "I thought you were so beautiful, with your raven hair and green eyes, that you had somehow a timeless look in the midst of your vibrant youth. And I was fascinated by your wit that flashed like silver, used on anyone who crossed you. Even Henry was not exempt from your sharp, funny gibes." William paused, then said more softly, "I always thought that you should have been Richard's wife and queen of England. And when I saw that Henry had been unable to resist the opportunity to have you himself instead, it seemed to me a dreadful injustice." He shook his head at some private thought.

"What else, then?" I asked.

"Truth to tell—and with the advantage of viewing the situation now from age and maturity—I was probably only jealous of the king." He had stopped pacing and stood, hands clasped behind his back, scanning my face. It demands effort to give no reaction in such circumstances, and I managed it only by looking down at my cold hare, now hopelessly congealed in its cheese.

William abruptly sat down opposite me. "You must forgive me for my arrogance at that time. Of course, I know now it was always your life, not for me to say what should or should not be for you. And truly, a grand passion, one such as I now understand you and Henry had for each other . . . Perhaps if such a passion arrives for someone, it is worth every sacrifice—even a crown."

"Even a child?" I could barely speak. Then, without waiting, for the question was more for myself, I spoke again. "You may be right about grand passion." A light danced in his eyes again, no more than the reflection of the torches. "Have you had such a grand passion, Sir William? Is it unrequited love, then, that drove you into a life of celibacy?"

He didn't respond, his face grave. I checked my tongue, of a sudden afraid of what he might say, and switched to a lighter topic. "And how did you manage to carry off your many disguises? Did the monks at Canterbury know you were not one of them as you sat in Hugh Walter's chair?" I couldn't keep the dry edge from my voice. I, who so prided myself on observation as an artist, had been thoroughly hoodwinked.

"Most did. They didn't care. As long as I was appointed as the abbot's vicar, they accepted me. I lived often at Canterbury over the years. I have taken Hugh Walter's place before. When I was there, the monks would invite me to participate in the liturgical ceremonies. I did so on high feast days, but I always chose not to consecrate the host, since I myself have not been consecrated into that priestly service."

"But there must be some reason you gained such acceptance in a community when you are not even ordained? Not even, it seems, a permanent member of the community."

William once again pushed his chair away from the table, propping his feet against a table leaf and crossing his hands easily behind his head, as if resting his back.

"You asked me some questions about my past several nights ago. Canterbury is a part of that past. I was attached to Canterbury as a young man, first for studies because I was of Becket's household, and then, during Becket's exile, I was sent there because Henry wanted me even better educated. But I never chose holy orders. Henry had other plans for me."

"Let me guess," I said unnecessarily. "The Order of the Knights of the Holy Temple." I was relieved that our conversation had left the personal and reverted to the much safer topic of politics. "You were among the men Henry sent to the Knights after Avranches."

He showed no surprise but instead responded genially. "Yes, I've been a Knight Templar since I was twenty years of age. I was terrified when Henry sent me, but it didn't turn out so badly. I became a member of the Order of Templars in the king's stead and am so to this day." He paused. "In a way, in the early years, I was Henry's eyes and ears within the Templars."

"You were a spy?" I was nonplussed. Would the revelations never end?

"Oh, not exactly that. The Templars knew I was Henry's man. But it suited everyone to have that alliance. And when Henry would call me back into service, the Knights were happy to lend me to him. Or perhaps it was the other way around."

I shook my head. The arrangement made me dizzy. I didn't want to probe further. I had no idea what Aristotle or Marcus Aurelius would say about the ethics of all this.

"But can you deny that the Templars have now decided finally to bring John's term as king to a close? And to use whatever means at hand to do it?"

His feet fell to the floor, and the chair made a clatter as it, too, hit the wood. His surprise was genuine. "Who told you that?"

"I've surmised it from all the responses that have come from everyone every time the conflict between John and the Templars comes up. And trust me, it has come up with wild frequency nearly every time someone addresses me! You and my aunt Charlotte hinted at it, and Isabelle, John's queen, also in the tower. And then William Marshal, at Sir Roger's estates. When he told me you were a Templar,"—I pushed away from the table and stood up, looking at him steadily—"he also warned me of you. He said I had stumbled into the middle of the quarrel between the Templars and John and that either side would use me for its own ends, including even yourself."

"William Marshal knows better than that." The flat of William's hand hit the table. "He must be losing his wits in his old age. He knows I would guard you from harm, no matter what the political intrigue. It's true that I am a Templar. Their grand master in England. But that has no bearing on my intentions toward you."

I stood looking down at him, torn between my doubt and my need to believe. Suddenly I was distracted. I recalled where I had seen such a ring before. On the finger of my uncle at the inn at Havre.

"That is the very ring of the Templars, is it not?"

He looked startled. "How do you know that?"

I pressed forward. "And now do you answer my question, for this surely has to do with me. Do the Templars intend throwing John off the throne of England and replacing him with my son?"

William rose and faced me, forcing me to look up to him. "I am bound by blood oath to Henry to protect François. I would never allow him to be used as a pawn by the Templars or anyone else." He reached across the table and grabbed my wrist, only the second time he had touched me in haste. "Do you understand me?"

Then he loosed his fingers, and I pulled my hand away.

"Then how did—"

"England must not have another civil war. The cost is too great. All sensible men know that. But it will have such a war if John doesn't stop raiding the treasuries of the great abbeys to pay for his ill-designed adventures in northern France." He sat again, as if he had discovered a momentary lapse of manners in his lunge toward me.

"But how did John get information that my son was living?" I spoke so intensely that my teeth barely parted. "How could he have known? It must be from the Templars."

Now it was William's turn to confront me once again. "The Templars need not resort to using threats against children to manage their diplomacy. How do *you* suppose John learned of your son?" I didn't answer. He asked again. "Have you learned nothing in the past weeks to answer that question?"

"Eleanor?" I questioned first, in disbelief. Then repeated with absolute certainty, "Of course, Eleanor!"

William's face lightened. "Yes! Eleanor. She began this current stir by getting wind of the Templars' refusal to lend John any more money until he stopped pressuring the abbeys. She wrote John before she went to Spain, reviving all those rumors about the bastard Henry supposedly had with some southern princess. She told him she had information that the boy might have lived, that the Templars knew about this child, and that John should beware antagonizing them, for they might use the child against him. Apparently the news had an effect opposite to that intended, of settling John down. Instead, John set out to find the boy himself and put an end to the threat. You must remember," he added with his customary irony, "John frightens easily."

"But why did she send me to Canterbury? So John could kidnap me?"

"You'll have to ask her that, if we ever get to see her in person. The answer may be less draconian than you think. It may just be that she truly wanted her Becket letters and—just as she told you—thought you were the one person who could safely retrieve them. She must have known where Becket hid them years ago. That was his special altar, and that's where Henry's rogue knights found him in prayer when they came to kill him. She may have honestly thought that if the letters came to light, they would cast a further shadow over John's throne. Or that if John got his hands on them, he might do something foolish that would harm his own cause even more."

"Like revealing them to protect himself?"

"Exactly." Amusement spread across his face. "Or at the very least, embarrassing her in her older years."

I considered this information for a moment. "When did you find them?"

"About fifteen years ago. When we redid the masonry at the

side altars after the great fire." He grinned. "I always kept them myself, because I thought they might be useful someday. Charlotte knew I had them. So did a few others. She trusted me not to use them against the Plantagenet house. But she also knew I would not give them up without reason. They were one more check held against John's baser instincts."

"Or Eleanor's," I murmured. I looked at William as if seeing him for the first time. "Unlike John, you don't seem to have any fears, William of Caen."

It seemed as though he would speak, but he only shook his head slowly. Then, after a minute, he said, looking over my left shoulder as if he could see the past woven into the tapestries that hung behind me, "For years I had nightmares so severe I woke screaming, in a cold sweat. I had them when I was a child—a burning cottage, a clash of steel, the pounding of hooves. They increased when I was in *Outremer*, killing Saracens."

"And now?"

He looked at me. "They left me when you arrived at Canterbury."

There arose a silence so large that it seemed to take up all the available air. I waited until I could successfully breathe again.

"Templars are celibate."

"Ah, yes." He glanced heavenward, as if for aid. "That was the ideal of the founders. But things have changed in a hundred years. For some of us. We are now, after all, not defending citadels against infidels but managing the banking of Europe. Celibacy shrinks in importance."

"Are you, then, after all, no different than the old king?" I asked softly, fearing the answer.

"I am only a man, as King Harry was only a man. But it is different between you and me. We are grown now, not children. And we are of equal power. With me, now, you have a choice."

He reached across the table and this time took my hand gently in his. I felt my whole body stiffen. "Whatever your choice, *Princesse*, you cannot deny that the room is filled with angels at this moment."

He was right. Something in my heart was cracking open, so loudly I thought surely the sound, would expand beyond bearing. I let go his hand and stood, then walked slowly around the table. He followed my every step, until I was close enough to touch him. But of course I did not touch him. He rose yet made no move toward me, as if to give me one last chance to withdraw. But there are some times in our lives when we know we are carried forward on a tide larger than anything reason can explain. My last coherent thought was this: Why should I not, for once, follow my own desires?

As I moved to him, he opened his arms. My body drifted into his until I could feel no separation at all. His arms wound around me, pressing me to him, and his cheek rested upon my hair, and I heard him murmur softly, "A room filled with angels and a queen."

I made no move to stop him as he pulled the laces of my bodice and loosed my gown. Indeed, I helped him with my good hand, but still my fingers fumbled. His seemed quick and sure, and my gown slipped from me. When I stood in my chemise, he put me at arm's length. He seemed almost to drink me in, and I only knew that his body would welcome mine as mine would gladly host his. I stepped out of my chemise in an easy movement and began to undo his own shirt laces as he cast his doublet aside.

When we reached the bed, there seemed no more question of the past or the future. There was only the urgent present. Our first coupling was immediate, and when I felt him inside me, my body responded so quickly we rose to a climax within minutes. My breath mingled with his in perfect rhythm. Moments later I opened my eyes to find his open as well. I felt him still within me, and without pause we began again, more slowly and rhythmically. This time his hands moved over me, seeking those places that would make me moan with pleasure, and mine responded, wandering over the back of his body. We knew each other in a new way in those moments. And I heard him murmur, "*Caressa mia,*" over and over. Then we rested for some time, lying on our sides, talking of nothing but each other. And soon, in the manner of men, he led me back into our intimacy in new ways that pleased us both. And then it was my turn. My memory of the rest of the events of that night is clouded with both pleasure and release, for at last I had found my true wedding partner.

The storm outside that had built during the night did not abate until after dawn. Then a peacefulness descended. As I drifted off into sleep, I saw through the window the moon emerging from behind a cloud.

22

The Jewel's Value

It seemed only minutes later that I felt someone shaking me. I tried to respond, but I kept sinking back into sleep, reaching for the warmth I had felt beside me through the night.

The bed, however, was growing colder and the shaking of my shoulder more insistent. I opened one eye to find William, fully dressed for travel, sitting on the side of the bed.

"Why are you out there and not in here with me, taking your rightful due from me—yet again?" I murmured, stretching out my arm and encircling his thigh.

"Come, my wanton *princesse*. You must rise. We have an appointment."

"Appointment? I have nothing to do today." I rolled over and stretched my entire body as far north and south as it would go. "I am recovering from a long, stormy night wherein my sleep was disturbed constantly. And if you were any kind of gentleman"—I lifted my head over the featherbedding and leered—"you would follow the man who used me so and chastise him for keeping me awake so rudely."

"That man will never be caught. He has already been up for hours, written and sent off by courier six letters, seen that breakfast was laid for Your Grace, and given four sets of instructions on horses and our party for the day." He was back in his battle-commander mode, I could see.

"I can't help it if you are cursed with a need for activity, like a Sufi dervish," I replied, sitting up and wriggling under his arm, with some aid from him. "It's obvious that you have an imbalance of tempers. You must be choleric to be so active so early," and I pulled his hand to my cheek.

He only laughed and ran his fingers down under my gown and over my breast, and I felt my blood run. But then he moved gently away and left the bed.

"This will not be our only night, I promise you. It is our beginning. But the day has arrived, and we must attend to it. Come, lazy Highness. Take a look. The sun shines on all our enterprises."

He reached down and pulled me off the bed and toward the window with his hand around my waist, and, to tell the truth, I couldn't resist following. It occurred to me that I might regret making one so strong a familiar. But for now I enjoyed his lead.

He guided me to the window, where he threw open the shutters, making a great clatter. Outside, a recently drenched world seemed to sparkle in the welcoming sun. A riot of blooming flowers met my eyes. The royal purple of the bluet and the bright red coquelicot were growing wild, all over the border of the inn's courtyard. Casques de Jupiter grew beside the stables, I could see, and the bright yellow of gaillardes with their rust interior stood in clumps around the door to the inn, below my window.

I wondered how long it had been since I had noticed the brilliance of the color of flowers. How many spring seasons had passed since I had thought to count their names?

"You see, the world is busy. It has no time for slugabeds. Come, dress and breakfast with me."

"I'll have it as I am," I said, reaching for my robe to throw around me.

"As you will. But you may be embarrassed in front of the other knights and the servants," he said with great cheer.

"We'll not eat in this chamber?"

"Ah, no. I want you to breakfast with our little company. I want to see you lay eyes on François now that you know."

"Oh, God's breath." I pulled back, startled. The night of love-making had thrown into the background all thought of the conversation about François. "I don't know . . . perhaps it's best if I wait. . . ."

"Nonsense," William said, in that priorish way he had. "Come, they are waiting. And after I want you to accompany me to the House of Lyons."

"The financiers?"

"Yes. There are some transactions that require my approval." He paused, then stood once again, towering over me. "Alaïs, it's best if you don't postpone an encounter with François. Trust me on this." He regarded me with a grave expression, one that reminded me of him as I saw him at Canterbury. He must have seen something in my response that softened him. "But if you require time, know that he need not ride with us to the Lyons. We can make that journey alone, if you like."

I was touched. In spite of my resistance, I understood the wisdom of seeing my son without delay, before I had thoughts of avoiding it altogether. I nodded and turned to dress. William kissed the top of my head, smoothed my hair, and then left the room with that catlike walk of his. A moment later a gentlewoman appeared to help me with my toilette. Once again William had thought of everything, I realized, with mixed feelings.

The company looked up as I entered the breakfast room. They were still the same familiar faces, but now my gaze skimmed over Roland and the other young knight, whose name I kept forgetting, and came to rest on François. All of the young men were eating heartily, although as I entered, they scrambled to their feet. After they made cursory bows, I gestured for them to resume their seats. Their attention quickly returned to their meal.

I studied François from my place at the head of their small table. It was the same face I had watched for some days now, but I saw it newly. I looked for traces of Henry and found them shining through the now-obvious-to-me resemblance to Mathilda. How had I missed it? Although the face was diamond-shaped, the jaw had shadow lines of that definite square that all Henry's sons showed. That auburn hair was but a shade darker than the hair I remembered seeing on the king when I was a young girl. And those eyes, if one looked closely, although not Henry's icy, inscrutable gray, had the same steady gaze, which I saw now as he raised them to mine.

"Did you not enjoy the '*Débat entre le corps et l'esprit,*' Your Grace?" he was asking.

"Our night out in Chinon? Indeed I did. Are you looking for accolades for your performance?"

"But no, not exactly." Across his face, fleetingly, traveled that dry whisper of humor Henry would sometimes assume, the corners of his mouth held down to check the smile that sprang instead to his eyes. "We were debating the merits of acting when you came in. My comrades here believe that theater is a waste of time. They say that the only life worth living is that of the knight and fighting."

"It's true. The only honor in life for a man is to be a knight and fight for his liege," Roland said. I had forgotten how given to high-sounding pronouncements he was.

"That may be an honorable life," I replied, biting hard into the stiff brown bread, "but it's usually also the shortest." After I had chewed a morsel, I looked up to find them all watching me with expectation.

"You are all yet young. When you have seen the pallets dragged into the courtyard covered with men bleeding from fighting, as I have, you will not think the fighting life such high romance. And when it is your brother or your son, when you wish it could be you in his stead but it is not, the pain is even greater." They were very still.

"Besides," I added, attending to my food again with more interest than I felt, "acting is an honorable profession. Even the high-born are adept. I have never yet seen a king or queen of any consequence who was not a supremely confident actor."

William had come in behind me and heard only my last statement. He broke into laughter, and the tension lifted.

"You are all free for the day. The princess and I have business here in Poitiers. But report back tonight before dinner, for we may move early in the morning." William's directives were terse but popular. There were several huzzahs at the thought of a day for leisure, and the company broke up in good cheer.

William and I departed soon after. He set a good pace, and I kept up with him well, which I know pleased him. I thought would go immediately to the House of Lyons, but instead he took the road that skirted the city walls. I resisted the urge to question him and followed with untoward meekness.

I was troubled and had in mind to ask him certain questions when the time presented itself. Finally he pulled the horses up near a field and carefully picked his way into the woods that rimmed the road. He gestured for me to follow.

He had bread, of course, and cheese and good wine. We threw our cloaks onto the carpet of pine needles that welcomed us and sat in companionable silence, listening to the slight wind play the tree-tops like a lute. Truth to tell, although we had just spent the previous evening making love, I now felt close to him in some other way, as though he must know my thoughts.

After a silence, in which I leaned back against him matching the length of my legs to his, I began. "William, I would have some comment from you."

"On what matter?" He was still chewing the bread.

"What was the judgment on the man who died in the garden outside my guesthouse in Canterbury? Father Alcuin seemed to think it was a natural death."

"Not a foul death, if that's what you are thinking. My medical monks could find no marks on his body, nor wound of any kind. They concluded that his death was a matter of the heart." He paused. "Why do you ask?"

"Well, it *is* rather disconcerting to have a man die right outside one's window," I said in a huff. Men were often blind.

"*Princesse*, as I recall, you were not in the guesthouse at the time." He now concentrated on destroying an apple he had picked from a nearby tree before we sat down.

"Nevertheless," I said, "it is of interest to me. I think it connects to other events that have occurred recently."

"Such as?"

"I met my uncle of Orléans at Havre on my way to Canterbury. He was in a country inn at a rendezvous with company most interesting."

I could feel William stiffen slightly. "I recall that you said at the time you had seen the man before. Whom did your uncle meet?"

"Master Averroës of Córdoba."

"How do you know this?"

"My uncle introduced us. He was there expressly to meet the master. The duke had just come from Canterbury. You must have known something of this meeting."

William was silent, so I continued.

"Further, the master was most interested in the pendant that I always wore, the Arab jewel that Eleanor gave to Richard, who passed it to me."

"But you do not have it now."

"No, it was taken from me when I was abducted from Canterbury. But because the master was so interested in it, I could not help thinking that the man who died, who I am certain I saw with the master at Havre, was sent to steal the jewel."

"Why would Master Averroës want your jewel? He is a jewel of his own. His school in Toledo gives him everything he wants. He is master of teaching the skills of translation of any in our world."

"I don't know why. But I think it has to do with the Christian knights who were captured in a battle in the Middle Sea some five years ago."

"In what way?" Again that slight physical tremor and an ever so slight tightening of the voice.

"It has occurred to me that one or another of these caliphs, whether from Córdoba or Egypt, might want this jewel. And even might be willing to trade Christian prisoners for this treasure."

"Alaïs, you are falling under the spell of those Arthurian tales coming out of your sister's court in Troyes."

"Marie is only my half sister."

"Bah. You have romantic imaginings." He brushed the remains of the bread from his lap and made to rise, tipping me off balance. I nearly spilled onto the ground.

"William, I will be taken seriously." I righted myself and looked up at him. "Someone sacked my rooms at Havre and Canterbury, and someone has stolen my jewel. Do you not care to help me find out why?"

"*Princesse*." He was standing now, and his hands covered his face in weariness. "When I complete the work I have to do with the financiers, after we have confronted Eleanor, and when we have safely returned you to your brother's court, I shall turn my attention to the purloined jewel. But you must admit, it cannot be first on the list of things for us right now."

I already knew that William was a difficult man. I sighed and took the hand he offered—belatedly, I must say—to help me from the ground.

"As you will, for the moment," I said. But inwardly I resolved not to rest until I had my answers. And I thought William a trifle quick to dismiss my concerns. Mayhap he knew more than he was willing to say, at least at the present. He helped me mount and, with an air of preoccupation that discouraged conversation, led me a merry ride into the city straight to our destination.

The House of Lyons was one of the larger banking houses in France, although it had its origins in Lombardy. True to form as Italian financiers, this mighty house backed both the English and French indiscriminately in their constant struggles. At the French court, it was rumored that they were connected to, mayhap even owned by, the Knights Templar as part of their vast Continental banking operations. Whatever the truth of that allegation, The Lyons, as they were called, continued to keep a separate name and establishment.

Thus it was with some interest that I noted the modest exterior of the building we approached by horseback not an hour later. Whether the house was owned by the Templars or was an independent house of finance, the owners seemed to desire a minimum of public attention. The building in which they conducted their business affairs was one of nondescript stone typical of all common

houses in Poitou, with the peculiar roof of shingles, peaks, and little top nobs Eleanor's subjects had begun to build. These roofs were
derided in the north as reflecting the excessive taste for decoration
that existed in the south, but I rather liked them. Paris was too stern
for my taste. I had more of Eleanor in me than I liked to admit.
Perhaps I had been born to the wrong wife of my father.

We came upon the door to their business almost, it seemed to
me, by accident. We had been cantering down a narrow lane,
William as usual in the forefront, not bothering about whether I
could keep up—did he still remember those childhood horse races
we had with the Plantagenet children, where I won my fair share of
prizes?—when he suddenly reined in his horse. I pulled my reins in
sharply to avoid running into him, and I saw then that we were in
front of a single battered old wooden door.

"This is the House of Lyons?" I was incredulous. "It's so common. And there's no sign."

"It's not, after all, a public inn, *Princesse*." He rapped impatiently
three times with his riding crop on the door, not bothering to dismount. "You can hardly expect a lion's head over the portals." The
door swung wide to admit us, quickly, as if someone had been only
waiting for the signal to spring the door open. Then it closed behind us. But there was no one in sight.

"What a lot of secrets exist in the world," I murmured as I
glanced around the small courtyard banked with assertive weeds. A
fountain in the old Roman style—and in some state of disrepair, I
might add—settled comfortably amid its dilapidated stones in the
middle. No water sprang from the center shaft, although each of the
nymphs surrounding the bottom looked heavenward expectantly. It
appeared as though there may have been a garden blooming at some
previous time, but one couldn't be certain, since no bud or blossom
could be seen now through the tangle of brush. "The Templars
must own this house, too," I added, implying their ownership of all

the others of our recent experience. "They seem to have a penchant for the odd place."

William said nothing. A moment later a youth with tousled blond hair and clothes that looked as though he had slept in them in the stables came to lead our horses away. I was so distracted by this and wondering where the stables were—since they were not visible from the courtyard—that I missed the entrance of an older man who materialized from one of the many doors opening onto the courtyard. William dismounted with alacrity when he saw the man, and although at first I found nothing in our host out of the ordinary, I did likewise when the young man cupped his hand for my foot.

The man was old, for certain, but probably not as old as he looked. His body had a certain odd angle to it, as if he had spent too many hours bending over ledgers and had failed to take advantage of the horses the wealthy House of Lyons surely kept for riding and exercise. He had a well-trimmed beard in the pointed style of the Latins, rather full eyebrows matching his white hair, and the garb of a gentleman of means. He wore about his neck a heavy chain of gold with a jeweled medallion dangling from it, very much like those medallions I saw on William's men at the manor of Sir Roger. The old man's eye took notice of me and it seemed to me he suppressed a slight start. However, he bowed graciously to each of us as if we both had been expected.

"Seigneur Carlo, may I present the *Princesse* Alaïs," William said, bowing low in return. I was trying to remember the last time I had seen William bow when the old man spoke in his deeply resonant voice.

"You are both welcome in this house," he said, motioning for us to follow him.

Seigneur Carlo led us into a large room that was organized around a huge oval table in the center. Comfortable, carved-oak chairs, well cushioned for long sittings, surrounded the table. There were no other chairs in sight. The usual flowered and hunting tapestries hung on the walls, and scented rushes were scattered on the floor. One unusual piece caught my attention, however. The largest oak armoire I had ever seen, with the most complicated set of forged iron locks and hinges, stood against one wall. The room was much bigger than it seemed at first glance, because this piece took up so much space.

A good fire roared in the hearth. There was a spring chill on the air in Poitiers, and I was glad of a chance to warm myself. I passed by the table, since I had no part of the business to be done here, and seated myself on a bench against the wall beside the fire.

"Please, may I send for a comfortable chair, Your Grace?" Seigneur Carlo had a slight stammer, which—together with his bent form and noble voice—endeared him to me on the spot.

"The *princesse* waits for no ceremonies, Seigneur Carlo, as you can see for yourself," William remarked in an acerbic manner, glancing my way.

"My bench is quite good enough, Seigneur," I said, plumping the crewel-worked cushions that rested against the wall behind me. "But I would be glad of a small table if you have one. I may draw in charcoal to amuse myself as you attend to your affairs."

"But of course, Your Grace," and the seigneur snapped his fingers. The stableboy appeared and was given orders rapidly in a dialect I did not understand, but after one or two pleasantries, he reappeared with a small table, behind him a woman carrying a tray of mulled wine, some large pitchers that were placed on the long table in the center of the room, and two candles, which were added to my own small corner.

The table was one of the new kind that fitted over my lap and yet was large enough to allow me to spread several pages of parchment and my charcoals in front of me. Suddenly a smaller table was set beside my bench, and mulled wine and small almond cakes were placed on it.

I gratefully took a long draft of the wine and pulled my travel-worn leather sack toward me. From it I took out the charcoals, two of which had broken in the journey, and made ready to draw by smoothing the parchment sheets before me and placing two stones at the upper corners. Then I sat still. I was aware that the room was filling, but for the moment I had closed my eyes. The men's voices were well modulated with that calmness that prevails in houses of finance and banking, no doubt in reverence to all the silver whose whereabouts are known to the men who labor there.

I waited for a picture to form behind my closed eyes, a vision such as I sometimes saw sleeping or waking, some scene that begged to be drawn. But nothing appeared. Sighing, I opened my eyes and paused, hand poised. It was then I was distracted momentarily by an intense voice coming from the head of the meeting table. I had not heard the words, but the tone was challenging.

William made the next comment, in tones equally firm, calculated to end the exchange.

"The *princesse* is totally in my confidence. You may speak freely in front of her." A grunt was the only response.

Now my attention had been joined, and I scanned the faces of the men sitting around the imposing oak table. All thirteen chairs were filled. The men were all mature, two quite elderly. I saw several of them wearing the same medallions worn by the man who had greeted us. And I noticed a number of men with the black onyx ring that belonged to both my uncle and William. The sight of these rings put me in mind again of my own missing jewel, and I pondered William's reticence in our last conversation to even discuss the matter.

Seigneur Carlo sat at one end of the table and, not unexpectedly, William at the other. I sought the face of the man who had challenged my presence. He was sitting next to Seigneur Carlo and opposite me. By shifting slightly I could see his face well. He looked familiar, in a way I could not place. I wondered what had sparked his objection to me. Perhaps only a routine fear; those who handle large amounts of other people's money are known always to be guarded.

The men droned on, discussing items in several large, leatherbound volumes that were passed from hand to hand. Absent other inspiration, I began to draw my antagonist, for so I had begun to look upon him.

The form took shape quickly: a large head, florid cheeks, a strong nose that appeared to have been broken at one time. Then the high forehead, the— Suddenly I stopped. How could I have not seen! The nose, the forehead. I began to sketch feverishly. But instead of the shock of gray hair I saw before me, I filled in the lines for the hood of the gray cloak this man had worn the last time I saw him.

For it was indeed he, one of the three men who had followed me from Paris and whose hood had fallen back as I passed him in the inn at Havre the very night my room had been sacked. Now he sat here with the financiers and the Templar leaders, before my wide eyes. No wonder it was that he wanted me away from this room or that he would not meet my glance. What game did he play? Why the mystery? Could he have anything to do with the missing talisman?

My imagination told me the two were linked. Memory, images, connections, as the Greeks knew. Don't sort too quickly, keep moving, keep reaching. Keep drawing.

To expand my thoughts, I knew I had to consider many possibilities. Who had a stake in obtaining my pendant? True, it was valuable, but no more so than others. Why would it cause someone to go to all the trouble of stealing from the king's sister?

And there was the troubling issue of the theft at Canterbury. The thieves had evidently been searching for the same pendant. But when they did not find it, why did they steal my other jewels?

As I chased these questions, I was already drawing a circle on the next parchment, glancing from time to time at the man who was now looking increasingly annoyed with the world. He was slumped back in his chair, disconsolately tapping his ring on the edge of the oak table, his full lower lip thrust out.

What next? I began a circle of faces, sketching anyone who might have wanted my talisman. Isabelle was the most obvious to suspect. The lines fell on the paper, her oval face, her pert nose, her rather mean mouth. But what about John? It was his men who'd abducted me from Canterbury. They also had the opportunity to thieve it, and John might have reason to do this. The jewel, after all, was gold and ruby. And John was in dire need of silver. I quickly lined in the face of John, as I remembered it after he kicked the dog, the sickly, mean, defiant smile on his face.

Then there was the pouting financier, or whatever he might be, sitting opposite me. I sketched him as I saw him now, in his Brabant wool robe, wearing the fur-lined cape that currently graced the high back of his chair; and Eleanor, who might want her jewel back but might also doubt that I would give it to her; and Charlotte, who loved jewels, any jewels.

Why would someone want *my* jewel? Not for the market price it would bring. It must have some other value.

For a long moment, I held the charcoal, then began to draw the pendant. I remembered every line of it, for it had been my most cherished possession for years after Richard gave it to me. The graceful gold filigree of the setting, the oval ruby in the center, the tiny flashing gems that surrounded it. Then next to it I drew the back, the gold oval on which was etched the line of *poésie* from Ibn al-Faridh: "Death through love is life."

I, who so recently found life through love, was not prepared to contemplate death as part of the affair. But the thought of love reminded me that there was one face conspicuously absent from my circle, one other actor in this drama. And I filled in the last circle of faces of those I suspected with that of the man who sat at the head of the table, the grand master Knight Templar in England, the man who had become my lover but whose depths were still unknown to me.

It was rather a good picture, if I did say so to myself. William, the ultimate arranger, the cleric, the resourceful man, the man of the world. Survivor and politician. Suddenly I had a thought that, not examined too closely, seemed brilliant. I remembered the ancients' description of drama: *inventio, memorio, actio. Inventio*—the creation of the new idea; *memorio*—the rehearsing of it; and *actio*—the presentation with vigor.

At nearly the same moment, the room began to rustle with movement. I looked up and was surprised to see most of the men around the table closing their large books and rising to their feet. There was no time for *memorio*, but I had the idea, and I moved with it. My quarry was already up and speaking quickly to the venerable man who had welcomed us, who seemed to have a position equal to William's in this gathering.

William himself was at the opposite end of the table, gathering some papers and stuffing them into his leather travel sack. Several others stood around the table in groups of two or three, talking in urgent murmurs. It was now or never, I decided.

I stood so suddenly that the small pine lap table turned over, scattering parchment and charcoal and creating a noise that drew everyone's attention. All conversation stopped. Every eye came my way, which was exactly what I desired.

I moved that table aside with my foot and walked quickly forward, ignoring William, who—how knew I this?—would move toward me as soon as he recovered.

"A word, sir, before you leave," I said loudly to the man with the large nose.

He had already pulled his cloak from the back of his chair and was swinging it over his shoulders in a deft motion. He did not meet my eyes but mumbled something as he turned to go. I stepped deliberately in front of him. I heard William say my name, but I pressed on with my event.

"Hold, sir. I said I want a word with you." My voice was as hard and demanding as years of royal training could make it. Now I knew that the others were all regarding us. The man looked like a deer confronted by Henry's hunting party. Short of knocking me down to get to the door, he must attend.

"Madam, this meeting is over. Please do not meddle in affairs that do not concern you." I heard some breaths sharply indrawn in the room behind me but saw only this man. I left space between us so that he could not tower over me, but I felt no fright. Despite his size, I felt that I was the hound and this fox was run to ground. For we both knew what he feared.

"I'll have my jewel, sir."

"What are you talking about?" I could see beads form on the high, broad forehead that had given him away.

"I know that you followed me from Paris, and I know that you sacked my chamber at the inn at Havre." I waited. No one in the room moved or spoke. "You wanted my jewel. And I know that it is in your possession. Now, give it back."

In truth, I knew not what this man would do, for I had not had the time to work out the plan in full. I knew only that I had to confront him before his confreres left the room. When I saw his reaction, I decided quickly to press on.

"Why would I want your jewel, madam?" He looked down the long, uneven nose at me.

"Because of its value," I said simply.

"But, madam, I am a financier. I am a Knight Templar of high office. I can buy jewels ten times the value of any you might have by snapping my fingers or signing my name. Why would I lurk in lowly inns or ransack rooms to get some pendant you possess?"

The silence in the room grew unbearable. The blood drained from the man's face as he understood what he had said.

"Jacques?" Seigneur Carlo moved swiftly to stand between us.

"Who told you it was a pendant?" I whispered. Everyone in the silent room heard.

"Destriers?" William's voice shot across the room like an arrow as he moved forward.

The ill-tempered Jacques Destriers threw his riding gloves onto the table and burst out in anger, "Well, what are you all looking at? You said we had to find a way to make the exchange for the Knights. You knew that the caliph was being difficult. I was just carrying out your scheme." He stared around the table at the faces, all open in surprise.

"None of you wanted to do it—oh, no. You said to get the agreement from the caliph however it had to be done." He gestured in my direction. "Now you all want me to explain it to the *princesse*."

"So, as I suspected, the value was in its trade." I spoke softly. "Monsieur, the jewel was mine. You had no right."

He looked away from me, pressing his full lips together.

"You actually followed the *princesse* and sacked her room at an inn?" William's face was visible over Destriers's shoulder. The astonished expression on it exonerated him far more than any denials he could have given me. "That's outrageous, man! I'd given strict instructions that the pendant was not to be taken. How dare you! What ails you?"

"I've already explained." The large man stepped back, as if physically afraid of William's advance. "Master Averroës was in the north, meeting with the Frankish Templars. He saw the jewel. The pressure on our lodge to obtain it was renewed. The order came from the grand master in France himself."

"Ho!" I couldn't help the sound that came forth. The grand master in France had given the order after Averroës had seen the jewel and before the man was found in my garden. Horses could not ride that swiftly. The order had been given by my uncle, Duke Robert.

Destriers folded his arms defiantly across his chest and continued speaking beligerently. "And besides, I wasn't the one who stole it after all."

"Oh, no, it wasn't possible for you to steal it, because it was always around my neck. But you finally found someone who helped you out, didn't you?" I gestured with my withered hand, and Destriers flinched. Then he flung himself into the chair and half turned from the table. "The lovely Queen Isabelle slipped the jewel from my neck when I was drugged at Old Sarum. And you made it worth her while, didn't you?"

I was stabbing in the dark with my guesses, but his whitening face told me I was right.

"You had social concourse with Isabelle of England?" Seigneur Carlo's olive skin was like to become as pasty as Monsieur Destriers's. "Are you mad to give her a weapon like this?"

Destriers waved his hand. "She had no idea why I wanted it. I used an intermediary as a messenger. When John's men abducted the *princesse* from Canterbury, we were staying at the town inn, trying not to arouse suspicion. I was growing short of time. The caliph said if he did not have the jewel by high summer, he would stop receiving the Temple's messengers. The knights would die. I'd been working on this the whole year long. So I sent a messenger to Isabelle at Winchester to ask her to obtain the jewel for me." He nearly smiled and waved his hand casually. "We had known each other when she was yet at Angoulême."

"You knew I had the jewel, but you couldn't touch me while I was at my brother's court." I was unwilling to let this fish off the hook.

Destriers shook his head. "Too risky. Philippe's men are loyal to a point of foolishness." He looked up at me, for the first time a hint of respect playing across his features. "You're very safe there, my lady. The Paris court protects its own."

William was now standing next to me, his hands on his hips, looking down at his increasingly uncomfortable colleague. "Where is the jewel now, Destriers? Does Isabelle still have it? Mayhap John will hawk it to the caliph, and the gold we planned to use to pressure him will be used against us instead."

"Don't be absurd, William. Of course it came to me. Isabelle had no idea of its real value. She only needed pocket money. John keeps her on a tight leash, and she is a lady with high fashion needs." He smirked. "She also likes pocket money to bribe people to get things. I simply accommodated her."

I had had enough. This man made me queasy. "I want my jewel back, Monsieur whoever-you-are. Where is it now?"

"I'm afraid, dear lady, if you want it back, you need to go to Egypt. The jewel was sent on as soon as I had it in my possession. I could not afford, after all, to risk having someone find it and give it back to you." He glanced at William. "If you want it now, you'll have to petition the caliph."

If the man had been standing, I think William would have struck him. His face was stormy, but I felt, of a sudden, very calm.

"Damn you, Destriers. You presume too much," William said.

I sensed that most around the room, whether sitting still or standing, were as surprised to see William's customary reserve breached as at anything else that had happened. But I was equal to the challenge.

"Why did the caliph want that particular jewel?" I asked,

staring down at the man flopped in the chair. "Why is he willing to trade the lives of Christian knights taken in battle for that pendant?"

He made a small gesture with one shoulder. A little man in a large body, pretending to be careless. "His grandfather adored the Arab poet Ibn al-Faridh, who created the jewel. That caliph gave it to William, Duke of Aquitaine, when he was his prisoner. The duke, in turn, passed it on to his *petite-fille* Eleanor, who gave it to *Richard*, who gave it to you." He pronounced "Richard" in the French way, as Eleanor always did, and it distracted me. "The caliph knew that you had it. He's making a life project of calling back all the works of this poet, who was also a master jeweler."

"Aah." William turned away in disgust. Every eye in the room was now on him. "We will talk of this later." He faced me. "*Princesse*, I am sorry. The jewel seems to be out of our reach for the moment. I will do what I can to remedy the situation, but it will take some time." He shook his head. "*Je suis désolé*. And the Temple—the English Temple"—he glanced down at Destriers—"regrets this flagrant act immeasurably."

I felt a curious distance from his words. The pendant that I had worn for so many years, the talisman Richard had given me on our betrothal day, seemed but a distant memory. The importance of discovering its whereabouts, which had been almost overwhelming when I first recognized the man from the inn at Havre only a short time earlier, did not seem so present. There was a lightness about this feeling, as if somehow memories were lifted from me.

"Don't disturb yourself, Sir William," I said. "These things all belong to the past. As long as I know what happened to the pendant, and why, I am satisfied. And if its purpose now is to save the lives of Christian knights, perhaps that exalts the keepsake beyond any value I could give it."

He threw me a look of such surprise and pleasure that I was

startled. Mayhap he thought I had been nigh on to throwing a fit, like some fishwife in Dover, and was gratified at my restraint. But what I said was true. And if it pleased him in the passing, so much the better.

It was the clatter of hooves in the courtyard that broke the silence that followed. The door burst open without ceremony, and two men entered. They bore themselves as if from a royal house. I recognized immediately the livery of Queen Eleanor herself. William also knew the coat of arms and turned to them with an inscrutable expression on his face.

"My lady Alaïs," the two said, both going down on one knee. I nodded in reply, but they were already turning to William.

"My lord William," the front-runner said, bowing briefly. I watched with interest, thinking, Lord William? "I bring you greetings from Queen Eleanor."

"The queen is well, I trust?" William asked.

"Yes, well, my lord. She is well and here at Poitiers."

"Is she now?" His voice registered no surprise, only a slight, quizzical lift at the beginning of the sentence.

"She asks you to come to her today. She is in residence at the ducal palace."

"How convenient," I murmured. William pretended not to hear.

"What is her suit?" He perched himself casually on the corner of the table at which he had so recently labored, unmindful of his colleagues, who now seemed spellbound by the new drama unfolding.

"She wishes to speak with you and the *Princesse* Alaïs."

"What does Her Majesty want with us?" he asked again, ignoring the fact that we had planned just that morning to visit Eleanor, whether she welcomed us or not.

"Now, wait a moment . . . ," I began.

"*Princesse*, you cannot think for a moment that, with John's men surrounding Fontrevault, the queen is here without his knowledge? And if that is the case, we would do well to—"

"You mean *I* would do well, since it is my skin we imagine to be at risk," I replied. "What is Her Majesty's desire?" This to the couriers.

"The Lord William is to bring you to the ducal palace this afternoon. She has certain business she wishes to discuss with each of you." The courier who spoke paused, looking around for the first time at the assembled men of finance. "She said it was important that you come together."

"I'm going," I announced, speaking to William over the couriers. "You can come if you like. It's liable to be a better show than we saw in the town square in Chinon. I wouldn't miss it to get the Vexin back for France." I walked back to the bench I had occupied earlier and picked up my cloak.

I was eager to be gone and not afraid to face the old queen alone, but in truth, knowing that John had his men out looking for my party, I would rather have had William's company on the ride.

William returned to his place at the head of the table and scribbled a message, which he gave to the couriers. They departed in haste. Then he came to me and took my cloak, placing it around my shoulders with great gentility and care. I scanned the startled faces turned to us and nodded to the assembly. When I raised my head, there was not a man in the room, with any portion of sense, who did not know that I was now William's and he mine.

The fresh air revived me. Once mounted, I made it my business to keep up with William. "What is this 'Lord William' business?" I asked as soon as we were cantering. "I don't remember hearing that you had a title."

But he didn't answer, only shook his head. Instead he led me a merry chase down side streets of uneven cobblestone, where I was forced to pay attention to my horses' hooves or risk being tossed.

I had not been in Poitiers since that memorable occasion when Henry had descended with a fury on Eleanor and closed down her court, sending his sons scattering and Eleanor to prison. Nearly a quarter of a century had passed since then. The town bustled, and the crowded cobblestone streets and lanes were unfamiliar to me. Either they had changed or my memory had faded.

Then I saw La Maubegeonne rising straight up over the roofs of the buildings ahead of me, and I had my bearings. This famous tower had been built by Eleanor's grandfather for the woman he'd abducted from her husband and loved until the end of his life. The dukes of the Aquitaine had always been incurable romantics. One doesn't imagine dukes behaving like that, not for women anyway, but there you are. Eleanor had come from interesting stock.

As we rode into the courtyard of the ducal palace, the gates were opened for us without our request. Here, too, they were obviously prepared for our visit. But what Eleanor did not know was that *I* was ready for *her*.

23

Eleanor at Last

It was my first sight of her in many years. She stood tall and regal as ever, framed in the grand entrance to the palace. But as I came closer, I was stunned at her fragility. Although she was standing upright with no help, she looked so brittle I thought her bones might break before we got to a greeting. I saw also that she was shaking like a reed in the wind with a kind of palsy. And I felt my animosity shrink alarmingly.

The full, cascading, burnished hair I remembered was now thin and gray. She still wore it high on her head and, as was her custom always, with no covering other than a single jeweled diadem.

As I approached, she held out her hand for me to kiss. It was freckled with age spots, clearly visible in the sun, which at just that moment decided to spread out like butter over us all.

I realized that I had remembered her mostly as the young woman of my childhood, and the sight of her in this state caused some blurring of my vision with tears, despite my best intentions.

"Queen Eleanor." I bent low.

"Princess Alaïs," she responded, as if we had parted only that day after breakfast. She looked over my shoulder. "Lord William," she said dryly, as if she were announcing something unnecessary. I knew he was bowing, too.

She said no more but beckoned to us to follow as she turned to enter the palace. To her side, immediately, came an old man who offered her his arm, which she took. Without that arm, I saw with dismay, she could not have made her progress.

Inside the palace we went not into the great hall, where traditionally visitors were received, but into one of the smaller, private rooms off to the side. There I was not particularly surprised to see my aunt, the ubiquitous Abbess Charlotte. She looked spectacular as usual, in a heavy silk shantung gown that shimmered when she moved. And move she did, quickly, to embrace me. I returned her warmth of greeting without hesitation.

"Niece, I am glad to see you are safe and back in France."

"Dear aunt, if I had taken your advice at Canterbury, I would have been safer at an earlier time, but I would have had a far less exciting visit to England."

Eleanor motioned us to sit around a table, as if we were a family, which indeed in some odd way I guess we were. Servants came and went with wine and ale, bread and cakes and platters of cold poultry, but no one ate anything or said anything for some time.

Finally I spoke. "I trust that Your Highness's journey to Spain to fetch the Princess Blanche was not too difficult and well rewarded by my brother, Philippe, when you arrived in Paris?"

The queen smiled at me, almost a real smile out of the past. "Thank you, Alaïs, for the thought. Blanche is safely installed at the court of your brother, and the two children seem to like each other.

It may be a marriage more successful than many that have been arranged by politics." And I knew she was thinking past me, to that time when she was married to my father because their fathers had decreed it. But then, I recalled, she later married Henry for love, and that didn't work out too well either.

"We have asked you here to discuss several matters," she said in William's direction, when most of the servants had withdrawn from the room.

"Good," I said with alacrity. "And when we have finished, I have some questions for you."

"They may not be necessary after certain things have been discussed," she said, turning that ever-so-slightly shaking head stiffly in my direction. "But we are most willing to hear your questions at the end."

Then she returned to William. "I am trying to save my son's throne. I am interceding with you to make that possible. If you, as Templar grand master in England, will agree to it, it will happen. If you do not support him, indeed if your Knights persist in rattling their collective sabers in his direction, his own fears may cause actions that will bring him down. And," she added, "you know well that could make a new civil war in England."

William sat back in his high, velvet-paneled chair, leaning his head carelessly on the cushioned backrest. He studied the beams on the ceiling for a brief period before he spoke. When his words came, he looked directly at the queen.

"Madam, the whole order of the Knights Templar is not exactly mine to direct." The dry quality of his voice was inescapable, without exactly being impudent.

"You know what I mean," she countered. "You are their general here in France, their grand master in England. You have the power to stop this threat to my son."

Again he demurred ever so slightly. When he spoke next, it was slowly, as if he were thinking each sentence out carefully before giving it voice. "I will agree to some things," he said finally. "I will agree to speak for John in our senior councils and attempt to persuade my brothers to give him another chance."

He sighed, then continued. "And I will sign the papers that will expedite the major loan that John needs. But these agreements are on one condition: and one condition only: John will have my bond on it, provided he gives up this misguided search for the phantom bastard of Henry Plantagenet, once and for all." William looked hard at the queen. "I want you to tell John that you know the child is dead."

"John is frightened. You know that is why he has created a stir." Eleanor waved her hand, as if discarding trailing cobwebs.

"Herod was frightened, too, and the consequences for a number of children are reported to have been most unpleasant."

Eleanor's eyes narrowed, but she kept them on William. For my part I loosed the scarf around my throat and unclasped the jewel that held my cloak. I was beginning to feel very warm. I bit hard on my tongue to hold it. For perhaps the first time in my life, I knew I would choose my words extremely carefully, since now I had something besides their effect on my own life to consider.

"What stake do you have, William, in this matter?" Her voice held that old peremptory habit and note of familiarity in her address to William by his given name.

"Eleanor, leave it alone," the abbess's tart voice cut in. "You must let it rest now, after all these years."

"*Au contraire*, Aunt. Let us talk about it," I interposed. "The topic of the child seems to have John quite beside himself. And why shouldn't he be?"

"*Princesse*—" William began, but Eleanor raised her hand again, this time quite purposefully.

"I will not be tempted into argument over this matter. I have nothing more to say on it, except to assure you, Lord William, that if the harassment of the king does not stop and the needed bond for silver to pay his troops is not forthcoming, you and your order will have much to answer for." Eleanor folded her hands regally in front of her, staring straight ahead, as if her announcements were addressed to God and simply might be overheard by some worldly representative of his. I for my part wondered which order she had in mind, the Benedictines or the Templars? Or perhaps there was a third, an Order of the Mysterious, which I had not yet stumbled upon.

"Well, I have something more to say," I announced, pulling her Sarum letters from my pouch. I threw them across the table, and they slid to a stop in front of her. William began to rise out of his chair, then thought the better of it. "You knew about my child, all these years you knew, and you never told me. You harbored your secret well."

The queen looked down at the letters, which lay quivering in the wind in the middle of the table. Slowly she reached out her index finger and her thumb and drew them toward her, as if they were alive. She pulled her Italian eyeglasses from inside a pocket in the front of her gown, carefully set them on her nose, and looked down at the handwriting on the parchment sheets. We watched her pick them up, glance at them, and discard them, one after the other, which she did with almost ritualistic movements. Her beautiful, oval, aristocratic old face remained expressionless, giving away nothing, as always.

"You sent me on a phantom mission to Canterbury so John could abduct me and find out where my child was. But the joke was on you. For I found these in Old Sarum, and now I know the secret of your soul."

She looked up from the letters and over her eyeglasses with her most regal stare.

"And what, pray, is that?" she asked.

"Your soul is mean," I said, surprising even myself.

"And what led you to that conclusion, Alaïs Capet?"

"Not that you foiled my marriage to Richard, although you did that; not even that you sent me into a trap at Canterbury so that John could get his hands on me, although you did that as well. But your soul is mean because you knew that my son was alive and you let me think he was dead all those years. If you had any kindness in you, you would have——"

"Alaïs, this conversation can have no good ending," Abbess Charlotte interrupted, stretching her long arm in its jeweled sleeve across the table at me, almost in supplication.

"No, let her go on," Eleanor said. I was looking straight into her eyes, but they gave no signal to me. "Let her read to me the legend of the wrongs I have done her."

I had the sense to pause here. A voice in the back of my head was murmuring, Well, yes, if we speak of wrongs . . .

"Perhaps I have done you some wrongs as well," I admitted, mitigating the frontal assault I had been mounting. "But there is no wrong comparable to keeping a mother from her child."

At this Eleanor stood, pushing back her high oak chair.

"Unless it is the wrong of the child who murders the love of the mother." The room became silent. Outside the open window, the birds were still. Suddenly her palsy seemed to disappear, and she walked around the table toward me. I stood to face her, not afraid but with a fast heart. "Unless it is the wrong of the child who is nurtured by the mother and then turns on her, to the very act of taking her own husband from her."

I said nothing.

"You ask me why I prevented your marriage to Richard? You dare to ask me after you replaced me in my own marriage bed?" She had reached me now. I did not even see her arm come up, so swiftly did she strike me across the face. To my credit I moved not one whit backward at the strike. She could have done it again and I would have remained as motionless. For one long moment, I thought she might. But instead she turned away.

Both William and Charlotte had risen, but I held up my left hand to them. With my live hand, I grabbed the queen's arm and forced her to turn back to me, though not enough to hurt her at all.

She opened her mouth to speak, but I held up my withered hand to her as well. It was always—as I have said before—an act that arrested conversation.

"You know I had no choice with the king." I spit out my words. "I was his prisoner every bit as much as you were. It wouldn't have mattered whether I wanted to be his concubine or not. He would have what he chose. But what matters, in the end, is that he was good to me at a time when I had lost everything."

To my complete horror, I heard my voice breaking and felt hot tears rising, tears I had felt only twice before in all the years since my child was taken from me. But I pressed on, through my sobbing.

"You have reason in your anger. I did a terrible thing, and I ask your pardon. But at least in my actions, confused as they were at the time, I had an honest heart. I came to love the king. And I knew you had not loved him for a very long time."

The queen stood impassively before me, but it was my aunt who came to my side and put her arm around me. She spoke to the queen in a matter-of-fact manner as she held my shaking body.

"Truly, Eleanor, there is enough blame on all sides. Alaïs is right. Your love for Henry was dead. Indeed, you hated him. You know it was only your pride that was wounded." The abbess gently pressed me to her. I saw William standing, his arms folded, watching me gravely across the table. "Why not stop this high-handed playacting and tell Alaïs honestly what you knew. Put this matter

335

behind you both." My aunt could feel me in danger of collapsing, and she guided me into the chair.

I buried my head in my folded arms, my face hidden, silent now but unable to stop the warm water flowing from my eyes. Then I felt the queen's hand briefly on my neck, a gentle brushing action as she passed by. When I looked up, I saw her back in her chair. I saw also what the effort to confront me had cost her, with the shaking of the palsy back and more pronounced than before. She passed her slender, blue-veined fingers across her eyes and then looked at me. She began to speak in quiet, measured, almost musical tones, as if chanting plainsong.

"At the time, Alaïs, I did not know that your child lived. If I had known, I would have told you. Although I was angry with you, I never meant harm to either you or the child." She pulled a piece of lawn from her inner sleeve and passed it across the table to me. I took it, as a sort of peace offering, and used it to blot my hot, wet face.

"I heard of your affair with the king while I was imprisoned in Old Sarum, as you know from the letters you found. But I, too, was told by him that the child had died. He swore to me on his father's grave. He was most convincing. He had one of his famous temper tantrums when I questioned the truth of his avowal. I think"—she paused here, as if searching in the dim reaches of her mind—"that he genuinely wanted to protect your son. If everyone thought the child dead, he would be safe, Henry reasoned. And so he was, for years."

"But I was the child's mother," I almost wailed, ashamed of my lack of control even as I spoke. "Why did he keep this from me?"

"You? You were the most dangerous of all," she said in that hard, quiet voice. "You were the one who could least be trusted, for keeping the babe would be your concern above all. And if you did so, others were bound to learn of it. And therein lay the threat."

"How did you find out he was still alive?"

"John uncovered the secret in recent weeks. As he was gathering information on the Templars, to use to persuade them not only to relent in their pressure on him but to back him financially, he was told by a trusted informer that the highest officers in the Templar ranks were shielding one who could be a threat to the throne." Here her eyes flashed at William, who seemed unperturbed, examining his fingernails.

"If John spent more time governing the country as a good king should and less time running around trying to identify and hold up his enemies, he'd have fewer of them," he drawled.

"John is trying to be a good king," Eleanor said, "and anyway, who do you have in your officers' trust who has such a loose and flapping tongue? I suggest you look to your own house and straighten it before you inspect mine." She had no sooner begun her harangue than William brought his fist down on the table.

"God's bones, Queen Eleanor! Stop shielding that overgrown juvenile from the consequences of his own actions. It's going to wreck the kingdom that you and Henry worked so hard to consolidate. Do you want to see your own efforts lost in your lifetime? Whose side are you on? You can't be wanting that impetuous little rabbit Philippe Auguste to take all of England too?" He seemed to remember us momentarily and glanced my way. "Sorry, *Princesse*," he muttered. "Sorry, Abbess."

Eleanor sighed. My aunt rolled her eyes heavenward. And the earnest, intelligent face of François crossed my vision. For just a moment, I felt a brush of sympathy for Eleanor, the mother of so unworthy a son.

"All right, suppose I do agree to convince John that there is no child, no little bastard brother that grew old enough to threaten him. Suppose I tell him that such a child, in truth, lived once but died in his infancy. John will ask me how I have come upon this information." She placed her hands upward on the table. "What do I tell him?"

"The grave has been found," William said without a pause, as if he had been thinking of nothing but this since he rose that morn. "The grave was in the north of England, with markings that are unmistakable. And a letter from the grand master of the Templars was intercepted and delivered to you, acknowledging these facts. I myself will pen the letter, if you bring me parchment," he added.

"Write the letter," Eleanor said as she signaled one of two servants hovering by the doorway to approach the table. "John will have it by nightfall, along with my own."

"Once he has convinced you that he believes, and gives up this wretched search, I'll sign the bond for his loans." William folded his arms in front of his chest. Almost as an afterthought, he added, "Oh, and he must release the abbeys from the quarantine he has placed on them. They must be free from this unfair tax he levied last year."

"That may be even more difficult," Eleanor said, a smile breaking her somber expression. "John loves to oppress abbeys."

"John has always loved to oppress anyone," I said, joining uninvited.

She turned her head stiffly toward me, as if she suddenly remembered something. "Alaïs, I did not send you to Canterbury so that John could abduct you."

"No? Then why?"

"Tell her why, William. It was your doing." Her voice quavered, as if her palsy extended to her throat.

"I must confess it was," he said cheerfully. "I let it be known at Fontrevault that certain letters from Queen Eleanor to Becket had been discovered but that we were allowing them to rest behind the altar where they had been found."

"For what reason did you give out this information?"

"So that John would be distracted from this business about Henry's son and come in pursuit of the letters for his mother. He would not want anything damaging to come to light about his mother's relationship with Becket whilst he was in such a tenuous position as king. The people might revolt."

"So you thought John would take the bait and raid Canterbury. And then what? You would catch him in the act and embarrass him?"

My voice must have betrayed my amusement, for William looked momentarily chagrined. Then he shrugged, a benighted look on his rosy face.

"God's good feet, a stupid plan if I ever heard one! And this is what the great Templars produce when they play at cloaks and daggers." I had to laugh out loud.

"Eleanor could see through that one," Charlotte said. "So we decided to send our own messenger to retrieve the letters. One we could trust. And one who would not arouse suspicion."

"I never dreamed she would send you," William said to me, not laughing now.

"And to get you to go, we had to promise dramatic news." Eleanor added. "I had only the rumors about the Templars to go on, but it was something."

"And would you have told me that?"

"Yes, I would have kept my word."

"But John's throne . . ."

"I didn't think you would truly find any other news. The Templars are a close-knit group. I never thought they would give you enough information to find the child." She looked at William with her imperious expression. "I hadn't counted on you."

"Life is full of surprises for all of us, Your Highness." He spoke to her but looked at me.

"So I will have those Becket letters now, as part of our agreement here," Eleanor said, tapping her fingernail on the table. And as if he expected it, William produced a small roll of letters from his worn leather purse.

"All right, so the child is dead and I have the letters to Becket. You will sign the bond before you leave this house."

"No. I will sign the bond when I have John's assurances that he will lift the tax on the abbeys and accept that there is no one who can threaten his throne other than himself. I will let you know where I rest for the next fortnight. You can send the papers there." William began to rise.

"What is to stop John from finding you and cutting your throat in your sleep?" I could not forbear from asking.

"Even John is not so great a fool as to kill the grand master of the Knights Templar of England and Normandy." The corners of William's mouth twitched. "I have one more piece of news for you, which Queen Eleanor may not be able to give you."

I rose, too, although, to tell the truth, I did not even know if I was to leave with him or stay with the old women.

"Eleanor did not prevent your marriage to Richard, as you said earlier. It was Henry himself who refused. Even though you were no longer living with him, he would not allow Richard to have you."

"Henry?"

"Yes. I was there. He and Richard had their last confrontation before Henry's death at Chinon. I was there and witnessed all of their conversations. Philippe was there, too, and both Richard and Philippe demanded of Henry that he allow the betrothal to be ful-filled. Richard was to have you as his bride. And Henry absolutely refused to give you up. Richard knew that you'd had Henry's child, but he wanted you anyway. Whether it was a deep love or that his pride was wounded, he demanded you. When Henry refused, Richard vowed that his father had now broken every oath and promise he had made to him and that it would be a fight to the death." William picked up his heavy velvet-and-fur cloak, which had fallen to the floor, shook it out, and threw it over his shoulders. "It's hard to forgive Richard's turning on his father in his last days, but in some ways that scene always made it easier for me to understand."

"And so it was," Eleanor said softly, catching my attention. "A fight to the death between them."

"And so it was," William repeated.

"Alaïs." It was my Aunt Charlotte who broke the silence. "I have letters your father wrote me years ago when he was married to your mother. I think you are entitled to know what is in them. Wait, and I will have the servants bring them from my chamber."

I thought about my father and my mother, and my uncle Robert, who had been rumored to love my mother. I thought about the mysteries surrounding all those who went before us. And I thought, briefly, of the rights of the dead to keep their own counsel. Perhaps that was what *requiem in pace* truly means.

"Stay, aunt," I said, busying myself with my own cloak. "I think I will leave those letters with you." She looked puzzled. "After all is done,"—I knew that my sadness shone through the smile I managed—"the dead must keep some secrets. I no longer have wish to know them."

"Come, *Princesse*," William said. "I'll see that you are returned to Paris."

But we had to pick our way to the door, for the women insisted on accompanying us. And the queen's walk was mightily slowed.

When we came to the doorway, each of the women in turn embraced me, my aunt and my stepmother. And in my sincere return, I knew I was embracing the whole of my life.

.24.

Opportunities

We mounted and waved back to the old women, a royal portrait in their elegant colors, with sleeves trailing as they raised their hands in farewell. As we rode out of the courtyard, I could see that William was in a hurry, as always, and I was challenged to keep up with him.

When we came to the edge of Poitiers, I knew not which road we would take. I rode up alongside William and stopped him with my hand on his bridle. "I would like a favor," I said.

"Only ask." He looked at me with that grave, courteous expression he assumed from time to time. "What is it?"

"I would like to ride in the fields before we continue."

"And what fields would those be that you seek?"

"I know a place, not two leagues from here, where the wheat is cleared and the trees are sparse and the horses could have their heads."

"But you haven't been here since you were a girl."

"No, but I have faith that this field is unchanged. I know that it is in the same spot and that it looks the same still."

William looked long at me. "You're full of surprises. And full of faith. All right. Let us see if the field is still there." He wheeled his horse around and followed my lead, and we cantered down a side road for some time.

We found the meadow, and it was as I remembered. Then we raced our horses together, hooting and shouting like children. We would no sooner finish one race than one of us would shout out a new target and we would begin again. William always won, of course. But I made a fair showing and once nearly pulled in front of him.

Finally I called a halt, partly because I was laughing so hard. We dismounted, and I threw myself on the good, rich meadow grass. He followed suit. First we embraced, and then we lay like children side by side. The sky had cleared, and all traces of the rain washed away. Hefty white clouds beaten about by the wind made patches in the sky.

"Are you content, then, *Princesse* Alaïs?" he asked, his mouth close to my ear.

"Yes, close to content." I smiled.

"And you no longer desire aught but me?"

I didn't answer immediately.

"Ah." He withdrew, just slightly, so he could see my face. "You still want the jewel."

"No," I said slowly, in full knowledge that I spoke the truth. "I no longer need the talisman. But I am still stunned that my uncle gave the order to steal it."

He rolled on his back to scan the sky.

"He is grand master in France, is he not?" I persisted.

"Alaïs, you know more about the Templar order than most of the Knights by now. Yes, he is. You heard that fool Destriers. But I cannot punish him, for he was acting under orders from his own commander that countered mine. And he belongs to the Frankish Knights. Duke Robert and I will have a talk. It is a delicate situation."

"And you forbade your knights to take my jewel?"

His voice softened. "Call me a fool. I knew that Richard had given it to you. It seemed unfair that it should be taken from you just to serve the whim of a tyrant. Like stealing a piece of your past, your very heart."

I turned to him. "All of the past is but a memory. And that memory shifts every time I understand something new about those long-ago events."

"I hope none of my men sees me here," William said, his hands comfortably locked under his head. "Resting in the grass with an errant princess is not the kind of leadership activity they expect."

"If they raise the question," I said with a sly look, "just tell them you are making plans."

"And what plans are those?" he asked. "Have they to do with you?"

"I don't know how they could," I said. "The Templars are committed to celibacy."

"As you have seen, that principle is honored more in the breach, even by their leaders." He seemed to be reading the clouds, not looking at me, so I turned my attention back to the sky.

"William, I have a question that has been burning for the better part of this afternoon."

"Ask anything, *Princesse*. My life is an open book."

"Hmm." I gazed upward. "It's true that Jacques Destriers followed me from Paris and had my room searched looking for the pendant he so wanted."

"Yes, and so cleverly unmasked he was by you this very afternoon. So much has happened that I neglected to compliment you on your astute reasoning."

"Well, that same astute reasoning leads me to another conclusion."

"Which is?"

I rolled on my side to look at him. "Today at the House of Lyons, I saw by your face that you were surprised when I accused that man of the theft."

"Alaïs, I would never have countenanced his actions. Thieving from women is not how the Templars accomplish their negotiations." William now turned his body to face mine. "And I would never have allowed such an invasion of your privacy."

"I do believe that. But there is one thing we still need to discuss. My room was sacked twice. Once at Havre and once at Canterbury."

"And neither time was the thief successful."

"But Destriers could not have been the person who tore my belongings apart at Canterbury. He was in the town, but he wasn't at the abbey. You would have known."

"Mayhap it was the Arab who was later found dead."

"No, he would not have been lurking in the garden when he was killed if he had a chance the previous evening to search my room."

"So what do you think?" His tone committed him to nothing.

"Whoever searched my possessions at Canterbury was not a thief. That performance was for another reason altogether."

"But who did it? And why?"

"Why, you did, of course."

"I did not!" Outrage laced his voice. "Do you think I had nothing better to do when I was running the abbey for Hugh Walter than ransack the rooms of guests? A fine demonstration of the Benedictine value of hospitality!"

"William. If we are to have honesty between us, we must start now." I propped myself on my elbow and looked into his eyes, those remarkable ice-blue eyes that could stop even rogue financiers in their tracks. He broke into a smile.

"Well, all right, then. But I didn't do it myself."

"But you had it done. And I can guess your purpose. You wanted to frighten me."

"It's true." His arm reached out and pulled a lock of hair loose from my braid. "I wanted you not to keep your vigil in the cathedral. I wanted you not to be accosted by John, and truly, I feared harm could come to you. But I have the jewels I took, Alaïs. And I did plan to return them."

"And, if I mistake not, you have already begun to make amends. It was you who sent to my room the beautiful chain of jewels for me to wear at Baron Roger's dinner party."

"Yes, what happened to it? I haven't thought of it since."

"I kept it. We can make an exchange one day, my own jewels for the one chain I have."

"I have a better idea. You keep the chain, and I will take my time returning the rest of your jewels . . . one by one, over many a year."

He pulled me toward him, and for a moment we lay a breath apart. "I don't want to lose you again," he whispered. "In some way you have always been in my life as a dream. Now that I have discovered you, I need you there in the flesh as well."

"But we have different paths," I said, as simply as I could, disengaging myself.

"What would you do? Go back to Philippe's court? But you are not happy there."

"I will go back for now. But I will leave the court soon. I have property in Ponthieu. I think it is time for me to move my household to my own estate."

"Philippe will not be pleased." We lay now, side by side.

"No, I expect not. He has always wanted me close. But I am tired of the life his family and friends live. And I will visit him often. In truth, he is so busy he may think I still dwell on the Île de la Cité even if I am off in Picardy."

"What about François?"

"I have to think about him. It would be good if he could join me, but I wouldn't want to deprive him of a life at court. Or better yet, a life on the stage." I had to laugh, but then I suddenly sobered. "I would like him to be with me for some while. Mayhap, when we have got to know each other, he could make his own decision."

"A good course of action." William turned to me. "You really are wise, you know." He paused for effect. "For a woman."

"Oh, you are a fine one." I began to tear off the long grass and throw it at him, in a most unroyal way.

He grabbed my hand, this time with great glee, and drew me close. And after we had kissed long, I said to him, "And what of your future?"

He rolled onto his back once again. "I have a commitment to the order as grand master in England for three more years. Then I have been thinking of retiring to the country. I am tired of power and its responsibilities."

"Retire to the country? You? To do what? Be a country squire, after all this excitement? I think not, Sir William. Oh, excuse me— *Lord* William, whatever that's about."

"I have land in the north of England, left to me by Becket, and a title that I never use, left to me by Henry before he died. Oh, and one manor in Normandy. And, to tell the truth, although I still like the planning and intrigue, my bones are weary of the days when I must ride the road from sunup to sunset. And many meetings on finances, like the one with the House of Lyons, require my presence. Three more years will be more than enough. Someone else can take over."

"Perhaps in between your travels, you will find your way to Ponthieu."

He rolled onto his side to face me. "If you were there, I would find my way with alarming regularity."

"If you come, I will be there."

348

My heart was joyful at these words, although I would not have admitted it for all the almond cream in Poitou.

We lay watching the sky together in silence. A huge wild falcon wheeled overhead, then spun off into the distance. At last I said what was in my heart. "When I was a young woman, I used to ride in these fields with Marguerite and our stepbrothers. I was so in love with Richard, and I looked forward to what our life together would be."

"But things turned out differently."

"Yes, you are right. And what I have learned from this remarkable journey is that those memories belong to the past. They are out of another time. Holding on to them, and the anger around them, has done me little good." I turned my head and pulled the fuzz off the dandelions that stood next to my cheek. When I opened my hand, the wind captured the ephemeral, cloudlike clumps and drew them up into the air. "That is why I could let the talisman go. I don't want it back. It has served its purpose for me, and now it can serve another purpose for someone else."

I turned close, my breath on his cheek now. "I promise you, William grand master, that I release all those memories. That the whole of me is in the present, not lurking in past times or with ghosts. And that in the future, those who give me joy will be those on whom I spend myself."

He propped his head up on one elbow, looking down at me. The sun shone now in his face, and I could see the etchings of age on it, those deep lines that ran from under his eyes to his mouth on each side. I realized he could see my face clearly also, in all its honest age. And the idea gave me some amusement.

"And I promise you that in however many years we have left, whatever we do, we will not lose each other again."

And that was sufficient for the moment.

Afterword

The royal princess Alaïs Capet (pronounced Al-ah-ees Ka-pā) is a true historical figure. Born to Louis VII, called le Jeune, and his second wife, Constance of Castile, Alaïs and her elder sister, Marguerite, were actually sent to live with the court of Henry II and Eleanor of Aquitaine, Louis's first wife and the mother of his first two daughters.

Alaïs was betrothed at an early age to Richard, later to be called Lionheart, and Marguerite to the elder Plantagenet brother Henry Court Mantel. King Henry did indeed take Alaïs as his mistress after he imprisoned Eleanor in Old Sarum. And, as one might expect, the marriage to Richard never took place. Following Henry's death Alaïs was returned to Philippe's court, where, after some time, she apparently married someone named William. More than that, historians do not tell us, but several say that the chronicles of the time hint that there was a child born of Henry and Alaïs.

Setting aside the magnificent soap opera of the Plantagenet family and its ongoing dance with the royal house of France, what lover of good stories could help but be arrested by the possibilities offered in the real scenario? And so, as I read medieval history for several years to amuse myself, often while traveling in France and England, I began to wonder. What if Alaïs was not the pawn she appeared to be, buffeted between her betrothed and his powerful father? What if instead she was cut of the cloth of some other women of her time: Eleanor of Aquitaine, who married two kings and mothered two more; Marie de Champagne, Eleanor's eldest daughter by Louis, who patronized Chrétien de Troyes and thus gave us the incomparable Arthurian cycle of stories; Christine de Pizan; Hildegarde of Bingen; Eleanor de Montfort; Blanche of Castile? These were powerful women of the twelfth and thirteenth centuries who changed the course of history with their wit, their resourcefulness, and their courage to be themselves. That question—"What if?"—is the beginning of every fictional exploration.

Much of the history in this book is accurate, although I have taken great liberties with the Knights Templar in creating Lord William. In most cases, I have tried to stay close to actual historical dates. I want to acknowledge, however, that Henry's mother, Matilda, is reported to have died in 1167, and thus could not have raised François herself. Also, Master Averroës is said to have died in 1195, and thus could not have attended the significant meeting with Duke Robert in northern Europe in 1200, the year of this novel's action. I am grateful for the many books that fed my understanding of these times. This novel would not have been formed without W. L. Warren's towering biography *Henry II* and Amy Kelly's classic work *Eleanor of Aquitaine and the Four Kings.* Also worthy of mention are Marion Meade's *Eleanor of Aquitaine* and *Richard Coeur de Lion* by Philip Henderson. Many works by Georges Duby were helpful, in particular *William Marshal: The Flower of Chivalry.*

Several books by Jacques le Goff had an impact on my understanding of the Middle Ages: *Intellectuals in the Middle Ages* and *The Medieval Imagination* are two such. For further understanding of the mysterious Knights Templar, *The Temple and the Lodge* by Michael Baigent and Richard Leigh is a great general history, and for a more serious treatment, the classic by Malcolm Barber, *The New Knighthood,* is a good resource.

For those interested in the Spanish-Arabic connection, a most complete accounting may be found in *The Great Medieval Civilizations,* volume III, published by Harper & Row, the international authors of which were assembled by a commission of UNESCO. It is from this work that we understand that eyeglasses came from Arab invention and were used as early as the twelfth century in western Europe.

Canterbury Cathedral aficionados will enjoy *The Quest for Becket's Bones,* especially the part about the fire and the removal of Becket's remains, as well as the penance Henry performed at the site.

Two other books deserve mention for their assessment of the place of women in the Middles Ages: Denis de Rougemont's *Love in the Western World* and R. Howard Bloch's *Medieval Misogyny and the Invention of Western Romantic Love.* Although de Rougemont's thesis of the origins of Western romantic love has been bitterly challenged (so much so that in the last edition he added an appendix consisting of twelve extra chapters to defend it!), his understanding of the influence of Arabic poetry and learning on the courts of southern France and subsequently on the whole of Western Europe remains a significant contribution.

I have visited and been moved by nearly every place described in this novel. The Conciergerie on the Île de la Cité in Paris is, in part, still the same building from which Alaïs departs on her fateful mission. The ducal palace with its great hall still stands in Poitiers. And while Canterbury is much changed, and Chinon and Old Sarum are now just ruins or outlines of buildings long gone, one can imagine what they were like in former times. Indeed, it was the monastery of Moissac in southern France that was the true model for the Canterbury scenes in this book. The Montjoie *château* near Chinon still stands and is now a very classy *Relais et Château* establishment. Still, there are echoes of other voices when one visits.

Historical Note

We know a great deal about the Middle Ages, but there remains disagreement among historians on some of the peripheral details. A case in point is the sobriquet "Court Mantell." My sources indicate the usage for the Young King, the son of Henry and Eleanor, to distinguish him from his father as a young man, before his crowning. The elder Henry was called Henry Fitzempress, in honor of his mother's title from her first marriage. Other sources have been called to my attention, in which this appelation is given to the father, Henry II. I hope the reader will bear easily with these differences, and enjoy the story for what it is.

Acknowledgments

I owe many, past and present, a debt of gratitude for ideas and encouragement in my happy search for these characters and this story: to John Berryman for suggesting years ago that I read Denis de Rougemont; to Emilie Buchwald, Jonis Agee, and John Desteian; to early (and sometimes often) readers Lynn Cowan, Pat Cummings, and Alice Buhl, thanks for their suggestions and encouragement; and to Jon Hassler for helping me understand the joys of rewriting. Special thanks to Dee Ready, friend, writer, and editor, for all her help.

My gratitude also goes to the sisters of the Monastery of St. Benedict in St. Joseph, Minnesota, for their hospitality over several weeks, which allowed me to finish and revise the book. Sisters Ruth Nierengarten and Margaret Van Kampen, wonderful artists both, contributed materially to the manuscript, and for that I am grateful.

Thanks also to my sons, Sean, Paul, Mike, and Colin, for interest and encouragement. Without the able assistance of my agent, Marly Rusoff, and the superb editorial direction of Carolyn Marino, the book would not have come to completion. Special thanks to my husband and best reader, Michael, for loving the story.